ODDS OF DYING

Judith Janeway

ISBN 13: 978-0-9850521-1-9
ISBN 10: 0985052112
ODDS OF DYING

Published in the United States of America

Cover design by Paul Roesch of *Fix8 Media*

DEDICATION

To Doreen

A pillar of support, always there so I could lean instead of falling down.

Perennial pep squad without the dancing and short skirts.

My own personal Dumbo's feather, who gave me a place and space for writing in the dark times.

And

To Lon

My other pillar of support, who always showed up. Always.

The guy in the stands who forever brandishes the sign BELIEVE!!

The only person, besides me, for whom no time is too dark for laughter.

Sick laughter. But laughter nonetheless.

There is no end to my love and gratitude for you both.

CHAPTER ONE

June 6, 1994
Oakland, California

Finding a dead body can ruin your whole day. At least it ruined mine. Not that I had much room to complain. Someone had ruined Stevie Number's whole life.

I found him in the Center's recycling dumpster sprawled on his back, arms outflung as if to embrace the gray dawn. Even alive, Stevie had smelled bad, and dying had done nothing to improve his body odor. I turned my face away and took a deep breath.

Okay, I'll admit it wasn't just the smell, pungent though it was. As a hospice nurse, I'd seen a lot of people pass from this earth to the next plane, but they'd done it on their own steam--or actually by running out of steam. Stevie had been helped along his way to the next world. Someone had crushed in the side of his skull.

The sight of that large dent alone acted as a visceral reminder that we're all made of the same fragile bone and flesh. So I breathed slowly through my mouth until I was sure I wasn't going to lose the half cup of coffee I'd had instead of breakfast.

What in the world was he doing here in the back alley of my place of work? Stevie Number, part-time street person and full-time schizophrenic, belonged on Berkeley's Telegraph Avenue. Granted, that was only two miles away, but it was a whole universe apart from the Center's office in Oakland.

No question, he was dead. Was dead before he was dumped here. There was nothing I could do for Stevie except show his battered body a little respect before I called the police. Moving him was out, but covering his face wasn't. All I had to offer was my jacket—the new navy one with a matching skirt I'd put on like armor for the face-off with my boss. If I used it, I knew I'd never be able to wear it again.

Stevie lay on top of a forest's worth of shredded computer printouts. All of it was destined for recycling to ease our guilty consciences over the destruction of innocent trees, and that was why I was here so early in the first place. My boss had given me the assignment, though it appeared nowhere in my job description, of making sure the recycling company and not the garbage service collected the paper from the bin. I couldn't see using the shredded paper to cover his face, though. It would be too much like packing him for UPS shipment. I spotted a few lined legal-sized pages that had somehow escaped the shredder and spread them gently over his face. "Rest in peace, Stevie," I whispered.

"I didn't kill him."

I nearly jumped right out of my skin even though I knew instantly who it was. I jerked around. GI Joe, Stevie's constant shadow, didn't look much better alive than Stevie did dead. His filthy army surplus camouflage fatigues hung from his skeletal frame. A few years of methamphetamine addiction had worn his body down to the fewest possible cells needed to sustain life, including the neurons in his frontal lobes which functioned rationally only to make sure he had enough meth for his next fix. The remaining gray matter retained the dialogue from every war movie he'd ever seen, which he re-lived in a daily, delusional exercise.

"I didn't kill him," he said again, his gaze darting in every direction and his hands and feet in a constant twitch. If you didn't know him, you'd suspect that he was guilty no matter what he claimed. If you did know him, you'd be confident in your suspicions. Meth had not only relieved Joe of every extra gram of fat and flesh, it had also stripped him of his conscience and possibly his soul as well.

"You gotta believe me," he whined.

I didn't have to do anything except call the police but wasn't going tell Joe that. He had a thing about cops. "Okay."

Strangely enough, I almost believed him. Stevie alive was Joe's meth ticket. It wasn't likely that Joe would kill off the only regular source of money he had. But then, speed freaks weren't known for their rationality.

Joe's twitching grew into a jerking, jiggling dance, which pulled him backward away from me. I'd already conducted the longest conversation I'd ever had with Joe. Usually he could focus on only two things, war movies and methamphetamine, but I didn't want him to leave if he knew anything about Stevie's death. "If you didn't kill him, who did?"

That got his attention. He held still for a full count of one. He opened his mouth, but whether to tell me something important or not, I never found out.

A garbage truck roared down the alley toward us. Its engine backfired twice, and Joe threw himself at me in a great swan dive. I tried to move aside, but only succeeded in making a quarter turn before he landed on me, sending us both down onto the pavement with me underneath, taking the impact on my knee, hip, shoulder and cheekbone in that bruising order.

"Get off me, you stupid freak."

"It's Charley. Omigod, it's Charley. Those gooks are gonna get us. Stay down."

Great. He was tweaking and now lived in the celluloid swamps of *Platoon*, or maybe *Full Metal Jacket*. I'd thought that Stevie had a bad smell, but it was nothing compared to Joe. At least Stevie showered once a month on check day. I was going to get the heaves if I didn't get away from him soon. "Get off *now*."

"It's okay, Loot. I'll take care of him."

I heard running feet. The cavalry, at last. "Help!"

"Take it easy, buddy," a man called out. "Why don't you put down the gun and talk to me?"

"Gun?" I yelped and twisted my head around as best I could. I couldn't see much, just the corner of Joe's jaw and his outstretched arm, and at the end of it, a hand with a gun. Maybe it was the angle of my vision, but it looked big, really big. A "found" object, no doubt. He'd never have spent money on anything except drugs.

"Mademoiselle, parlay voo English?" Joe asked.

Christ, what movie were we in now? "Oui, a leetle," I gasped, playing for time.

"Hold still. I won't hurt you. We've got Jerry at two o'clock. Comprenez?"

Okay, I got the picture, if you know what I mean. Maybe I could get the other guy to play along. "Non, non, monsieur," I said as loud as my crushed lungs would allow. "You are meestaken. Zat ees my brother. He ees a member of the Maquis. He risk hees life to bring you l'information about zee German tanks."

"Whyn't you say so?" Joe lifted his weight from me, and I scrambled to my feet. Joe, carrying the gun with its barrel pointed down, was already heading toward the dumpster the garbageman was using as a shield.

"Monsieur, wait." I limped after him, my bruised hip keeping me at a halting half-trot. "I must translate for you."

Unfortunately, the garbage truck driver, who'd stayed behind in the cab, decided to take matters into his own hands. He shifted the truck into drive and bore down on us. The roar of the engine reverberated against the walls of the buildings in the narrow alley and drowned out my words.

Joe probably wouldn't have listened to me anyway, but the truck's rumble guaranteed deafness. He leapt off the ground and spun an airborne one eighty, his legs already pumping before his feet hit the asphalt. Stupidly, I didn't get out of his way. Instead of zigzagging around me, he hit me with a shoulder block, and I went down onto my already injured hip.

As he ran away, I pushed myself to a sitting position

and swore. I knew how to swear at length, thanks to my years of volunteer work with street people like Stevie Number and GI Joe, and I'd used my entire vocabulary by the time the garbageman made his way over to me. He was a big guy somewhere around my age, which means still on the safe side of thirty-five, with dark curly hair and a goatee.

"Are you okay?" he asked.

"What do you think?" I came back.

"I think you know a lot of curse words for a foreigner. I guess we should see if anything's broken."

"Nothing's broken. Help me up?" I held out a hand, which he took, and without any effort on my part, nearly lifted me straight up into the air.

The garbage truck driver hurried over. He was a big guy with a beer belly, but also with plenty of muscle showing around his arms and shoulders. "I sent Izzy to call the police," he said.

"Thanks, Lou," Dark and Curly said.

"Izzy? You mean there are three of you contenders from the World Wrestling Federation, and you let a guy who doesn't weigh a hundred pounds beat me to the pavement?"

Lou pulled at his ear. "Yeah, but he had a gun."

I shook my head. I'd seen the gun, too, but it just didn't fit with anything I knew about Joe.

Dark and Curly cocked his head to one side. "One thing I don't get. What happened to your accent?"

"What accent?" I replied out of pure contrariness. It wasn't fair to blame him because my hip hurt like hell, or because I'd discovered the murdered body of someone I knew, or because I was going to have to talk to cops for hours instead of facing off with my boss. But then, as Stevie Number himself would have told him, life wasn't fair.

The cops came quickly and in full force, ready to deal with a hostage situation. Some of them looked let down when they finally figured out that they only had one dead body, one bruised woman, three confused garbagemen and no gun-toting bad guy in sight.

When one of the older cops asked him, Dark and Curly told him his name was Tony Dezzutti and made sure the cop knew that it was spelled with two Zs and two Ts. When it was my turn, I told him my name was Alison Weaver and let him figure it out for himself. I also told him that I knew Stevie and Joe from volunteering at the Mobile Clinic in Berkeley, that I didn't know what either of them would be doing this far from Telegraph Avenue, and that I didn't know why anyone would want to kill Stevie. I didn't bother to add what he knew as well as I. In Stevie and Joe's world, almost anything could serve as a motive for violence—a sneer, a misunderstood mumbled word, a refusal to share a cigarette.

Tony stood nearby while I gave my version of what had happened. Beyond him two cops unwound a roll of yellow crime-scene tape around the bin and across the alley. Lou negotiated with them to let him continue with his garbage pick-up route. The cops said something I couldn't hear, but it couldn't have been good news. Lou's shoulders sagged, and he headed back to his truck shaking his head.

I felt sorry for him, but sorrier for myself. It wasn't possible that Lou's boss could be any worse than mine. Daniel Dunston, PhD, founder, director, and absolute dictator of the Center for Biostatistical Studies, would blame me for every bit of inconvenience to him and his staff, every second of lost work time, and every column inch of unwanted publicity this murder was going to cost him. I just wished I knew what would make him angrier—calling him now to tell him what had happened outside the Center's back door, or letting him find out for himself when he came in at his usual time.

The cop closed his notebook and tucked it in the breast pocket of his uniform. "Would you like me to call the paramedics, or do you want to be seen by your own doctor?"

I resisted the urge to rub my backside. "My hip hurts, but I'm sure nothing's broken."

"What about those cuts?" He gestured first to my face and then my leg.

"Cuts?" I echoed. My hand went to my cheek and came away smeared with blood. I looked down. Blood oozed from my knee, over a jagged tear in my pantyhose and down my leg.

I hadn't felt the pain on my face or knee until I saw the blood. I bent over to inspect the damage. Adrenaline's a funny thing. Pumps you up in a second. Deflates you just as fast. When I straightened up, the ground tilted under my feet, and I had to take a little stagger-step to regain my balance. The cop grabbed me by one elbow, and Tony took the other one. With his free hand, the cop unhooked his radio from his belt.

"I'm okay. I don't want the paramedics." I pulled my arms free from both men to demonstrate that I really was all right.

Tony tilted his head to one side and gazed at me. "You ought to have those cuts seen to. They might get infected."

"I'm an RN. I'll take care of it. I'm going to get my bag, okay?" Without waiting for him to reply, I crossed to the recycling bin, picked up my shoulder bag, and came back to rejoin the two men.

The cop slid his radio back into place, retrieved his notebook and jotted something down. "I need to ask you both to stay around until the homicide team has a chance to talk to you. You can wait in the squad car." He led the way to the black-and-white.

Tony went back to the garbage truck for his stuff. The cop opened the back door of the squad car and I slid in. He disappeared from sight, but in a few seconds he came back and held out a first-aid kit to me. "You can use this, if you want."

I took the kit and said, "Thanks," though I didn't mean it. Nurses are a peculiar breed. We're really good at taking care of other people and terrible at looking after ourselves. If given a choice, I'd ignore the cuts as long as I could.

Tony, lunchbox cooler in one hand and thermos in the

other, eased himself into the back seat next to me and stowed his lunch things at his feet. I moved over to make room for him, and he shot me a look. "Hope this is okay with you. The cop said I should wait in here."

"Sure. Come on in. Plenty of room."

Tony gazed at me intently. He was pretty good-looking—an Italian-American hunk with brown eyes, nearly black hair, and the goatee-type beard currently preferred by about seventy percent of men in his age bracket. He rested his arm along the top of the seat and leaned toward me. "I have the weirdest feeling we've met before. Don't I know you from somewhere?"

"That's not a very original line, but I guess the circumstances are unusual enough to give it a fresh twist."

He straightened and looked away from me, then back again. "I didn't mean it like that. I meant...just...you know." He stopped trying to explain and sat silent, looking embarrassed.

If there'd been enough room in the back seat I would have kicked myself. Almost two years after my husband had left me for another woman, my bitterness still leaked into everyday social encounters with men. I needed to watch myself. "Sorry. I'm a little jumpy."

Tony relaxed a little. "I don't blame you. Freaked me out, I'll tell you, seeing that body and the weirdo waving a gun around."

"I was pretty shaken up myself, and I didn't thank you for trying to help."

"Didn't do much. It was Lou who scared him off with the truck."

"You both helped," I said not quite truthfully, because I was concentrating on improving my social skills with the opposite sex. "I don't think we've ever met, but I do volunteer work with the Mobile Clinic. Maybe you've seen me on the street." I offered my hand. "I'm Alison."

He shook my hand. "I'm Tony, and I'm pretty sure we met face to face." He gave his head a shake. "It'll come to me later, I guess." His gaze dropped to the cooler and thermos at his feet.

"Hey." He picked up the thermos and unscrewed the top. "How about some coffee?"

"Thanks." I took the steaming cup he handed me. The warmth from the cup seeped into my hands and then, as I took gulp after gulp of coffee, trailed down inside me. The chill, both from the morning fog and the morning discovery, slowly dissipated.

He opened the lunchbox and pulled out a couple of sandwiches. "Hungry?" He held out one of the sandwiches.

Hunger hardly described the ravenous demon that the sight of those sandwiches awakened in my stomach. "Well," I hesitated.

"Go on." He offered me a big deli sandwich, the kind with more meat than bread.

Controlling the urge to snatch it out of his hand, I traded him the coffee cup for the sandwich, peeled back a corner of the plastic wrap, and took a monster bite of French roll with an inch-thick layer of honey-roasted ham slices, provolone cheese and all the fixings.

Hunger aside, I'm more than partial to sandwiches of any kind, and this one was the good kind.He tossed off the remaining coffee and unwrapped his own sandwich. We chewed in a comfortable silence. My early morning terror receded. My apprehension about the immediate future faded. I relaxed against the police car's vinyl upholstery, and just at that moment, my boss showed up. I turned my head, looked out the back window, and spotted him arguing with one of the uniformed cops guarding the yellow-taped barrier across the alley.

I handed the untouched half of my sandwich to Tony. "My boss. Got to go."

"Sure you don't want the rest of it?" Tony asked, offering the sandwich to me again.

I shook my head and tried to find the door handle. Of course, the back seats of police cars don't have working door handles because usually that's where the bad guys ride. Tony had to get out to make way for me. I banged my knee on the door and started it bleeding again.

One glance at Daniel, pressing his lips together in that pissy way of his while he listened to the cop telling him he couldn't cross the police line, told me that a little scrape on the knee wasn't going to win his sympathy. In fact, probably no injury short of complete decapitation would impress him at all.

If Daniel Dunston weren't a genius and a humanitarian who'd already made a difference in public health policy, I wouldn't have been standing there in the first place. But he was. And more to the point, I was using his data in my dissertation. If he decided in one of his infamous attacks of pique to withdraw support for my work, I'd be up a creek without a PhD.

"Daniel," I called. He looked my way and made to duck under the yellow tape, but the uniformed cop took him by the arm and restrained him.

I hurried over and lifted the tape over my head. "Daniel," I said again and stopped. I shifted my weight from one foot to the other. I'd been stuffing my face with ham and cheese when I should've been rehearsing my story—something concise that would put me in a good light but didn't sound defensive.

Daniel gazed at me and pointed to the scene in the alley. "What's going on? What happened to your face?"

"I got here before the garbage truck." No, that wasn't right. Too self-justifying. It was a just-the-facts-ma'am kind of situation. "I found a dead person in our recycling bin."

I was going to go on, explain further, but Daniel gave a jerk with his whole body, a movement that gave the phrase "doing a double-take" a whole new meaning.

"Dead person?" It came out in kind of a squeak, as if his vocal chords weren't working well.

"Yes, well—it was kind of a shock, I guess you can imagine. Daniel? Are you all right?" His skin had gone a sickly yellow color, and his eyes bulged behind the lenses of his glasses. The problem with having worked around dying people is that I forgot that most people have an irrational fear of corpses. They don't like being reminded that we're all terminal cases.

"Do they know who it was?"

"That's the weird thing. I knew him. He was one of the street people I'd treated at the Mobile Clinic. People called him Stevie Number. I don't know his real name."

"You knew him, but he wasn't one of our employees." He stated it as a fact, but waited for me to confirm.

"He's... he was mentally ill. He didn't work anywhere. He lived in Berkeley."

"Have you checked the offices?"

"The offices? No. I... "

"The back door, was it locked, unlocked, broken into?" His voice rose with each word.

So that was it. Before my time, they'd had a break-in at the Center. Some of the stolen computers hadn't been backed up, costing Daniel some crucial data and many federal dollars in replicating a completed study. The experience had turned Daniel into a security freak, in spite of the fact that currently even the backup systems were backed up. He was upset at the possibility of another robbery, not for the lost life of a poor street person. "I didn't notice anything."

He pressed his lips together in disapproval. "You didn't notice," he said and sniffed. "What about the front entrance?"

"I haven't looked."

"You haven't looked." He echoed me again and repeated the sniffing routine.

His rotten attitude made me forget that I wanted to be placating. "Look, I get here before the garbagemen, per your instructions. I find a body in the dumpster. Then I'm knocked down by this crazy speed freak. The garbagemen come and call the cops, who tell me to wait here until some other cops come. So, no, I haven't looked at the doors or the offices, and how could anyone break in there anyway, now that it's more secure than the Pentagon?" I ran out of breath about this point, and it was none too soon.

Daniel ran a hand over his precisely combed, wavy brown hair and sniffed once more, loudly.

I spoke again, hurriedly, before he could get a word in himself. "However, if you'd like, we could go now and check."

"Anytime you're ready, Alison." By which he meant the exact opposite--as in, I'd better come immediately, and, if I didn't, I was in deep doo-doo.

CHAPTER TWO

Daniel made for the back door, but I could tell we weren't going to get past the cop guarding the yellow tape across the alley. "Let's go in the front," I said. "We can check the back door from the inside."

I told the cop on guard duty where I was going and why. Daniel led the way at his usual fast clip up the street and around the corner to the Center's official entrance. My knee hurt, my hip had stiffened up from sitting in the police car, and I couldn't keep up with him. I brought up the rear in a hurried half-limp.

"You say that you discovered the body and then someone attacked you?" Daniel asked me over his shoulder.

"Mmmph." I was short of breath, and I wasn't too fond of doing the three-step-behind submissive march. If he wanted to ask questions he could slow down.

When we reached the painted metal front door with its discreet brass nameplate, Daniel punched in his access code to turn off the alarm, first shielding the number pad with his body. Ever security-conscious, our Daniel. I had my own access code, what could I possibly want with his? I leaned against the wall and rested my sore hip.

An electronic alarm and two dead bolts later, we were inside the suite of offices. Daniel's office and the data room ran along one wall, restrooms and lounge lined the opposite side. The large windowless expanse that remained had been divided into a maze of cubicles with only fluorescent fixtures buzzing overhead to illuminate the darkness.

If thieves ever succeeded in breaking in again, they'd wonder where the treasure was buried. Our computer equipment represented a haphazard collection of used hard drives, dysfunctional keyboards and ancient printers, and our office furniture would have made a poor showing at a garage sale.

Granted, we had two newish computers with hefty memory, which were used as servers, two more nearly as big computers for running large statistical analyses, a state-of-the-art scanner, and a super-duper copying machine. All of this fancy stuff was bolted down and locked up in the fishbowl, a large room with thick acrylic picture window on the interior wall that let everyone, especially Daniel, see who was working in there.

"Shall we talk in here?" Daniel led the way to his private office. He went through the same routine with the access code and multiple locks on his office door, and held the door open for me, while he switched on the lights.

I sank into one of the two little-used visitors' chairs. Daniel didn't entertain company in his office. You mainly came in here if you'd messed up. I guess I qualified in his eyes.

He hitched one hip onto his desktop and gazed down at me. "What can you tell me about this situation?"

"What I've already told you. That's all."

"Do you have any idea why this street person should have crawled into our recycling bin and expired?"

"He didn't expire. He was murdered." I hated that word—expire—as if death were nothing more than running out of time on your earthly parking meter. I had a memory-flash of Stevie's crushed skull and wrapped my arms around my middle. "I was going to call you. I didn't think you'd be here this early."

He stood up and moved to sit behind his desk. "I came in early to review your dissertation proposal."

"My proposal?"

"For analyzing the refinery study data. You were expecting to discuss it today, weren't you?"

"Yes." The dissertation was the final requirement for my graduate degree. Two years ago, I'd given up my nursing job with shorter hours and three times the pay, because Daniel had assured me I could use data from the refinery study for my dissertation. All he asked was that first I do data collection in the field. Okay, no problem. I scurried around for months, convincing people to participate in the study, interviewing them and doing a mini-medical exam.

After that, Daniel had said that all I had to do was enter data into the computer, crosscheck and double-check it for accuracy. Again, no problem. I was going to use some of this very data in my dissertation, so I should do the work. Then, Daniel said, since I was so good at that, and, as it turned out also good at a number of other low-grade scut-work tasks, he'd assigned me to work for two other researchers at the Center, with the result that work on my dissertation had been stalled for eight months. All the while, Daniel had dangled access to the study data like the proverbial carrot and jerked it away from me as soon as I tried to take a bite.

He reached into his out box and extracted some typed sheets of paper. "I find your proposal quite acceptable. I've made a few comments and minor revisions." He handed the pages across his desk to me. "Your analysis fits quite well into the over-all goals of the study, and I'd like you to begin as soon as possible."

My mouth fell open. I'd prepared a speech to give him this morning, almost an ultimatum, to convince him to let me start working on it, but he was handing it over to me without a single protest. "I'm glad you like it," I managed to say.

"It's urgent that we proceed with all data analyses at once."

"I understand. I'm ready to start right now."

"Very commendable attitude. However, under the circumstances... " He paused, tilted his head back and gazed at me. "I hope you don't mind my saying it, but you look terrible. How do you feel?"

I felt a throbbing above my right eye and a sharp flash of pain from hip to knee every time I shifted in the chair, but these counted for nothing against the amazement, elation, and relief that welled up in me. Daniel was giving me access to the data. "I'm fine. Honest. Just give me a minute to clean up these scrapes, and I'll look a little better."

"I'm sure you will, but will you feel better? You've sustained a shock. I know I was appalled simply to learn a stranger had died outside our back door. What must you feel after actually finding him, someone you knew?"

"Sure, it was a shock, but... " I hesitated. But what? Shit happens? Life must go on? I could only conjure up inappropriate clichés. I didn't know how to act with a concerned and compassionate Daniel, since he never was. At least, not with people who worked for him. He reserved his humane impulses for the people he helped through his research.

A buzzer sounded, our doorbell for the uninitiated without a door code. "That must be the police. Do you feel up to talking to them?" Daniel asked, rising from his chair.

I lurched to my feet. "Sure." Where had this new, concerned Daniel come from?

"Very well, why don't you do that while I check the back door?"

A second buzz jarred me into action, and I headed down the corridor. The door opened before I could reach it, and Flo, the Center's administrative director, entered followed by a uniformed policeman and a heavy-set man wearing a well-tended mustache and a wrinkled sports jacket. "Alison, there you are," Flo said. "How could someone have been killed outside our back door? And what's this about you being attacked? You're bleeding." She made it sound like an accusation.

"Alison Weaver?" the sports-jacketed man asked. He reached into his pocket and held up his identification, complete with silver badge. "I'm Detective Stans. Is there somewhere we can talk?"

"Wait just a minute," Flo interrupted him. "You can see that she's been injured. She needs medical treatment."

Detective Stans glanced at Flo. "I was told that Ms. Weaver refused medical aid. Is that correct?" He directed the last to me.

"Yes, but I'd like a chance to clean myself up, if you don't mind."

"Good idea," Flo said and placed her body between the detective and me. "Let me grab the first aid kit and help you."

"Is it all right if we check around?" Detective Stans asked.

Flo hesitated. I could tell she was dying to ask me what had happened, but she also needed to protect the premises from invasion. I decided to help her out of her dilemma. "You'd have to ask Dr. Dunston about that. His office is just down that way." I pointed Detective Stans and his uniformed sidekick in the right direction, and they headed down the corridor.

Flo shepherded me into the ladies' room, then ducked out for a second and returned rolling a desk chair with one hand and carrying a first aid kit in the other. "Now you sit right down here," she said.

I felt like a fraud. Sure, I could have spoken with the detective right then and there, but I wanted to find out why Daniel was so suddenly ready, even eager, to have me work on the refinery data. Who better to tell me about it than Daniel's right-hand woman, Flo?

"Why don't you take off your pantyhose so we can clean that scrape? It's really too bad, they have such a big hole in them, I think you're going to have to throw them out."

I stripped off the torn and bloody pantyhose and dumped them in the trash. Then I plopped down into the chair. Before I could brace myself, Flo began patting the scrape with disinfectant-soaked gauze, and I hissed on an in-drawn breath at the sharp sting.

"It must have been simply awful, finding a body like

that." She glanced up from her disinfecting work.

I had my teeth gritted against the stinging pain in my knee and didn't want to unlock my jaw to reply, so I just nodded.

"They said he was in our recycling bin?" She made a question out of the statement.

Flo was after details, looking forward to being appalled, repelled, and horrified. A natural reaction. If I'd had a different set of life experiences, I'd probably have felt the same way. I loosened my clenched teeth and said, "Yes, he was lying on top of all our discarded paper. And yes, it gave me a jolt." I paused for a beat before changing the subject. "Guess what? Daniel told me I could start on the refinery data today."

"About time."

"That's what I say."

She straightened and doused yet another gauze pad in disinfectant. "Your poor face," she moaned, like the makeover expert at a cosmetics counter who'd found the limits to her art. "I hate to tell you, but you're probably going to get a black eye. I just hope these cuts don't scar."

I jerked my head around and checked out my face in the mirror. I saw a very puffy cheekbone and a fairly minor scrape. I was in no danger of disfigurement, but I have a secret vanity about not being vain, so I threw out an off-hand, "Scars lend character."

Then it hit me. Flo's comment "about time" couldn't mean the same thing it did to me. Flo was on Daniel's side in absolutely everything.

"Flo," I said softly. I didn't want to arouse her defenses. "What did you mean when you said it was about time Daniel gave me the refinery data?"

"He told me to leave a section open in the Center's annual progress report to NIPH for the up-date on the refinery study, and that was three weeks ago. The report's due at the end of the month, which means I'll have to work weekends to finish it."

"Why did he wait three weeks to give me the go-ahead to start working on it?"

Flo pressed her lips together. Even if she knew, she wouldn't be telling me. She reached with the gauze toward my face.

At the first jolting sting, I jerked my head away. "That's okay, Flo." I pushed her hand away from my face. "I'll take it from here." I'd let her torture me only because I thought she'd tell me something useful.

Flo started putting things away in the first aid kit. "I forgot. You're an RN, and I'm probably not doing it right."

Now I'd hurt her feelings. "I'm sorry. I didn't mean it that way. To be honest, I'm really worried about my dissertation. My advisor said he was giving me just one more month to show him I'm making progress. If you could give me some idea of Daniel's thinking about this, it would really help."

Flo kept fiddling with the first aid kit, fitting and re-fitting the bandages in place. "I'm certain Daniel will tell you everything you need to know," she said cryptically.

I should have guessed she'd stonewall me.

The door opened a crack and Kenji, one of the Center's star researchers, peeked in. "Knock, knock. I heard that you got roughed up, and I just wanted to check on the accuracy of the rumors."

"Kenji," Flo scolded. "This is the ladies' restroom. You can't come in here."

"Whoa, baby," he said to me. "You're going to have some shiner. Look at that eye." He came all the way into the room, ignoring Flo who fluttered her hands at him as if to shoo him away.

"Really, Kenji, this is not appropriate."

"Why not? It's sexist to assume that I can't render care to the fallen."

"I didn't mean your helping Alison. I meant it's not appropriate for you to be in the ladies' room."

"But Flo, I have to check out all rumors. It's in my job description."

"It is not."

"Yes, it is. My tacit job description. Just as defending Daniel against all comers is in your tacit job description." Kenji gave her his famous beguiling grin. He never hesitated to use his exotic good looks or his charm to reach any ends he thought worthwhile. He could say outrageous things, even to Flo, and get away with it. It wasn't fair.

Before Flo could think of a reply to this, Kenji turned to me. "Did you get a good look at the killer?"

"Who?"

He looked at me, eyebrows raised in surprise. "You know—the killer. The guy who did this to you." He gestured at my face.

"Oh, him. He didn't kill anyone."

"How do you know?"

That was a good question. Because Joe told me he hadn't done it? Probably not. Joe's word was completely worthless, but, somehow, I believed him anyway. "Joe's pretty crazy, mainly because he's an amphetamine addict, but even so I don't think he killed Stevie."

"You knew him? You knew them both?" Flo asked. She made it sound more like an accusation than a question.

"Yes. That really was what made finding the body so shocking. It was someone I knew."

"But I heard that he was a bum," Kenji protested. He sounded upset.

"He was mentally ill. I knew him from doing volunteer work in Berkeley."

"And the other guy? The mugger? You knew him, too?"

I nodded. "He isn't a mugger. He got scared. He didn't knock me down on purpose—or not exactly on purpose."

"But he *is* a drug addict," Flo said, as if that alone confirmed his guilt on any other count. "And you know him personally."

I stood up and straightened my shoulders. "What's that supposed to mean?"

"You were assigned to monitor the re-cycling. One of your friends shows up murdered in our bin, and your other friend beats you up. Obviously the matter concerns you personally and not the Center. But the police are here, inside our offices, and wanting to question us about it. It's going to reflect very badly on the Center when word gets out."

"Word? What word? He wasn't my friend. I knew him, that's all. It's pure coincidence that he ended up in our dumpster. His death doesn't have anything more to do with me than it does with the Center."

"Now, now." Kenji stepped between us. "No need to get worked up. I'm sure the police will leave us alone as soon as they talk to Alison. And, I nearly forgot," he added, turning to Flo. "Daniel wants you to organize an informational meeting in the fish bowl. He'd like to get the facts of this business out to everyone so they can go back to work. Right now, it's just one big water cooler scene out there."

"Why didn't you say so before this? Everything's going to be chaotic today because you found that body, Alison."

I gritted my teeth. "I didn't do it on purpose, you know. Tell you what. Next time, why don't *you* monitor the recycling pick-up? Then, if there are dead bodies lying around, you can carefully avoid noticing them."

Flo turned away and closed the lid on the first-aid kit with a snap. Kenji raised his eyebrows at me—a silent admonition against ruffling the feathers of the one person who always had Daniel's ear.

"You go on, Flo," Kenji said. "Tell Daniel we'll be out in a minute."

Flo left without saying a word.

"Hell," I muttered.

"You'd better think of a peace offering. That was a little too brutal. She'll find a way to let Daniel know that you hurt her feelings."

"What about my feelings?"

Kenji shrugged. "Unfortunately, your feelings don't

count for much in the sacred pecking order of the Center for Biostatistical Studies."

Kenji was right. Flo would be nice to me just as long as I supported the ongoing work of the Center. Still, it rankled that she'd turned on me so quickly simply because I knew Stevie and Joe. Something else bothered me, too. Just beneath my self-righteous indignation nibbled some guilt that I'd so vehemently denied that Stevie had been my friend. In fact, to the limited degree that a schizophrenic could have friends, I think I was a member of his small inner circle.

I rubbed my face as if I could wipe out the thoughts inside my head. I managed only to remind my cheekbone that it was bruised and sore, and I winced at the pain.

"You okay?" Kenji leaned toward me.

"I'm fine." Sure I was fine, considering I'd managed to get on Flo's wrong side. I'd have to figure out a way around Flo later. Right now I needed information, and Kenji was the gossip-meister of the Center. "Did you know that Daniel asked Flo to leave a section open in the NIPH report on the refinery study, and he still hasn't filled it in?"

"That so?"

"Yes, and listen to this. Daniel gave me the go-ahead to start work on the data for my dissertation. Said that work had to start ASAP. Of course, I couldn't be happier, but why the hurry all of the sudden?"

Kenji shrugged. "I don't know exactly, but I heard... " He paused.

"Yes? What did you hear? Come on, Kenji, you're the source, you know that. If there's a rumor, you've heard it."

"I don't know anything definite, just that Daniel was concerned about being scooped."

"Scooped? You mean, there's another study on the health effects of living near oil refineries?"

He nodded. "Something like that."

"But who? Where'd they get their funding?"

"Hey, I'd tell you if I knew. It's just something I

heard, that's all. Why don't you ask Daniel?"

I made a face. "You know how he is. He plays his cards so close to his chest I think sometimes he has trouble reading them himself, but I guess I might as well try."

"You go, girl." He held open the door and I marched out into the corridor, ready to do battle, or whatever else needed doing.

Detective Stans was waiting for me outside the ladies room, his arms folded across his chest and resting on the expanse of belly below that his sports jacket made no effort to hide. He had a tired face, lined with an expression of permanent resignation, but also with a certain doggedness in the set of his mouth. "You feel well enough to talk to us now?"

Daniel bustled up to us. "I'm sure Alison will do all she can to help you with your inquiries."

"I'll tell you anything I can," I said, "but there's not much I can add to what I told the first policeman."

"It helps us to go over it again."

"Perhaps I could come down to the station after work." I glanced at Daniel out of the corner of my eye. He'd be glad to see my work ethic in action.

"It would help if we could talk to you now."

"Sure, but you can see that there's not much privacy here, and I don't want to interrupt anyone's work." Not that there was any risk of interrupting anyone, since no one had even started working. In spite of Flo's instructions to hold an informational meeting, the entire crew of the Center stood around in small groups or peered over the tops of their cubicles at us. They clearly preferred to get their "information" from front row seats.

"Of course, you can't talk here," Daniel said flatly, ruling out any possibility of our using his office for the interview. "I assumed you'd take the day off after such a horrific experience."

I stared at him. Who's side was he on? "I'm fine. I'd really like to get started on the refinery data."

"That can wait. The police need your help right now. I expect you to take the day off. Tomorrow, too, for that matter. Rest and recover."

I'd been counting on him to take his usual line of the work being too important to take second place to anything.

"Thank you for *your* cooperation, Dr. Dunston," Detective Stans said. "If you don't mind, Ms. Weaver, we can talk outside in my car."

I minded. I saw the long-deferred work on my dissertation being delayed yet again. Maybe I had to abandon the field of battle now, but I'd be back.

CHAPTER THREE

Detective Stans took me out to his unmarked police car and opened the door on the front passenger side. So I sat down and looked around while Stans circled the car and got in on the driver's side. This cop car boasted the crime-fighting equipment of the modern age. No metal screen separated the back seat from the front. Instead of a shotgun, a laptop computer mounted on a swivel occupied the space between the two front seats.

Another detective opened the back door and slid in. "This is my partner, Detective Carney," Stans said. I twisted around in my seat and nodded to him. He was younger than Stans and tougher looking. Like Stans and all the uniformed cops at the scene, he sported a mustache. Unlike Stans, he didn't have a soft belly straining the buttons on his white shirt, and his sports jacket lacked the permanent-press wrinkles. Possibly he was more of an action-type cop and didn't spend a lot of time in warm cars questioning witnesses.

Stans got my address and phone and asked me all the expected questions. I found myself repeating almost word for word the story I'd told the uniformed officer earlier. I'd just found the body when Joe had appeared out of nowhere. He'd spoken to me briefly, then knocked me down when the garbage truck showed up.

"I've known Stevie Number and GI Joe for about two years, through my volunteer work at the Mobile Clinic."

"Where's that?" Carney asked.

"Lots of places. It's a converted Winnebago. We drive it to different parts of Berkeley and Oakland. Nurses and physicians donate their time to provide free medical care to those who need it."

"You mean homeless people?"

"And new immigrants, and parents without insurance, and prostitutes, and runaways. Anyone who needs basic medical care."

Stans nodded. "I've heard of it. Stevie Number, GI Joe—what are their real names?"

"I don't know. You should ask Libby Honeck. She's the force behind the Clinic. If anyone knows their names, it's Libby. I do know that Stevie and Joe spent a lot of time on the street, but they aren't, or weren't homeless. Stevie had an apartment."

"How'd he pay for it? SSI payments?" Stans asked.

I shook my head. "I don't think so. I heard that he got money from his parents. Once a month he'd get back on his medication for a week, take a shower, put on clean clothes, and go pick up his check." I sighed and looked through the windshield at the windowless stucco wall of the building that housed the Center. "He seemed almost normal when he was cleaned up and on meds. What a waste."

"Do you know for a fact that he was schizophrenic?" Carney asked from the back seat.

I turned to gaze at him. He held a pen poised over an open notebook in his lap. "Yes, why?"

He shrugged and jotted something in the notebook. "Seems pretty in touch with reality to be able to hit up his folks for money every month."

"That was Joe's job. He made sure that Stevie had his head straight on check day. He got the money for drugs from Stevie, plus a place to live."

"Why didn't he make sure Stevie was okay the rest of the time?"

"Joe's a meth addict," I said. "He just wanted the money for drugs. Sometimes he sold Stevie's unused medication or traded it for speed or crystal."

The rest of their questions followed a predictable course. Did I have Stevie and Joe's address? Did I know anywhere else Joe might have gone? Did I know anyone who might know besides Libby Honeck? After the third "no" answer, they seemed to lose their enthusiasm for asking questions.

We sat in silence for about half a minute. In the passenger side mirror I saw the city morgue van pull up. Stevie had been left lying in the dumpster while the police did all the necessary evidence-gathering. His body would be in full rigor by now. Just the idea of the black bag forcibly zipped around his unwieldy form made my insides clench. "If that's all you have to ask me, I'd like to go now."

"One last thing," Stans said. "We'll need your signature on the complaint form."

"What complaint? I have to file a complaint, because someone killed Stevie?"

"No. It's a complaint for assault. We probably don't need it, but just in case we find this GI Joe before we have enough material evidence, having a complaint on file will help us hold him for awhile." He made it sound completely reasonable. In fact, he sounded too reasonable, and maybe that's why my bullshit sensors went into overdrive.

"But I told you, Joe didn't attack me."

Sounds of pages being turned from the back seat, then Carney said, "'He knocked me over and held me down on the pavement.' That's what you said happened right after you found the body. The other witnesses confirm it."

I twisted around in my seat and looked at him, "I also said that he wasn't trying to hurt me. He thought he was protecting me."

"From what? The garbage truck?" Carney asked. I couldn't be sure but it looked as if he was smirking behind his moustache.

"He's delusional because of the drugs. He told me he hadn't killed Stevie. He would've told me more, but the garbage truck pulled into the alley just then and scared him."

"So he knows something about the murder, right?" Stans asked. "Even if he didn't kill Stevie." He made it sound as if he was willing to entertain any theory, no matter how far-fetched.

"Look, if you arrest Joe, all you'll get out of him is his name, rank and serial number plus some dialogue from Saving Private Ryan. Stevie was my friend, and I want his killer arrested, but jailing Joe on a phony assault charge isn't going to help."

Me and my big mouth. I knew right away I shouldn't have used the word "phony." Stans straightened in his seat, and Carney began rapidly flipping through his notebook.

"You said you were acquainted with the deceased from volunteering at a clinic. You didn't mention that you were friends," Carney said.

"Well, we weren't friends in the usual sense of the word. I never invited him to my house for dinner or anything, but when he was on meds, we'd talk about statistics."

"What d'you mean, statistics? Like baseball?" Carney asked.

"No, I mean as in mathematical ways of figuring things out."

They both stared at me blankly.

"Say you drink contaminated water," I said, trying to think of a simple way of explaining my work. "And later on you develop cancer. If some of the other people who also drank the water got cancer too, a statistical test of how many people developed cancer versus those who didn't could tell you how likely it was that it happened by chance or because of the water."

Carney narrowed his eyes at me. "So you're saying you talked with a crazy guy about contaminated drinking water?"

This cop was getting on my nerves. "No, we didn't talk about drinking water. I already told you, we talked about statistics, a kind of mathematics."

"That so?" Stans asked. "He could actually carry on a conversation about mathematics?"

"He was schizophrenic, not retarded. He was a brilliant mathematician when he wasn't delusional. That's why they called him Stevie Number."

"No kidding?" Carney said from backseat.

I didn't see any point in responding.

"So, about the complaint," Stans said.

"I just told you why I won't sign it. One, Joe didn't intend to hurt me. Two, he won't tell you anything useful if you put him in jail. So why should I help you arrest him? Don't you think we should try to find out what he wanted to tell me instead?"

Carney leaned forward from the back seat and spoke next to my ear. "There is no 'we,' Ms. Weaver. This is strictly a police matter."

"So what am I doing here?"

"You're a witness giving us information that could make a difference in the case," Stans said, "but, give us information only. You shouldn't approach the suspect on your own."

"I'm not going to," I said with complete insincerity, which I hoped didn't show.

"Good," Stans said. He reached into his breast pocket and pulled out a business card, which he handed to me. "If you change your mind about filing the assault charge, let us know. You may think you are doing the best thing, but remember, he was armed and irrational. If you see him, I repeat, do not approach him yourself. Call us."

I stuffed his card into my bag without looking at it. "Sure. If that's all... " I didn't wait for them to say anything before I opened the door and slid out of the car.

I headed up the street, away from the cop car, the morgue van and the Center. It was only a mile from the Center to my house. Even so, I usually drove my ancient but still road-worthy Toyota and parked as close as I could to the building. Yesterday, though, I'd loaned it to Libby because her car was in the shop.

I'd have to call Libby as soon as I got home and tell her about Stevie. She was going to be upset. She'd put a lot of her immense capacity for caring into Stevie. I started rehearsing different ways of breaking the news to her, but gave up after about five minutes. There were no words to ease the pain of hearing someone who mattered to you had died. If I hadn't learned anything else in my years as a hospice nurse, I'd learned that.

I walked a little slower, because of something I'd rather not do looming when I got home. I wasn't paying attention when I strolled around the corner onto my street and nearly collided with one person I never wanted to meet. The man who had nearly single-handedly turned my neighborhood into a nightmare of yuppification--Mitch the carpenter. I didn't know his last name and didn't want to know it. I took pride in the fact that in the nearly two years since he'd moved into the house across the street, we hadn't exchanged a single word.

I'd never seen him up close, although I'd recognize him anywhere. He always looked the same--tall and lanky in baggy khaki shirt and pants, long blond frizzy hair tied at the nape of his neck, untrimmed red beard and an A's baseball cap pulled down to his eyebrows. He usually girded himself with a leather tool belt, slung low on his hips like a Western gun fighter. Maybe that was how he saw himself, as the single-handed enforcer of city building codes.

I jerked to a stop, did a quick left face and cut across the street. I could see the brown-spotted lawn, peeling trim and weatherworn shingles of my house down the street. Run-down as it was, it was still the most coveted house on the block. In its original incarnation, it had been a small farmhouse, encircled by trees and fields. The fields had gradually been sold off. In the 1920's a developer bought the remaining property and put up as many small stucco bungalows as he could crowd in.

My house had remained intact on a much-reduced lot, which was still large in comparison to my neighbors'. The bungalow owners didn't even have the dignity of a real front yard, just two small rectangles of dirt flanking cement steps that descended directly from the front door to the sidewalk.

By the time I'd moved here five years ago, most folks had cemented in those patches of ground rather than struggle to maintain the fiction of a front lawn. A few homeowners had opted for an original touch with astro-turf covering the cement or, my personal favorite, colored gravel in shades never seen in nature.

That all disappeared when throngs of young professional couples had decided to flee the suburbs, starting a local real estate boom rivaled only by the Oklahoma Land Rush. When home prices in all the desirable districts were inflated beyond reason, they began buying houses in working-class neighborhoods like mine. With Mitch the carpenter's help, they painted, refinished, refurbished and added onto their houses. They replaced the cement in their nominal "front yards" with extravagant displays of blooming shrubs and perennial flowers as if they were finalists in a House Beautiful contest. But, they never sat outside on the front steps and watched the kids play catch in the street. They never stopped to gossip on their way to drop their utility bill payments in the mailbox on the corner. Or offered to give their neighbors' battery a jump when they'd forgotten to turn off their headlights. My street had been a real neighborhood when I first moved here. Now it was pretty, but socially as barren as arctic tundra. My eighty-five- year-old neighbor Rose and I were the last holdouts on the block.

I reached the front edge of my lawn, and something caught my attention, a furtive movement or a rustle of leaves. I stopped and looked around. A kid, not a day over ten, dropped out of a tree, and for the second time that day I found myself staring at a large hand gun. The only difference was that this time it was pointed directly at my heart.

He dropped into a crouch and held the gun in the Hollywood-approved two-fisted grip. "Put your hands where I can see 'em," he barked at me. Sort of a high-pitched bark, like a Chihuahua or a Pekinese.

I slowly lifted my right arm above my head and gripped the strap of my bag with my left. As soon as his gaze shifted to track the movements of my hand, I slung my bag at him. He saw it coming, turned his head to look, and staggered back a step at the last second to avoid being hit. As soon as he looked away from me, I moved in and twisted the gun out of his hand.

"Hey, gimme that back." He reached for the gun.

I held it away from him, but the feel of it was all wrong. "What the hell?" I spread my palm and hefted the gun. Some liquid dripped from the barrel. "A water gun? You were going to hold me up with a water gun?"

"You shoulda done what I said. If it was a real gun, you'd be dead by now."

He was right about that. He'd gotten off a shot. I could feel my wet blouse pressing against my chest. "Okay. I'd be dead, and you'd be a murderer. Which is worse?"

He stared at me open-mouthed. Apparently he hadn't faced too many existential questions in his short life. I tried an easier one. "What's your name?"

"Tyler. And I want my gun back." He tried to twist his arm free, and I tightened my grip.

Now I could place the kid. He'd moved into the neighborhood just before my divorce. My ex-husband, Frank, had buddied around with him, given him occasional rides on his motorcycle. Frank was very big on being hero-worshipped and knew just how to cultivate it in susceptible souls. "Frank doesn't live here anymore."

"I know." He gave me a resentful look, as if he blamed me for Frank's unfaithfulness.

"Why aren't you in school?" I wasn't asking, so much as telling him I knew he was a truant.

"There's no school. It's professional development day." He rattled the words off as if they were supposed to mean something to me.

"School has really changed since my time. We never got days off to train as hit men."

He sneered in disgust. "It's professional development day for the teachers, not for the kids."

"That so? Looks to me that you were seizing an opportunity to develop some criminal tendencies. Why else were you trespassing on my property?"

"I wasn't trespassing. I was guarding it. I thought *you* were a trespasser." He popped the counter-accusation right back at me. Maybe I'd guessed wrong about his career goals, and he had aspirations to be a lawyer, not an assassin.

"You'll have to do better than that. You already admitted that you knew I lived here."

"I couldn't tell it was you from up there." He glanced at the tree where he'd sat in ambush. "I could only see the top of your head. Besides, you're supposed to be at work."

"So it's all my fault? I can see that Frank has taught you well."

He tried to pry my fingers from his wrist with his other hand. "Lemme go. Frank's a nice guy."

"Yeah, and so was Ted Bundy."

He narrowed his eyes at me. "Who's he?"

"Listen up. I already found the dead body of one person I knew this morning, and it put me in a very bad mood. I don't know you all that well, but I assure you it would really piss me off if you got killed." I waved the gun under his nose. "Sticking up people with this could accomplish that."

"It's not real. My dad brought it back from Hong Kong for me, and I'm going to tell him that you beat me up."

I released his wrist. "You do that." I retrieved my purse from the ground, tucked the gun into my waistband and headed for my house.

"Hey," Tyler yelled. "That's mine. Give it back."

I kept on walking. "I'll give it to your dad. You send him over to pick it up."

I unlocked my front door and slammed it behind me. Sure I'd give the gun back to his dad. After I gave the irresponsible son of a bitch an educational lecture on what gunshot wounds did to children's small bodies. Maybe I'd even give him a slide show. I knew a forensic pathologist who'd be more than happy to help with that. Photos of dead kids who cops had believed were armed when they opened fire.

I stomped into the kitchen, looked in the refrigerator and closed the door again. I was hungry and thirsty, but couldn't calm down enough to focus on fixing something. I settled for a glass of water. My hand shook as I held the glass under the tap. I put the glass down on the counter without taking a drink. The late morning sun slanted through the window and spread out on the kitchen counter. I pressed my trembling hand palm down onto the warm tile and let the heat seep into my fingers, but the wet spot on my blouse still felt cold against my skin. About as cold as Stevie Number had felt when I'd found him in the dumpster. When I'd covered his face with discarded paper instead of my jacket.

My mind veered away from the memory. I let my thoughts buzz and evade. There'd be a reckoning about what I'd seen and done—and hadn't done—when I'd found Stevie, but it didn't have to be now. Particularly not when my blouse clung clammily to my chest from Tyler's direct hit, and my hand could still recall the temperature and texture of Stevie's skin.

I stepped out of my shoes, strode barefoot to the other end of the kitchen, and threw open the louvered doors that hid my washer and dryer. I quickly stripped off my jacket and blouse and dumped them on top of the washing machine. When I unzipped my skirt, the water pistol clattered to the floor. I picked it up and tossed it next to my clothes and shut the folding doors. I make gestures like that. Shut the door. Hide any reminders out of sight. It never works in the long run, but I was only interested in the short run that morning, in shaking off the nagging feeling that I'd behaved badly when it had counted, and that I'd pay for it later.

CHAPTER FOUR

Hot showers are wonderful restoratives. Naps are even better. I took both, but got a little carried away with the nap. The sun had shifted to the other side of the house when I dragged myself out of bed, pulled on a tee-shirt and a pair of old jeans and staggered into the kitchen.

If I'd been hungry before, I was ravenous now. I rummaged through the refrigerator and the breadbox and put together a quick sandwich of cold spaghetti with tomato sauce on crusty sourdough. I'd learned the basic rule of the sandwich from my first foster mother—namely, there's nothing edible that can't be put between two pieces of bread. Even after I'd been moved on to my second, third and fourth foster family, a sandwich, any sandwich, remained my personal comfort food.

Leaning over the sink to spare my kitchen floor from random loose strands of spaghetti, I chomped my way through half a loaf of sourdough, noodles, and red meat sauce. I'd just crammed the last bite into my mouth when the doorbell rang. I padded barefoot across the living room and opened the door without bothering to peek through the little spy hole in the door first. Since nine times out of ten my visitors are people soliciting for a good cause and the tenth time they're Jehovah's Witnesses, I was pretty surprised to find Tony Dezzutti standing on my doorstep.

"Hi." He shoved his hands into the pockets of his jeans. Clean jeans, I noted. In fact, everything about him, from his combed wet hair to his ironed sports shirt was spanking clean. You'd never guess by looking that he made a living collecting garbage.

I stared at him for a few seconds, still chewing my last mouthful. What was he doing on my doorstep?

He shuffled his feet. "I just thought I'd stop by... " he said and stopped. "I wondered how you were doing," he started again. He paused and did the thing with his feet once more. "But, if you don't want to talk about it, that's okay."

I finally managed to swallow the last of the spaghetti sandwich. "I'm fine. I was eating and didn't want to talk with my mouth full. Usually, people who come to my door have a whole long sales spiel, so I'm not used to having to say anything right away."

He chuckled as if I'd said something funny and flashed a dimple in his right cheek. I'm a sucker for dimples. "Would you like to come in?" I took a step back from the doorway and waved my hand in the general direction of the living room.

Maybe it was the dimple, or maybe the fact that he was the first good-looking man to show up on my doorstep since my divorce. Okay, he was the only man, period—except for Kenji, and Kenji was just a buddy, so he didn't count. Whatever the reason, I invited him in and let him sit on my couch while I sat in my unmatching easy chair.

He looked around the living room, taking in the shabby, pre-owned furniture and the well-worn rug. I never noticed how beat-up everything looked until I had people over, but whatever anyone really thought, they always said, "Nice place." We sat there in silence while he checked out what he could see of my house from his seat on the sofa.

"Nice place," he said.

"I like it." I smiled, but he didn't grin back this time, so I asked the question I'd wanted to ask when I opened the door. "How'd you know where I live?"

"I heard you tell the cop."

Could this hunky guy actually be interested in me?

That flattering notion sank down into my middle and formed a warmish sensation. It lasted for about fifteen seconds, when I realized that Tony had run out of small talk. I'd always been a complete flop at chitchat myself, so the silence stretched out between us.

"Would you like a cup of coffee?" I finally broke the silence. At least fooling around in the kitchen would give me something to do other than sitting there thinking about the fact that I couldn't think of anything to say.

"Sure, if it's no trouble."

"No trouble at all." I was on my feet and in the kitchen before he'd struggled to a standing position. "I was just going to put on a pot when you rang the bell." There. I'd told a small social lie. I might make it as a conversationalist after all.

I performed the ritual of the electric coffee maker—insert filter, measure coffee, pour water. Tony watched my every move in silence.

"You get off work early today?"

"What?" He jerked his gaze toward me, as if I'd interrupted some very important thought. "No, we were late. Because of the cops and everything."

"I guess you must start pretty early."

"Yeah, we leave the yard at three-thirty, make the first pick-ups at four. I stopped by at your work, and they said you'd gone on home. But you're okay?"

"I'm okay." I fingered my right cheek. "I got a black eye out of it, but no permanent damage."

"Sorry I didn't stop that guy from knocking you down."

I don't know where the conversation would've gone from there, because the doorbell rang.

"Two visitors in one afternoon. I think that's a record." I walked into the living room, and this time I stopped to look through the little peephole in the door. Good thing I did. My ex-husband stood in front of the door, his hand poised to push the bell again. I jumped back just as he rang it. I hadn't seen Frank in two years. Not nearly long enough for me.

"Who is it?" Tony asked.

The doorbell rang again. Longer this time.

"It's okay. It's just my ex-husband. Ignore him and he'll go away."

"Your ex-husband?" Tony whispered.

Frank gave up on the bell and pounded his fist on the door. "Al, open up. It's me, Frank."

"Don't worry. He's harmless, unless you happen to be married to him."

No sooner were the words out than Frank pounded even louder. "Al, are you all right?"

"I was until you showed up," I muttered under my breath.

"What?" Tony asked, his gaze darting from me to the front door.

"I think the coffee's ready." I ushered him back into the kitchen.

Frank continued to pound on the door. His blows reverberated through the house.

"It's okay, really," I said soothingly. I'd practiced that encouraging tone of voice during my years as an RN.

Tony looked as reassured as a patient about to undergo surgery without anesthesia.

"Al, I know you're in there. I need to talk to you."

"Go away," I yelled. I turned to Tony and spoke in a normal voice, "Do you take milk or sugar in your coffee?"

"Maybe you'd better open the door."

I shook my head. "No way. For some reason, he's making a scene. It's kind of a habit with him, but since I'm not married to him any longer, I don't have to put up with it."

No sooner were the words out than Frank's pounding changed to an ominous thudding, slower in rhythm, but so strong it made the windows rattle. I ran into the living room in time to see my front door smashed open by Frank's booted foot. The boot was soon followed by the rest of him—a short, paunchy middle-aged man wearing a leather motorcycle jacket and sporting a bandito mustache. The mustache was going gray, just like the long ponytail he affected.

"Al, are you all right?"

"Have you completely lost your mind? Look what you did to my door."

"I thought I heard you call 'help.'"

"Yeah, right. 'Go away' and 'help' sound so much alike."

"I knew you were home. Why didn't you answer your door? Christ, look at your face. What bastard did that to you?"

"It was an accident, which is more than I can say for what you did." I pointed to my wrecked front door.

"Can you blame me? God, ever since I heard the news, I've been worried sick." He moved toward me, arms open for an embrace.

I backed up and held my palm outward, traffic cop style. "Take another step, and you'll regret it."

He stopped in his tracks and gave me a pained look. "Al, it's me, Frank. What's with the threats?"

"Gee, I can't imagine. Do you think it has something to do with you having one of your destructive tantrums and breaking my door in for no reason whatsoever?"

"I had a damn good reason."

"I see. I must be overreacting—again, as I'm sure you'll tell me if I let you stay inside my house for more than thirty seconds."

Tony appeared in the kitchen doorway and cleared his throat.

"I didn't know you had company," Frank said in his typical evade-the-issue style. "Hi, I'm Frank Avery." He walked past me and held his hand out to Tony.

Maybe Tony was relieved that Frank hadn't pulled

out a .45 and started blasting away. Or else he was simply confused that the same person who had just violently destroyed a door could, the very next second, act like a perfectly normal person. Whatever the reason, Tony shook hands with Frank, and even favored him with a glimpse of his dimple. "Tony Dezzutti." He pumped Frank's arm up and down several times.

"Okay, social hour is now officially over, and you can leave." I crossed to the door that hung crookedly from the splintered doorframe on one hinge. I tried to straighten it by lifting it by the knob, but the remaining hinge screeched in complaint when I did. "How much cash do you have on you, Frank?"

Frank shrugged. "A couple of bucks, I guess. Are you short this month?"

"Yeah." I faced him with my fists on my hips. "I'm short the cost of repairing my front door. You're going to have to pay for the damage you did." I turned back to the door to see if I could at least get it to close, but it resisted my efforts.

Through the doorway I could see my neighbor Rose and Mitch the carpenter, standing on the sidewalk in front of my house, watching me. I waved at them so Rose would know that I was all right. She didn't harbor many good opinions of Frank and was probably debating calling the police.

"I'm sorry about the door, but after I heard about what happened this morning, I was worried about you. When you didn't answer the door, I thought the worst."

"What a coincidence. I always think the worst of you, Frank. And since I can't seem to remember a single time before this that you worried about me, why don't you tell me the real reason you broke down my door?"

Frank turned to Tony. "She talks tough, but don't let it fool you. She's a very caring person, very caring."

I gritted my teeth. Of all the things Frank could have said, that was the worst, because it was true. And that was the essence of Frank Avery. He could recognize the truth, but use it so manipulatively that it became a lie. He should have known better than to pull that number on me again. For some reason he was trying to jerk my chain with his door-smashing, his phony concern, and repeatedly calling me Al, his version of a pet name that I'd never liked.

I turned to Tony. "Frank sounds like a nice person, but don't let it fool you. Underneath he's a pure slimeball."

"So, how do you know Al?" Frank asked Tony, as if I hadn't said anything.

"We met just today, as a matter of fact," Tony said.

"Over a corpse, as I think you already know." I broke in before Tony could continue.

"Someone you knew, right? What happened to him?" Frank asked, a bit too eagerly. That's when I got what he was up to.

"Forget it. I'm not going to tell you a thing," I turned to face Tony. "Let me explain something. Frank is an experience-vampire, otherwise known as a novelist. Nothing profound, moving or even interesting ever happens to him, because he's too shallow and self-absorbed. So he goes around sucking up the lives of other people, puts them down on paper and claims that everything came out of his imagination."

"I think I'd better go," Tony said. "You two sound like you have some things to work out."

"No, we don't," I said.

"Al's right," Frank said. "There's no problem here, and, besides, we're not going to get you in the middle of anything. Al still has some issues over our break-up. That's why she talks like that. But there's no reason we can't all sit down like adults, is there?" Frank clapped Tony on the shoulder, and Tony nodded and grinned.

I don't know if it was what he said so much as the way he said it, but it pushed me over the edge. "You condescending piss-poor excuse for a human being. *We* can't all sit down like adults, because one of us, namely you, never got past the emotional age of four."

Frank turned to me with a gleam of victory in his

eyes. He'd made me lose my temper, in spite of my resolve not to. The way he played the game, that made him the winner. He was probably counting on my apologizing now, the way I used to, and agreeing to tell him all about Stevie. Stevie had to be the reason he'd gone to the trouble of creating so much drama. But he had a surprise coming. I'd taken my marbles and gone home a long time ago. Much worse from Frank's point of view, I'd taken all my stories, too. He'd ripped off my life for the last time.

"This is my house, not yours, and I do the inviting. You weren't invited. You invaded. You will pay me for the cost of getting my door repaired. Now. And then you'll leave."

"You have some tools? I could probably fix it."

"You haven't fixed so much as a burned out light bulb since I've known you. I'll take whatever cash you have on you now, and send you a bill for the rest."

"You've already bled me dry, Al. I'm not paying you another cent." Frank might have played it differently if we hadn't had an audience. Poor Tony still stood there, although I'd guess he'd stayed only because we stood between him and the doorway.

Frank should've known better than bring up the money he'd never provided, even when we were married. His only contribution had been to sign over his half of the house when we divorced—the house he'd never made a single payment on. His mentioning it reminded me who I should ask to pay for the damage he'd done. I strode into the kitchen, picked up the phone with one hand and flipped open my address book with the other. Before the divorce, I'd written down the work number of the woman he'd been fooling around with. He had since married her.

Frank followed me into the kitchen and watched me from the doorway as I punched in the number of the San Francisco art gallery she owned. I kept my gaze fastened on his face as the receptionist answered my call with a cool, "M.J. Gallery."

"Marcia Johnson, please," I said.

Frank took a step forward. "What the hell do you think you're doing?" He jerked the receiver out of my hand and slammed it into the cradle.

I reached for the phone. He bumped me out of the way, hitting my hip with his. My sore hip.

"Now, be reasonable."

I rubbed my hip. I'd had it with him. I grabbed the first thing that came to hand—the large black-handled butcher knife I'd used to cut the bread for my sandwich. "Okay, I'm feeling much more reasonable now. So back off."

I must have sounded convincing, because he retreated to the doorway. "What's gotten into you? Come on, put down the knife."

I hit redial and asked for Marcia again.

The receptionist asked, "Who shall I say is calling?"

"Her husband's ex-wife." I didn't know if Marcia would recognize my name. She came on the line instantly.

"Alison?"

So she knew me by name, after all.

"Yes, Alison Weaver here. I need to discuss an emergency situation with you. It concerns Frank."

"Has something happened to Frank?"

"He's fine, but I'm not. If I weren't holding a knife, I don't know what he'd do. He kicked in my front door."

"What?" she said so loudly I had to jerk the phone away from my ear.

Frank made a move toward me, but I gestured with the knife and he stopped.

"Here's the problem. He refuses to pay to have my door repaired. It's a complete mess. I can't even close it. So, knowing you to be a reasonable person, I thought I'd give you a choice. You can agree to pay the costs of repairing my door, or I'll call the police and have Frank arrested."

"Put Frank on the phone." She had the voice of someone used to giving orders, low-pitched and definite. It probably went with the territory of owning her own art gallery, hobnobbing with artists and their wealthy patrons.

"You can call him on his cell phone after you tell me what payment option you're choosing."

Frank turned away from me and rubbed his hands over his face. I knew that Marcia had been keeping him in a style to which he'd always wanted to become accustomed. He was undoubtedly already planning how he was going to weasel out of this mess.

"I must speak with Frank."

"Bye, Marcia."

"Wait. Of course, he'll pay for the damage to your door. Just get some estimates and send them to him."

"I have two points to make, then you say either 'I'll pay' or 'Call the police.' First, Frank has never spent money on anything except his own self indulgences since I've known him, so let's agree that you'll pay, as I'm sure you've been paying ever since you were unlucky enough to fall for his line the first time. Second, no estimates. The door won't even close, not to mention lock. It has to be fixed now. I'll probably be paying someone time and a half overtime. That's it. Your turn."

After a brief pause, she said, "I'll pay."

"Thank you." I hung up before she could say anything else.

"All right," Frank said, "you've made your point. I apologize for kicking in your door."

"I'll know you're sincere if you leave now."

He didn't move. "I just wanted to make sure you were all right."

"So much for sincerity. You're still leaving."

"To tell you the truth, I'm more worried now that I've seen you." He eyed the knife. I held onto it. I liked the effect it had on him. "You're not acting like yourself. Finding the body of someone you know is a big shock for anyone, even more so for you."

I tightened my grip on the knife and waved it back and forth in front of him, knife-fighter style. "Stop right there, you son of a bitch. You know nothing, absolutely nothing."

"But I do know, Alison." He made his voice soft and confiding. "And I hope that you will someday forgive yourself for telling me."

"I will never forgive *you* for stealing my life and pretending it was 'art.' This is the last time I'm telling you to get out." I advanced toward him with the knife in front of me.

He backed away from me into the living room. I followed him to make sure he managed to get all the way out of my house, but the exit was blocked. Tony had not only stayed, when I'd thought he was long gone, he was holding my battered front door steady while Mitch the carpenter fiddled with the last working hinge.

"What do you think you're doing?" I demanded.

CHAPTER FIVE

"That should do it," Mitch said, which was no answer at all as far as I was concerned. He stood up, took the now unhinged door from Tony and carried it out onto the porch.

"That should do what?" I stalked out after him.

Tony and Frank followed in my wake. "I'm going to take off now," Tony said.

I turned to him. Of the three men standing on my front porch, he was the only one I wanted to stay. He hadn't been much help with Frank, but he'd hung around when I'd assumed he'd duck out.

Frank shook his hand, like they were old buddies, and they mumbled good-byes to one another.

"Thanks for coming by." I tried to give a casual goodbye wave, but forgot I was still holding the butcher knife, and more or less ruined the effect. I didn't add anything about seeing him again. That was probably too much to hope for.

"Looks like you've already found someone to fix your door." Frank gaveMitch his sincere look and extended his hand. "Hi, I'm Frank Avery."

Mitch didn't move, speak or smile. In fact, for a moment, I thought he'd deliberately wiped all expression from his face. Not that it was easy to tell on a man with a full beard and a baseball cap pulled down to his eyebrows.

Frank gave a chuckle and dropped his out-stretched

hand. "I can see Al's been talking about me."

"Who's Al?" Mitch asked.

Frank chuckled again. It was all part of his show and usually a pretty effective icebreaker, but I'd seen it all before. Mitch acted as if he'd seen it, too.

"Guess I'll be going." Frank's jolly pose seeped out of him like air out of a balloon.

I copied Mitch and didn't say anything.

Frank stepped awkwardly down the front steps, his feet clumsy in their steel-toed motorcycle boots. He paused at the bottom of the steps, pulled out his wallet and extracted a card. "I have to talk to you. It's important. You can reach me at this number anytime."

I remained motionless, staring at him. No point in telling him I hoped never to speak to him again in my life. Some men just won't listen.

He placed the card on the porch, sketched a wave and walked down the path. I watched him head down the street. He must have parked his motorcycle around the corner so I wouldn't hear him coming.

"Who is he?" Mitch asked.

"My ex."

"Besides that. He said, I'm Frank Avery—like I should know who he is."

I almost laughed. "I wish he could hear you. He's a writer. He's had two books on the New York Times bestseller list. He thought you'd say 'not *the* Frank Avery, the famous novelist?' A lot of people do."

"He calls you Al?"

"His idea of an affectionate nickname. You know, pretend intimacy."

Mitch didn't comment, just waited a beat as if to make sure I was done talking before he turned back to inspect the door frame. He pulled a hammer from his tool belt and began to pry loose a splintered board.

"Wait a minute. What are you doing?"

"Fixing your door." He didn't pause demolishing the doorframe.

"That's not fixing. That's wrecking."

He didn't respond.

"Hold it. Just stop everything."

He slowly lowered the hammer and turned toward me.

"I didn't ask you to repair my door."

"Mrs. Fiorelli sent me over."

"Mrs. Fiorelli? You mean Rose?"

He nodded.

He had to be making it up. Rose was on my side against all gentrifiers. "Why would Rose send you over to fix my door?"

"I'm doing some work for her. Fixing her screen door."

That tore it. This man had to be stopped. "She can't afford to have you fix her screen door. She's eighty-five and lives on social security."

"She drives a hard bargain, too. I said I'd fix it for some of her tomato and pepper seeds. She agreed to the tomato seeds, but just for the door. She'll give me the peppers if I fix the second step on her back porch, too." He said all this with a straight face, but I had a feeling he was laughing inside.

Rose prided herself on her heritage vegetable garden and carefully saved seeds from her plants every year. "Those tomato seeds are rare. Her father brought the original seeds with him from Italy."

He nodded as if all this was old news to him.

"Rose is my friend, and I know she means well, but I'm not sure I want you to fix my door."

"You don't want it fixed, or you don't want me to fix it?"

"You haven't even told me how much it will cost," I temporized. "I'm not sure I can afford it. And I'm sure you won't do it for tomato seeds in my case."

"I thought Marcia was going to pay for it."

"You heard me talking to her?" He didn't reply, simply stood there. His capacity for stillness wore on my nerves. "I only said that to get Frank to leave. He was acting as if he could still push my buttons and get me to do what he wanted. I pushed his instead."

"What did he want?"

I opened my mouth to say that I thought it had something to do with my finding Stevie's body, then I remembered who I was talking to. I'd been about to confide in Mitch the carpenter, after I'd avoided even saying hello to him for two years. "Is this how you do it?"

"Do what?"

"Worm your way into people's confidence. You catch them off-guard when they need their front doors reattached. And the next thing they know, their house is painted some designer shade, their yard's a botanical garden, and a realtor from Century 21 is holding open house."

He gazed at me for a long five seconds before he said "No," and took up destroying the doorframe again.

"Didn't you hear me? I told you to stop."

"Mrs. Fiorelli said you might give me some trouble." He pried a board loose, and the nail holding it to the wall screeched as it gave way.

"Why won't you stop?" I raised my voice over the noise the nail made.

Mitch pulled the loosened board free and heaved it over the porch railing before he turned to me. "I'm kind of between a rock and a hard place here. As a rule, I never argue with a woman holding a knife, but Mrs. Fiorelli made me promise I'd fix your door no matter what you said."

I looked down at the knife in my hand. Funny that I kept forgetting I was holding it. "Wait a minute." I hurried into my house, put the knife away in a kitchen drawer, and returned empty-handed to face down Mitch. "I'm unarmed. You're still holding a hammer."

He slipped his hammer into his tool belt. "Now I'm

not."

"Good." I folded my arms across my chest. "I need my door fixed. I don't need my house dismantled. Just get some new hinges and put the door up again."

"If I do that, even Mrs. Fiorelli will be able to kick it in. Door was worthless to begin with, and now it's busted. Door frame's busted. And the deadbolt's… " he paused.

"Don't tell me—busted."

"I was going to say bent. I might be able to fix it."

"What's the bare minimum that needs to be done?"

"To fix it right?" he asked.

I nodded.

"New door frame, new door, new lock. Door doesn't have to be brand new. I think I can get a good one from salvage."

"Okay. Meanwhile, how do I close off this gaping hole?" I gestured to the open doorway.

"Thought I'd nail the old door in. You can use the back door for a day."

"Okay, and since Marcia's paying for it, be sure to charge time and a half for the hours you put in today."

"I don't usually do that."

"Think of it as preventive medicine. If she has to pay out a lot for something Frank did, she'll keep him on a shorter leash."

"Or make his life hell."

"Do you have a problem with that?"

He shook his head. "I'll fix the door so no one'll be able to kick it in again, but he might go for something other than your door next time."

"Like what?"

His gaze drifted to the right side of my face which now hurt so much every time I moved a facial muscle, I didn't need a mirror to tell me how swollen it was.

"Frank didn't give me this black eye, if that's what you're thinking."

"It's none of my business."

"You're right. It's none of your business, but apparently it's already been on the news. Someone knocked me down this morning, not really on purpose. I'd just found a dead person."

"Where?"

"At work. Actually, in the alley behind where I work. In our paper-recycling bin. His head had been bashed in. I feel pretty bad about it, because I knew him. He was sort of a friend."

"I'm sorry about your friend. It wasn't on the news."

"Yes, it was. That's how Frank heard about it."

"I listen to the noon news every day when I eat lunch, and it wasn't on the news."

"Some station or other aired the story, because that's why Frank came over and kicked in my door."

He shrugged, the way people do when they know you're wrong, but they don't feel like arguing.

I might have taken issue with him about it, but Libby pulled into my driveway, and all I could think about from that point on was that I hadn't called her to tell her about Stevie. One more regret to keep me from sleeping at nights.

"I'm going to get some two by fours over at my place. Be right back." Mitch headed down the steps.

Libby hurried out of the car, sparing a brief glance at Mitch as he cut across my lawn. She was a large woman, both graceful and awkward at the same time, and I could never figure out how that could be. She hurried toward me the way she hurried through everything she did except talking to people who needed help. Her long brown-going-to-gray hair flowed down her back and lifted away from her face as she rushed up to me. Without question she'd heard about Stevie already. Her eyes were red-rimmed and puffy. You'd think that after all the tragedies in her life, she'd have run out of tears. I'd had only one, and I hadn't cried since.

"I'm so sorry." She enveloped me in a hug.

"I'm sorry I didn't call. I should have been the one to tell you."

She released me from her embrace but kept her hands on my shoulders. "What happened to your face?"

I reached up and patted her hand. "That's part of the story of my finding Stevie. GI Joe was hanging around. I think he wanted to talk to me, but this garbage truck came along and scared him off. He knocked me down trying to get away," I said.

"The police think that Joe killed Stevie." Libby made a face like someone who's tasted something disgusting and wants to spit it out.

"I know. They're like that. A crazy street person gets killed, it's not going to be a high priority case. They went for the easiest out—another street person."

"I think I straightened them out on that score. Stevie's murder has just gone to the top of their list. Come on." Libby started moving down the path. "I'll tell you about it in the car."

"Are we going somewhere?"

"To the clinic."

"It's not one of my nights," I protested. Libby and Jerry, our driver, were the only ones who received a salary and worked full time for the clinic. Everyone else worked as volunteers in addition to their day jobs.

Libby stopped in her tracks and turned to face me. "Our first stop tonight is People's Park. Stevie's death is going to hit some people very hard. I took it for granted you'd want to be there." Her words carried an edge of impatience, and that, more than what she'd said, persuaded me. Working in the clinic when even the reliably steady folks would be bouncing off the walls with anxiety was a challenge I could do without, but I couldn't stand up to Libby when she lost her forbearance.

"I have to wait till Mitch gets back. He's fixing my door."

"Leave him a note."

So I wrote Mitch a note, grabbed my purse, and hurried after Libby to my car. I carried my shoes in my hand. It would be faster to put them on in the car, since Libby was already in the driver's seat with the engine running.

Libby drove the way she moved, rolling through stop signs at about ten miles an hour, revving the engine at red lights, and not slowing down for turns. Even belted in, I had to hang onto the dashboard with one hand and the side of my seat with the other to stay upright. I kept my mouth shut as we powered our way through traffic.

Speed, even at the legal limit, wasn't a possibility once we crossed the invisible line that divided Oakland from Berkeley. The city of Berkeley had been waging war against cars for decades. By the use of diverters and blockades on key sidestreets, all cars trying to get from one side of Berkeley to the other were funneled onto just a few streets, none of them adequate to the traffic demand.

We turned down Haste—a misnomer if ever there was one since every corner had a boulevard stop. Drivers on Haste could hurry only from stop sign to stop sign, which, of course, Libby did. Once we'd slammed to a full stop and were waiting for the cross traffic to clear, I asked Libby, "How did you convince the cops to make Stevie's murder a priority?"

"I simply told them who he was—Stephen Lind. His family lives in Piedmont, and I think they're wealthy and socially connected."

My chin dropped. I didn't know why I was so surprised. Lots of street people originally came from good, solid families. Somehow or other, though, I hadn't imagined wealth as part of the picture for Stevie. It fit with the monthly check I knew he got, though.

Once we arrived at the church where we kept the Mobile Clinic van, I didn't have time to think about Stevie's family. Jerry, our three hundred-pound driver, all-purpose mechanic and backup muscle in case of trouble, was already in the church's basement storeroom, filling boxes with the night's worth of supplies.

"Hey, Jerry." I grabbed a box in each arm. "How's it going?"

He glanced at me and raised his eyebrows. "Me? I'm fine. You look a little rough, though."

I grimaced. I'd be fielding questions about my black eye all evening. I should have stood my ground with Libby and not come. I turned away and carried the boxes into the Winnebago without telling Jerry how I'd come by my bruises. Libby could explain everything once the crew was assembled.

I climbed the steps of the van. Vanessa, that night's regular volunteer nurse, was already inside, wiping down all surfaces with disinfectant. She took one of the boxes from me with a hurried, "What happened to you? Wait, let me guess—I should have seen the other guy," and headed to the examination room at the rear of the van to stow the supplies.

I bent over to put the remaining box on the small pull-down table that Libby used as a desk, and my shoulder bag's strap slipped from my shoulder. Damn. I always locked my bag in the trunk of my car before I started work, but tonight I'd forgotten. I gritted my teeth. Everything was off-kilter. I didn't want to take the time to walk all the way back to my parked car, so I'd have to cram my purse into one of the locked medicine cabinets. Space was at a premium in the clinic. Libby preferred us to use most of it for our clients' needs.

Dr. Bill showed up just as we'd finished the last preparations, with apologies for his lateness. We didn't give him a bad time about it, since he'd already worked a full shift in the ER at Alta Bates Hospital. Divorced, in his late fifties and with his kids in college, Bill Edwards spent most of his leisure time either volunteering for the Mobile Clinic or helping Libby with fundraising.

We crammed ourselves into the van for the usual pre-clinic briefing. Libby told the others about Stevie Number. No one there was a stranger to death. The clinic's clients lived on the ragged edge of life where poverty, disease, substance abuse, mental health problems, and plain bad luck combined daily to shorten life expectancy. Even so, the staff wasn't ready to deal with this particular death. Libby's voice cracked in the telling of events. Jerry cried. Vanessa cursed. Dr. Bill tipped his head back and blinked hard at the ceiling. I again wished that I hadn't come.

Jerry slid into the driver's seat. We drove in silence to People's Park. We had our assignments. Jerry kept the line in order. Libby did all the paperwork, including referrals to various social service agencies. Vanessa took care of minor complaints herself and sent the serious or complicated cases to Dr. Bill in the exam room in the rear of the van. Dr. Bill, in turn, rotated patients back to Libby for follow-up appointments or referrals to other clinics.

Once the clinic opened for business, there was no room for me in the crowded Winnebago. Libby had assigned me the dual job of town crier and scout. "Tell them about Stevie. There's going to be so much rumor going around. And ask about Joe. Maybe someone knows where he is. They'll tell you, even if they won't talk to the police."

Libby had the right idea. I should've thought of it myself. GI Joe had tried to tell me something that morning. I needed to find him and ask him what he knew. I walked up and down the line answering questions about Stevie and taking a lot of ribbing about my black eye. No one knew, or admitted knowing, where Joe was. I went farther afield, circled People's Park, and even strolled a few blocks up and down Telegraph Avenue. Still no luck. When I returned to the clinic, Jerry waved me over.

"Check out Doris, will you? She's hanging around like she needs to see someone in the clinic, but won't talk to me."

Doris often didn't talk to anyone. Weathered and worn from years lived in the open air, she looked over sixty, but was probably only in her early forties. She had a dog and a rusty shopping cart crammed with her earthly possessions, and she used them both as her excuse for not entering any enclosed space. She suffered from an array of mental health problems, one of which was claustrophobia.

I strolled in Doris' direction, taking care to maintain a careful distance. She panicked if people came too close.

"Hi Doris. How's it going?"

"Stevie Number died. He went to heaven to be with Jesus and Mary."

"I know, and I'm very sad about it."

"Doris is worried."

"You're worried?"

"No, I'm not worried."

"But Doris is worried."

She nodded.

"This is another Doris, not you?"

She pointed to her dog, a multi-colored cross between a mutt and a mongrel, who lolled on top of a bundle of blankets in the grocery cart.

"Your dog's name is Doris, too?" This was news to me. I didn't know the dog even had a name.

"She spells her name with two R's. That's how you can tell us apart."

"I'm sorry that she's worried. Can you tell me what she's worried about?"

"The clinic might go away."

"She's wrong to worry about that." I turned and spoke to the dog. "Dorris, trust me, the clinic always comes back, no matter what bad or sad thing happens during the day."

Dorris stood up and wagged her tail in that encouraging way dogs do when they want you to think they know what you're talking about.

I turned to Doris. "Is Dorris concerned about anything else?"

"Stevie was nice to Dorris."

"She's going to miss him, isn't she?"

Doris nodded.

"Know what? I'm going to miss him, too. Know who else is really going to miss him? GI Joe. You haven't seen Joe by any chance, have you?"

"You're mad at GI Joe." She stated it as a fact.

"No, I'm not mad at him."

"Yes, you are. He told me you were very mad at him. You and Charley."

I stared at Doris. "You talked to him today? Do you know where he is?" I took a step toward her. I knew better, but I acted on impulse. This was the first lead I'd had on Joe.

Doris took a quick step backward and frantically grabbed for her cart, knocking Dorris off her perch in the process. She didn't wait for Dorris to jump back onto the blankets, but started marching down the street bent over with the effort of pushing the cart.

I forced myself to stay put. "I'm sorry, Doris. I didn't mean to startle you. Please tell me about Joe."

She stopped about ten feet away and half-turned toward me.

I shoved my hands into my jeans' pockets and let my shoulders slump—the posture of someone who wasn't about to make any sudden moves. "I want to help Joe. I think he needs help, don't you?"

"You should take better care of your skin."

I cocked my head to one side and waited for her to give me some clue about what the hell she was talking about. Conversations with Doris were always a little tricky. Sometimes I enjoyed the challenge, but that particular night I couldn't muster any enthusiasm for skin care lectures from someone with a face like old brown shoe leather. Doris remained silent.

"What should I do?" I finally asked.

"Moisturizer."

"Okay." I nodded in outward agreement. "Anything else?"

"Forget about sunscreens. They keep out the vitamin D. You should wear concealer, too. You'll scare people with that eye."

"That's a good idea. I'd hate to scare anyone. Did you hear how I got this a black eye? Joe knocked me down by accident, and I bumped my face on the ground. He didn't do it on purpose, that's why I'm not mad at him. I'm worried about him, though. Do you by any chance know where I could find him?"

"Stevie's in heaven with Jesus and Mary."

Wasn't this where I came in? "Yes, we're all sorry about Stevie."

"He gave Dorris a big bag of dog food, but it's all gone now."

Was that what this rigmarole was all about? Doris hitting me up for dog food? I sighed. "I'll find some more dog food. Come by the clinic next week, okay?"

She gave a curt nod, grabbed the push bar of her grocery cart and headed down the street.

"Wait a minute. What about GI Joe? Where can I find him?"

She kept moving but called over her shoulder, "He's with Jesus."

"I'm not talking about Stevie," I yelled after her. "I'm talking about Joe."

She kept marching forward as if she hadn't heard me.

"Damn." I turned back to the Clinic.

The rest of the evening was just as unproductive. No one else had seen Joe for days. I asked the more reliable people to keep an eye out for him, letting them know that if I didn't find him first, the cops would arrest him.

I de-briefed the clinic staff on our ride back to the church parking lot. Libby said she'd contact a group that helped the pets of homeless people about food for Dorris. Everyone else agreed to keep their eyes and ears open for word about Joe. I left as soon as we'd parked the Mobile Clinic. Libby and the others assured me that I wasn't needed that night for the unloading and locking up process.

I drove home, making one stop at an all-night drugstore for concealing make-up. Doris was probably not far off about my black eye. I doubted that I actually scared people, but I probably put them off. The teenage girl on the register sent me back to get another brand that cost twice as much as the one I'd picked. "Yeah, it's like expensive," she said, "but that stuff, like, totally works." I thanked her for her help when I paid for it, and she told me to have a nice day. Even though it was now night, I thought what was left of my day might be nice, just because she'd been friendly and helpful.

Funny how a few words exchanged with a complete stranger can change your whole frame of mind. Of course, I'd forgotten about my front door. I also didn't know that someone had lifted my flashlight until I opened the glove compartment. Had I left my car unlocked when I stopped by the drugstore? Without a light, I tripped and stumbled my way in the dark through the side gate and down the path to the back door. Fitting the key into the lock by feel alone required the talents of a safecracker. I made it on the seventh try.

Once inside, I knew it was bed for me. When had I ever felt so completely drained? The red light on my answering machine flashed, the siren call of the current age, beckoning me to check my phone messages. I couldn't resist. I punched the new messages button.

"Al, I have to talk to you. Please, if you're there, pick up. I'm sorry about your door. I don't know what got into me, except that I'm desperate. I mean it. Call me back. Anytime. Please."

I jabbed the message erase button. *Call you back, Frank? Yeah, right. In my nightmares.*

CHAPTER SIX

I woke up before my alarm went off, sat up with a jolt, and swung my feet over the side of the bed. My hip joint twinged and the side of my face felt tender. No matter. Today belonged to me, because yesterday Daniel had finally given me the go-ahead to work on the refinery study.

I dashed into the bathroom and speed-showered, but I couldn't move as fast as my imagination. I pictured myself at my desk, already reading the printouts, the results nearly leaping off the page: Living near the refineries was hazardous to your health, and I could prove it. Or maybe it was more subtle than that, and I'd have to do some complicated analyses that took account of wind patterns.

I towel-dried my hair and pulled on khakis and a knit top while lost in a fantasy of how my dissertation was nearly going to write itself. I'd reached the point of receiving the dissertation-of-the-year award at graduation, me very modest in my acceptance speech, thanking all the people who'd helped me, when the sound of the doorbell stopped me cold.

I checked the time. If I got rid of whoever was at the door and settled for a quick cup of coffee, I could get to work early. The sooner the better, as far as I was concerned. Whoever it was gave up on the doorbell and took up knocking. I hurried into the living room. Could Frank have come back for another door-destruction maneuver? If so, he was in for a big surprise. Mitch had sealed the door on both sides with strips of lumber. It would take more than a kick with a booted foot to break it in now.

I pressed my eye to the peephole. The two detectives who'd interviewed me the day before stood on my porch. I groaned. Just what I didn't need—cops with my coffee.

"This door doesn't open," I yelled to them through the door. "You'll have to go around to the back."

I heard them step off the front porch and saw their shadows as they passed by the living room window, going the wrong way around the house. I hurried to the kitchen, out the back door and up the path. "Hey. You have to come through the gate on this side. I'll unlock it for you."

It wasn't really a lock. Just a simple metal bar that disengaged the latch mechanism on the other side. I pushed the bar aside and opened the gate.

After a few seconds, they came around the corner of the house, ducking to avoid the low hanging branches of the holly tree.

"Remember us from yesterday, Ms. Weaver?" Stans asked, coming to a halt in front of me.

"Sure, you're Stans, and he's Carney." I gestured with my chin towards the younger cop who'd stopped behind Stans.

"That's right. We'd like to talk to you." He stood still, his feet planted hip-width apart, his hands hanging at his sides. Carney stood a little behind Stans on the path and shifted from one foot to the other.

"I'm just on my way to work."

"Your boss will understand if you explain you were helping us."

"I still won't file an assault charge against Joe, if that's what you want to talk about."

"It isn't," Stans said and left it at that. He hadn't moved. I got the impression that he wouldn't stir until he had what he wanted.

Irritation swelled up in my throat like a bad case of indigestion. These cops were going to screw up my entire morning. I could miss getting a jump on analyzing the data.

Daniel might get antsy if I was late getting to work and change his mind—again.

I folded my arms across my chest. "Well, what do you want, then?"

Carney moved forward. "We'd like to ask you a few questions."

"Different questions from the ones you asked yesterday?"

"Is it all right if we come in?" Carney moved forward even as he spoke.

I didn't budge.

"It will only take a couple of minutes."

"Yeah, right. I bet you say that to all the girls."

Carney narrowed his eyes at me and pressed his lips together in a tight line. Maybe I'd touched on a sensitive spot.

"Inside, outside, it's up to you if you," Stans said. "But the sooner you answer our questions, the sooner you can get to work."

He had a point. I said, "Okay, you can come in." I led them through the kitchen into the living room. "Want to sit?" I asked and waved my hand at the sofa. I took the easy chair, but perched on the edge of the seat. Gave them the body language of a busy woman whose time was valuable.

Stans sat and took a notebook and pen out of an inside pocket of his sports jacket, but Carney remained standing, twisting his head this way and that, checking out the room.

"What happened to your front door?" he asked.

I hesitated for a second, then settled for a non-committal, "I'm doing some remodeling."

He raised his eyebrows. "Yourself?"

I didn't like his automatic assumption that I couldn't do basic carpentry, even if it was true. "You can learn a lot by watching those do-it-yourself programs on TV. Is that what you wanted to ask me about?"

Stans flipped open his little notebook. “We’d like you to tell us about yesterday morning. What’s the usual time you leave for work?”

“On mornings that I’m the one who checks on the recycling, I usually leave at ten of six.”

“That when you left yesterday?”

“No. I left at five thirty, because I walked to work.”

“Do you usually walk?”

“Occasionally I walk. It’s not very far. I’d loaned my car to a friend the night before, so I couldn’t drive.”

“Is that your car in the driveway? The Toyota?”

I nodded.

“Who did you loan it to?”

I stared at Stans. These questions were getting weird. “Why do you want to know?”

“Just answer the question,” Carney said.

“That’s not a response designed to elicit cooperation,” I said, looking at Stans.

“You discovered the body, so naturally we’re interested in the timing of events. The fact that you walked to work affected the timing,” Stans said.

“What does that have to do with who I loaned my car to?”

“It probably doesn’t. We just like to cover all bases. Saves us time in the long run. Do you mind telling us?”

I shrugged. “Libby Honeck. You talked to her yesterday.”

Stans nodded. “We did. She didn’t mention your car.”

“Why would she?”

“When you found the body in the dumpster, did you touch it?”

“No. He was clearly dead.”

“Did you know who it was right away?”

“Yes.”

“Even though his face was covered?”

"His face wasn't covered. I did that. With some paper."

"So you did touch the body." Stans said.

I shrugged. "I may have brushed his face with my fingertips, that's all."

"Why'd you cover his face?" This from Carney.

I gazed at him. "Out of respect for the dead."

Carney stared at me as if he'd never heard of such a thing. "It would've been better if you hadn't tampered with the crime scene."

If he wanted to irritate me, he was doing a good job of it. "That wasn't the crime scene. It was just where the body was dumped."

Carney narrowed his eyes at me. "How do you know that?"

"The lividity in his hands and arms. He was on his back with his hands up. I could see that the blood had pooled in his palms and inner arms. He must have been lying on his back with his arms at his sides for a period of time after he was killed."

"You know this because you're a nurse?"

"Because I worked as a hospice nurse for some years, both in a hospice itself and as a visiting nurse in the home hospice program."

"You're saying you've seen a lot of dead bodies."

"More than some people. Maybe not more than you. I understand the murder rate in Oakland is pretty high."

Stans ignored the gibe. "When did you last see Stevie alive?"

"I'm pretty sure that he came to the clinic a week ago Monday."

"Was he sick?"

"No, he asked me some questions. He acted a little weird, but he wasn't delusional."

"What did he ask you?"

"I don't really remember. It was a busy night. I

remember one—he asked me what my middle name was. I thought that was strange."

"Why was that a strange question?"

"Not the sort of thing Stevie would typically ask. We go by first names or nicknames only in the clinic, to preserve our privacy. Sometimes patients ask us our last names. No one's ever wanted to know my middle name."

"Did you tell him?"

"I told him I didn't have a middle name."

"Was that the truth?"

"Yes."

"You never told him your last name?"

"No, and he never asked."

Stans and Carney exchanged a look.

"Are you going to let me in on the secret? Or are you the only ones with the question-asking privilege?"

Stans reached inside his sports jacket and produced a folded sheet of paper. "Have you seen this before?" He handed it to me.

I unfolded it and scanned the page. It was a do-it-yourself will. Form 10-b it said at the bottom of the page. Right below Stevie's signature. He'd signed it, "Stephen Lind A.K.A. Stevie Number." It was a smudged photocopy of the original, but even so I could make out the notary stamp and witness signatures. He'd filled in my full name, first and last, in the relevant blank at the top of the page, bequeathing me his entire estate. He'd asterisked that part and hand-written in the margins "including ALL of my papers, including those at my parents' house."

"No, I've never seen this. Stevie didn't say a thing about it." I looked up at Stans and moved my gaze to Carney. They were both staring at me. Carney had stopped his nervous scanning of the room and stood completely still. It gave me a distinctly creepy feeling.

I tried to hand the will back to Stans, but instead of reaching for it, he said, "Check the date."

I did as he said. "It's fairly recent."

"A week ago Monday. When you say you last saw him."

"When I did last see him—alive." I held out the will. This time Stans took it.

"You're sure you haven't seen this before?" Stans asked.

"Yes, I'm sure. I'm also sure that I didn't tell Stevie my last name. I didn't even know his real name until Libby told me last night. I guess that's why you guys are out so early in the morning. Libby told me that the Linds are a wealthy family who live in Piedmont. Guess you're feeling the pressure. This isn't just one worthless street person killing another worthless street person anymore."

"We put the same effort into solving every homicide," Carney said.

"Excuse me for expressing cynicism. It's a bad habit of mine."

"The reason I asked about the will," Stans put in as if Carney and I hadn't had our little exchange, "is because it was found on the body."

I gave him my full attention. "He carried it around with him?"

"We're not clear about that. When the coroner's people were undressing the body for autopsy, they found it tucked into the front of his pants. You admit that you touched the body, so we wondered."

"You wondered what? Did I check out his pants, just to see if he'd left his will there?"

"He didn't leave his will there," Carney said. "Somebody put it there after he'd been left in the dumpster. You'd be helping us, and yourself, if you'd just tell us the truth."

I stood up and looked him in the eye. "I already told you the truth, and you didn't want to hear it. You couldn't have cared less about Stevie Number, a Berkeley street person with a terrible mental illness. But Stephen Lind, son of a prominent Piedmont family, that's another story. The truth, Detective Carney, is that Stevie's family, the media, your boss and possibly the mayor are going to be breathing down your neck. The truth is that you are desperate to find someone to arrest, whether they did it or not, so you could close your case. Sorry to have to tell you one last truth, but I didn't have anything to do with his death, if that's what this is all about. I just had the bad luck to be the one who found him."

Stans hoisted himself to his feet and tucked his notepad and pen back inside his jacket and inserted himself between his partner and me. "Maybe it was just bad luck that you found him, but it's also true that you had the good luck to be named his sole beneficiary."

I rolled my eyes. "Right, the sole beneficiary of a diagnosed schizophrenic. With luck like that, maybe I should start playing the lottery. The odds of winning are even better—only eighteen million to one."

Carney looked ready to say something, but Stans flashed him a look—a warning? I couldn't tell, and what was more, I didn't care. They'd pissed me off and, even worse, made me late for work. "If that's all?" I stood up.

Stans nodded. "For now. Thanks for your time." He headed toward the kitchen with Carney right behind. I saw them out the back gate, then scrambled around the house grabbing up my jacket, keys and purse, and left by the back gate myself.

I drove to work in record time with Stans' words echoing in my head. His thanks had seemed hollow at best. I couldn't imagine what Stevie had been thinking when he'd written that will, but clearly he'd had some sense that his life was in danger. And what papers could he have meant? I stopped at a red light and closed my eyes for a second. I needed to forget about the cops, forget about Stevie. I had a big day ahead of me, even if I'd lost that great feeling of happy anticipation I'd had when I woke up.

Flo was the first one who spotted me as I came through the door. She immediately checked her watch. "There you are. We didn't know if you were taking today off or not. We got worried when you didn't call."

I gritted my teeth. "I'm only a little late. The police

came by to talk to me, otherwise I'd have been early." I breezed on past her and into my cubicle, stowed my purse under the desk with one hand and switched on my computer with the other.

Flo followed me all the way into my cubicle and hovered next to my desk. "The police? What did they want?"

"Just more details about how I happened to know Stevie. Is Daniel in his office?" I asked, hoping to distract her. I didn't feel like being interrogated twice in one morning.

But Flo wasn't going to be put off. "What do you mean 'more details?' What more is there to tell them?"

Kenji popped his head around the corner of my cubicle. "What's this about the cops?"

"It turns out that Stevie has—had rich parents. So the police have to look like they're really trying to solve his murder."

Flo straightened and gave me a shocked stare. "I'm sure it couldn't matter to the police who his family is."

"Remind me to introduce you to Detective Carney. You two would really hit it off."

"What's that supposed to mean?"

I didn't need to stand around chatting with Flo, but it wouldn't be a good idea to be directly rude to her. Especially not after yesterday. "Detective Carney told me to thank you and Daniel for all the cooperation you gave them yesterday." It was a lie, but she'd never know that.

"Really? Nice of him to say so, but we only did our duty as citizens."

"Excuse me, Flo," Kenji said, "I hate to interrupt you, but I have to consult with Alison about a work-related matter."

I bit my lip to keep from grinning. Kenji had just used Flo's own favorite excuse for breaking up a gossip session.

"You're not interrupting a thing. I just wanted to make sure that Alison was up to working today." She turned to me and inspected my face, cocking her head first to one side, then the other. "Your eye looks worse today than it did yesterday, but I suppose it doesn't feel as bad as it looks."

I reflexively put my hand to my face. I'd been in such a rush to get out of the house, I'd forgotten to put on the concealer I'd invested in the night before. "You're wrong. It's very painful," I said straight-faced.

"Oh." She blinked twice. "Well, good thing you're such a stoic," she said and sailed off towards her own cubicle several cubes away from mine.

I waited until I saw the top of her head sink out of sight behind the partition as she sat down at her desk before I turned to Kenji. "I can't believe she said that," I whispered.

"Do you have a few minutes to look at this data?" he said in a voice loud enough for Flo to hear, then in a quieter voice said, "I told you she'd make you pay for yesterday."

"I'd be glad to help you," I said and eyeballed the pages he was holding. I could see from the date at the top that they were old printouts, nothing more than an excuse for him to come along and grill me. Kenji always had to be the first to know everything. "But I need to talk to Daniel first."

"He's not here yet." Kenji slid into the second chair. Kenji's cubicle had towers of books, articles and papers piled in every available space, so we always met in my cubicle. "Maybe he's sleeping in. I worked late last night, and he was still here when I left."

"What were you working on?"

"It's the end of the funding year. I have to get a draft of the project report ready for Daniel." He looked grim. Everyone hated writing grants to get funding and then yearly reports to account for their use of grant money, even though they depended entirely on the financial support they got from agencies like the National Institute of Public Health. If I was lucky, and ever got my PhD, I'd be able to apply for grants myself, instead of working on other people's. Then I could gripe about fiscal year-end reports like all the other principal investigators.

"Sorry, but I'd have traded yesterday for having to write a year-end report."

"What was worse, finding the body or getting roughed up by the other guy?"

"Neither. It was having to hold my ex off at knife point after he kicked in my front door."

"What?" Kenji leaned forward in his chair. "Why'd he do that?"

I shrugged. "I don't really know. He said he'd heard about my encounter with Stevie's body on the news, and he'd come over to see if I was all right. When I wouldn't open the door, he kicked it open. Wrecked it. Then wouldn't pay for repairs. I got a knife... "

"What do you mean you 'got a knife?'" Kenji interrupted. "What are we talking about here--letter opener, switchblade, machete?"

I gave him a quick recap.

"Remind me never to cross you," he grinned.

"I take that as a compliment. Now I have to ask you to get back to what you were doing, because I have dissertation data to analyze at last." I swung around to face my computer.

"Daniel didn't call you?"

I swiveled back to face Kenji. Something was up, I could tell by his expression. "No, what was he going to call me about?"

"He wants you to talk to him before you start."

"He told you that?"

Kenji nodded.

"When?"

"Last night. He said I should go home and that you could help me with the report today. You know my study inside out, so he thought it would be no problem. He wants to talk to you first before you do anything with the refinery data."

I gritted my teeth. “I don’t believe this. Yesterday, he gave me the go-ahead and today I’m on hold again?”

Kenji gave me a sympathetic smile. “Looks that way.”

“Why?”

He shrugged. “You know how he is. A brilliant guy, but difficult to work for.”

I turned back to my computer and logged on. “It can’t hurt anything for me just to do some of the basic analyses I’m going to need.” I tried to pull up a data file. An “access denied” box flashed on the screen. I tried again, with no luck. “The bastard,” I muttered. All our data were stored on the large servers locked up in the fishbowl. With many studies going on simultaneously, only those people directly involved had access to a particular study’s data. “He locked me out.” I slumped in my chair and crossed my arms over my chest.

Kenji cleared his throat. “He must have figured you’d try to do the work anyway. He knows how stubborn you are. Maybe he’s come up with a whole new slant on how to approach it. You know he did that with the schoolyard lead studies last year. If he hadn’t, the city council would still be dragging its feet about doing the clean-up. Think of all the kids whose IQ’s aren’t going to be lowered by lead poisoning because Daniel had one of his strokes of genius.”

“You’re right. He cares a lot about the people he helps, but not very much about the people who work for him.” I sighed. “All right. I’ll help you with your report. But only until Daniel shows up.”

I ended up writing half of Kenji’s report while keeping an eye out for any sign of Daniel. I asked Flo hourly if he’d checked in with her. The last three times she gave me a brisk shake of her head before I could get the question out. At five o’clock Daniel still hadn’t showed. Kenji put a copy of the finished report in Daniel’s box, and I headed home.

CHAPTER SEVEN

I stopped by the grocery store on the way home. Kenji had offered to buy me dinner to thank me for helping, but I took a rain check. I wouldn't have been good company. I needed the solace that only my own special combo of sliced meats, veggies and cheese on sourdough could provide.

When I pulled into the driveway, my house looked the same as it had when I'd left that morning, and Mitch was nowhere in sight. I trudged around to the back of the house, unlocked the back door and dumped my purse and groceries on the kitchen counter. How much longer was I going to have to use the back door? In daylight it wasn't so bad, but I hadn't liked finding my way in the dark the night before. Mitch hadn't given me a timeline for replacing the door. What if I had to live with a non-functional front door for weeks? Discontent settled over me like fog over the Bay Bridge.

I quickly unpacked my bag of groceries and lined them up on the counter. I'd probably feel a lot better after I ate. I hacked wide slices from the middle of the round loaf of sourdough. Mayo and mustard went on next, followed by layers of turkey breast, ham, Jarlsburg Swiss, lettuce and sliced tomatoes, olives and cucumber. I put some more turkey and ham on top for good measure.

I had the other piece of sourdough prepped and ready to top it all off when someone rang the doorbell. I put down the bread and headed for the living room, muttering to myself that it had better not be the cops again. "Who is it?" I called through the door.

"It's me, Tyler."

Just what I needed—a visit from my local assassin-in-training. "The front door doesn't open right now. You have to go around to the back."

I retraced my steps to the kitchen and opened the back door. Tyler found his way there more quickly than the cops had, probably because he'd already cased the joint. I didn't invite him in. "What's up?"

"I want my gun back."

I tried to remember if I'd closed the louvered doors that closeted the washer and dryer on the wall behind me. If not, all Tyler had to do was look past me and he'd see his gun sitting on top of the dryer. "What did I tell you yesterday?"

He shrugged.

"Does that mean that you don't remember what I said or that you don't care?"

He shrugged again and chewed on a dirty fingernail. "My dad's out of town."

"Then you'll have to wait until he comes back. He's the one who gave you the gun, so he's the one I have to talk to."

He sighed. "Okay."

I gazed at him silently for a moment. He'd given up more easily than I'd expected. Most kids would have whined a little, just to see if it got them somewhere. Not that I particularly wanted to stand there and listen to whining. My sandwich beckoned from the kitchen counter. "See you" I moved to close the door.

"What about the guy who died?"

"What about him?"

He shrugged, his bony shoulders poking up like broomsticks under his tee shirt.

"He's still dead."

"I saw the cops come by this morning."

"So?"

"So, what did they want? Like are you going to pick the perp out of a lineup or something?"

"I think you've been watching too much TV."

He shrugged again. Maybe it was his favorite cool-guy gesture.

"Anything else on your mind?"

"Frank was here yesterday."

"Yes, and if we have any luck at all, that visit was his last."

"Frank's my friend."

"You should try to hang out with a better class of people."

"Frank's a nice guy."

"Didn't we already have this conversation? I think we have different working definitions of 'nice.' In my book, nice guys don't kick in other people's doors for no reason. It's been great talking with you Tyler, but my supper's calling me, and I have to go." This time I closed the door without waiting for him to say anything else.

I nearly dove across the kitchen. The sight of my perfect monster sandwich waiting only for the top slice of bread to crown it had me salivating already. I quickly put the bread on top and sliced the sandwich in half so I could manage to pick it up. I took a bite from one side, cramming my mouth so full I could barely chew. It was a good thing I lived alone. My table manners weren't designed for public view. Still chewing, I grabbed a napkin and a plate, loaded on the sandwich and carried it to the kitchen table. I took a smaller second bite and leaned back in my chair. I could feel my spirits lifting already.

A light knock on the back door stopped me in mid-bite. That darn kid. I got up and crossed the kitchen. Through the glass panel in the top of the door I saw, not Tyler, but Mitch. Great. Not only had I been forced to hire Mitch to fix my door, apparently I also was going to have to speak to him from now on. I jerked the door open and snapped, "What?"

Mitch took a step back. "If it's not a good time, I'll come back later."

Never was a good time, except that I needed a timeframe for my door repairs. "You're here now. Might as well come in."

He stepped into the kitchen. He looked different somehow. Maybe because he wasn't wearing his tool belt. "I don't want to interrupt anything." His gaze fell on my plate.

"I was just having a sandwich. What's up?"

He continued to stare at my plate. "That's a sandwich?"

I followed his gaze. "It's my own invention. I call it The Monster."

He wandered closer to the table and examined my dinner, taking his time. I folded my arms and waited. He looked at me under his eyebrows. "You eat like this all the time?"

"Yes, if it's any of your business, and I'm not bulimic, if that's what you're getting at."

"Bulimic? What's that, one of those astrology things?"

I rolled my eyes. "It's an eating disorder."

"No, I didn't mean anything like that. This," he gestured at the plate, "is a feat of construction. I'm impressed."

"You wanted to talk to me about something?"

"Yes, but I don't want to interrupt your dinner. I can come back later."

"It's all right. We can talk now." As much as I disliked him, I couldn't bring myself to eat in front of him without at least making a gesture of common hospitality. I pointed at the food array on the counter. "The sandwich makings are over there. Help yourself, if you want." I sat down and stuffed a big bite of sandwich in my mouth.

"Thank you. I believe I will."

I nearly choked. Couldn't he tell the difference between an empty gesture and a sincere offer?

He strolled across the kitchen, picked up the bread knife and deftly cut the bread. His slices came out even, not jagged like mine. "I have a line on a door for you. A guy I know who does salvage said he's pretty sure he has one the same vintage as the house."

"I don't understand. Don't you just go to the door store or wherever and buy one?"

"I could, but with an old house like this you want to preserve its integrity."

"You mean that *you* want to preserve its integrity."

He paused in spreading mayo on his well-sliced bread and looked over at me. "You don't?"

"The house isn't going to run for mayor, so I'm not too concerned about its integrity, but I would like to be able to enter and leave through the front door. This going around to the back lost its charm last night when I discovered that someone had taken the flashlight out of my car."

"Maybe I should put up sensor lights out there," he said as he built his sandwich. "Your driveway and backyard are pretty dark. Lights would make it safer."

"How about just fixing the front door so I don't have to go around the dark side of the house?"

He found a plate for his sandwich and carried it to the table. "I thought you might feel that way." He put his plate down and fished around in his pants pocket. "So I brought this over for you." He produced a padlock and a key and put it down next to my plate.

"What's that for?"

"The gate. Your back door is pretty flimsy. If you padlock your gate, it'll make it harder for someone to get to the back door." He sat down, bent over his plate and took a bite out of his sandwich.

I chomped on my own sandwich and stared at the padlock as I chewed.

"I have a job I have to finish tomorrow, but I'll find

out if this guy has the right door or not. If he doesn't, I'll go to the lumber yard and get a new one. One way or another, you'll have a working door by the day after tomorrow."

I lifted my gaze from the padlock to look at Mitch, and I figured out why he looked different. He'd trimmed his beard. He'd made it a lot shorter and even around the edges, but evened up or not, it still hid the bottom half of his face while the permanently placed baseball cap obscured the top half. Maybe he was balding. Lots of guys grew their hair long and wore hats to cover their bald spots.

Mitch glanced up just then and caught me staring at him. "What?"

"Nothing," I said quickly. "I mean, okay about your plan for the door."

"What about the sensor lights?"

"No. My neighbor has those. Every time a cat walks by, the lights come on. Some nights they're on and off all night long. They shine through my bedroom window and drive me crazy."

Mitch didn't say anything to that. He was probably the one who'd fitted up the entire neighborhood with sensor lights. Then everyone had had to put up blackout shades so they could get some sleep. We ate our sandwiches in silence. Mitch finished before I did and sat without fidgeting until I swallowed the last of my monster.

"Thank you for sharing your dinner. It was excellent."

"Nothing beats home cooking," I said with a straight face. I pushed the padlock toward him across the table. "I appreciate the thought, but the latch has a built-in lock."

"It does?" He picked up the padlock and slipped it into his pocket. "Mind showing me?"

I led him out the back door to the gate. "This little bar slides over, and then it can't be opened from the other side."

Mitch looked at it and moved the bar back and forth himself. "Okay. He went through the gate and closed it behind him. "Lock it."

I slid the bar over. I saw his fingers grasp the top of

the gate. He jiggled the gate from his side and the bar popped out of place.

"Shit," I said under my breath.

Mitch pushed the gate open and held out his hand. The padlock with the key inserted lay in his open palm. "This will work on either side, so you can lock it on the outside when you're not here."

"You already knew that you could open the gate latch, didn't you?"

"I figured I could. Look, your back door has a glass panel on the top. Anyone could break it and get in your house."

"I've lived here five years and never had any trouble."

"Until yesterday."

"I don't want to start being paranoid. Padlocks today. Tomorrow it'll be searchlights, barbed wire and round-the-clock armed sentries."

"Nothing's going to stop anyone who really wants to break into your house. The padlock on your gate might slow him down, though."

"Him? You mean Frank?"

"Whoever."

We stood staring at one another for several long seconds. He blinked first. "Just take the damn padlock, Alison." He put the lock on top of the fence post and strode away.

I left the padlock on its perch, closed the gate, slipped the bar into place, and retreated into my kitchen. He'd called me by name and somehow that made our connection more personal. I didn't like that at all. No way was I going to be friends with the man who'd ruined my neighborhood.

I set about cleaning up the kitchen. I had too much on my mind to waste time thinking about Mitch the carpenter. There was my dissertation, for example. If Daniel didn't surface tomorrow, I was going to face down Flo and make her tell me how to reach him. She had to know. Making that resolution helped me feel better. I read for awhile and was just about to turn in when Libby phoned. "The Linds are having a memorial service for Stevie the day after tomorrow at ten."

"That's pretty fast. Have the police already released the body?"

"They don't need a body. It's a memorial service, not a funeral. I'll pick you up at nine-forty."

"It's a work day, Libby." Funerals, even disguised as memorial services, were not my thing, although I'd been to more of them than your average citizen.

"I'm sure you can take off a couple of hours for this. How many friends do you think he'll have at the service?"

As usual, Libby occupied the moral high ground. Besides, she'd buried two children and a husband. If she could face Stevie's memorial service, I could, too.

"Okay, meet me at the Center. I'll be out front."

It was hard to settle down after Libby's call, but I finally drifted off to sleep. I don't know what woke me up, but I went directly from sleep to wide awake, sitting up straight in my bed. I couldn't tell if I'd actually heard a noise or if the sound had been part of my dream. I held rigidly still, listening, but all I could hear was my heart pounding and the blood rush in my ears. I forced myself to lie down and breathe slowly so my heart rate would return to normal. Didn't work. I lay encased in fear, unable to move an arm to turn on the light or shift my legs and get out of bed.

How stupid could I be? It was all Mitch's doing. He was the one who'd insisted that my house wasn't safe. My rational, conscious mind rejected it, but my sub-conscious thrived on threats of danger. Any old reason to strike terror into my soul would do.

Damn that Mitch. I had good mind to go right over to his house and give him a piece of my mind. Maybe I'd run around his house once and get all of his anti-burglar lights to come on. Make it look like a major home invasion. I almost laughed out loud at the panic I'd cause.

Then I heard a noise and had my own moment of

panic. Was somebody inside my house? I held still and waited. Several minutes passed with no sound. Then it came again. Definitely outside the house. I got quickly out of bed and moved across the room to the window without turning on the light. I peeked through the crack between the window frame and the shade. It was completely dark outside. Not even a glimmer from my neighbor's sensor light.

I walked barefoot into the living room and made the same careful survey of the outside. I hesitated before going into the kitchen. I didn't have curtains in there. Would someone be able to see me even if I didn't turn on the light? I moved carefully into the kitchen and stayed a few feet away from the window. I still didn't see anything. Then a shadow moved in the front yard.

I didn't look directly at the spot where I'd noticed the movement. I'd learned at foster home number three that you see better with your peripheral vision in the dark. The shadow resolved into the shape of a person, who moved deliberately on a diagonal across my yard to the sidewalk and then disappeared from sight. Whoever it was had been near my house on the driveway side. Had I locked my car? I couldn't remember.

I did clearly recall, though, that I'd left the padlock sitting on the fence post after I'd closed the gate and shifted the useless bar across. No point in my going out in the dark and locking it. Whoever had been there was gone now.

I went back to bed, but couldn't make my body relax. Images of a large man holding a belt loomed over me as I lay helpless in bed. A ghost from the past coming back to haunt me. How was I ever going to get back to sleep? I got up, grabbed the heaviest book from the stack next to my bed, and still without turning on any lights, checked all the windows in the house. It didn't take long. Only two windows actually opened. The rest were permanently shut thanks to a combination of bad paint jobs and broken sash cords.

I checked the back door, although I'd tested the dead bolt on my way back to bed the first time. The lock looked pretty flimsy to me now. I pushed the kitchen table against the door. It would at least slow down anyone who tried to break in that way. It would slow me down, too, if the house caught on fire, but I wasn't going to think about that right now. I'd take life one terror at a time.

I leaned against the table and hefted the book I'd brought along as a defensive weapon. I couldn't see getting close enough to an intruder to hit him on the head with it. I needed a weapon that worked at a distance—like a gun. Not to shoot anyone with. Just to scare him into going away. And it just so happened that I had one.

I crossed the kitchen and opened the louvered doors that closeted the washer and dryer. I located Tyler's water pistol by feel. I left the book on the kitchen table and took my weapon into the bathroom, closing the door before I turned on the light. The bathroom window faced the back yard. If someone were watching the house from the front, he wouldn't see the light go on.

I inspected the gun. Would this fool anyone? It had fooled me, but I didn't know anything about guns. I fired until the gun was empty and refilled it again, only this time I topped it off with some bleach. I turned off the bathroom light and felt my way back to bed, weapon in hand. If anyone broke into the house and refused to leave after I announced that I had a gun, he would get a blast of bleach in the face. With that violent and yet comforting thought, I drifted off to sleep.

I was awakened by pounding on my back door. I checked my clock. Damn, I'd slept through my alarm. And what was that smell? In the morning light filtering through my windowshades I made out the shape of Tyler's water pistol lying next to me on the bed. I sat up with a start. The gun had leaked, and not only did it smell god-awful, but now I had two quarter-sized white spots on my blue blanket from the bleach I'd added. Served me right for my paranoid reaction to the midnight bogeyman scare. How could I have even considered the possibility of deliberately blinding someone?

The pounding on my back door resumed. "Police.

Open the door."

What could they want now? "Just a minute, I'm coming," I yelled. I grabbed the water gun with one hand and shoved it under the bed. "I'm coming," I yelled again, and pulled on a sweatshirt. I staggered into some jeans while heading for the kitchen.

I strode toward the back door and smacked into the kitchen table. Whose stupid idea was it to put the table there? Detective Stan's face peered through the glass panel in the back door. I definitely needed curtains in here. I wrestled the table aside and opened the door.

"Good morning, Ms. Weaver. Glad you're home."

I stood blinking in the glare of the morning light. "Don't you know it's bad manners to drop by without phoning first? I guess I should have told you that yesterday."

"This is more in the way of a courtesy call. We're going to have to impound your car, and we were hoping we could enlist your help in taking a look at it before the tow truck gets here."

I stared at him. "Impound my car? Why?"

"We have reason to believe that your car was used to transport the body of Stephen Lind."

"Says who?"

"We have a citizen's ID of your car by license plate number."

"Wait a minute. Anyone could give you my license plate number. For this, you're going to impound my car? Don't you need a search warrant for something like that?"

"Not if we have probable cause to believe that it contains evidence, or was an instrumentality of a crime."

"Mind giving me that in ordinary English?"

"We interviewed a neighbor of the deceased. Three hours before you found Stephen Lind, the neighbor had called the Berkeley police. Your car, which he identified to them by license plate number, was blocking his car, and he needed to leave for work. Your car was gone by the time he went back outside."

"So, you're just going to take my car? Shouldn't you be telling me I can call a lawyer?"

"No need to. You're not under arrest. You're free, of course, to consult an attorney. He'll tell you the same thing I am. We can take your car for forensic testing. I was just hoping you'd help us out right now, and let us take a look inside it. You'd be helping us out a lot. I know that Stevie was a friend and that you really want us to find out who killed him."

Smart Detective Stans, going for the emotional hook, but he should've used it to begin with, instead of handing me all that cop talk. "Okay, I know there's been some mistake here. No one took Stevie's body anywhere in my car, but you can look. Just give me a couple of minutes, okay? I need to put on some shoes, and I'll be right out."

I moved to close the door in his face. He put up a hand and held the door open. "Bring your car keys, will you? I'll detail one of the officers to question your neighbors while we're waiting."

"Why do you have to do that?"

"Just standard procedure," Stans said mildly.

"Fine," I snapped. "Be sure to shut the gate behind you." I closed the door in his face, a gesture that would have been more effective if it hadn't been a glass-paneled door. We stared at each other through the glass for a couple of seconds, before Stans moved away.

I hurried into the bathroom and tried to achieve the equivalent of my morning shower by standing in front of the sink and using a washcloth. If they impounded my car, how would I get to work? I was late already and walking would make me impossibly late. It was all such bullshit. And questioning my neighbors. What a joke. No one ever saw anything on this street anymore. They were all too busy working to pay off the home improvement loans they'd had to take out after Mitch got hold of them. A morning visit from the cops would have all of them in a frantic state about my bad influence on neighborhood home values.

All except Rose. She'd simply be upset. Rose didn't need dumb cops worrying her and raising her blood pressure. I shoved my bare feet into some sneakers, grabbed my keys and rushed out the back door. I slowed down when I reached the gate. Trying for some dignity.

Stans leaned against an unmarked cop car parked at the curb, a cell phone at his ear. A black and white was parked across the street. One of the uniformed cops stood on the sidewalk in front of my house talking to Rose. She turned when I came through the gate and called out to me. "Alison, are you all right?"

I cut across the front yard, ducking under the low branches of the tree Tyler had dropped out of two days ago. I crossed to where she stood, hugging herself with her arms as if shielding herself from the cold, although it was a very mild morning. "I'm fine. The police are checking something out. It's nothing for you to worry about."

She reached out to me with one hand. I took it into both of mine. We often stood like this, holding hands while we talked and gossiped. Today, though, her hand was icy cold and kept clenching and unclenching mine. "This policeman is asking me if I saw you leave your house the day before yesterday. Why does he want to know that?"

Stans approached us. "If you're ready, Ms. Weaver, we'd like to take a look at your car." He held out his car keys to the cop standing with us. "Get the kit out of the trunk, will you?"

Rose turned a worried gaze at me. I patted her hand. "It's okay. I'm helping the police with their investigation."

"Is it about that friend of yours who was murdered? Mitch told me you found his body."

I nodded. "That's it." I lowered my voice and leaned closer to her. "I have a question of my own. Have you been messing around with your medication again?"

She pursed her mouth the way she always did when I brought up a topic she didn't want to talk about. "Those pills make me so lackadaisical. I don't have any oomph at all when I take them. I hate it."

"You'd hate it more if you had a stroke. Look, call your doctor and tell him the dosage isn't right for you, but for now just take your regular dose, okay?"

"Whenever you're ready, Ms. Weaver," Stans said again.

I ignored him. "Why don't you go in now, Rose? I'll drop by before I go to work."

She nodded in agreement, gave my hand a squeeze, and headed toward her house.

I turned toward Stans. "All right, I'm ready now."

They followed me up my driveway. My car was parked under the branches of a Japanese plum tree. A few leaves decorated the hood and windshield. The uniformed cop carried a black case he'd taken from the trunk of Stans' car and deposited it on the ground nearby. "Anything else, sir?"

"I'll need the flashlight and gloves out of there first," Stans said. "You take the Polaroid and get shots of the car from all four sides."

The cop squatted down, opened the case, and removed a flashlight and surgical gloves, which he handed to Stans. Stans tucked the flashlight under his arm and pulled on the gloves. He stood back from the car while the cop circled and took pictures.

"You loaned your car to a friend the night Lind was killed, right?"

"Yes, that's right. Libby had it the entire time, so there's no way it could've been used to move his body."

"Did you notice anything different about your car when she returned it?"

"No... nothing, except my flashlight was missing. But it might've been missing before that, and I didn't notice it."

"Where do you keep the flashlight?"

"In the glove compartment."

Stans moved toward my car. "Will you unlock the driver and passenger side doors for me?"

I stepped toward the car, keys at the ready.

"Don't touch anything or open the door. Just turn the key in the lock. Okay?"

I did as he said, although I felt a little silly. But if that was the way he wanted to play it, I'd go along.

He opened the door and shined the light around the interior. He opened the glove compartment and glanced at the registration and local area maps I kept in there. He looked under the dashboard and under the seats, tipping the front seats forward delicately with one gloved finger so he could scrutinize the rear seating space. He backed out of the car and straightened.

"How in the world do you think anyone could fit a body into that car?" I asked. "The back seat is so tight that live people don't want to get into it. The front passenger seat's a possibility, I suppose, but still hard to manage, not to mention risky."

"Can I look in the trunk?"

"Sure, but you'll see there's no way Stevie would fit into my trunk." I slotted the trunk key into the lock and turned it. The lid rose sluggishly, propelled by a failing hydraulic pump in the hinge. Stans and the uniformed cop lined up on either side of me and waited for the lid to complete its upward arc.

I gazed into the trunk. "Oh shit."

CHAPTER EIGHT

"Is there a problem?" Stans asked.

I stared at my empty trunk. "You bet there's a problem. I've been robbed."

"What's been taken?"

"All my emergency supplies. My tent, sleeping bag, camp stove, fuel, food, water, medical supplies, tools. This really ticks me off. It took me months to get it all together."

Stans leaned over and peered into the empty recesses at the back of the trunk. "What kind of emergency were you expecting?"

"What do you think? A seven pointer on the Hayward Fault."

He straightened and exchanged a glance with the uniformed cop.

I sensed doubt, even ridicule. "You think I'm a nut? Wait until you're cut off for a week with no food, water, shelter or medical care."

"Except for the missing supplies, does your trunk look as usual to you?"

"As usual? It looks empty, and that's not usual."

"What about that stain?" He pointed at a dark patch on the brown carpet lining of the trunk.

I shook my head. "I don't know. I don't remember it, but it could have been there before. It's an old car."

Stans pointed the flashlight beam into the back of the

trunk. “What about that hat? Was it there before?”

I recognized it. It looked like the green and blue striped knit hat that Stevie Number used to wear. What was it doing in my car?

“Ms. Weaver?” Stans prompted.

“It’s not mine.” The flash from the camera went off, and I jumped. The camera whirred and ejected a print, a blur of muddy green that would resolve within a minute into a clear, defined picture. If only the blur in my mind could change so quickly.

“Take one more of the inside of the trunk,” Stans ordered the other cop, "then get as much as you can of the car interior.” Stans turned to the open case on the ground and retrieved a paper bag, while the cop snapped the picture. Stans fished the hat out of the trunk, dropped it into the bag and used a twist tie with a tag attached to close it. He wrote something on the tag and stuffed the bag in his coat pocket while the cop kept pointing and shooting with the camera.

The roar of an approaching motorcycle drowned out the camera’s buzz. The motorcycle pulled into my driveway and braked inches away from us. Frank had arrived to make my life even more miserable than it already was.

He dismounted and pulled off his helmet. “Hey, Al,” he said, walking up to join us. “What’s going on?”

I put my fists on my hips. “What are you doing here, Frank?”

“I’m here to help. Want to fill me in on what’s going on?”

“Excuse me, sir,” Stans said. “We’re conducting an investigation here. I’ll have to ask you to remove yourself and your vehicle to the sidewalk.”

I had to admit that Stans was good at the cop talk, although it wasn’t particularly effective with Frank.

“Are you in some kind of trouble, Al?” Frank asked me.

Stans signaled to the uniformed cop, who put down

the camera and approached Frank, saying, "Come with me, sir." He walked directly towards Frank, forcing Frank to walk backwards away from him.

"You don't have to say anything to these guys, Al. I'll call my lawyer for you."

Just what I needed—advice from a lawyer who specialized in literary contracts. "If you show up here one more time, Frank, I'm filing for a restraining order."

"Boyfriend?" Stans asked.

"Ex-husband."

"He been giving you trouble?"

"Trying to, that's all." I turned to Stans. "Did you announce over your radio that you were coming here this morning?"

"No reason to. Why?"

I glanced back towards Frank, who was now standing at the curb, earnestly bending the ear of the cop.

A movement behind some bushes across the street caught my eye. I gazed at the bush and asked Stans, "I've been meaning to ask you—did you release my name and details of my finding Stevie's body to the news media?"

"We never release witnesses' names without their permission."

"Excuse me," I said. "I'll be right back." I strode down the driveway and crossed the street without glancing at Frank. I found Tyler crouched behind the bushes.

"When did Frank ask you to spy on me?"

Tyler slowly got to his feet. Dirt and dried leaves stuck to the knees of his pants. He glanced toward Frank.

I moved to block Tyler from Frank's view. "Don't look at Frank. Look at me. You see those cops? You want them to question you instead?" My conscience gave me a little kick. I'd never approved of parents who used threats of police intervention with their kids. On the other hand, it seemed likely that Tyler was going to have an encounter with the police at some point before he reached adulthood, so maybe I was doing him a favor by injecting some fear at an early age.

"I wasn't spying. Frank's worried about you."

"Okay, let's say I buy that. How long has he been worried?"

"A couple of months, I guess."

"So you called Frank after you held me up with the squirt gun, because I told you I'd come across a dead body that morning, and Frank came right over." I spoke as if I knew this for a fact, and Tyler didn't contradict me. "When did you call him this morning?"

"After I saw the police cars in front of your house. Why's the cop talking to Frank? He didn't do anything."

"Frank's helping the police, just like I am. Did you see anything last night?"

"My mom doesn't let me go out after dark," he said quickly, but his gaze slid away from mine. He hadn't perfected his lying techniques. There might be hope for him, after all.

I glanced across the street. Stans appeared completely engrossed by my car's empty trunk. If Stevie's body had actually been in the trunk of my car, my friend Libby was going to be in trouble.

I turned back to Tyler. "Let's talk some more later, okay?"

He gave me his classic shrug.

I re-crossed the street and paused by Frank and the cop. "Using a kid as a spy is pretty low, even for you. You know I meant it about the restraining order, and I'll make sure Marcia hears about it, so back off."

I didn't wait for him to respond, but hurried up the driveway to rejoin Stans.

"I found something else," Stans said. He slipped a wrinkled piece of paper into a plastic document sleeve and held it up for me to see. "Is this yours?"

I stepped closer to look. It turned out to be a sheet of lined paper with handwritten lists of numbers under cryptic headings. I nearly said "oh shit" again. "No, it's not mine.

That's not my writing."

Stans didn't say anything. He simply remained still, holding out the paper for me to see.

I found myself adding, "But I've seen pages like this one. I covered Stevie's face with them when I came across his body in the dumpster."

"How do you suppose it came to be in the trunk of your car?"

"I have no idea." I hoped that I was telling the truth, because any idea I might have had was unthinkable.

We stood silently staring at one another for a long five seconds. I probably would have blinked first if the tow truck hadn't arrived in a roaring cloud of hydrocarbons. The uniformed cop pointed out my car to the driver. Frank started to walk back up the driveway toward me, but the cop stopped him. He must have said something persuasive, because Frank reversed direction, got on his bike and took off.

"We're going to need the keys to your car," Stans said.

I turned to him. "Is it true that I don't have any say in this?"

"We have cause to believe that your car was used in the commission of a crime. That gives us the right to seize the vehicle. We don't need the keys to tow your car, but, if we have them, it'll make it easier for us to lock it up and keep it safe until we hand it back to you."

He made it all sound so reasonable. I fished my keyring out of my pocket, unhooked the two keys and handed them over.

"Thanks. I appreciate your cooperation. Just wait a second, and I'll get you a receipt."

I moved away from my car and watched Stans organize the towing operation. I needed to talk to Libby and find out how the hell my car had come to have Stevie's hat and that sheet of paper in it. Maybe someone had just put them in the trunk, and Stevie's body had been transported some other way. Possibly it was just coincidental that my supplies had been stolen. I couldn't see how Libby could have been involved.

The preliminaries took forever, but the actual towing happened in a bare minute. When Stans headed in my direction, I moved toward him and met him half-way.

"Here you are." He held out the receipt for my car.

I took it and folded it. "When can I have my car back?"

"Depends on what forensics turns up. We'll get back to you about it."

"I'd better get going." I backed away from him.

"Before you take off, I need to ask you some questions."

"Can we do it this evening? I'm already late for work."

"I'm sure your boss will understand," he said, making it clear he wasn't going to be put off.

I folded my arms across my chest. "Okay. What do you want to know?"

"I wonder, would it be all right if we went inside? Be a little more private, more comfortable for you to sit down. And me, too."

I suppose I could have said no, except Stans had this way of acting as if his requests would be completely acceptable. As if I had nothing at all to hide. So I took him around to the back door and let him into my kitchen. Some people are slow learners.

I'd pushed the chairs aside the night before so I could jam the table against the door. I hastily pulled them back around the table. "Have a seat. I'll be right with you. I have to call in to work."

I crossed to the phone and dialed work. I would have given anything to call Libby, but couldn't picture carrying off that conversation in front of Stans. Flo didn't pick up so I had to settle for leaving a brief message.

I joined Stans, taking the empty chair opposite him. Stans had commandeered my table, invading my private space. He'd placed the bag holding Stevie's cap and the plastic sleeve containing the damning sheet of paper in the middle of the table. He reached into an inside pocket, pulled out a mini-cassette tape recorder, and placed it on the table with the rest.

"This is so there's no misunderstanding later on," he said, pushing the record button. He spoke into the recorder, identifying himself, me, the time and date.

"Who cares about later on? I don't understand right now what's going on. Am I a suspect? Should I get a lawyer?"

"You're not under arrest, if that's what you're asking. If I did place you under arrest, I'd advise you of your right to an attorney. Right now, I just want to ask a few questions, fill in a couple of pieces of missing information."

"Like what?"

"When was the last time you looked in the trunk of your car?"

I locked gazes with him. "The night before I found Stevie's body. Nothing was missing."

"You told us that you'd loaned your car to your friend that night."

"That's right, but believe me, Libby couldn't have had anything to do with Stevie's murder. She couldn't harm anyone."

"Would she have taken your supplies without telling you?"

I hesitated, and saw that Stans noticed it. How to explain a saint like Libby to a cynic like Stans? "If there'd been some dire need, she would've given my supplies away, knowing that I wouldn't mind. But she also would've told me about it when she saw me and replaced everything as soon as possible."

"When was the last time you saw the deceased?"

"I told you, a week before he was killed."

"You got along with him pretty good?"

Another unanswerable question. If I couldn't explain Libby, how could I describe my friendship with Stevie? I settled for a curt, "Yes."

"What about your ex-husband? What's the relationship like with him?"

"What does Frank have to do with Stevie's murder?"

"I don't know. Maybe nothing. But he's been trouble for you, and you're involved directly or indirectly with a homicide. I find it's always better to get as much information as possible. Sort out what's relevant and what's not later on."

"One of the neighbors told you that Frank kicked in my door?"

"What was that all about?"

"I don't know. Ask Frank. My guess, based on past experience, is that he wants something."

"I take it you don't get along?"

"We have no relationship at all."

"He showed up today."

"Second time I've seen him since the divorce. He hired a neighbor kid to spy on me. The kid called Frank when he spotted the police car out front this morning."

"Think he could be stalking you?"

"Why don't you ask him what he's up to? Not that I think you'll get the straight story."

"What about the things we found in your car?" Stans asked, in a swift change of subject. He gestured at the hat and paper on the table between us. "Anything else occur to you?"

I pulled the plastic sleeve holding the paper toward me and bent over the table to examine it. "I don't know what else to tell you."

"You recognized the paper, right?"

"Yes, because it's like the ones I used to cover Stevie's face."

"That your handwriting?"

"No."

"And yet out of a whole bin of trash paper, you can tell me that this piece is like the ones you put over the deceased's face."

"They were the only pieces of paper that hadn't been shredded. My boss is very particular, almost obsessive, about security. We're supposed to shred every piece of paper before we toss it into recycling. But you have the other pages. Why don't you compare them?"

"What about what's written on it? That tell you anything?"

I gazed at the page. It showed three short columns. Variable names at the top and numbers lined up beneath. "That it's handwritten and not a computer printout tells me that it's probably someone's notes. I don't recognize the handwriting or the variable names. It's not from any study I've worked on, but that doesn't mean anything, because there are a lot of projects ongoing all the time."

"Variable names?"

I pointed to the first column.

"R-B-P-C-E," Stans spelled out the first variable. "That's a name?"

"An abbreviation of a variable, although, as I said, I don't know what it refers to."

"And a variable is... ?"

"Something you measure that might vary from one time to another or from one group to another, or both," I said and grinned when he frowned. "It's not hard to understand. Your weight can be a variable. If you eat less or eat more over a period of time, you'd expect your weight to change or vary as a result of your different eating pattern. Only the variables researchers like me look at are things having to do with the environment that might affect health, like contaminants in drinking water or in the air. We compare the level of contaminants to different rates of illness in people exposed."

Stans waved his hand as if brushing away flies. "Okay, okay. So you don't recognize exactly what these notes refer to, but they look like the sort of thing that's done where you work?"

It was my turn to frown. "Yes. Where else would they

have come from?"

"You said Stephen Lind was a mathematician. I wondered if this could've belonged to him."

"I just assumed it was from the Center." I bent over the page again and examined it more closely.

"In my work it's generally not a good idea to assume."

I studied the page for a few more seconds. "I suppose it could've been Stevie's, but I don't think so. He was a mathematician, not a statistician. These look like statistical results. They aren't whole numbers, and they're taken to four decimal points, the way our statistical software calculates it. We round to two places when we present our results formally."

"You told me that the two of you talked about statistics."

"That's true, but we talked about it abstractly, like what kind of analysis would you do with a certain kind of data. What were the limitations of that approach."

Stans put a finger on one corner of the plastic sleeve and drew it towards him. "So, let's say this is from your trash can."

"Not mine," I corrected him. "The Center's."

He shrugged. "Okay, the Center's trash. How do you suppose it got into the trunk of your car?"

"I have no idea."

Stans let the silence hang in the air between us. I held his gaze and waited him out. He reached over and turned off the recorder. "That's all the questions I have for now." He stood up and gathered up the recorder, hat and paper, and stuffed them in his sagging jacket pockets.

"What about the neighbors? Anyone see me leaving for work day before yesterday?"

"We'll have to check again in the evening. No one's home right now, except one babysitter who only speaks Spanish." He headed for the back door.

I'd followed him as far as the gate when it hit me. "Wait a minute."

He turned and looked at me.

"If no one's home, who told you that Frank kicked in my door?"

"You did." He turned away and opened the gate.

I watched him walk down my empty driveway and tried not to grit my teeth. No point in getting upset. He'd warned me not to assume, and I'd gone ahead and done it anyway.

As I stood there, no longer assuming anything and making sure that Stans actually got in his car and drove off, Libby arrived. She pulled into my vacant driveway, slammed out of her car and hurried toward me. Stans had already opened the driver side door, but he paused and watched us over the roof of his car.

Libby's face was creased with concern. "Alison, I'm so sorry. I had to tell them everything."

CHAPTER NINE

"What do you mean—everything?" I kept one eye on Stans, who was in no hurry to get away.

"About your car. I'm so sorry," she apologized again.

"Let's go inside." I hurried her through the gate and into my house.

I waited until we were inside and I'd closed the door. "Now tell me what happened."

"I'm so…"

"Please, don't apologize one more time. I just want to know what the cops told you, and what you told the cops."

"He came by my house this morning."

"Who?"

"The young detective I'd talked to before."

"Carney?"

She nodded.

"He said he needed to ask me again about the night I'd borrowed your car, which it turns out was the night Stevie was killed. He wanted to know everything—why I needed it, where I'd gone, how long I'd been there."

"And?"

"I should have mentioned it when I returned your car, but all I could think about was poor Stevie, and when I remembered, I thought it didn't matter, because everything had worked out okay."

I gritted my teeth. "Libby, you're still not telling me. What about my car?"

"I lost your keys. So I didn't take your car after all. I borrowed my neighbor's, which I didn't want to do, because it doesn't have an automatic transmission, and you know I hate driving a stick shift on hills, and I had to go to San Francisco."

"But you returned my car with the keys in it when you came over the night before last."

"Yes, I hadn't lost them permanently. I'd simply misplaced them, but still I felt terrible about it. There they were the next day, lying right in the middle of my desk. I felt ridiculous, the way you do when you do something stupid like that."

"My keys were in your house the whole time?" I said, my voice rising.

"No, not my house. They were on my desk in the mobile clinic, where you left them for me. Well, actually under some papers, which is why I'd thought I lost them, I suppose, although I thought I'd looked there."

I paced the kitchen. We always parked the clinic van at Holy Savior, because the parish priest supported our work and his church had a secure parking lot. It would be hard to steal the mobile clinic from a barricaded parking lot, but not necessarily that hard to get into it. We didn't store any important supplies inside the clinic, but stocked up with what we needed for each outing and removed any unused supplies at the end of each run.

"I left my car on the street in front of the church. Was it still parked in the same place the next day?"

"I'm sorry. I don't remember. I didn't really pay any attention to your car once I realized I didn't have the keys. I got a ride home with Jerry and called my neighbor. Do you think someone took it and then returned it?"

"I know it."

"I still don't understand what your car has to do with Stevie's murder."

"The police found Stevie's hat in the trunk and think

Stevie was in there, too. Which means that someone stole my car, took all my emergency supplies out, put Stevie's body in, drove to the Center, dumped Stevie, and then returned the car minus the emergency supplies."

"And when I couldn't find the keys... "

"They were gone."

"But that means that someone broke into the clinic to return the keys. Alison, there wasn't any sign of a break-in. Honest."

"Of course not. My keys to the clinic were on the same key chain as my car keys." I closed my eyes. I needed desperately to think the whole series of events through, but my head was spinning and my stomach hurt. I focused for a few seconds on my stomachache. I hadn't eaten all morning, and here it was noon already, no wonder I felt like little animals were inside, gnawing their way out. "I don't know about you, but I need to eat something right away. Let's hit Polish Joe's. It's not that far from here. Then, I need you to drop me off at a car rental place. The cops impounded my car."

Libby looked relieved to have a task at hand. "Polish Joe's it is. As for car rental—I know just the place. It's owned by a friend of mine." We drove to the home of the best Polish sausage in Oakland where we both ordered Joe's Supreme Sandwich. I need to go to Saag's and get a description of their menu offerings. Maybe also trace the route from the police station to the restaurant, and how often police officers themselves might go there.

My insides felt better after we ate, but my brain still struggled with the weird events around Stevie's death, and how I'd become entangled in them. I told Libby about Stans finding Stevie's hat and the piece of paper in the trunk. She gave me a worried frown. "I don't think you should talk to the police again without an attorney present."

"I'm not under arrest." The word "yet" remained unspoken between us.

"Promise me you'll get a lawyer."

"Okay, I promise, but first I have to rent a car. You

mentioned a friend?"

Libby took me to "U-Use-Used Cars," a place only she could have known about. The cars were a lot older than the ones on the Hertz lot, but they were also cheaper. On top of that, I was given a major discount because Libby had helped reunite the owner with his runaway son. Libby introduced me as a friend, but he kept checking out my black eye, so he probably felt he was doing his charitable bit for a battered wife. I ended up with a six year old Buick Century, which was acres more car than I needed, but still within my budget.

I left Libby with a promise to see her at the clinic on my next usual night. I decided to go home before proceeding on to work. I'd call and reconnoiter with Kenji first, and I'd also do something about my black eye.

As I pulled into my driveway, I could see that Mitch had made some progress on repairing my door. Lumber of varying lengths leaned against the porch railing and a can of paint rested on the bottom step. I got out of my car and crossed to the front porch to inspect what Mitch had left there. Besides the paint and lumber, I found nails, screws, and a paintbrush, tucked away in a corner of my front porch, but no door. Okay, so I didn't have a basis for complaint. Mitch had told me he'd be working on another job until tomorrow, but still a rasp of irritation added itself to the morning's accumulation of aggravations.

I retreated down the front steps and around the house to the padlocked gate. In the light of day with Polish sausage lining my stomach and no police dangling incriminating evidence under my nose, the padlock looked a little silly. I'd always used the usual urban precautions of deadbolts and window locks, but realistically speaking, it would take a very mentally challenged burglar to target my old place over all the spiffed-up houses on the street. It was a clear case of what you saw was what you got, because I didn't own anything theft-worthy—at least not now that someone had lifted my emergency supplies.

I let myself in the back door and shut it harder than necessary. The loss of my stockpiled provisions rankled more than I'd wanted to let on to Stans. Those stores were my hedge against calamity. I'd learned at an early age that there were more unnatural disasters than natural ones in life, and they usually involved loss of shelter or food or both. I'd taken the squirrel and the ant as my role models.

I'd have to start making a list to replace everything. I'd have to go to the police station to fill out a theft report, because an insurance claim would require a police report number. I nearly grabbed up a notepad and started writing a to-do list but remembered in time that I absolutely had to call work.

While I was punching in Flo's number, Mitch knocked on the back door. I opened the door and motioned him to come into the kitchen. He came in carrying a thick orange extension cord.

Flo answered on the first ring. "Center for Biostatistical Studies, Flo speaking."

Mitch gestured toward the living room, and I waved him through.

"Hi Flo. It's Alison. Is Daniel in?"

"No, he isn't. Are you still *helping* the police?" She leaned on "helping" in an unpleasant way, as if either she thought I'd lied to her about why I couldn't come in to work, or she considered my helping them to be one step away from being arrested.

I ignored the sub-text. When Flo decided you weren't pulling your weight at work, she'd beat you into submission with her sarcasm. "I'm done—for now. How can I reach Daniel?"

"You can't. However, I'll be happy to pass along any message."

Noisy banging came from the living room followed by a loud screech.

"What was that?" Flo asked.

"It's nothing. Is he picking up his voicemail?"

"I'm sure I don't know."

Great. I had Flo at her most snippy and Daniel

incommunicado. She said something else at the same time as another screech came from the living room.

"I'm sorry I missed that. What did you say?"

"Who is that screaming?"

"No one. What did you say?"

"I said, 'Who is that screaming?'"

What I didn't need right then was several rounds of "Who's on first?" with Flo. "No one's screaming. I'm having some repairs done on my house. Would you transfer me to Kenji, please?"

"Kenji's not here. He *said* he was sick," she said, again with the implication of malingering. At least I wasn't the only suspect in her personal line-up of slackers.

"I'm sorry to hear that. Well, I have to go now. I'll see you tomorrow."

"You're not coming in?" she asked, her voice rising.

"I'd love to come in, but I'm completely at the mercy of Daniel's erratic schedule. I can't do anything until he gives me access to the refinery data. So what's the point? I'd do better at this point to sit down here at home and brainstorm the best approach to take on the data."

"*I* hire only honest people I know I can trust to do repairs for me."

It took a few seconds for me to get it—she thought I was staying home simply because I didn't want to leave while my house was being worked on. "You're very lucky to have good workers you can trust around you." I said with as much sarcasm as I could lace into my words. At that moment, Mitch passed through the kitchen, minus the extension cord, and headed out the back door. "I just don't understand why you don't trust me as much as you do your plumber. I'm working at home for the rest of the day, and I'll see you tomorrow." I hung up without waiting for a reply. A mistake for sure, but I couldn't help myself.

I'd deal with Flo tomorrow. Right now I wanted to find out what Mitch was up to. I looked into the living room. He'd succeeded in opening one of my formerly sealed windows, although judging from the noise I'd heard, the window had put up a good fight. Since both sash cords were broken, he'd propped it open with a hammer. He'd plugged the heavy-duty extension cord into the outlet beneath the window and passed the rest of the cord outside.

I followed what was becoming a well-worn path out the back door and around the house to the front porch. Mitch knelt on the porch next to one of the long boards, measuring it with a steel tape measure. I shared the general public's tendency to regard construction work as a spectator sport and stood watching Mitch mark the board with a pencil, shift it until it stuck out over the front steps, and slice off the end with an electric hand saw. He switched off the saw and glanced over at me.

"Hi," I said and came closer.

He nodded without speaking.

"I thought you were going to be working on another job today."

"Finished early." He picked up the newly trimmed board, leaned it against the porch railing, selected another piece of lumber and proceeded measuring, marking, and sawing until it matched the first board.

He propped the second board next to the first and turned towards me. "I found a door for you."

"Great. Where is it?"

He came down the porch steps without saying anything and led me across the street to his truck. He reached into the bed of the truck and whipped a tarp to one side to reveal a paint-encrusted door. Through the layers of paint, which were chipped away in places to show as many as eight different colors, I could just make out a curlicue design in the wood.

"It looks like it was pretty nice—once," I said. "I suppose one more layer of paint won't make any difference."

Mitch jerked the tarp back over the door. "You don't want to paint it."

"I know I don't, but I was hoping you'd do it as part of the deal."

He folded his arms across his chest and squinted at the horizon like a cowboy looking for the dust raised by rustlers' horses. "The door should be stripped and the wood treated with a sealant. It's solid oak and about a hundred years old, with hand-carved designs on both sides. It's not a standard size. Your door opening will have to be adjusted to fit."

"Okay, sounds good to me. So is all this paint-stripping and doorway-refitting extra? Just give me the bill. I'll send it on to Marcia."

He didn't reply, but lowered his gaze to study the toes of his boots.

"I get it. You're trying to tell me it's going to take even longer for me to have a functioning front door. How long do you estimate?"

After another long pause, he lifted his gaze to meet mine. "You have no commitment to have me finish the job. If you want to bring in someone else, I'll hand over the door and a bill for my work so far."

"I'm a little confused. I thought we agreed that you'd fix the door. Are you telling me you don't want the job?"

"I like to finish what I start, but not if you're uncomfortable having me do the work."

"Mitch, don't go all weird on me now. I have enough bizarre things going on in my life as it is. Someone killed Stevie Number and used my car to take his body to my place of work and dump him so I could be the first one to find him. The police think I had something to do with it, because Stevie, who happened to be a diagnosed schizophrenic, left his papers to me in his will. I'm sad about Stevie. I'm mad as hell at the cops, and I'm also terrified that they're going to arrest me, because then my boss will fire me, and I'll never finish my dissertation. So there's no room left over in my life for mild sensations of discomfort." I stopped and took a breath. "And what gave you the idea I was uncomfortable about you fixing my door anyway?"

"You did. Just now on the phone."

"On the phone? I was talking to the biggest pain in the ass who ever managed an office. It was her idea that I didn't trust you, because she doesn't trust me, or anyone else who works there, except our boss, of course. He's more infallible than the Pope."

"So what are you going to do?"

"Convince you to fix my door, I hope."

"I'll fix it. I meant about the other problem, with the cops."

"Find a lawyer, fast. You don't happen to know a good one, do you? Someone who handles criminal cases?"

Mitch gave me the strangest look, as if I'd just sung the first eight bars of "Un bel di," or spoken to him in Cantonese. Then I had to wait while he did the squinting at the horizon thing again. He finally said, "Yeah, I know a guy who does that."

"Great. Who is he? Do you have his number? Do you have any idea what he charges?"

He went to the back of his truck and lowered the tailgate. "Help me stow the door, would you? I don't want to leave it in the truck."

"Sure. Where do you want to put it? In my backyard?"

He climbed into the bed of the truck and pulled the tarp off the door. "Let's put it in my garage. I'll do the stripping over here." He hoisted his end of the door and slid it towards me.

I grabbed the end when it cleared the tailgate. It was heavier than I expected. Much heavier. "What did you say this was made of—lead?" I said as I backed up carrying the door.

"Solid oak." He stepped down from the truck holding the other end of the door. "If the door frame is put in solid, no one'll ever kick your door in again."

"They won't need to use the door." I grunted with effort as I walked backwards, holding my end of the door. "They can just crawl in through the window. Piece of cake, now that you've unsealed it."

"Still hard to open with both sash cords broken."

"Well, that's some comfort." We carried the door up his driveway and propped it up outside the garage while he slid the door open. Mitch's garage bore testimony either to a careful craftsman or to someone with obsessive-compulsive disorder. I did an inspection tour of the interior. A wall of pegboard held the tools of his trade arranged by type, purpose and size. Dymo labels on drawers named the contents, and shelves held paint cans grouped by color.

"Looking for something."

I turned around. He'd arranged two sawhorses in the middle of the garage while I'd nosed around his tools. "Just being impressed."

He gave me a sidelong glance that I couldn't read as he walked out to get the door. He lifted it without my help, carried it in and rested it on the sawhorses. I'd always thought of him as lanky bordering on thin, but there had to be some significant muscles lurking under his khaki work clothes. He straightened and faced me. "So what impresses you?"

I got the distinct feeling that he didn't think I could be. I decided not to mention his muscles. I didn't want to get too personal. "Your garage is neater than my kitchen. It might be cleaner, too. Do you scrub the floor in here?" I gazed down at the pristine cement.

"Certain kinds of jobs, like sealing your door, you can't have any dust around."

I nodded as if I knew what he was talking about. "Speaking of my door. What kind of timetable are we looking at now?"

He led me out of the garage, pulled the door down and secured it with a padlock. A larger one, I noticed than the one he'd given me for my gate. He stood and regarded the cement of the driveway, as if there was a calendar carved into it. "Two days, maybe three. Depends on… a couple of things."

"Okay." What else could I say, anyway? Mitch had control over the whole project. I gazed across the street at the work in progress and saw Tony Dezzutti sitting on my front steps. "I don't believe it," I breathed. I waved at him and headed across the street. Mitch crossed with me.

"Hi," I said, as I approached Tony.

He stood up and brushed off the seat of his pants. "Hi." He smiled, giving me a brief glimpse of his dimple. "I thought that was you over there."

"Mitch was showing me my new door. I guess you two met the other day, right?"

Mitch said, "Hey," to Tony and walked past him up the porch steps.

Tony said, "Hey," in turn, but Mitch had already gone back to work, sorting through the remaining uncut boards. Tony turned his attention to me. "I wondered if you'd like to go out for a ride or something."

"Sure," I said immediately. Who was I to hesitate? The last time he'd seen me, I'd been waving a knife, but he'd come back for a return visit anyway. I wasn't going to argue with chemistry. "Mind coming in for a minute while I get my purse?" I might not argue with chemistry, but I might help it along. It was time for a judicious application of the concealing makeup I'd bought and left in my bathroom. With luck, it would work as well as the salesgirl had said.

Tony waited in the kitchen while I rushed into my bathroom and dabbed on the makeup. She hadn't exaggerated. It hid most of the discoloration completely. Success in covering my black eye inspired me to put on some lipstick, too, but I didn't dawdle over it. No point in keeping the man waiting.

I hurried into the kitchen. "I'm ready." I ushered him out the back door and then through the gate. "Will you need to get into the house?" I asked Mitch as an afterthought. "I locked the back door, but I'll unlock it if you like."

He'd been about to cut another board. He straightened and let his gaze slide from me to Tony and back again. "That's okay. I'll shut the window when I'm through here." He looked as if he had something else to say, but he didn't add anything. Just stood looking at me.

Tony touched my arm. "Ready?"

"Sure." We walked down the driveway to his car and got in. As we pulled away from the curb, I looked back at the house. Mitch was still watching us.

"You feel okay leaving your house while he's there?"

"Who, Mitch? Of course. Why?"

"I don't know. Something about him makes me uneasy."

"I don't know him very well, but all the neighbors think he tap dances on water. Hey, where are we going?"

"I thought maybe a walk somewhere like Point Isabel. What do you think?"

"Point Isabel's pretty, but it's a bit too much like Wild Kingdom since it's the only place people can let their dogs run off leash."

"Okay, Point Isabel's out. How about Tilden Park?"

"Tilden's good." I didn't add anything about watching out for poison oak. I didn't want to seem difficult to please. He'd been going west on Alcatraz Avenue, but made two right hand turns and headed east on Ashby. I couldn't think of anything to say, so I sat trying to look interested in the urban scenery that was as familiar to me as my own house.

"You aren't a dog person?" he asked.

"I don't know. I've never had a dog. I thought I'd have a kid first and get some practice before I tried a dog."

"Isn't it usually the other way around?"

"The way I look at it, kids get potty trained after about two years, but with a dog, you're picking up poop forevermore. If I couldn't take it with a kid, then I'd know for sure not to get a dog."

He didn't laugh. I tried not to sigh out loud. I also tried not to rush into judgment. He might have a sense of humor, just a different one from mine. I mean, what was the point of having a killer dimple if you never smiled? We both fell into silence again.

He turned left at Claremont Avenue and took the road that circled behind the Claremont Hotel. I craned my neck around and caught a brief glimpse of tanned couples running after yellow tennis balls before the white dome of the hotel blocked my view. The road rose steeply. We passed a bicyclist pedaling hard in low gear. Eucalyptus and pine trees grew in thin stands, broken here and there by wide sweeps of tall yellowed foxtails. A carved wooden sign told us that we were entering Tilden Park. Trees and brush grew more thickly here, climbing up the side of the hills.

Tony tried to get the conversation going again. "So you and Frank didn't have kids?"

"No. Frank decided that he wanted to be an only child."

Tony frowned a little at my reply, but didn't comment, and silence settled between us like a third passenger in the car. We possibly could have spent the entire outing not speaking another word, if I hadn't seen Jesus.

Chapter Ten

"Oh, my God." I sat up straight in my seat. "It's Jesus!"

Tony jerked the steering wheel. "What?"

I pointed to the figure walking up the road ahead of us. "It's Jesus. There!"

"Who? That black guy in the long robes?"

"Yes. Pull over."

"You scared me, yelling like that," he said and kept on driving.

"I'm sorry. Honest. I was surprised to see him. Can you stop the car? I have to talk to him." How could I have missed it? Doris had said Joe was with Jesus.

"You sure?" He didn't take his foot off the accelerator. "He looks kind of crazy to me."

"That's because he is crazy, but Doris told me that Joe was with Jesus, and I think this is who she meant. So will you stop the car?"

"Who's Joe?" he asked, as he drove past Jesus.

"The guy who knocked me down while you hung out behind a dumpster. Now *stop the car*." I twisted around in my seat, trying to keep an eye on Jesus out the back window. The road curved, and he disappeared from my line of vision.

"That guy had a gun. You mean the guy with the gun?" Tony sounded worried, but he slowed down.

I had my hand on the door handle and tugged on it as soon as Tony put his foot on the brake. "Will you leave off about the gun? Joe knows something about Stevie's murder."

Tony swung the car to the side of the road and jammed on the brakes. Good thing I still had my seatbelt on. I struggled for a second trying to unfasten the belt and open the door at the same time. I got out of the car and started at a lope back down the road. I cleared the curve where I'd last seen Jesus, but there was no one in sight. Not that it would be easy to spot him. The road was lined on both sides with trees and underbrush.

Tony trotted up to join me. "Where'd he go?"

"Into the park. He lives here."

"Where?"

"How should I know? It's not like there's an address. Just in the park somewhere." I walked to the spot where I thought I'd last seen him before we went around the curve. "He must have taken off somewhere around here. Look for tracks or something."

"You know how big Tilden Park is? It covers thousands of acres. We could get lost if we don't stay on the trails," Tony said, but he bent his head and scanned the shoulder anyway. "You don't think Joe killed Stevie?"

"He's not dangerous," I said, skirting the question. "He was going to tell me something about who killed Stevie when your friend decided to run us down with his truck."

"Lou was only trying to help."

"Whatever."

"Look at this." Tony pointed to some broken brush and trampled foxtails. "Do you think he went in there?"

"Maybe. It won't hurt to see." I stepped on the flattened weeds and saw a barely discernable path through the brush.

"Wait," Tony said behind me. "Do you think this Jesus guy could get violent?"

"He believes he's Jesus. How violent do you think

Jesus was?" I continued following the path, alternately examining the ground underfoot for the slightly worn places that showed the trail, and looking ahead for a glimpse of Jesus. Gradually, we entered into a thickly wooded area, with less brush and more eucalyptus debris on the ground. I could hear Tony crunching along behind me. Jesus was going to hear us before we saw him.

I stopped and held up a hand to halt Tony.

"What is it?"

"Shhh," I hissed. I waited for a few seconds, but didn't hear or see anything. We weren't going to find him in these woods, but maybe I could convince him to come to us. "Jesus, only son of God," I yelled as loud as I could. "Hear our prayer. We seek your help in our time of trouble."

I glanced back at Tony. He stared at me as if I'd completely lost my mind. I put a finger to my lips to warn him to stay quiet. "We are poor sinners, it's true," I shouted at the trees, "but a mother weeps, and we long to help her."

I'd only spent a few months in foster home number two, but a lot of it had been passed in church. I'd tried hard not to let it make much of an impression on me. Too bad. I should have paid more attention, because now I couldn't think of another thing to say that might draw Jesus to us.

I stood as still as I could, straining to listen for the slightest rustle. Nothing. Then, suddenly, Jesus just appeared, as if out of nowhere, standing not ten feet from us, clothed in once-white robes belted with a rope.

"Christ!" Tony swore.

Jesus inclined his head slightly in acknowledgement. He looked at me, and I thought I saw a glimmer of recognition in his eyes.

"You know me, Jesus," I said, hoping it was literally true. "I'm Alison, a poor sinner, but I try to help the sick and the needy, just as you have taught us to do." I paused, but Jesus didn't respond. "Now I seek to help the mother of Stevie Number. She weeps because her son was murdered. GI Joe also has great sorrow over the death of his friend, and he has sought comfort from you." I paused again and waited to see if he'd confirm this. Nothing.

"Joe wanted to tell me something important, something about Stevie's death. Will you take me to him?"

Jesus didn't respond, but I took it as a good sign that he was still there, listening.

I gave it one last shot. "I give my solemn promise not to tell anyone where he is."

Jesus flicked a glance at Tony.

"This is Tony. Joe has seen him before. He is an honest workman on the garbage truck. He is my friend and helper."

That seemed to do it. Jesus smiled benignly at us and turned his hands palms outward. "Suffer the little children to come unto me," he said in a rumbling basso and disappeared.

I ran forward and reached the spot where he'd been standing in time to see him disappearing into the woods. I took his words as an invitation to come along and started off after him. I had to run to keep up. He stayed just barely in my line of vision for the next ten minutes, while Tony crashed along behind me.

I tried to increase my pace to catch up, but my breath came in harsh rasps and I couldn't get enough oxygen into my lungs to make my legs go faster. It didn't help that he led us on an uphill route most of the way. I needed to get into better shape if I planned on doing cross-country running on a steady basis. With any luck, one visit to Jesus would be enough to get Joe to tell me what he knew.

"Where's... he... going?" Tony gasped in my ear.

I shook my head. I didn't have any breath left over for talking. I lost track of Jesus but kept on heading in the direction he'd taken last and finally burst into a small clearing, sheltered on one side by a rise of boulders. Jesus sat on top of the highest one. He wasn't even breathing hard.

Someone had set up camp in the clearing. In the flattest spot, a pup tent rested on a tarp with some stuff piled up next to it.

"Joe?" I called out loud. "It's Alison. I want to help."

No answer.

"What… " Tony started to say.

I waved him to be quiet, went over to the tent and pulled back the flap. It was empty except for a familiar-looking green sleeping bag and an army blanket. "I'll be damned," I muttered to myself.

I dropped the tent flap and turned to the pile of stuff next to the tent. Backpacking stove, portable lantern, and packages of freeze-dried food. All of them formerly known as Alison's emergency supplies. If Joe had lifted my supplies, then either he'd used my car to move Stevie's body, or he'd cooperated with whoever had done it. He'd been there when I arrived in the morning, waiting near Stevie's body. Would he have done that if he'd killed Stevie?

Tony crouched down and picked up one of the packages and inspected it. I crossed to the boulder and looked up at Jesus. "Do you know where Joe is?"

He gazed at me and intoned. "'Come unto me all ye that labor and are heavy laden, and I will give you rest.'"

He had the "heavy laden" part right. I didn't know how Joe had managed to get all that stuff up the hill. "I can see that you gave him protection when he was afraid. You know, though, that Joe is driven by more than the fear that brought him to you. He's a drug addict, and his need for drugs will lead him back to the streets."

"'Wide is the gate, and broad the way, that leadeth to destruction.'"

I knew the rest of that one. I'd heard it from foster mother number two every single day I'd spent with her. "'Strait is the gate, and narrow is the way, which leadeth unto life, and few there be that find it,'" I quoted. "But you and I might be able to help Joe find the narrow way. I want to try, but I need to find him first."

Jesus appeared to ponder this for a while, then he said, "'Ask, and it shall be given you. Seek, and ye shall find.'" And, with that, he stood up and dropped out of sight behind the boulder.

I turned and joined Tony by the tent.

"Aren't we going to follow him?" Tony asked.

"No. We won't get anything more out of him. At least we know this is where Joe's been staying. He stole all this stuff out of my car, and I think he's also the one who left Stevie's body in the dumpster. I think he knows who killed Stevie."

"Really? That means we've almost solved the case. We just have to find Joe, right?"

I wasn't sure where he got off with this "we" business. He'd been a less than willing participant. I scanned the trees around the clearing, "First, we have to find our way back to your car. Do you have a clue about that?"

As it turned out, Tony wasn't any better at re-tracing our steps than I was. It took us an anxious half-hour to find the road again, and then we ended up a quarter of a mile away from where we'd gone in. My only edge was my ability to spot poison oak. Unfortunately, I didn't always notice it until we were in the process of plowing through it. By the time we reached the car, we were both sweaty and had leaves and foxtails clinging to our pantlegs. Tony tried to brush them off before he got into the car.

"I wouldn't do that, if I were you. We've been walking through poison oak. You'll get it on your hands, if you haven't already."

"That's okay. Poison oak never affects me."

"Famous last words," I mumbled to myself as I sank into the passenger seat.

Tony got in behind the wheel. "Sorry, I didn't catch what you said."

"I said, I bet you wish we'd gone out for coffee instead of a hike."

He turned to me. "Are you kidding? We're that close to finding a murderer." He held his thumb and forefinger a half an inch apart to show me just how close we were. "You were amazing with that Bible talk stuff. How'd you know to do that?"

I relaxed against the seat. It was nice to be admired. "I've talked to him a couple of times when he's been down on Telegraph. He'll only quote Jesus when he talks to you. He must have all the gospels memorized."

"You're amazing," he said again. He started the car and pulled a U-turn to head the car back down the hill. "When do you think we should go back. Tomorrow?"

"Tomorrow's out for me." I had both work and Stevie's memorial service to face. "Besides, I think Joe's gone back to the streets to score some meth. It might be easier to find him down there than to trek through the poison oak again."

Tony didn't pursue it, and we spent the rest of the trip back to my house in silence. He seemed preoccupied, which was fine with me. He'd taken it for granted that we'd look for Joe together, but I needed time to decide if I really wanted Tony as my co-investigator.

When we pulled up in front of my house, I got out of the car in a hurry. I didn't want to have to invite him in, because I still stood a good chance of not catching poison oak if I could get out of my clothes and wash with my special lotion immediately. I bent down and stuck my head into the car. "Thanks for stopping by. I appreciate your helping me to track down Joe today."

"You lead a pretty exciting life. It was fun. We'll have to do it again soon."

I smiled to cover for not answering, straightened and closed the door.

He drove off, and I turned to walk up my driveway. What was wrong with me? Tony was cute and a hunk. Both definite pluses. And, for some reason, he liked me. Why else would he keep coming back after each disastrous meeting? He'd even called me "amazing." My new billing--the Amazing Alison.

I sighed. For some reason, I didn't feel that great rush of hormones or whatever when I was with him. In fact, until I spotted Jesus, the entire outing rated a complete zero. Maybe my years with Frank had permanently wrecked my hormonal responses.

"Alison?" Mitch said, right behind me.

I jumped about a foot off the ground. "Don't creep up on me like that." I turned around to face him.

"Sorry." He took a step back. "I saw you drive up."

I waited for him to go on. "Yes?" I prompted.

"I wanted to talk to you before you went inside."

Another long pause. "Mitch, please just get it off your chest. I've had a long hard day. I thought I was going to have a little walk, and ended up chasing a crazy man cross-country."

"What happened? Did that guy try something?" He reached his hand out toward my arm.

"Don't touch me." I stepped away.

He jerked his arm back. "Sorry, I didn't mean… I just… are you hurt?"

"No. I've been plowing through poison oak. My clothes are probably covered in it, and you might get it on you. Now, what's on your mind?"

"I put up lights. It's just temporary. I'll take them down after I get your door fixed, if you don't want them." He stood with his legs apart, like a sailor braced for a gale.

"Lights? Really? That sensor kind you talked about before?"

"Yeah, one over the gate, another over the back door. Just until you can use your front door again."

"Thanks." I hadn't been looking forward to going to bed that night, worrying about someone creeping around again.

"You're not mad?"

"I thought I didn't want them, but I changed my mind."

He stared at me.

"Really. I appreciate it. Will they shine on my neighbor's house, too?"

"Who? Mrs. Fiorelli's?"

"No. The ones on the other side."

"You mean the Bowens."

"Is that their name? I hope you pointed the lights right at their bedroom window."

"No."

"Damn. Well, you can't have everything, I suppose."

He stared at me for a beat before a slow grin spread across his face. At least I assume it was a grin. The beard disguised his face so well.

I fished my keys out of my purse. "See you." I turned to go.

"One more thing."

I turned back.

"I saw that guy you were with, talking to your ex-husband." He gestured with his thumb over his shoulder.

"Tony?"

He nodded. "The day your ex kicked down your door. I had to get some lumber from my garage and your friend had just driven up?"

"I remember, but Tony left before that."

"I know. But I saw them talking. Down the street."

"Maybe he was telling Frank to stay away from me," I said, even though it didn't fit with anything Tony had said or done so far.

"They were very friendly. Like they knew one another pretty well."

I shook my head. "No, they hadn't met before. It's just Frank's way. He tried it on you, but you weren't buying any."

"Yeah, well... Mrs. Fiorelli thought I should mention it, so I did."

That got my attention. "You talked to Rose today? How did she seem? I could kick myself. I should've gone over to see her. She didn't look well this morning."

"She's okay. She took your advice, she said, and went back on her medicine. She's going to see the doctor tomorrow." Mitch gazed briefly in the direction of Rose's house, then consulted the toes of his work boots. "She worries about you."

"It's mutual. If you see her tomorrow before I do, tell her I'm fine. I know—tell her all about my new outdoor lighting. She'll like that."

"She already knows."

I narrowed my eyes at him. "You didn't tell her about my problems with the police, did you? I wanted her to think I was helping them with the case."

"I didn't think you'd want me to say anything, but that reminds me." He reached into his back pocket. "You were asking about a lawyer." He handed me a scrap of paper.

"Ron Kelso," I read out loud. There was a phone number too, but no address. "Is this his office phone number?"

"His pager. You can reach him any time, day or night."

"Thanks. Luckily, I found out who used my car to move Stevie's body, so I can clear myself with the police, but I'd better keep this for Joe. He's going to need a good lawyer." I tucked the paper into my purse.

"Who's Joe?" Mitch asked.

"A long story. I'll tell you some time. Thanks for the lights and the lawyer."

"You're welcome."

Neither of us moved. "It's funny… " I started to say, but stopped myself in time.

"What?"

"Nothing. See you." I turned and headed for my gate.

"See you," Mitch said behind me.

I gave him a wave over my shoulder. Strangely enough, it didn't bother me at all that Mitch had gone ahead with the lights, even though I'd told him in no uncertain terms that I didn't want them. It didn't even bother me that Mitch and Rose had formed a friendship and discussed me when I wasn't there. But I was concerned that

I felt more comfortable talking with him, my sworn enemy for two whole years, than with someone who thought I was amazing. Worse yet, I'd almost told him so. Maybe I was losing my grip.

CHAPTER ELEVEN

I arrived at work early the next morning. It helped that I hadn't had to deal with policemen pounding on my door, finding incriminating evidence in my car, or interrogating me about a schizophrenic's last will and testament. I only had to get out of bed, dress and show up. Nothing to it. As with many things in life, perspective is everything.

I set immediately to work. Daniel had seen the proposed plan for my dissertation, but what I needed to give him was my plan for analyzing all the data from the refinery study. In the months I'd been sidelined with other tasks, I'd given it a lot of thought. I quickly typed up a full-scale proposal, specifying each hypothesis and the best approach for testing it.

I'd nearly finished when Kenji stopped by my cubicle. "Did you see the morning paper? Your friend's in it." He held out a newspaper and rattled the pages.

"Which friend?"

"The dead one. Doesn't say much—just the bare bones. The body's been identified and his family resides in Piedmont."

I stretched out my arm. "Let me have it for a bit, okay? I want to read it when I have time. Right now I have to finish this proposal before Daniel gets here."

Kenji handed over the paper, folded back to show the article, and I went back to the computer. I was still making minor changes in wording when Daniel arrived. He stopped at the entry to my cubicle, announcing himself, as usual, with a sniff. “Alison,” he said and sniffed again. “You’re here. Good.”

I quickly clicked on “print” and jumped to my feet. “I’ve prepared a data analysis plan for the refinery study. Do you have time to look it over?”

“I understand from Flo that you had some problems with the police yesterday,” he said, ignoring my question entirely.

His statement invited, even required, comment, but I didn’t want to mention that the police knew my car had been used to transport Stevie’s body. At least, not until I’d cleared Libby and myself with the police. “I had to help them identify some of Stevie’s belongings. That was the man who was killed—Stevie Number.”

“Are they satisfied with the assistance you’ve given them?”

“Yes. Entirely. Completely.”

“Very well, perhaps now you can concentrate on your work?”

“I intend to give it my full and complete attention.” I hesitated briefly. “Except for two hours this morning. I have to attend Stevie’s memorial service.”

“You’re required to attend?”

No question about it—Daniel could be a bully. “I want to attend. I feel morally bound to attend. Stevie was a friend.”

“Are you acquainted with the man’s family?”

“No, but I want to show his family that there were people who cared about him.”

Daniel pursed his lips and sniffed. “Very well. I would like to see your thoughts about analyzing the refinery data. There’s a great deal to be done, and I know you’re going to need some assistance.”

I blinked, opened my mouth to speak but nothing came out. What a bonanza—Daniel was offering his personal help, not just giving distant supervision. “Thank you," I finally managed to say. "You don't know how much I appreciate this."

"It's in my own self-interest to ensure the highest quality work is done here at the Center."

He had a point, but even so, I felt blessed. "I printed out my ideas about how I'd like to proceed." I gestured in the direction of the corner printer that everyone at my end of the office shared in common.

Daniel stepped back to let me pass, and I hurried to the printer. My hands shook a little as I gathered up the pages. Even though, as a person, Daniel irritated me with his attitude and put my back up with his bullying, as a researcher, he embodied the best that had been done in public health—the highest standards of research on some of the most pressing health concerns of the community. I'd given up my regular nursing practice to do that kind of work, to make a difference on a large scale, instead of person by person.

I carried the printed pages back to Daniel and managed to hand them over with a casual, "Here you are."

The front door buzzer sounded.

"Would you get that, Alison?" Daniel asked, even though there were several people closer than I, including Flo.

I headed for the door, checking my watch as I walked. It was still too early for Libby, and she'd wait outside for me anyway. Could it be the police—again?

I opened to door to a very pretty young blond in an extremely short skirt. "Hi." She flashed a bright smile.

"Can I help you?"

She studied me for a second and peered at the small engraved brass sign on the door, as if she'd mis-read it the first time. It still read "Center for Biostatistical Studies.

"I'm looking for Dr. Dunston."

I stood back and waved her through the doorway. "Come in. He's probably in his office."

I was wrong. Daniel was bearing down on us even as

I spoke, a broad smile across his face and both hands outstretched as if he planned on taking the blond into his arms. Too bad I didn't have a camera. Daniel rarely smiled, and I'd never seen him hug anyone.

He stopped short of actually taking her into his arms. He settled for her hands, which he held in both of his. "Carolyn. You found us."

"I didn't know we were lost," I muttered.

"Pardon?" the blond said and frowned. So did Daniel.

"Alison," he said, "this is Carolyn Dahlstrom. She'll be doing her post-doctoral work with us. Please help her get settled in, would you?"

"Sure. Where?" We were always a little cramped for space.

"I thought it made sense to put you two together, since you'll be working with her on the refinery data."

I stared at him. Didn't he mean that she'd be working with me? And how should I translate "put you two together?" If we were to be in adjoining cubicles, someone was going to get bumped. He couldn't possibly mean we'd both be crowded into mine, could he? I opened my mouth to ask, but he turned to Carolyn. "Alison will give you a little tour of the Center, and then I will get you started on the beginning analyses we talked about yesterday. He turned abruptly and left us together.

I didn't look at her. "This way." I took off toward my cubicle. Several curious people popped their heads over the top of the cubicle dividers, Kenji among them. I waved and gestured for him to join us. Kenji moved as fast as he could without actually running. "Here's someone you should meet," I said to Carolyn as he drew near. "Kenji Fujimora-Sanchez, a researcher here at the Center. Kenji, this is Carolyn Dahlstrom."

Kenji had offered to shake hands before I finished the introductions. "Nice to meet you, Carolyn."

"Would you introduce her around a bit? I'll be right back." I headed straight for Daniel's office, knocked on the door and went in without waiting for him to invite me.

He was seated at his desk, mail stacked up in front of him. He looked up, his face a blank. "Yes?"

"Please explain what's going on."

"We are making the refinery study a top priority now."

"What's Carolyn Dahlstrom's role?"

"She'll be leading the team—under my direction, of course."

"You promised I could use the refinery data in my dissertation."

"I hope you will use some part of the data. It would be mutually beneficial if you did. You didn't think that we expected to produce merely one dissertation from a million dollar grant, did you?"

"You know I didn't. I did expect you'd honor our agreement that if I delayed starting my dissertation and helped with Kenji's study, I'd take the lead on first analyses of the refinery study. I did all the work in the field. I convinced the residents at the atmospheric study sites to help collect air samples, and to be interviewed as well as complete the repeated physical exams."

"Don't forget that we also had a group of phone interviewers conducting the larger survey on the health of the general population in the area. You did very fine fieldwork. With your nursing experience, you are eminently qualified to do hands-on public health work."

I gritted my teeth. "I think I'm also qualified to do the data analysis."

"You will participate in the data analysis. It is urgent that we begin work immediately and proceed very quickly. Delays will be disastrous."

"I've been ready for months."

"And now you are involved in a murder investigation. The Center has been mentioned in the newspapers and television reports as the site of a crime. It all reflects very badly on the Center. It's not the kind of publicity funding agencies like to hear about. The NIPH was extremely concerned when we had a burglary here that compromised the security of our data."

He wasn't telling me anything I didn't already know. We'd had an unscheduled site visit from the folks at the National Institute for Public Health and were grilled mercilessly on every aspect of our operation. "We answered every question posed by the NIPH. They've expressed their support for our work."

Daniel tilted his head. His glasses caught the reflection from the overhead fluorescent lights, and I couldn't see his eyes. "They could change their minds at any time." Which pretty much summarized his own position. He turned his attention to the stack of mail on his desk. "Would you please tell Carolyn I wish to speak with her," he said, without looking up.

I left his office and didn't slam the door. I also didn't scream, curse or throw things. I may have looked as if I intended to, though, judging by the looks my co-workers gave me as I stalked by their cubicles. I found Kenji and Carolyn seated at my desk, drinking coffee. Carolyn had hers in my Oakland A's souvenir cup, while sitting in my chair with her legs crossed. Her skirt had worked its way nearly to her hipbones.

"Daniel wants to see you, Carolyn. His office is that way." I gestured with my thumb over my shoulder. "You can't miss it."

"He wants to see me?" she said, all wide-eyed.

I nodded and moved aside to make way for her. She jumped up and gave a little wriggle. Her skirt gained a full inch in length—just enough to cover her butt—and she made for Daniel's office.

I turned to Kenji. "We have to talk," I whispered and gestured for him to follow me to the women's lounge. Luckily it was empty. I pulled Kenji inside, closed the door and leaned against it. "Okay, what's going on?"

He gave me a palms up shrug. "I don't know. I was out sick yesterday."

"Daniel says that Carolyn Dolly-face is going to work

here as a post-doc, taking the lead on the refinery data—my data. You got cozy with her. What did she say?"

"Daniel spent the last two days down at UCLA convincing her to join his team. She just completed her PhD there. She's multi-published in all the right journals, and UC Press wants to publish her dissertation as a book."

"What is she, a prodigy? She can't be legal drinking age yet, and she looks like a bimbo."

He gave me a sympathetic smile. "Come on, Alison. You know Daniel doesn't hire bimbos. She's smart. She's gorgeous. I think I'm in love. Really."

"You let her use my coffee cup."

"What was I going to do? She said she hates drinking out of cardboard."

"Traitor."

"Come on, you know you'll always be my best buddy."

"Did she tell you that Daniel has put her in charge of the data analysis for the refinery study, after all his promises, all his reassurances and all the crappy work I had to do for the last six months?"

Kenji stared at me. This was clearly news to him. "Are you sure?"

I nodded.

He patted my arm. "I'm sorry. That sucks. Do you want me to talk to him?"

"Thanks, but I don't think it would help. I need some time to think it through. Time… " I said and glanced at my watch. "Hell, I have to go now. Stevie's memorial service is this morning."

"It's pretty bad timing. Can't you give it a miss?"

"No, I can't, and I don't want to. Try to think of some way I can change Daniel's mind, okay?"

"I don't know if that's possible, but I'll try."

I crossed to the door.

"One thing, though," he said.

I turned, my hand on the door handle.

"If you're going to be working with Carolyn, don't make an enemy of her. It'll just make everything worse."

"I wouldn't think of it," I lied. I walked out of the lounge and hurried toward my cubicle. I found Carolyn seated in front of my computer. "Do me a favor and don't read my e-mail."

She gave me a startled, wide-eyed look. "Is this your computer?" she asked, as if she didn't know. "Daniel said I could use it. He had the password, so I assumed it was one of his."

"In a manner of speaking, they're all his. He has everyone's password. That's Daniel's version of *droit de seigneur*. You'll get used to it. I just need to get my purse." I pointed to her feet, which rested under the desk right next to my bag.

"Sorry." She quickly pushed her chair away from the desk. "I didn't notice it."

Yeah, right. I eyeballed the monitor screen as I bent down to grab my purse. She was networked into our main data computer, which meant that Daniel had already given her access to the refinery data files. I straightened and gave her what I hoped would pass as a friendly smile. "I have to go to a funeral this morning."

"I'm sorry. Someone close to you?"

"A friend who was murdered. I found his body right outside the back door of the Center."

A crease formed between her two perfectly arched eyebrows. "Murdered? Here?"

"Yes, but don't worry. You're perfectly safe. You saw the special locks on the front door?"

She nodded slowly.

"It would take a bazooka to get past them. Maybe even a rocket launcher. And there aren't too many of those around Oakland. Probably not more than a dozen."

"I don't know the area at all. You say it isn't safe?"

"No! I never said that. It's safe, perfectly safe. Completely safe." I carefully didn't meet her gaze as I said this. "I have to go now, but I'll be back in a couple of hours."

I left her gazing at me with the little worry frown still forming a crease between her brows. With any luck, she'd be re-thinking Daniel's job offer all day. I turned a corner, winding my way out of the maze of cubicles, and nearly collided with Flo. She eyed my purse. "Taking an early lunch?"

"No. I'm going to a funeral."

"A funeral? Really? You didn't mention that you'd had a death in the family."

"I'm going to Stevie's memorial service."

"Who? You mean that bum who died in our dumpster?"

"He wasn't a bum. He was my friend, and I'm going to tell the Linds that, too."

Flo stared at me. "Who?"

"His family. Their name is Lind. They live in Piedmont. It was in the paper." I brushed past her and headed out the door.

Libby was waiting for me when I came out. She drove us to church in Piedmont where Stevie's memorial service was to be held. The number of cars in the parking lot surprised me. I hadn't expected that that many people would come to say good-bye to Stevie.

Libby pulled into a slot between a Jaguar and a BMW. "Do you want some tissues?" she asked, as she reached into the back seat to retrieve a box of Kleenex.

"No, thanks. I suppose I should warn you—I never cry at funerals." In fact, I never cried at all, except over an occasional onion.

"You don't? I cry buckets. It's pretty embarrassing sometimes."

"It's more embarrassing not to. People expect it."

Libby checked her watch. "We're just exactly on time. We'd better hurry."

We got out of the car and started toward the church when a kid in a white Mercedes convertible took a tire-squealing turn into the parking lot. I grabbed Libby by the arm and jumped backward pulling her with me.

The kid turned sharply into a parking place, slammed on the brakes, and brought his car to a stop two centimeters away from the car parked just opposite.

"Good heavens," she said. "Did you see that? He didn't even swerve. If you hadn't pulled me back, he'd have run us down."

I released Libby's arm and strode over to the Mercedes. The kid got out of the car, and I did a double take. "He" was a "she" and also not the sixteen year-old I'd first thought. More like early twenties and wearing the casual chic of jeans with a blazer over a tee shirt. Her short haircut emphasized the androgynous jut of her nose and chin. She flicked me a glance. The kind of look people get on their faces when accosted by panhandlers on the street.

"Nice car." I blocked her path. "You nearly ran us down with it."

She edged around me.

"You should drive more carefully. I said to her back. "You wouldn't want to mess up the paint job with blood.

She gave me the finger over her shoulder and kept on walking.

Libby motioned me to come along. I joined her and followed the wannabe hit-and-runner up the front steps of the church. A well-dressed middle aged man stood just inside the door. He gestured to the young woman to hurry. She didn't speed up by any noticeable degree. When she reached him, the man put his arm around her shoulders and hustled her across the foyer and through two wide doors to the church. Strains of muted organ music wafted out through the doors when he opened them.

We caught up with them before the doors swung shut again. I held one of the doors open and motioned Libby in ahead of me. The church was about half full of people, most of them ranged in pews in the front half of the church. I let Libby lead the way. She paused by a pew near the back with only one occupant, a woman with the worn look of long-time grief. Libby went to her like a homing pigeon.

The man we'd seen outside was still guiding the young woman with his arm around her shoulders. They proceeded without hesitation to the front row of pews and joined the lone woman seated there. Stevie's mother and father? And that would make the young woman a relative, too. I leaned toward Libby. "Do you think she's Stevie's sister?"

Libby nodded. "He once said he had a younger sister."

Stevie had also once said that he was a direct descendant of King Tut, but in this case, the family resemblance between Stevie and the girl was pretty convincing. She'd plopped down between her mother and father.

I could only see the backs of their heads, but even from that angle, I recognized the imprint of money and taste. Stevie's mother had blond hair, artfully streaked, pulled straight back and fastened at the nape of her neck. She leaned towards her daughter, spoke directly into her ear. I could see her lips moving. The daughter jerked away and glared at her mother. She said something aloud. I couldn't hear, but the people near them clearly did. I saw heads turn. The daughter stood up and moved to sit on the other side of her father. The father slid closer to his wife to fill in the gap, but still, from the back, I could see the distance between them.

The organ music swelled. The minister appeared in the front of the church, wearing the full regalia of an Episcopal priest, his hands folded in front of him as he waited for the organ music to come to its conclusion.

I'd attended the funeral of every patient of mine who'd died, which, since I'd worked in a hospice, meant more funerals than I could remember. This kind was one of my least favorite—every aspect ordered in advance, every word and gesture restrained and formal.

My mother had died when I six. My father chose the day of her funeral as an opportunity to add to his long list of DUI's by driving our car into a tree. The accident had cost me a month in the hospital, a childhood in foster homes, and a persistent longing to know what my mother's funeral had been like. I was pretty sure it'd been nothing like this one.

The organist brought the music to a close. The minister spoke into the ensuing silence, "I am the resurrection and the life, saith the Lord." With rustles and muffled sounds, the congregation opened printed programs or reached for prayer books. Libby had the program, so I pulled a black book out of the rack in front of me. Just what I needed to help distract me and block out the minister's voice.

"He that believeth in me, though he were dead, yet shall he live," the minister continued, his voice rolling out over the bowed heads with smooth confidence.

I leafed through the prayer book. Maybe I'd find some good quotes in here I could use with Jesus. Convince him to get into treatment. In the hop-scotch way thoughts go, no sooner had Jesus popped into my head, than my mind leapt to Joe, where it stayed a mere fraction of a second before an image of Stevie's body surfaced and seemed to float above the page I held open in my lap.

I closed my eyes, which didn't banish the picture at all. It brought the image of Stevie into clearer focus. What else could I have expected? Stevie and I had unfinished business. I kept my eyes closed and deliberately pictured Stevie as I'd last seen him. My one true skill, learned the hard way at age six—how to be with a dying person. If I'd been with Stevie when he died, what would I have done? I clasped my hands together and imagined that I held Stevie's hand between mine. I took my time, keeping the image of Stevie in my head while I let the sounds of the memorial service drone on in the background. I don't know how long I sat like that, but finally the right words came to me—the words I would have spoken, if I could have been with him.

Stevie, it's me, Alison. I'm here. You're not alone. I'm sorry you're dying. I'll miss you. Thank you for thinking of me as a friend. I'll be your friend after you're dead. I'll find out who killed you. I promise.

Libby poked my arm. I opened my eyes and looked at her. Had I spoken aloud? How embarrassing.

"They're not going to have a eulogy," Libby hissed in my ear.

"Huh?"

"They're just going to let that old windbag pontificate and recite prayers. I don't think he even knew Stevie."

Thank God, she hadn't heard me making promises to Stevie. I had no idea where the harebrained notion that I could find a murderer had come from. Probably guilt, because I hadn't actually been there when Stevie died. I smiled sympathetically at Libby. "The minister's only doing what the family asked him to."

"It's supposed to be a memorial service, for goodness sake," she whispered louder this time. A few heads turned in our direction, although we were seated three rows away from the rest of the mourners.

I shrugged. I'd made my own personal peace with Stevie, and I didn't care what anyone else did.

The minister stopped droning on. "Amen," the congregation said in unison. The organist started up some Bach-sounding piece, livelier than the one he'd chosen for the beginning of the service.

"It's not right," she muttered. "What comfort can his family have if they don't hear from others who cared about him?" She stood up and motioned me to shift my legs so she could move past me. I swung my feet out of her way. She edged by and made her way up the aisle.

"Excuse me," Libby said over the sound of the music. "I want to say a few words about Stevie." The organist came to a faltering halt. The minister stared at her open-mouthed. Libby reached the front of the church, turned and spoke directly to Stevie's parents, but loud enough so we could all hear.

"I didn't know Stevie when he was a baby or a little boy, or even as a teenager. I imagine, though, that he was delightful and charming and also maddening and frustrating. He was so incredibly smart."

The woman sitting next to me nodded her head in agreement.

"I know the tragedy of his mental illness changed him and made him unlike the child you knew. As for me, I only knew Stevie as the young man he became after his schizophrenic break, but I can tell you that he was often delightful and charming, and also maddening and frustrating.

"Once he'd worked out some very complicated mathematical system that he told Alison about. She said it could be useful in epidemiological studies. The next time we saw him, he'd decided to use his system to trace genealogies. His own genealogy, he said, showed that he was a direct descendant of Tutankhamen. He told me that I'd descended from a long line of very hard working slaves. I was sorry to hear it. I'd hoped at the very least for a royal handmaiden, if not Nefertiti herself."

I laughed softly and heard some others join in.

"I'm very sorry that Stevie's gone. Even when he cleverly frustrated our efforts to help him, he was always gentle and kind. I'm going to miss him." That said, Libby made her stately way back down the aisle and slipped in next to me. I smiled my approval to her.

The minister signaled the organist and the music rose up, louder and faster this time, as if to hurry us out of the church. The minister escorted Stevie's family out a side door at the front of the church. The rest of us followed them slowly.

The door opened onto a small patio, landscaped with blooming plants around the perimeter. Overhead, a vine-covered trellis filtered the sunlight. The daughter leaned sulkily against a wall, but Mr. and Mrs. Lind stood in the middle of the patio, accepting condolences and thanking everyone individually for coming. Their every gesture held just the right degree of expressiveness and restraint. They didn't look ravaged by grief, or even mildly dented by it.

Libby and I stood in line with everyone else, waiting our turn. The woman we'd sat next to waited with us. Libby must have made some connection with her when they were seated side by side, because Libby said to her, "Isn't it wonderful that so many of the Linds' friends came today?"

The woman raised an eyebrow. "These aren't their friends. What friends they still have stayed away in droves. These are all people Lucianne has helped through the Foundation."

"What's the Foundation?" I asked.

"You haven't heard of the Lind Foundation? They've organized support groups for parents of mentally ill children all over the world. They also raise money for research on new treatments. She heads it. Everyone thinks she's a saint." The way she said it, I could tell she didn't agree.

"You've known them long?" Libby asked.

"We're neighbors. Our sons were best friends from the time they were in pre-school."

I had about ten more questions I wanted to ask, but we'd reached the head of the reception line. The Linds' neighbor stepped forward. Stevie's father took her hand. "Barbara," he said, "thank you for coming."

Stevie's mother finished talking to the person ahead of Barbara. She turned and gazed at her without any of the warmth her husband had shown. In fact, instead of greeting her, she turned her face deliberately away.

Barbara's shoulder's sagged, but she stood her ground. "I'm so sorry Lucianne. I just wanted you to know that."

Lucianne didn't relent, but kept her face averted until Barbara had moved away. Her husband touched her arm, and she turned toward Libby, her face again smooth, even serene. She reached for Libby's hand. "Thank you so much for your kind words. I don't believe we've met before."

"Libby Honeck," Libby said. "I'm glad you weren't offended. I just wanted you to know that Stevie had friends who cared about him."

"I knew that, of course, although I couldn't meet you before. Are both of you from Conway House?" Lucianne Lind included me in her question.

"Conway House?" Libby asked, a puzzled frown on her face.

"Am I mistaken? I assumed you worked at the residential care facility where Stephen lived."

"No, we're from the Mobile Clinic," Libby said.

Mr. Lind stepped forward, partially blocking his wife from our view. "Let me add my thanks to my wife's," he said. "It would give me great pleasure to make a serious contribution to your organization. Perhaps we could step over here and discuss it?"

At the word "contribution," Libby snapped to attention. "That would be wonderful."

She probably would've said more, a lot more, since Libby was most articulate and persuasive when talking about the Mobile Clinic. But, Lucianne Lind stepped forward. "That can wait, Jack. I want to hear how Ms. Honeck knew Stephen."

A brief spasm of irritation passed over Jack Lind's face. Like temporary interference on a television screen, it blurred his features for a second, then it cleared, and he was again in perfect focus. "First, why don't you thank the rest of the people who came today, darling?"

"Come on, mom," the daughter spoke for the first time. "Let Daddy take care of this."

Lucianne gazed in turn at her daughter and her husband. "I wasn't aware that there was anything to be taken care of anymore. Please explain what you mean, Gina."

"Don't upset yourself again, Lucianne," Jack Lind said.

I'd have happily stayed and watched the family threesome air their private business, but Libby spoke up. "Why don't I give you my number, Mrs. Lind? You can call me whenever you feel like it, and we can talk."

She directed her blue gaze on Libby like a laser beam. "I want to talk now. What is the Mobile Clinic?"

"It's a clinic run entirely on the donated services of

physicians and nurses, like Alison here. She gestured to me. "We provide medical care to under-served populations in Berkeley and Oakland. People below the poverty line, street people, and the homeless."

"Conway House is in Napa, and the residents aren't under-served, or normally allowed to wander about the streets alone. It's clear why. The one time Stephen eluded his companion, he somehow traveled all the way to Oakland and was—murdered. She stumbled on the word, then regained control. "Please tell me. How did you come to know Stephen?"

"Stevie came to the Clinic for emergency care once."

Gina burst into the conversation. "You're lying. You didn't know him at all. No one called him Stevie. His name was Stephen, and you'd better get out of here before I call the police."

Libby didn't even look at Gina, but kept her gaze on Lucianne Lind. "After he came to the clinic the first time, we tried to keep in touch with him. We usually saw him on Telegraph Avenue when we did our weekly stint there."

Lucianne Lind shook her head back and forth repeatedly. "No. Stephen had his own private physician who made monthly visits to Conway House."

"He told us he had a private doctor," Libby said, "but wouldn't tell us who. He shared an apartment with a friend somewhere near the Avenue."

With every word Libby spoke, Lucianne's composure cracked a little more. "No, no, no," she repeated, but without conviction.

"I'm afraid it's true. Stevie was his street name," Libby said. "Everyone called him Stevie Number. I'm so very sorry."

Lucianne Lind's mouth twisted in a rictus of pain. She swayed, as if she might crumble to the ground, but instead, she swung around and hit her husband's cheek full force with her open hand. "You lying bastard," she choked out. "You killed him. I never want to see your face again."

CHAPTER TWELVE

Jack Lind pressed one hand to the side of his face and extended the other towards Lucianne, whether reaching for her or holding her off, I couldn't tell. Lucianne stood with her hands at her sides while tears coursed slowly down her face carrying eyeliner and mascara in black streaks.

Libby reached out towards Lucianne, but Gina rounded on her. "Get away from my mother, you stupid bitch. Haven't you done enough?" She gave Libby a shove. Libby staggered a little, but kept her balance. Gina pushed Libby again, harder this time, knocking her against a post. Neither parent appeared ready to stop their daughter. Lucianne covered her face with her hands. Jack pulled out his cell phone and talked into it, snapping out an order to "get over here now." The funeral guests who'd remained just stared at us.

I stepped between Libby and Gina. "That's enough."

"Get out of my way, bitch." She tried to push me aside so she could get to Libby.

I gave her a body check, canceling out her momentum with mine, and blocking her from Libby. "I'm not moving, brat."

I don't know what would have happened if we'd been allowed to continue. I probably would've ended up with another black eye. Given a choice, I'd have taken the black eye over a re-match with the Oakland P.D., Homicide Division, but no one asked me. Instead, Detectives Stans and Carney appeared and hurried toward us.

They stopped to confer with Jack Lind, who'd pocketed his cell phone and now held a white handkerchief to his mouth. When he removed it to speak to Stans and Carney, I could see that Lucianne's slap had split his lip. He gestured toward me with the hand that held the bloodied handkerchief.

The urge to duck and run had my legs moving me backward before Stans and Carney had even glanced in my direction. I might have actually made such a pointless maneuver if Gina hadn't grabbed my arm above the elbow and tried to pull me toward the cops.

"Here she is, officers. The other one's over there." She pointed to Libby, who now stood with her arm around Lucianne's shoulders.

Stans and Carney came my way without a glance at Libby. They didn't look the least bit bothered at being called "officers" instead of "detectives." I tried to shake off Gina's hand, but she dug her fingers even harder into my biceps.

"Hey, Detective Stans," I said. "Do me a favor. Tell Miss World Mud Wrestling Champ here to let go of me immediately or I will file charges against her for assault."

"Arrest me?" she said on a rising note. "You're the one who has no business here. Arrest her for trespassing," she ordered Stans and Carney.

"I believe you witnessed the incident in the parking lot," I said to Stans and Carney. "You had to be watching the church, so when Mr. Lind gave you the signal on his cell phone, you could rush to the rescue. Would you have been so quick to call an ambulance if Gina had succeeded in running over us with her car?"

"You're not helping yourself any, Ms. Weaver," Stans said.

"And you don't intend to help me, either?" I looked pointedly at Gina's hand on my arm.

"I think," Carney spoke up, "that Ms. Lind's understandably concerned about the attack on her father."

"What? You see that he's bleeding and she's got my

arm in a death grip, ergo I hit him? For that, Detective Carney, you just flunked Basic Detection 101. Ask your partner his guiding rule—it's 'never assume.' Now if you don't tell her to let go of me right away, I may require surgery to get her fingernails removed from my arm."

Stans looked at Gina. "We need to talk to Ms. Weaver alone."

She glared at Stans and didn't let go of my arm. I could have told her not to get into a staring contest with Stans. He could make the Sphinx blink first. After a few silent moments, she scowled at the three of us, gave me a push as she released her grip, and stalked away.

I made a show of rubbing my upper arm and wincing. I gazed around the patio. The guests had all disappeared. I couldn't blame them. I would've vanished, too, if I'd had the chance. Libby stood with her arm around Lucianne, who leaned against her, head bowed, weeping. At almost the opposite side of the patio, Gina held forth to her father. I couldn't hear her actual words, but she kept gesturing toward me.

"I don't believe the Linds invited you, so why did you come today?" Stans asked me.

"I didn't know it was an invitation-only affair."

"Answer the question," Carney said through clenched teeth.

"I told you before. Stevie was a friend. Libby found out about the memorial service. She thought it was appropriate for us to come pay our respects. How about you? This is Piedmont, not Oakland. Aren't you stepping on local law enforcement toes?"

"Unlike you, we're here at the Lind's request," Carney said.

Jack Lind strode over to join the detectives, Gina trailing along behind him. "Please escort these two women from the premises." He gestured to me and then to Libby.

Lucianne lifted her tear-stained face and glared at her husband. "Still giving orders, are you Jack? Arranging other people's lives to suit your own convenience? Tell me, how did you manage to arrange to have Stephen killed? I know you must have, because it was the most convenient arrangement of all, wasn't it?"

Jack gave Stans and Carney a beleaguered look. "My wife's understandably distraught."

"Don't you patronize me," Lucianne said. "Just for the record, and in front of witnesses, tell me, was Stephen ever in Conway House?"

Jack reached for his wife. "Try to understand… " he began.

Lucianne recoiled from his outstretched hand as if it were a venomous snake. "You're so low, so debased, you're not even human."

"I did it for you. You were killing yourself trying to care for him."

"You liar. I'm going make you wish I had died."

"Mom, you're not being rational," Gina said, adding her pointless two bits. "Daddy did it for you. He made sure Stephen had money and a place to live."

Lucianne turned to her daughter, her eyes filling again with tears. "You knew? You let your own brother be cut off from his family?" She choked on the last word. She turned her back on her daughter and stumbled toward Libby, who caught her by the arm and steadied her.

Gina took a step as if to follow her mother. "You're going with them? Don't you know who they are? This," she gestured to me, "is Alison Weaver, the one who conned Stephen into putting her into his will. She claimed she found his body. She probably killed him in the first place."

Lucianne turned slowly to face me. "You're Alison Weaver? You found Stephen?"

I swallowed hard and nodded. It was one thing to stand up to the cops about Stevie, quite another to face Stevie's mother.

"Didn't Libby mention your name during the service? She said that Stephen talked to you about his ideas?"

"Yes," I said.

Lucianne held out her hand. "Come with me and tell me about Stephen. Please."

As I moved toward Lucianne, I resisted the urge to stick out my tongue at the cops, Gina and Jack. Instead, I hurried to Lucianne's side without a backward glance. Libby and I escorted her between us to Libby's car and, with Lucianne giving directions, we drove into the wealthiest corner of Piedmont. I sat in the back seat of Libby's car and gawked. Every house ruled a mini-kingdom, enclosed by wrought iron fences, shielded by electronic gates, and protected by private, twenty-four hour patrolling security police.

I checked my watch. We'd already used up one of the two hours I'd told Daniel I'd be away from the office. And, all the time I'd been gone, blondie had been sitting at my computer, working on my data.

I shifted uneasily in the cramped back seat. I owed it to Stevie to forget about my dissertation for a few minutes and talk to his mother, since she'd asked me to. But what could I tell Lucianne about Stevie's life that wouldn't bring her more pain? What comfort could anyone derive from hearing that her son had ended up ragged, filthy and dead in a dumpster?

We pulled into the curving drive of one of the estates, got out of the car and followed Lucianne into her home. I tried not to gape, but I'd never actually been inside a house like it. The front hall was big enough to house a junior prom—with a live band. A wide doorway on one side led to the living room. I could have fit my entire house in there.

A housekeeper appeared, wearing a plain gray dress with a white apron. I'd seen her at the memorial service, dressed differently. I'd noticed her because she was the only non-white person there. She must have come straight back without waiting for the floorshow outside the church. "I've set up the buffet in the dining room, Mrs. Lind."

"Thank you, Mary," Lucianne said, and turned to us. "Would you like something to eat?"

I opened my mouth to say something like "Thanks, but we have to get back to work," but Libby spoke before I could. "Only if you'll eat something, too."

Lucianne lifted her hand and touched her fingers to her tear-reddened cheek, as if she could sense without looking in a mirror that the perfect veneer of serenity had washed away with her makeup. She'd aged twenty years in an hour. "All right, but would you mind starting without me? I have two urgent phone calls to make." She turned to her housekeeper. "Take care of my guests for me, will you Mary?" Without waiting for any of us to reply, she turned and hurried up the wide, curving staircase.

"Won't you come with me?" Mary asked. She led us into the dining room. The expanse of polished mahogany in the middle of the room could have been called a dining room table the same way you could call a stretch limo a car. The table went on forever, and held an array of food that set my stomach rejoicing. Roast beef, ham and turkey occupied center stage, surrounded by bowls of salads and trays of little pop-in-your-mouth goodies in tiny pie shells. Mary gestured to the table like a magician producing a rabbit. "Please help yourselves."

Libby smiled her gentle, soul-warming smile. "Didn't I see you at the memorial service?"

Mary nodded and her eyes filled with tears. "I was glad you spoke up. I've never been to a funeral with no eulogy. It didn't seem right to me at all. That preacher didn't know Stephen from Adam."

"But you knew him," I said.

"Since he was a baby. Me and the family, we were the only ones there except you, who knew him. All the others, they're just the folks that Mrs. Lind helps, so they came to pay their respects." She glanced a little uneasily towards the front door, visible through the wide arched entrance to the dining room. "Mrs. Lind thought they'd be coming back here afterwards. That's why she had me set up the buffet. Maybe they're coming along with Mr. Lind and Gina?"

Libby and I exchanged a glance. We'd been counting on not having to see either Jack or Gina Lind. We'd be in a pretty awkward position if they showed up now. Another reason why I should find a way to politely excuse myself and get out of there.

"Mr. and Mrs. Lind had a difference of opinion after the service," I said.

"You mean they had a fight? What about?"

I couldn't see any reason not to tell her. "It turns out that Mr. Lind hadn't told Mrs. Lind the truth about Stevie. He wasn't a patient at Conway House."

Mary's eyes widened. "Where'd he been staying all this time then?"

"He had an apartment in Berkeley and wasn't always on his medication. He hung out on the streets of Berkeley, on Telegraph Avenue, if you know it."

"I know it," Mary said with a grim clench to her jaw. "You ladies go on and help yourselves to something to eat. I'll be right back. I just want to check on Mrs. Lind." She hurried out of the room.

I turned to Libby. "I'm going to have to get back to work pretty soon. I told my boss I wouldn't be out for more than two hours."

"We can't just leave without saying anything to Lucianne. Besides, I'm worried about her."

"I'm more worried about being here when Stevie's sister shows up," I said

"Why don't you eat something while we're waiting? Food always makes you more optimistic."

I eyed the table. I guess Libby knew me pretty well. I headed for the food. The doorbell rang and stopped my forward momentum but didn't cause panic. Jack and Gina would have just walked right in, so this had to be company.

Neither Mary nor Lucianne showed up to answer the door. The bell rang a second time. Libby and I looked at one another. "Shall we?" I asked. As soon as Lucianne had friends in place, Libby would feel free to leave.

We went together to answer the door and opened it to a balding man in work clothes, carrying a clipboard. His shirt had "A-1 Locksmiths" embroidered on the pocket. His van, parked next to Libby's in the front drive, not only had the same logo as his shirt, but also said "radio dispatched," which must've accounted for how fast he'd showed up. The Piedmont address probably motivated him, too.

He looked from me to Libby. "I got a call about changing locks from... " He consulted the clipboard and looked up at us again. His gaze slid from my face to just over my shoulder. "Mrs. Lind?"

I turned my head. Lucianne had reached the foot of the stairs without my hearing her. Mary followed on her heels.

"Yes, I'm Mrs. Lind," Lucianne said, crossing the hall and stepping in front of me. "Thank you for coming so promptly. I need the locks changed immediately."

"Why don't you let me see what you need, and I'll get on it right away."

"Mary?" Lucianne said, turning to the housekeeper who'd followed her down the stairs. "Would you show him every entrance to the house?"

Mary moved closer to Lucianne. Worry creased her face. "You sure you want to do this? You don't want to think about it a bit first?"

"There's nothing to think about, I assure you. Oh, and keep an eye out for Andrew Duggan, will you? I need to know the second he arrives."

The locksmith had already bent to inspect the front door deadbolt. He made a note on his clipboard. Mary waited for him, her arms folded across her chest. Jack Lind was in for an unpleasant surprise when he finally decided to come home, and I needed to get out of there before that happened. I'd had enough family drama for one day.

Lucianne gestured for Libby and me to return to the dining room. "Please come along here. There's something I want you to see."

I caught Libby's eye and pointed surreptitiously to my wristwatch. She nodded in understanding.

Lucianne crossed the dining room to a sideboard and beckoned us to join her. "I had Mary put these out this morning. I haven't even had a chance to go through them yet, but after your eulogy, I thought you'd like to see them." The sideboard was covered with photos, both framed and unframed, of a Stevie that Libby and I had never known. A grinning baby, hands and face covered with birthday cake frosting. A toddler with his arms held out for balance as he took an unsteady step.

"That's when he graduated from Berkeley." Lucianne pointed to a photo of a boy in graduation cap and gown standing in a line with much older kids. "He was fourteen."

"He went on to do post-graduate work there, too, didn't he?" I asked, although I knew the answer.

"Yes." She picked up a group snapshot. "Here's one of... " She stopped short, and her face hardened as she gazed at the photo. "This," she gestured with the photo, "is the reason Stevie had a mental breakdown when he did. I didn't realize he had any pictures of her. I'd have burned it if I'd known."

I peered over her shoulder at the picture. Stevie stood with three college-aged men and one woman. She had her arm around Stevie and her head on his shoulder. "But that's Flo!"

"You know her? Florence Bing?"

I nodded and reached for the photo. "May I see it?"

Lucianne handed it to me. "You can keep it. I certainly never want to see her face again."

I examined the picture. Flo looked remarkably the same in her features, same black hair, thin face, pointed nose and chin, but everything about her conveyed softness. The way her head rested on Stevie's shoulder, the carefree smile. Now that I thought about it, I couldn't remember ever seeing Flo smile like that since I'd known her. I looked up from the snapshot. "What happened, if you don't mind my asking?"

"It's no secret. She seduced him. She was ten years his senior, and he was underage at the time. He'd never had a girlfriend. Never even been on a date. He'd moved ahead in school so rapidly that he didn't have a same-age peer group. Naturally, he was very susceptible. He believed that he was in love. Young people so often mistake physical passion for love. She dropped him cold, with no warning. He was devastated. The next thing we knew, he'd been picked up by the police and taken to the psych ward at Herrick Hospital." Lucianne's voice cracked. "He was never the same again."

Libby put a comforting hand on Lucianne's shoulder.

Lucianne sighed. "The doctors said that given the right amount of stress, Stephen could have experienced a psychotic break at any time. All the research indicates that in cases like his, it's a genetic predisposition. Even so, I blame her." She nodded at the picture of Flo. "I wanted to have her charged with statutory rape, but Jack talked me out of it. I suppose she went on to become quite successful. Stephen said she was brilliant."

I shook my head. "No. She never even finished her PhD. She doesn't do any original research. She's basically just an office manager."

Lucianne gave a cold little smile. "Good."

The doorbell rang and Lucianne swung away from us. "Excuse me, will you? I think that's my attorney." She moved toward the front hallway.

"Flo works at the Center," I whispered to Libby, holding up the photo.

Libby's eyes widened. "Do you think she had something to do with Stevie's death?"

"I don't know, but I'm going to find out. Are you ready to go?"

Libby shook her head. "I can't leave yet. Not one friend has come by. She's throwing her husband out of the house. Maybe her daughter, too. She'll be alone." She reached into her purse and pulled out her car keys. "Here, you go on. I can always call a cab."

I took the keys just as Lucianne rejoined us with a short round man in tow. He wore a three-piece suit and carried a leather brief case. "Alison and Libby, I'd like you to meet Andrew Duggan."

Andrew Duggan frowned at me from under shaggy

black eyebrows. "Ms. Weaver, is it?"

"None of that, Andrew," Lucianne said sharply. "Alison was Stephen's friend. He made her his sole heir, and I want you to make sure that she's fairly treated."

"Look," I said. "Until yesterday, I had no idea Stevie had even written a will, much less named me in it. I couldn't take Stevie's papers. Those are part of your memories of him, and you should keep them."

"So you don't want Stephen's papers," Duggan said to me. "Just his money."

I stared at him. "What money?"

Duggan raised a skeptical eyebrow. "Please, Ms. Weaver, there's no need for dissimulation." He turned to Lucianne. "Would you mind if Ms. Weaver and I spoke in private?"

"I don't want to talk to you in private. I don't want to talk to you at all. Whatever Stevie owned belongs to his family."

"No!" Lucianne spoke sharply. "I'll never let Jack get one penny of that money. My father gave it directly to Stephen, and Stephen intended for you to have it."

I sighed. "Mrs. Lind."

"Please, call me Lucianne."

"Lucianne," I began again, "I am so profoundly sorry about your loss. Stevie was a very special person, but... " I would've gone on, but Lucianne interrupted me.

"Then honor his memory and accept that he wanted you to be his heir. Don't let that monster benefit from Stephen's death."

"I know you're angry and upset with your husband, but, rightly or wrongly, he believed that he was protecting you."

"Listen to me. Within a year of his breakdown, Stephen was living at home, on medication and functional. He had good days and bad days, but overall he was doing well. Then I fell ill, but it had nothing to do with Stephen. I had surgery followed by complications, and was in the hospital for several weeks. When I returned home, Jack told me that Stephen had been placed in Conway House. He showed me psychiatric reports stating that I was too overbearing and smothering, that Stephen himself wanted to be away from me. The recommendation was that I not be allowed any direct contact with Stephen, for his own good. I was devastated, but it was all so... plausible.

"You always look back and wonder if you could have done something different. Here was evidence that Stephen's illness was at least partially my fault. So, I accepted that I couldn't see my son, for his own sake."

"That bastard," Libby growled.

I jerked around and stared at her. Libby never, ever cursed or used what she called "strong language."

Lucianne nodded in agreement. "Precisely. So will you please help me ensure that nothing of Stephen's goes to Jack?"

"I'd like to help, but realistically speaking, what are the odds of a court upholding the will of a diagnosed schizophrenic?"

"That's Andrew's department. And Andrew is extremely good at what he does, which is why Jack called him the second I left the church today. Do you think anyone but you could break our pre-nuptial agreement, Andrew?"

"Probably not," Duggan agreed.

"Look," I said, "if you're going to try to break your pre-nuptial agreement, do you also want to get into a big court case about the will?"

"I don't want to break it. Jack does. Andrew designed it in the first place, at my father's insistence. Under the agreement, if we get divorced, which we certainly will, Jack gets what he came with, which is nothing. But, if Stephen's will doesn't stand up to challenge, then he'll get half of Stephen's money."

"So you're saying Stephen had a lot of money?"

"Depends on your point of view, I suppose," Duggan answered. "Does a fortune that generates half a million dollars in annual interest seem like a lot to you?"

Libby gasped.

"More than a lot," I said.

"Will you help me stop Jack from benefiting from Stephen's death?" Lucianne asked.

"I want to, but I need time to think." I also needed some breathing room. I paced over to the windows that overlooked the front drive. Just as I halted in front of the window with my back to the room, Gina screeched into the drive and nearly sideswiped the locksmith's van. An unmarked police car followed her Mercedes, minus the screeching and near collision. I could see Stans behind the wheel. I jumped back from the window.

"I changed my mind," I said to Duggan. "I do want to speak with you privately." I turned to Lucianne. "Company's coming. Your daughter and the cops. Where can Mr. Duggan and I speak for a few minutes without being disturbed?" Or arrested, or beaten senseless, depending on who gets to me first, I might have added, but didn't.

"This way," she said without hesitation and led us across the dining room, through the kitchen, down a hallway and into a small sitting room, completely different in character from the rest of the house. The slightly worn furniture and personal possessions on every surface made it cozy. "This is Mary's suite. I'm sure that she'll forgive our intruding without permission. Lock the door behind me. No one will bother you here."

She left. I crossed to the door and turned the lock. "Okay," I said facing Duggan. "Let's put our cards on the table."

"An excellent idea. Do you mind if we sit down?" He crossed to an overstuffed chair and sat down, placing his briefcase at his feet.

I followed suit and settled into a matching chair. I dumped my purse, Libby's keys and the photo on a coffee table. We eyed each other.

"I assume that it's part of your job to do a quick read on people," I said. "In fact, I'm counting on it. I'm going to tell you what you need to know about me to make a decision whether this thing with the will is a good idea or not. For my part, I have pretty good bullshit sensors, but I don't have a take on you yet. So tell me, what's your cut?"

Duggan gave me a sharp look. "That's negotiable."

"Is it negotiable with me and Lucianne alone, or is Jack Lind included in the bidding?"

He folded his hands and rested them in his lap. "I'm very fortunate in this situation that my moral feelings don't have to war with financial necessity."

I glanced at my wristwatch. "Speak English. I'm already late getting back to work."

"Even if he inherited from Stephen, Jack wouldn't possess one-tenth the wealth that Lucianne controls. For my part, I've never liked Jack. His behavior toward Lucianne and his own son is repugnant to me." He nodded to me. "Your turn."

"The police consider me a suspect in Stevie's murder because my car was used to transport his body. His will is supposed to be my motive, and I guess now I know why. But I didn't know until two days ago that he'd written a will and made me his beneficiary. And even then I had no idea that Stevie was rich."

"I see. Have you obtained legal representation in this police matter?"

"Not exactly."

Duggan raised one of his bushy eyebrows and waited for me to go on.

"I got the name of someone, but once I found out who'd used my car to haul Stevie's body around, I thought I wouldn't actually need a lawyer. Now, with the will thing, I guess I do. So can I hire you?"

"I would be pleased to represent you as the sole legatee of Stephen Lind's estate. I don't, however, accept criminal cases."

"You think you can make the will stand? Stevie had a serious mental illness."

"It's possible that he was mentally competent at the

time he signed the will. There are precedents that stipulate that a diagnosis of previous mental illness does not invalidate a will completed at a later time."

This was news to me, and I'd watched a lot of Perry Mason re-runs in my formative years. "What if I get hauled off to jail? Wouldn't that give Jack Lind a weapon to break the will?"

"If you're convicted of Stephen Lind's murder, you cannot benefit from your crime." He paused and gazed at me a moment. "Do you agree that I'll represent your interests as regards Stephen Lind's will?"

"How much do you charge? I don't have a lot in my bank account."

"The reimbursement for probate is set by law--four percent of fifteen thousand dollars, three percent of the next eighty-five thousand, and two percent of the remainder."

"I guess you won't be retiring on that."

He gave me a thin smile. "I could comfortably retire now, but I like my work. However, you didn't let me finish. If the will is contested, I would charge my usual hourly fee, contingent upon the will being upheld."

"So, I don't inherit, you don't charge?"

He nodded. "Correct."

"All right, you're hired."

Duggan half-stood and held out his hand. I stretched out my arm and we shook hands. He settled back into his chair and said, "We now enjoy attorney-client privilege. Did you kill Stephen Lind?"

I stared at him. "No," I said flatly. I'd always wondered what it meant to 'enjoy attorney-client privilege.' Now I knew. It was one of those trick words—enjoyment didn't mean having fun. At least, not for the client.

"Good. That makes everything much easier. We'll need to meet to formalize our arrangement." He reached into his coat and produced a business card, which he handed to me. "Call my office and make an appointment." He reached for his briefcase and stood up.

"Hold everything. You represent me now, right?"

"That is correct."

"I take that to mean that you work for me, not vice versa. So sit down and take some notes."

Duggan blinked, opened his mouth, closed it and sat down. He opened his briefcase and extracted a yellow legal-size pad and fountain pen. He uncapped the pen and looked at me.

"This is what *I* call enjoying attorney-client privilege. I want everything I inherit from Stevie—after your cut—to be divided between the Lind Foundation and the Mobile Clinic."

CHAPTER THIRTEEN

"Surely not," Duggan said.

"Surely yes," I said and gave him the hard eye.

"As your attorney, I must urge you not to be impetuous. You might later regret your generous impulse."

"Look, I didn't hire you to give me grief."

We went around this issue twice more before he started writing. Once he caved in on his objections, everything went pretty smoothly. Duggan fired questions at me and wrote several pages of notes, mostly about the Mobile Clinic. I kept an ear out for Gina and the cops, but Lucianne had been pretty smart to stash us in Mary's rooms. It didn't occur to Gina to look for us here.

I hadn't reckoned with the cops' *modus operandi*, though. Libby told me later that when Gina couldn't find me, Stans just relied on the ordinary citizen's unwillingness to lie to the police and asked Lucianne up front where I was. He was smart enough to do it out of Gina's earshot, and to have Mary come along with him to knock on the door. We could hardly deny her access to her own rooms, could we?

I opened the door to an apologetic Mary and an imperturbable Stans. "I'd like a word with you, Ms. Weaver."

"I'm conferring with my attorney."

Duggan gathered up his notes, slid them into his

briefcase and rose to his feet. "I believe we're done for now." It looked like the attorney-client relationship didn't extend to supporting me in delaying tactics. Well, he'd been up front about not doing criminal law. I stepped back from the door to let Duggan out. He paused as he reached me. "Please call my office at your convenience, Ms. Weaver. I'd like to have all the necessary papers drawn up immediately, but I need to see proof of the Mobile Clinic's non-profit status first."

He didn't need to be so pedantic. We'd already covered this ground. "Sure. Thanks, Mr. Duggan." I turned to gather up my things from the coffee table.

"We're going to ask your client a few questions," Stans said to Duggan.

"With regard to?" Duggan asked.

I turned and stared at Duggan. What was he up to?

"With regard to the murder of Stephen Lind."

"Is Ms. Weaver a suspect?"

"We're not charging her with anything at this time," Stans replied, slippery as ever.

"Is Ms. Weaver considered a suspect?" Duggan repeated.

"There are suspicious circumstances surrounding her involvement in the crime."

"It's my understanding that she has cooperated with the police investigation to date and that her 'involvement,' as you call it, concerns her personal vehicle, which was not in her possession at the time of the murder. Am I correct?"

"Her involvement includes her being named in the victim's will."

"Ah," Duggan said a bit theatrically. "Now you touch on a matter that is of concern to me, in that I represent Ms. Weaver as the sole legatee of Stephen Lind."

Stans goggled at Duggan. I grinned. I'd thought nothing could startle the unflappable Stans. "You're not going to try to probate that will?"

"I shall probate the will. I have here," he brandished

his briefcase, "Ms. Weaver's instructions for the disposition of the estate, which, naturally, I cannot discuss. She can tell you the details if she wishes." He turned to me and offered his hand for the second time that afternoon. When I clasped his, he gave me the barest wink. "Good-bye, Ms. Weaver. We'll talk soon," he said and left.

Stans narrowed his eyes at me. "Okay, what's the deal here? What was he talking about?"

"He's Andrew Duggan, big-time lawyer. Check him out. Lucianne Lind's one of his clients. He's convinced there'll be no problem with Stevie's will, because, one, he knows I didn't kill Stevie, and two, crazy people's wills have held up in court before."

"A guy like that wouldn't sign on unless there was a lot of money involved. Am I right?"

"Enough investments to provide half a million a year. His cut actually isn't that big. I'm giving what I get to the Lind Foundation and the Mobile Clinic."

"So that's how you got around Mrs. Lind. Pretty smart."

"I didn't want to take the money in the first place, but Lucianne wants to keep her husband's hands off Stevie's inheritance. Know why? He lied to her about where Stevie was. Gave her fake doctor's reports, too, so she'd think she was one of the reasons Stevie was crazy. You might consider checking out daddy's motives. As for me," I made a show of looking at my watch, "I have to get back to work."

Stans stood in the doorway, blocking it with his substantial bulk. I don't think he would have moved aside if Jack Lind himself hadn't put in an appearance at the front door, yelling loud enough for us to hear all the way at the back the house.

I cocked my head to listen, but couldn't make out specific words beyond the unprintable. "Speak of the devil," I said. "Lucianne's divorcing him. That's why the locksmith and the lawyer are here. Under the pre-nup, he gets nothing. She keeps the multi-millions she inherited from her side of the family. Think Detective Carney should handle that situation all by himself?"

More loud words drifted to us from Jack Lind and some indistinguishable rumbling in reply from Carney. Gina added her expletive-rich vocabulary to the conversation. She mentioned my name a couple of times, couching it in obscenities. Stans gave me a sharp look. "Maybe you'd better go out the back way."

"Okay by me." I had no wish to go *mano a mano* with Gina.

Stans hesitated. "We still need some answers from you. You're going be at work all afternoon?"

"Either that or having tea with the Prince of Wales on his yacht. You should probably check work first."

The voices from the front of the house grew louder. Jack, Gina and Carney were all trying to talk over one another. Stans headed down the hall toward them.

I went in the opposite direction and found a short staircase that descended to a door at the back of the house. The locksmith had been there before me. An empty hole gaped where he'd removed the deadbolt lock mechanism. I followed a flagstone path that circled the house. When I reached the side of the house, someone tapped on a window. I jerked around, heart racing. Mary waved at me from the kitchen window and signaled me to wait. She emerged from the house carrying a paper bag. I backtracked to meet her halfway.

She held out the bag for me to take. "Libby said you wouldn't have time to eat, so I made you some sandwiches. Hope they're the kind you like."

"I never met a sandwich I didn't like," I said, taking the bag. "Thank you, Mary. You're an angel."

She gave a self-deprecating wave of her hand. "A body's got to eat."

"This body does at least." I scanned the windows on the side of the house. All clear.

Mary turned her head and followed my glance. "Don't worry about them. They're in the library now. They can't see you from there."

"I could hear Jack and Gina all the way in the back of the house."

"Probably the whole neighborhood heard—the mouths they have on them, and to a policeman, too." Mary frowned her disapproval.

I shifted the paper bag to my other hand. If Mary felt comfortable disapproving of Jack and Gina Lind in front of me, maybe she could be induced to gossip a bit. "Gina's an attractive young woman, but she seems awfully unhappy. Why do you think that is?"

"That girl was a terrible fusspot when she was little, but she'd come around if you talked to her a bit. Now it seems like nothing can please her. Of course, her folks spoiled her rotten. Gave her anything she wanted, and that just seemed to make her more miserable."

"Is she in college?" I guessed that Gina was about the right age.

"She was thrown out of three of them. Mrs. Lind tried to get her to help out at the Foundation. Gina told her she didn't 'give a damn about a bunch of crazy people,'" Mary mimicked Gina's snotty tone of voice.

"I guess she has enough money that she doesn't really have to work."

Mary gave me a steady look. Maybe I'd seemed a bit too nosy for her.

"I only ask," I hurried to add, "because she was so mad at my being named in Stevie's will. I want to give the money to the Lind Foundation and to Libby's Mobile Clinic, but if Gina contests the will, that probably won't happen."

"She got the money her grandpa left her, same as Stephen. But the way she spends it, I don't know. Maybe for some folks, there's no such thing as enough money. Besides… " she hesitated.

"Mmmm?" I murmured in encouragement.

"Nothing. I best get back. I hope you enjoy your sandwiches." She turned and headed back to the house.

"I know I will. Thanks for everything," I said to her

retreating back. I followed the flagstone path to the front of the house. When I reached the circular front drive, I avoided looking up at the windows and walked directly to Libby's car. I had her keys in hand so I could get in and drive off without delay. No one came screaming out of the house. Even if Gina had, she couldn't have followed me. Her father had parked his car directly behind hers and blocked her exit.

I slipped into the car, started the engine and sped out the front gate like a NASCAR driver leaving a pit stop. I was so busy checking my rear view mirror to see if either Jack or Gina was following, I nearly broadsided a motorcyclist coming out of the neighbor's driveway. My car screeched to a jerking halt just one layer of denim away from the driver's leg. I stared through the windshield. The motorcyclist had the face shield on his helmet pulled down, but I recognized the gray ponytail hanging down his back.

"What the hell are you doing here, Frank?" I yelled at him. Had he been tailing me all morning and I hadn't noticed?

His only answer was to gun the engine and speed off. I nearly followed him, but a figure standing in the driveway caught my eye. The woman Libby and I had shared a pew with during Stevie's memorial service stood at the foot of the drive looking at me. I parked the car at the curb and got out.

"Hi. I'm Alison Weaver. We talked at Stevie's memorial service."

"You were driving too fast for city streets."

"I know. You didn't stay for the excitement after the service, did you? Anyway, Gina has it in for me, and I guess so does Jack. I was afraid they'd seen me, but you're right, I shouldn't have been driving so fast." I was rattling on too much, practically jabbering, but I was shaken from the near collision with Frank. "That guy I nearly ran into—I think he was following me. Did you notice how long he'd been hanging out in your driveway?"

She gave me a funny look. "That was Frank Avery. He's a well-known writer, and he came to see me."

"Why? Did he want to pump you about Stevie?"

"No. Do you often worry about people following you?"

"Not just anyone—my ex-husband. For some reason, he's been acting completely nuts. He kicked in my front door, and he hired a neighbor boy to spy on me, so I don't think it's too off-base to think he's following me."

"Are you serious? You were married to Frank Avery?"

"Unfortunately, it's true. He's not really as nice as he seems. The charm wears thin the first time he doesn't get his way."

"Sounds like my ex." She gave me a wry smile and held out her hand. "I'm Barbara Reynolds. Do you have a minute to come inside? I think we'd better talk."

I shook her hand. How was I going to get out of this one? I was already very late getting back to work. "If you want to talk about Frank—all I can say is, whatever he's selling, don't buy it."

"What if I told you he was selling me my son?"

"That sounds over the top, even for Frank. I don't think I can help. You'd better call the police."

"It's more complicated than that. Please, come in for just a few minutes. I need your advice."

She led me up the driveway. The grounds of her house matched those of Lucianne's in size, but they weren't nearly as well kept. The grass was overgrown and the flowerbeds badly in need of weeding. The house was an enormous brown shingle that had to be a Julia Morgan. Once I crossed the threshold, the contrast to the Lind's house hit me with even more force. The house itself was lovely. Wood everywhere, floors, wainscoting and ceiling beams. It was clearly a family home rather than a showcase. Sports gear lay in jumbled piles on both sides of the front hallway. Barbara led me into a living room which redefined the term "lived in." Newspapers, magazines, kids' backpacks, sweatshirts and even dirty socks were strewn on the floor, chairs and sofas.

Barbara cleared space on the sofa and invited me to sit down. "I have six children. Four still live at home," she offered by way of explanation.

“It’s a beautiful house,” I said truthfully. “Not as intimidating as the Lind’s.”

“Nice of you to say so. I had to choose between comfort and perfection after the birth of my third child.”

“You wanted to talk to me about your son?” I prompted.

“No, I wanted you to talk to me about my son. You know him. He used to be Stephen’s best friend, and, according to Frank, still was, right up till Stephen’s death.”

“The only friend of Stevie’s I know, if you can call him that, is a strung-out meth addict, who’d rob his own... ” I stopped in mid-sentence. Barbara gazed at me steadily, and I had that choked-up feeling you get when you’ve just inserted your foot in your mouth.

“Rob his own mother for a fix? Yes, he did that. More than once.”

“Joe’s your son?”

“We named him Jason. Apparently he goes by GI Joe now.”

“Has he been in touch with you since Stevie died?”

“Indirectly, just now, through Frank Avery.”

“Frank! How does he know Frank?”

“A friend of Frank’s found him. Frank’s been researching Stephen Lind’s murder. He’s planning on writing a book about it. So he wanted to interview Jason, but Jason said he’ll only talk to Frank if I’m there.”

“Back up a minute. Who’s Frank’s friend and where did he find Joe... er, Jason?”

“I don’t know his name, but he tracked Jason down in Tilden Park where he’s living with a crazy man who thinks he’s Jesus.”

Suddenly things were coming together for me. Like a jigsaw puzzle, only it wasn’t coming out as a pretty landscape or cute kittens playing with yarn. I was the one who’d tracked down Joe, dragging Tony Dezzutti along with me. Tony, the guy Mitch had seen being friendly with

Frank. The guy who'd said he thought he knew me from someplace. Who'd even called me "amazing." I was amazing all right—the amazingly credulous Alison Weaver. When would I ever learn?

"Are you all right? You don't look well."

"I suffer from occasional bouts of gullibility. The only cure is a stiff dose of reality, which usually tastes pretty nasty."

Barbara gave me a sympathetic smile. "We seem to have some things in common."

"Maybe, but somehow I doubt that your ex could be worse than Frank."

"My ex-husband made it a condition of my having custody of the children that I never have contact with Jason—not even a phone call."

I winced. "Okay, let's call it a draw. So that's your dilemma? Whether to meet with Jason?"

"One part. The other part has to do with my own doubts about whether he can be salvaged. I haven't made contact with him for over two years, but you have. What do you think?"

She had me there. A week ago, I'd have said that Joe was beyond redemption, but I couldn't bring myself to say it to his mother. Besides that, I now had serious doubts about my own judgment. "Tell me about Jason and Stevie's friendship."

"They grew up together. Started kindergarten together. Stephen clearly had a genius I.Q., but he was also odd and didn't fit in socially. His parents encouraged him to be skipped in school. I'm sure he was bored in class, but it meant that he never made any friends. So he always turned to Jason."

"Why did Lucianne give you the cold shoulder at Stevie's memorial service today?"

"Stephen came to live at home after his breakdown. Jason was already experimenting with drugs—pot mostly, I think, but also hallucinogens. He gave Stephen some LSD. He said he thought it would be good for him. Stephen completely freaked out. Lucianne was in the hospital at the time. Jack had Stephen institutionalized. Lucianne blamed Jason and hasn't spoken to me since."

Up to that point, Barbara had spoken unemotionally, just telling the story as if it had happened to someone else. Now she turned her head and looked out the window, blinking her eyes rapidly. After a few moments she cleared her throat and went on.

"My marriage had been rocky for a number of years. The episode with Stephen fractured it completely. My husband blamed me. He threw Jason out of the house, then left me himself. Jason would show up every now and then and ask for money. When I stopped giving him money, he'd steal it, or something he could sell. One of the younger kids told my ex, and he filed the court order barring me from making contact with Jason."

She finished talking, and we sat in silence for a minute. Something didn't quite add up here. Finally I spoke. "You've seen Jason recently, haven't you?"

Barbara gave me a little half smile. "How did you guess?"

"You wondered if Jason could be 'salvaged.' You had to have seen what he looks like now to ask that."

"I've had a private detective keep tabs on him off and on. I've driven to places I was told he usually hangs out just to get a glimpse of him. He looks... " She stopped and bit her lip.

"Pretty bad," I finished for her. "But he asked to speak to you. That's encouraging, isn't it?"

"I suppose so. He knows why I haven't tried to make contact. I thought he'd hate me for turning my back on him. I'm sorry to have to ask you this, because it would mean your getting in touch with Frank, but would you talk to Jason for me? Find out what he wants. Please?"

"I'll do it, but not through Frank. I've been trying to talk to Jason since Stevie was killed. I was the one who unintentionally led Frank to him. Believe me, Frank doesn't care about him, about you or anyone except himself. The only complication is that the cops are very eager to talk to him, too, because Jason knows something about Stevie's death."

"You won't hand him over to the police, will you?"

"They might make me. Any message you want me to give Jason?"

"Just that I love him. Tell him I'll pay for a treatment program."

I thought the likelihood of Jason voluntarily going into treatment was small to non-existent, but didn't think I could say that to Barbara. Instead, I told her I was very late getting back to work, exchanged phone numbers with her and hurried out to my car. It had been an emotionally wearing day so far, and I still had the situation at the Center to clear up. I wasn't sure I was up for any of it.

I drove back to work at the posted speed limit, steering with one hand and pulling out Mary's sandwiches with the other. There was nothing like chewing away on a perfect roast beef sandwich to brighten my outlook, unless it was chewing on a roast beef sandwich knowing that I had a great ham sandwich still to go.

When I walked into the office, I went quietly, but quickly, the long way around to my cubicle so I wouldn't have to pass by Daniel's open office door. Blondie sat in front of my computer clicking through an array of numbers. The data analysis plan I'd given Daniel that morning lay on the desk next to the keyboard.

"Hi." I sank onto the visitor's chair. My cubicle no longer felt like my space. Carolyn Dahlstrom had turned it into occupied territory. "How's it going?" I'd rehearsed this bit in the car until I had just the right tone of casual confidence. I needn't have bothered.

"Fine." She went on clicking through rows of numbers.

I just sat there. After a full minute by the clock, she turned her head and asked, "Do you need something?" It wasn't a friendly question.

I considered asking for my cubicle, my computer and

my job back, but they really weren't hers to hand over. Daniel had that power, and it looked as if he'd already wielded it. Had he ever intended to let me run the analysis part of the study? Finding someone like Carolyn and convincing her to come work at the Center must have taken some time. In the end, Daniel would get first pick of the most compelling results to publish. Carolyn would get second pick, and I would get what was left over.

"Well?" Carolyn asked with a cranky look on her pretty face.

"No, I don't want anything from you."

"Do you mind waiting somewhere else, then? I have a lot to do."

I stood up and headed out of the cubicle.

"You can't expect me to be friendly after you tried to scare me like that," Carolyn said.

I turned around and looked at her. "What?"

"Telling me how dangerous it is around here. I talked to some other people, and they said it wasn't true at all."

I went to Kenji's cubicle. He was hunched over his keyboard reading email.

He looked up as I entered. "Where have you been?"

I put my fingers to my lips. "I told you," I whispered, "Stevie's memorial service. Look, I need a monster favor." I pulled out the photo Lucianne had given me. "Run this through the scanner." As a senior researcher, Kenji had access to the locked data room where Daniel kept the servers, scanner, color printer and all our other highest tech equipment. "I need to give this to the police, but I want to make an enlargement for myself first."

He took the picture and studied it. "Hey, that's Flo. Who're the other guys?" he whispered back.

"The one with his arm around Flo is Stephen Lind, the guy whose funeral I attended today. I'll give you all the details, if you'll make copies for me." Nothing could motivate him faster than the promise of hot gossip.

"Okay. Let's go." By tacit agreement, we avoided

going past Daniel's office. We walked hurriedly, Kenji carrying the photo discreetly shielded in the palm of his hand. This was just the kind of intrigue that appealed to him. When we reached the data room, he punched his code into the lock--8801088. A number palindrome. Easier to remember than my doorcode, and my code didn't also work on the fishbowl.

We walked into the room and the door swung shut on its own and closed with a click. Kenji headed for the scanner, but I stayed by the door and looked around. I'd been inside the data room only a few times before. We called it the fishbowl because of the large window in the wall that let everyone in the main room see in. The window was made of thick unbreakable acrylic—part of Daniel's paranoid reaction to the burglary we'd had. A long conference table occupied the center of the room. The main data computers, scanner, and color copier were lodged on one wall. Bookcases covered the opposite wall. I crossed to look at them while Kenji settled himself to his task.

The bookcases mainly held copies of scientific journals, but one shelf displayed thick volumes with gold lettering--bound copies of the dissertations of all the PhD's who'd ever worked at the Center, beginning with Daniel's. He'd won the Meadowes prize with it. I pulled it from the shelf and leafed through the pages. For two years now, I'd pictured placing my own bound dissertation on that shelf. There simply had to be a way to convince Daniel to keep me on the refinery study.

"Catching up on your reading?" Daniel asked.

A gave a startled jump and stared at him standing in the doorway.

"No," I said quickly and tried to jam the volume back onto the shelf. I only succeeded in knocking three other bound dissertations onto their sides.

Daniel crossed to me, lifted the volumes upright with one hand and deftly slotted his dissertation into place with the other. He turned to me. "If you're not reading, what are you doing?"

"Waiting for Kenji." What a lame answer. I should

have asked Kenji to give me some work to do before we came in here, then I could have at least had a plausible excuse, not to mention been able to look busy.

Daniel sniffed. "I see. I'm looking for Flo. I thought she might be in here. Has either one of you seen her?"

I shook my head.

Kenji said, "I haven't seen her since this morning."

"That's very strange. Apparently she left very suddenly without saying anything at all to me."

Flo always checked out with Daniel, even if she was just going to lunch. I'd simply assumed it was part of her self-image of being indispensable, but maybe Daniel expected it of her.

"Not only that," Daniel added with a sniff, "but her desk is a mess."

"That doesn't sound like Flo-type behavior at all," Kenji said. Flo was a complete neat freak. She straightened everything on her desk even if she was only going out for coffee.

"Maybe she got sick all of a sudden," I suggested.

"Possibly," Daniel said. "However, I was informed by the last person who saw her this morning that she had a newspaper clutched in her hand, and didn't speak when spoken to. Simply walked out the door."

Flo's behavior sounded completely normal, as far as I could tell. I could think of a number of occasions when she'd completely ignored me.

"I get it," Kenji said. "You know what was in the paper today, don't you?"

I gritted my teeth. Couldn't Kenji ever keep his mouth shut? I gave him a hard stare, but it didn't faze him.

"The article about Stephen Lind," he went on.

"Who?" Daniel asked.

"The dead guy Alison found in our recycling bin," he explained with an apologetic glance in my direction. "Alison told us his name was Stevie Number. I didn't know who he really was until I read the article. Probably Flo didn't either."

"Why should that information upset her?" Daniel asked.

"She used to know him."

"Indeed?" Daniel said and sniffed. "I'm surprised she confided in you. She said nothing about it to me."

"Actually, it was Alison who found out about it. She came across an old picture of the two of them."

"Is that the picture?" Daniel asked, pointing to the photo Kenji still held. "May I see it?" He took it from Kenji, and without glancing at it, said, "Let's move this discussion into my office, shall we?"

Kenji and I followed him out of the fishbowl and down the hall into his office. Kenji slipped me the scanned copy he'd made of the photo, and I quickly shoved it into my purse.

Daniel sat down behind his desk and placed the picture under the bright beam of his desk lamp. "Close the door, please."

Kenji pushed the door shut. We sat in the visitors' chairs in front of Daniel's desk and waited while he studied the photo.

"Which one is the man you found outside the Center, Alison?" Daniel asked.

"The one with his arm around Flo."

He studied it in silence for a few moments. "This looks to have been taken a number of years ago. I'm not sure I would have recognized Flo from it." He picked up the picture and handed it across his desk to me. "Where did you find it?"

"It was with some photos Stevie's mother had at her house" I tucked the picture into my purse.

"She had a particular reason for giving it to you?"

"I recognized Flo, so I asked to borrow it." I paused to see if Daniel would let it go at that, but both Daniel and Kenji gazed at me intently, saying nothing, waiting for me to go on. "According to Stevie's mother, Flo and Stevie were lovers. The police think I had some involvement in Stevie's murder, because his body was dumped here. The photograph shows that someone else at the Center knew him and, at least at one point, was a lot closer to him than I was."

Daniel pursed his lips. "Let me see if I follow you correctly. The police harbor suspicions about you simply because his body was found outside your place of work?" He sniffed loudly.

I nearly writhed in my chair. Trust Daniel to go immediately to the flaw in my reasoning. The short-cut method never worked with him. "There are certain other factors. I loaned my car to a friend, but someone else used it to transport Stevie's body here. The cops were tipped off about it, so they have forensic evidence that Stevie's body actually was in the trunk of my car. Also, for some reason I don't understand, Stevie wrote a will just a week before he was killed and left his entire estate to me."

"I believe you told me that he was mentally disturbed."

"Schizophrenic."

Daniel sniffed at my correcting him. "That surely invalidates the will."

"Andrew Duggan doesn't think so. He's Mrs. Lind's lawyer. She wants it to go through for her own reasons."

"Is there a significant sum of money involved?"

"Yes." I didn't go into Duggan's routine of how much counted as a lot.

"I see." Daniel sank into silent contemplation of the photo of Flo and Stevie. The seconds ticked by. I could feel sweat gathering in the small of my back. Finally, still gazing at the picture, he said, "I'm very concerned about the impact of these events on your work and on the Center." He raised his gaze to meet mine, adding, "And now you've involved Flo."

I gripped the armrests of my chair to keep myself from leaping to my feet and loudly defending myself. Daniel held strong opinions on the subject of raised voices.

"Just let me do the work I've waited six months to begin, and you'll have no reason for concern. I'm prepared to work seven days a week on the refinery data."

"Carolyn Dahlstrom seems to be progressing nicely on the preliminary work on the data. She's been working on it all day, and you, I believe, have just returned after being away from the office most of the day."

I gazed at him steadily and kept my mouth shut. I wasn't going to get into a pointless discussion about Stevie's funeral again.

"I had lunch with Brian Perry today," Daniel said.

I tried not to wince. Brian Perry was the self-designated "new broom" at the NIPH.

"He's in town for the Public Health Society meetings," Daniel continued. "He'd heard about the police investigation and expressed his concern. I assured him that the Center had no involvement whatsoever in the situation. It seems that I wasn't speaking the exact truth, was I?"

"Daniel," I said, but he held up a hand to stop me.

"I'm sorry. I really have no choice but to ask you to take a leave of absence until this matter is resolved."

"But, Alison hasn't done anything wrong," Kenji protested.

Daniel sniffed. "The legislature in Washington is looking for ways to cut funding for public health research. Anything that puts us in a negative light, even tangentially, threatens every project we have going here. Including yours, Kenji." Daniel turned his gaze to me. "Kenji will accompany you while you pick up any personal items from your desk. Then I must ask you to leave the building immediately."

CHAPTER FOURTEEN

I'd worried that Daniel might ask me to take a few vacation days if he learned how much the police questioned my involvement in Stevie's murder. None of my imagined worst outcome scenarios, though, had prepared me for an actual expulsion.

"I'm sorry," Kenji said as we walked toward my cubicle, "but it's just temporary leave. It'll be cleared up before you know it."

"Come on. You know that this leave of absence is just cover-your-ass talk. I'm on leave until he figures out how to get me to quit or to fire me without being sued."

Kenji muttered several more times how sorry he was. I gave him a "nevermind" wave of my hand and preceded him into my cubicle.

Carolyn stared at us, and then, as it became clear what was up, couldn't meet my gaze. She hovered just outside my cubicle while I performed the ironic gesture of placing only one object—my souvenir Oakland A's cup—in the cardboard box Kenji had found for me. I dropped all other personal items into the wastebasket. Everything I really needed was stored on the computer's hard drive and inaccessible to me now. "Cut your losses" had been my motto for my entire miserable childhood. I'd had to leave toys, mementos, even whole wardrobes behind more than once. Who'd have thought the Center for Biostatistical Studies would turn into just one more rotten foster home?

People in neighboring cubicles caught wind of my

forced departure and popped their heads over the tops of their space dividers to gawk. They just as quickly dropped from sight when I made eye contact. Lucky for me I'd passed a good part of my early education being sent to the principal's office. I'd acquired, if not immunity to humiliation, at least the ability to put on a good show of not caring.

It worked all the way to the curb. Then I it hit me that I still had Libby's car, which I'd parked directly behind my rented Buick. I wanted to dive into a car and drive away, but stood wavering between which car to dive into, until I felt the shakes set in—aftershock tremors from witnessing the destruction of my graduate career. I couldn't think. I just headed for the closest car, which turned out to be Libby's, got in and drove off.

Mindless driving is as effective a tranquilizer for me as any pill, except in this case, my driving wasn't so much mindless as unconscious. I found that I'd driven straight to Flo's. She lived in an in-law apartment in Berkeley—a tiny cottage built thirty or forty years ago behind a big old two-story stucco house. I'd been there once before—not on a social visit, but bearing papers she needed to see when she was home sick with the flu. Just the kind of extra scut work I'd been given during my time at the Center.

Flo's car was parked on the street, so she had to be home. Along the side of the big house, a cement pathway flanked by overgrown camellia bushes and an untrimmed hedge led to Flo's cottage. She had her privacy, I had to hand her that. Though a little sunlight might also be nice.

I knocked sharply on her door. No answer. I knocked again and called out, "Flo, it's Alison. I need to talk to you about Stephen Lind." I waited, but still no answer. I could picture her standing behind the door, holding her breath, waiting for me to go away. It made me so mad I grabbed the door handle and shook it. "Open the door, Flo. I'm not going away until we've talked."

The door yielded under my hand. It hadn't been locked. I pushed the door all the way open. "Flo? I'm coming in." I took a slow step into the room. The windows, shrouded on the outside by the high hedge, dimly lit the living room. A powerful fecal smell hit me, and that, even more than Flo's not answering, hurried me through the living room into the bedroom.

She lay on the bed, eyes bulging, mouth agape. The contents of her involuntarily evacuated bowels formed a dark stain on the bedspread beneath her. "Flo? Oh God, Flo. Flo, what happened? Flo?" I kept talking, as if I could resuscitate her by repeating her name.

I leaned over the bed and felt along her carotid. No detectable pulse, but her skin was somewhat warm to the touch and still quite pink. Blood-flecked foam lined her lips. I'd seen that with pulmonary edema before, but if she'd had an episode of flash edema and suffocated, why was her color so good?

The bedspread was rucked up around her in a very un-Flo-like mess as if some terrific struggle had taken place there. Flo had battled for her life, but not with another person. A half-full bottle of Jack Daniels stood on the bedside table next to an empty glass and an empty prescription medicine container. I picked it up to read the label. Seconal? Something very weird was going on here.

I put the container back on the table and picked up a framed photo that the Jack Daniels nearly blocked from view. Florence Bing and Stephen Lind smiled out at me from the silver frame. It looked to have been taken the same day as the picture Lucianne had given me, but this shot featured only the happy couple, arms entwined, faces radiant. Stevie looked so young and happy. And normal. I'd never had the slightest glimpse of this persona behind the face I'd known. Flo, too, seemed like a different person, her face aglow with love. It was like getting a glimpse of a parallel universe—same people, but very different from the ones I knew. I put the photo back where I'd found it. Something wasn't right. I didn't know what. I just knew that I didn't like it. I didn't like it at all.

"Ms. Bing?" a familiar voice called out. "Police officers, Ms. Bing. May we come in?"

"Detective Stans, is that you?" I moved into the living

room. Stans' bulk blocked the light from the open front doorway. I could make out the top of Carney's head behind him. "Thank God. I was just about to call you."

"What are you doing here, Ms. Weaver?" Stans asked, moving into the room, with Carney following.

Carney made a face. "Christ, what a stink."

Stans looked at me.

I jerked a thumb over my shoulder. "She's in the bedroom."

"You stay here," he said to me and headed for the bedroom. Carney went with him, but only as far as the bedroom doorway, where he stayed, glancing toward me once or twice as if to make sure I wasn't going to make a run for it.

Stans didn't stay longer than half a minute. He emerged from the bedroom with a purposeful stride, muttering something to Carney as he passed him. Carney gave a nod and exited through the front door. Stans glowered at me. "Let's go outside."

Flo had a postage-stamp patio outside her front door, its borders marked by a low brick wall to indicate where her domain ended and her landlord's back yard began. Flo hadn't furnished her patio with outdoor chairs, so I perched on the brick wall.

Stans stood in front of me, his hands shoved into his pants' pockets. "How'd you get in?"

"Door was unlocked. She didn't answer when I knocked."

"You touch anything in there?"

I nodded. "The pill bottle and the photograph, but I put them back where I found them."

"Why'd you come?"

"I wanted to talk to her."

"You told me you'd be at work."

I flinched. My forced leave wasn't something I wanted to think about right now. "What about you? Shouldn't you be working now?" I pointed towards the door to Flo's cottage. "In there, investigating, gathering evidence, whatever it is you do."

"Not my territory. It belongs to the Berkeley PD. I'm just holding the fort until they get here."

I stiffened. "What do you mean not your territory? Isn't any murder related to Stevie's yours?"

"Not necessarily, depends on cooperation between different police departments. But it's a moot point anyway, because that lady's a suicide."

"No, she's not."

Stans gazed at me steadily. "What makes you say that?"

"She was wearing her shoes. Every person I've known who's overdosed on pills has taken off their shoes before they lie down."

"So? She's the exception to the rule."

"Ask anyone who knew her. Flo was very fastidious, obsessively neat. She would never have put her shoes on the bedspread."

Stans shrugged. "After a pint of Jack and several dozen reds, people stop being fussy."

"She didn't o.d. on seconal."

"No? Then what?"

"I can't say. Nothing fits with anything I know. She thrashed around, tore up the bed. With seconal, you go to sleep. You're not conscious when your body struggles for breath. And that foam on her lips? That looks like pulmonary edema to me—you know, when the lungs fill up and you can't breathe. But look at her color. If she'd suffocated, she'd be blue."

Stans nodded. "Yeah, that pink color reminded me of some carbon monoxide cases I've had."

"But where would the carbon monoxide have come from?" I protested.

"Heater maybe. Anyway, if it's carbon monoxide, it's either suicide or accidental—still not murder. It might even be natural causes."

I gritted my teeth. Why was he being so obtuse? Sure, Flo was as capable of suicide as anyone else, but the scene I'd witnessed had too many contradictions. There was something else wrong, too, but what? It sat just on the edge of my consciousness. If I could only remember what.

I put my fingers to my forehead, closed my eyes, and tried to picture the scene in the bedroom. Big mistake. Instead of Flo, images of my mother surfaced. Now there was a real suicide—wearing her favorite dress for the occasion, her hair fanned out on the pillow and shiny clean for a change, except for the small matted section where some vomit had dried. People intent on self-destruction rarely anticipated that particular problem. What if all the pills and alcohol made you throw up? My mother hadn't let it stop her. She simply took an anti-emetic and swallowed some more pills. "Get me the brown bottle in the medicine chest will you? There's a dear" were her last words. A great epitaph to put on her grave marker, if I could ever figure out where they'd buried her.

"You okay?" Stans asked.

I opened my eyes and blinked in the sudden glare of sunlight. "Yeah, I'm fine."

"Thought maybe finding your friend dead like that made you feel sort of, you know, woozy."

"The only thing that can make me feel woozy is missing a meal. Besides, she wasn't a friend."

"Yeah? Then why'd you drop by?"

"Flo and Stevie were lovers before Stevie had his psychotic break. I wanted to ask her about him."

"We wanted to ask her about him, too. Only that happens to be our job. Mrs. Lind didn't tell us about Florence Bing until we'd convinced the husband to pack a suitcase and leave. We might've arrived on the scene before she o.d.'d if you'd given us this information earlier."

I'd considered that possibility myself. Another "if only" to add to my list of omissions. "At least you had a shot at interviewing Mr. Lind. Someone who can abandon his mentally ill son and lie to his wife about it seems capable of just about anything to me."

"Unfortunately being a scumbag isn't an indictable offense. And if I were you, I'd be careful what I said in public about the man. He has his lawyer's phone number on speed-dial. Anyway, he was out of town when his son was killed."

So Jack Lind had an alibi. Had they also asked Gina for one? I sat on the brick wall and stared at the ground until Carney strode into view, running point for a Berkeley uniformed policeman who disappeared into Flo's cottage, reappeared, went in search of reinforcements and returned, leading two plainclothes detectives. I doubted that Flo had ever had so many visitors in one day.

"What's going on?" I asked Carney, who'd joined Stans in the hands-in-pockets pose at one corner of the patio.

"Police procedure."

We waited in silence. I watched a line of ants struggle determinedly up one side of the brick wall and down the other, in search of some mysterious goal. Finally, one of the Berkeley plainclothes cops emerged from Flo's cottage and approached us. He didn't identify himself, but he wore the regulation mustache.

"You the one who found the body?" he asked me, pulling a notebook and pencil from his jacket pocket.

I said I was and then answered the other questions he asked about who I was, where I lived, and how I knew Flo. The question-answer routine reminded me a lot of the one I'd gone through with Stans and Carney after I'd come across Stevie's body, including my denying being Flo's friend, just as I'd denied being Stevie's. Only this time it was true.

"Did you have any reason to think that she might have been suicidal?" the cop asked.

"She didn't commit suicide."

The cop stopped writing and looked at me. "You know that for a fact?"

"Do you know for a fact that she did?" I shot back.

"She left a note."

I hadn't noticed a note. "What did it say?"

"We release the contents of suicide notes only to the family."

I suddenly felt too tired to say anything else. What was the point of constantly struggling against the official knee-jerk response? Note or no note, I just didn't buy suicide. And if it wasn't suicide, then someone killed her because she knew something about Stevie. The really hard part was that Flo might not have died if I'd shown the police where to find GI Joe. And if, somehow or other, I'd convinced Joe to tell them what he knew about Stevie's death. Instead, I'd become a patsy for Frank Avery—again. Frank wouldn't care that Flo had been lonely and unhappy. He'd be delighted to have more material for his book. Why hadn't I seen through Tony sooner? I was sinking into a mire of "if only's" today.

"Is that all?" I asked the Berkeley cop.

"For now."He handed me a business card. "If you think of anything else, please call the number on the card."

I took the card. "Tell you what. When the coroner says that she didn't commit suicide, why don't you call me, so I can say 'I told you so?'" I turned to Stans and gave a small sideways jerk of my head to indicate that he should follow me and headed up the walkway to the sidewalk.

The gathering of police cars at the curb had drawn neighboring residents out of their houses onto the sidewalk. They stood in small groups, alternately talking among themselves and staring anxiously in our direction. I stopped well short of the closest group and turned to Stans and Carney.

"I know where to find GI Joe. I'll take you. Though, I guess I should warn you that he might not be there right now."

"Why don't you just give us the address?" Carney asked.

"There isn't one. He's hiding out in Tilden Park. Also, the guy he's staying with knows me. He's... " I hesitated--

how to explain Jesus to them? "He's a little delusional, but he trusts me." I backed away from them. "Just follow me in your car," I said still backing away.

I somehow finessed the transition by not faltering as I moved toward my car. I slid behind the wheel and waited until they'd closed their car doors before I pulled away from the curb. I was pretty sure I'd recognize the spot where Tony and I had gone into the park after Jesus. And, since Tony had taken Frank there, too, the path should be easier to follow. The hard part wouldn't be finding where Joe was camped—it would be explaining to Stans and Carney why I hadn't told them about it sooner. Just how hard, I found out when we'd parked our cars and met at the side of the road in Tilden Park, and I'd given them the basic story of how I'd found Joe.

"You've known since *yesterday* that he was in there?" Carney yelled, leaning toward me like a marine drill sergeant chewing out a grunt.

I set my jaw. "Look, you guys have been treating me like a criminal. It doesn't infuse confidence, you know."

Stans held up a pacifying hand. "Wait a minute. Let's just get the story straight, okay? This Joe character is staying in the park with a guy who thinks he's Jesus. He's using your camping gear, which you say he lifted from your car. You also think he used your car to dump the victim's body in the alley, but you don't think he's the actual perpetrator. Finally, at least two other people have visited the hideout—the other guy we interviewed at the dump site and your ex-husband." He scratched the back of his head. "Funny how your explanations just seem to muddy the waters even more."

"That's not all," I said.

"I'll bet," Carney muttered.

"GI Joe's real name is Jason Reynolds. The Reynolds are the Linds' next door neighbors. Jason and Stevie have been friends since grammar school."

"So?" Carney asked.

"So, it keeps going back to Piedmont. To the family."

Stans shook his head. "Let us do the detecting, all right? We'll gather all the evidence, then see where it leads. You just take us to the witness."

I found the path easily. It looked like a whole contingent of hikers had preceded us. Even the poison oak had been trampled down. Lucky for me, because I wasn't really dressed for hiking. I still wore my funeral-going clothes, but at least I was wearing low-heeled shoes.

Stans and Carney followed me single file. We weren't breaking through brush or weeds this time, and, unlike Tony, they didn't talk at all, so we didn't telegraph our presence unnecessarily. It helped, too, that we weren't chasing Jesus, running uphill. I managed the climb this time without gasping.

The trees thinned out enough for me to see the top of the boulder Jesus had sat on, but from my downhill angle, I couldn't actually see the clearing where Joe had set up camp. I stopped and held up a hand. Carney and Stans halted in their steps and looked at me. "The clearing," I whispered and pointed.

Stans and Carney exchanged a look. Carney pointed to himself and made a circular motion with his hand. I guessed he meant to go around to the other side. He moved off silently, as if he'd been trained as a tracker. I hope he'd been trained to recognize poison oak, too.

I started to continue toward the clearing, but Stans stepped in front of me and motioned me to stay behind him. When we breasted the hill and entered the clearing, we found it empty. No tarp, no tent, no supplies--but mostly, no GI Joe. He'd completely cleared out.

Stans moved into the center of the clearing where the tent had stood. A flash of white flicked and disappeared behind the tall rock.

"Jesus?" I called out. "Is that you, Jesus?" I couldn't come up with an appropriate Biblical text, so I just blurted out. "Can you help us, please?"

I heard rustling, grunts and cursing. After a few moments, Carney emerged from behind the boulder holding

Jesus by the arm. Jesus struggled ineffectually to free himself. “Hold still,” Carney ordered. “We’re police officers. We want to ask you some questions.”

Jesus winced as Carney hauled him toward us.

“Don’t hurt him,” I said.

Carney gave me a disgusted look. Leaves and dirt clung to his jacket and pants. “Why don’t you tell him that?” He gave Jesus a little shake. “Where’d your buddy go?”

Jesus cast an accusing gaze at me and said nothing.

“I’m sorry,” I said to him, “but I had to bring the police with me this time. Won’t you please answer their questions?”

“Cast not your pearls before swine,” Jesus pronounced.

Carney’s face, already red from exertion, turned a deeper shade. “Watch your mouth, buddy.”

“It’s okay, Detective,” I said. “That’s just the way he talks. He’s Jesus, remember?”

I took a step closer to Jesus. “You know the man who came with me last time? I thought he was a friend, but he wasn’t. He brought another man to see Joe. Did you see them when they came?”

Jesus’ eyes gave a flicker. He knew what I was talking about. “Did you see Joe go with those men?”

“The good shepherd giveth his life for the sheep,” Jesus intoned.

“What the hell is that supposed to mean?” Carney asked.

“Will you be quiet?” I snapped at him. I turned to Stans. “I think Jesus knows that Joe left with Tony and Frank. He might have tried to stop them, because he knows that Joe is in danger.”

“You mean Joe told him what he knows about the murder?” Stans asked.

“Possibly,” I said. “But I don’t think he’ll tell us anything.”

"We told you before," Carney said. "There is no 'us.' This is a police matter."

"He's right, Ms. Weaver," Stans said. "You've obstructed us more than you've helped. If our witness won't talk to us here, then we'll have to take him down to the station." He gestured to Carney, who moved toward the trail hauling Jesus along by his arm.

"No, please don't take him in," I pleaded.

Carney marched on without pausing, but Stans turned to me. "Don't you think this man should get some help? Out here he's a sitting duck for any kind of exploitation."

"Yes, I think he should get into treatment, but if you take him to the police station, he's just going to be traumatized and withdraw even more into his delusion."

Stans shook his head. "I don't see how he could get any more into it than he is now." He turned and followed Carney down the trail.

I hurried after him. We marched in silence and reached the road a lot faster than Tony and I had. It helped that the trail was now so well traveled. Carney marched up to the police car and opened the back door for Jesus.

"Jesus," I said. "I'm so sorry. Just hang on. I'll tell Libby, and she'll send someone to help you with the detectives' questions."

Jesus lifted his eyes heavenward and said, "Father, forgive them, for they know not what they do."

Carney hustled him into the police car and closed the door. He circled the car and got in behind the wheel. Stans turned to me. "Anything else you haven't told us, Ms. Weaver?"

"You have Tony Dezzutti's address. You should ask him where he took Joe. He knows more than Jesus."

"We'll be talking to him, and to your ex-husband, but right now I want some assurances from you that you've told us everything."

"I have." As soon as I said it, I remembered the

picture. "No, wait. There's one more thing." I pulled the photo out of my shoulder bag without letting Stans get a glimpse of the copy I'd made. "This is the picture Lucianne Lind gave me. Flo had a photograph by her bedside. I think it was taken the same time this one was."

Stans took the snapshot. "Who are the other guys?"

"I don't know. Friends, maybe, or fellow graduate students." Then it hit me. "Wait. The picture. That's what wasn't right about the set-up in Flo's bedroom. She has a framed picture of Stevie by her bed, but she was the one who broke off the relationship, and that was years ago."

"She might have ended it for other reasons. He was a nut case, after all," Stans said.

"But what if she was still in love with him? So much so that when she learns that he's dead, she immediately goes home and kills herself? Why would she put the whiskey bottle in front of the photograph? She'd have held the picture, or at least put it where it would be the last thing she saw."

"Let's wait and see what the Berkeley coroner says. Meanwhile, my partner and I will stick to the unsolved cases we know for sure are homicides."

Carney started the car and revved the engine a couple of times. Letting us know he was impatient, waiting. Stans walked to the passenger side and got in. Jesus sat immobile in the back seat. He looked smaller, almost shrunken into his robes. He didn't turn his head or make any movement as they drove past me and down the road.

I kicked the dirt. A futile gesture, just like everything else I'd done that day. I succeeded only in raising a small cloud of dust that settled in an indistinguishable layer on top of the all the other layers that already coated my shoes.

I got in my car and drove straight to Libby's house. She was home and relieved to see me, since she'd already tried to reach me at work. I gave her the whole story, meeting GI Joe's mom, Tony's betraying me to Frank, my being canned, finding Flo's body, and leading the police to Jesus. She supplied me with a sandwich and a soda. When I finished both my story and the sandwich, she left me long enough to call in a favor on Jesus' behalf.

When she came back into the room, she pointed to two cardboard banker's boxes stacked by the door. "That's also part of your inheritance. Lucianne wanted you to have them right away."

"Stevie's papers?"

She nodded. "I think she hopes you'll publish some of his papers posthumously."

I groaned. "Great. Just what I need. One more person to let down. I can set a world's record for the number of personal failures in a seventy-two hour period."

Libby waved away my defeatism. "Come on. You don't know that there's nothing in there until you look. You owe it to Lucianne at least to try."

"I should have known I wouldn't get any sympathy from you." I stood up. "Come on. Grab a box. We'll drive back to the Center so I can pick up my car. I'm going to drive, though, because I have something more to tell you, and you won't be able to concentrate on driving once I do."

We stacked the boxes in the trunk of Libby's car, and once we were on the road I told her about my plans for giving half of Stevie's money to the mobile clinic. Libby was ecstatic. I just drove and grinned and listened to her roll out her plans. The day wasn't a total flop after all if I could make Libby happy.

I stopped next to my rental car in front of the Center. I transferred Stevie's papers from the trunk of her car to mine, and threw my purse in, too, to save the trouble of doing it when I reached the clinic.

"Meet you there," Libby said with a wave and sped off.

I lingered for a moment, waiting for something, though I didn't know what. The Center was closed down for the evening. It was closed to me for longer than that. I looked away from the metal door and the discreet brass nameplate, got in my car and drove away.

CHAPTER FIFTEEN

I've never been good at moping. I figure I'm a throwback to an earlier generation, because my parents were prize wallowers in self-pity. I've tried wallowing a couple of times, but just ended up feeling bored. Anyway, I woke up the next morning at the usual going-to-work time and got busy with all the yard work I'd been putting off for weeks.

I was already in my front yard, pushing my rusty lawn mower around when Mitch showed up, rolling my new door in front of him on a dolly. "I thought you'd be at work."

"I've been laid off." It wasn't as hard to say it as I'd imagined.

"Sorry." He looked about to say something else on the subject. Instead he said, "Here's your door."

I gave it the once over and said, "Nice," which hardly covered it. Mitch had transformed a paint-encrusted piece of wood into a work of art, the oak grain lustrous and the hand-carved scroll design vivid under a clear finish.

"If you don't like it, I can still get you another."

"Why are you always so touchy? The door's beautiful. It's going to make the rest of the place look shabby by comparison."

"No way. Trust me, it'll look like it came with the house."

"So you're going to put it up now?"

"As soon as a friend of mine comes over to help. He specializes in door hanging. It's sort of an art."

"I'll take your word for it. I'm going to clean up my yard today."

"Yeah? He looked around my front yard with a skeptical eye. Mowed or not, the lawn still consisted more of weeds than grass, and half of the grass part was brown.

"Not to your standards, of course. No one from House and Garden will show up to take photographs."

"Now who's being touchy?" He headed up the driveway pushing the loaded dolly.

His door-hanging friend arrived a few minutes later. I pointed him in Mitch's direction. He was the first of a series of visitors who dropped by while I mowed, trimmed, edged, pruned and weeded.

Tyler rolled up on his skateboard next. "Why aren't you at work?"

"Why aren't you at school?"

"I'm sick," he said and spun the board around while balancing it on the back wheels.

"Me, too." I bent over to unhook the grass catcher from the lawn mower. "Must be something going around."

"Can I have my squirt gun back?"

"Sure. As soon as your dad comes over to get it." I doubted that his dad would ever make an appearance. At some point I'd have to show up at Tyler's house and ask to talk to the dad, assuming he wasn't mythical. I might drop a hint about Frank Avery at the same time.

I headed toward the back yard to dump the lawn clippings on my compost pile. I'd accumulated a huge mound of compost, mainly because I never used any of it.

When I returned to the front yard, Tyler had left and Rose bustled up. "Your yard's looking very nice." She looked good, with color in her face and no anxiety lines showing on her forehead. "Do you think you might put some annuals in the bed along your front porch? Maybe something easy, like marigolds and zinnias?"

Rose had kept up a never-flagging campaign to get me more involved in gardening ever since I'd moved in.

"Sure, sounds good to me." Not that I knew what marigolds and zinnias were. I'd learned the names of a number of trees, but my expertise in identifying smaller plants started and stopped with poison oak. "I was hoping you'd help me with a problem, though. I have way too much compost. Could I bring some over and dig it into your garden this afternoon? Rose was the reason I had compost in the first place. She'd caught me dumping my lawn clippings in the trash several years ago and had given me a lecture about recycling.

"That would be nice. If you're sure you can't use it."

"I have more than enough for both of us." Especially since I wasn't going to go to the trouble to dig it into a flowerbed that would never see a flower. "I'll be over after lunch."

She beamed at me and left me to my lawn edging.

I'd progressed to pruning out dead branches from the Japanese plum trees, reaching up into the branches with my long-handled pruning shears, when Tony Dezzutti showed up, striding across my new-mown lawn. Man with a purpose. He also had a nasty case of poison oak on his neck and arms.

"I hope you're happy," he said with a sneering twist of his mouth to let me know he meant the exact opposite.

I lowered my pruning clippers. "Happy doesn't cover it. I'm thrilled, delighted, ecstatic. And I hope it itches a lot."

He blinked a couple of times before he got what I meant. He folded his arms across his chest. "Thanks to you, I just spent hours being questioned by the police. Made me miss work."

"You're breaking my heart. Why didn't you tell me you knew Frank?"

He did the blinking thing again. "I didn't remember at first who you were. I took a writing class from him four years ago. You showed up after class a couple of times. He introduced you. I didn't know you'd divorced him."

It was my turn to blink. "What? You're a writer? I

was stunned, and it showed.

"Don't sound so surprised," he said, the sneer back in place.

"I'm not surprised, just disappointed. I thought you were an honest working man, with a respectable job."

"Frank was an auto worker before he sold his first book."

"You fell for that? Frank's father was the autoworker. Frank has never done an honest day's work in his life."

Tony let his arms fall to his sides and puffed up his chest. "Frank Avery is a great writer. You're just too envious to admit it."

"I could never be envious of a liar and a cheat, even if his prose was remarkable, which it isn't. I'd warn you away from him, except that your handing Joe over to him proves that you have the ethics of an insect. You're probably just as bad a writer as he is, too."

"Frank was right about you. You're a bitch."

I tightened my grip on the handles of my pruning shears. "Frank's scum, and you're a scum sucker," I countered.

Tony moved toward me, but halted in mid-step. His eyes strayed just past my right shoulder.

"Is there a problem here?" Mitch asked.

"No problem," I said, turning my head to look at him.

He didn't return my gaze. He'd locked onto Tony, giving him the best bad-assed, dead-eyed, I'd-as-soon-kill-you-as-spit stare I'd ever seen. "How about you?" he asked Tony. "You got a problem?"

Tony took a step back. "No problem."

"You were just leaving?"

"Yeah." Tony turned to leave.

"Where'd you take GI Joe?" I called after him.

"Frank took him someplace," he said over his shoulder. "I wouldn't tell you where, even if I knew."

I waited until he reached the sidewalk before I yelled,

"Don't worry too much about that erectile dysfunction. It should clear up as soon as the rash goes away."

"Christ, Alison," Mitch muttered.

Tony slammed into his car and laid noisy rubber driving off.

I turned to Mitch. "Thanks for the back-up, but I had everything under control."

"Yeah, I noticed you'd armed yourself."

"Damn straight. I could've held him off with these, easy." I gestured with the pruning shears.

"I meant the mouth you have on you. Cut a man and leave him bleeding in the street."

"I trained in the old school. Insults R Us."

"What if he'd had a gun in his car?"

"That weenie? Never happen. He was just hoping he had a hanky, because he was about to cry. He's on his way home to mommy right now."

Mitch rubbed the back of his neck. He looked close to smiling. "Hope you never underestimate the opposition. What was his problem, anyway?"

"You were right about him. He knew Frank. He'd taken a writing class from him some years back. He thought I'd be a way for him to meet up with Frank again and get help with his literary career. Some writer he'd make—he can't think of anything more original to call me than 'bitch.'"

Mitch did smile this time, but turned away without further comment. I finished pruning the dead wood, while Mitch received more instruction in door hanging. I clipped and trimmed without stopping for over an hour. The face-off with Tony had freed me from niggling guilt feelings about Joe. The cops would have tracked down Frank by now and made him hand over Joe. He'd be safer in jail than out where Stevie's murderer could get to him.

At mid-day I grabbed a quick sandwich and headed next door to Rose's house. I used her wheelbarrow to haul compost and distribute it around her garden. Rose directed me to add more in some places and less in others and for goodness sake don't run over the tomato plants. As if I would. It helped that she pointed out again what tomato plants look like. They were harder for me to spot at this time of year when they were only a foot tall and didn't have ripe red tomatoes hanging on them.

By late afternoon, all my muscles ached in a pleasant way. I sprawled in one of Rose's rickety lawn chairs, and drank iced tea with her. We were quietly admiring the newly composted flower beds and vegetable garden, when Mitch slipped through a broken part in the hedge that separated my yard from Rose's.

He held out a key ring to me. "Want to try your new front door?" He sounded almost shy. Maybe he still wasn't sure I'd be pleased with it. Funny guy, Mitch the carpenter.

Rose and I hurried over to inspect it, opening the new lock with the shiny key. The door swung in perfect balance on its hinges. Mitch gave all the credit to his friend, the door-hanging artist.

"Yes, but you found the door in the first place. You saw the beauty underneath all that paint, and you transformed it. But, you were wrong about one thing. The rest of the place looks trashy by comparison."

Mitch opened his mouth to speak, but Rose got in first. "Haven't you heard of 'shabby chic?' That's what you have. Now why don't you both come over to my house. We'll sit in my back yard and drink a toast to your new front door."

We drank a toast to the door with iced tea. And then we toasted Rose's newly composted garden. One thing led to another, and somehow we all agreed to a potluck dinner. I brought over a loaf of French bread and some mozzarella. Mitch returned with fruit and a bottle of red wine. Rose made us wait outside while she did some magic in the kitchen. She emerged carrying a huge platter of crostini covered with thick homemade spaghetti sauce and melted mozzarella.

"Normally, I would have made pasta," she said, as Mitch leapt to his feet to take the platter from her. "But Alison will only eat sandwiches."

"I eat pasta, too."

"Between slices of bread," Rose laughed.

I laughed, too, because she was right, and because it felt so good to be sitting with neighbors, eating potluck dinner. I didn't even mind that one of those neighbors was Mitch the carpenter. We drank another toast to my new front door, this time with Mitch's very nice red wine, and proceeded to demolish both the crostini and the fruit. I couldn't have asked for a better escapist experience.

"I saw that you had a visit from that same young man who came by the other day," Rose said. It was a gentle probe for information from a friend, not a nosy neighbor.

"Tony Dezzutti, with two z's and two t's, if you please." I had a nice buzz going from the wine. "He won't be coming back. I should've spotted him for a loser. That stupid goatee is a dead giveaway." I turned to Mitch. "What is it with you guys and facial hair anyway? Frank has that ridiculous bandido mustache, thinks it makes him look like a real kick-ass guy. And the cops—every single one of them has a mustache. I've decided," I waved my glass for emphasis, "that I'll never again trust a man who has more facial hair than I do."

"I don't think you should generalize, dear," Rose said. "You trust Mitch, don't you?"

I studied Mitch for a moment over the rim of my glass, taking in the full beard, long fuzzy blond hair in a pony tail, and baseball cap pulled down to his eyebrows. "Okay, Mitch, you can be the exception to the rule. Besides, I don't think you're trying to look like something you're not. You're just hiding out." It was an *in vino veritas* moment. Mitch dropped his gaze. Rose went rigid in her seat. I'd hit a nerve I hadn't even been aiming at. Worse yet, I'd broken some unwritten law of hospitality and nearly destroyed the cloud of good feeling we'd all been floating on.

I'd underestimated Mitch's toughness, though. "You're right." He lifted his gaze to meet mine. "Any man who hangs out around you needs to keep a low profile." He turned to Rose. "First time I met her, she was holding off two men with a butcher knife."

Rose chuckled. "If one of them was Frank Avery, a little butter knife would have worked just as well."

Rose didn't harbor any good opinions of Frank. She'd seen him bringing women into our house when I was at work, and in her mind that made him a "no good," the bottom rung of her ladder of esteem. We all smiled at Rose's image of Frank shrinking in fear from a butter knife, and then the conversation slid onto more neutral topics. We lingered until the sun went down and I could just make out their faces in the gloom. It was time to go home.

I stacked our empty glasses on the equally empty platter and moved to carry them inside. Mitch tried to take the platter from me, and we had a silent tug-of-war until Rose shooed us away.

"Go home, both of you." She jerked the platter from my hands. "The day I can't carry a plate into my own house will be the day they carry me out of here. Feet first."

"Let me help with the dishes," I said.

"I don't want you messing about in my kitchen. Besides it's past my bedtime, and you're keeping me up."

She let Mitch open the back door for her and called "good night" to us from inside her kitchen.

"Good night. See you tomorrow," I called back. I turned to Mitch. "She likes her independence. Thanks again for the great job you did on my door. You want to give me the bill now or tomorrow?

"Tomorrow's soon enough."

We walked single file along the side of Rose's house to the front sidewalk. Mitch came to a sudden halt and I nearly bumped into him. He turned to face me, opened his mouth, closed it, lowered his head and studied his boots for a minute. "Don't take offense, okay? But if you need a loan or anything, I'm good for it."

"Why would I need... " I stopped in mid-sentence as it sunk in. "You mean because I lost my job? Thanks for the thought, but I'm fine. I'm an RN. I can get work any time I want."

"Mrs. Fiorelli said you were a student."

"I'm that, too. I just need to write my dissertation, and I'll have a PhD in public health. My job was supposed to give me the data I needed for my dissertation, but now… " I left the sentence unfinished.

"That's tough."

"I'll live. Thanks for the offer, though."

"You and Mrs. Fiorelli are two of kind, aren't you? You both like your independence."

"Let's say I've learned to prefer it to the alternative."

"What's the alternative?"

"Thinking you can depend on anyone else."

He didn't have anything to say to that. Just stood there looking at me, though I'm not sure he could really see my face very clearly in the dark.

Whether he could see me or not, it made me feel uncomfortable. I said, "See you," and headed up the walkway to my house. It was fairly dark now. I hadn't left my porch light on, and the entire front of the house lay in shadows. I could have gone around to the back door where the lights would come on automatically, but why would I do that now that I had a front door?

I had the answer two seconds later, when someone rushed out at me from the shadows and knocked me to the ground. I went down head first, breaking the fall as best I could with my hands. I tucked myself into a ball as soon as I hit the ground and rolled over twice. I dug in with my toes and sprang into a crouching stance. The next attack came instantly, but I was ready. I kept my head down, aimed my fists for a belly-punch, and drove out my attacker's breath and momentum at the same time. I did the leg-sweep I'd learned in self-defense class, but instead of running away, as I'd been taught, I went down on top, ready to start punching again at the sign of any resistance. No one mugged me in my own front yard and got away with it.

Running feet behind me, coming up the driveway. "Alison!" Mitch shouted. "You all right?"

"Yeah. Someone tried to jump me. I need a light here."

Mitch moved away and, in a second, the sensor light over my gate came on. Even with only indirect illumination, I could clearly make out Gina Lind's angry face. She made little frog croaks in her throat.

"What's the matter with her?" Mitch bent over for a closer look.

"Probably a character disorder. I'd guess something along the lines of a narcissistic personality." I shifted from lying full-length on her to straddling her so I could get a good grip on her wrists.

"She doesn't look so good. Should I call an ambulance?"

"No. I hit her in the solar plexus. She's trying to breathe. Getting a little panicky now." I watched Gina's eyes. "If I weren't so pissed off at her for trying to beat me up, I'd tell her to relax. Her body will remember how to suck in air before she passes out."

"You know her?"

"She's Stevie Number's sister. Gina Lind. Be grateful she can't talk right now, because she only speaks in curses and obscenities."

Gina took a long, squeaky inhalation of air and immediately began to struggle to free her wrists. I shifted my grip to her forearms and pressed on the brachial nerve. She had wrapped one hand in terrycloth, maybe that was her equivalent of a boxing glove. Hadn't done her a lot of good.

"Let go, you fucking bitch," Gina said, still struggling. She turned her head and looked at Mitch. "Help me. She's hurting me."

"Mitch," I said, "do me a favor. Go sit on my front steps. Gina and I need to have a private conversation."

"Anything to be of help," he said with more irony than I expected of him.

I waited until Mitch was out of earshot and said quietly. "Pay attention. Your arms are starting to go numb. If you answer my questions quickly with no swearing at me, I'll let you up, and the numbness will go away. If you stay like this very long, though, you'll incur permanent nerve damage. You don't want that, do you? I didn't mention that it would take many hours before that happened. In this case, her ignorance was my bliss.

Gina continued to struggle, but with a little less force. "What the fuck are you doing to my arms?"

"I said, no swearing, remember? And, did you see that man who was asking about you? He didn't help you, and he won't. In fact, he's my bodyguard. His middle name is Rottweiler, if you get my drift. So start answering now. Why did you attack me?"

"You deserved it. Let go, you're hurting me."

"Wrong answer. Start worrying when it doesn't hurt anymore, because then, you'll be permanently paralyzed. Tell me what you're doing here."

"She should never have given you Stephen's papers. They don't belong to you. He wanted me to have them."

"He didn't put you in his will."

"He told me after... " she hesitated. "He said I could have his journal, and I want it."

"He told you after he wrote his will? When?"

"The week before he died."

"You saw him? Where?" I shook her by her arms. I would have pinched the nerves harder, but my hands were beginning to tire.

"At Daddy's office, when he came to get his money. Daddy had to go out of town. He asked me to give Stephen his money."

"What did he say? He didn't just say, 'oh by the way, you can have my journal after I die,' did he?"

"He said he was getting a job."

"Where?"

"Where do you think? Nowhere. Who'd hire him? He was crazy. He'd couldn't get a job flipping burgers."

"Is that what you told him?"

She didn't answer.

"What else did he say? Come on, tell me."

"He wanted me to tell Mother. He thought she'd agree to see him if she knew he had a job."

"What? She'd have seen him job or no job. You knew that, too. Did you tell him that Lucianne would have done anything to have seen him?"

No answer again. Disgust and dislike rose up in me like bile. I breathed in and out slowly to clear my head. I wouldn't get any information out of her if I couldn't think straight enough to ask the next question.

"Why did he say you could have his journal? In fact, why would he want to give you anything?"

"He said I'd always been special to him, that he'd written about me in his journal, and I could have it after he died."

"Did you kill him?"

"No. Did you?"

"No." I loosened my grip and stood up. "I was his friend, which is more than I can say for you."

She sat up, rubbed her arms and flexed her fingers. "You'll never see any of his money." She struggled to her feet.

I took a step back in case she decided to go on the offensive again. "That money is intended for two very good causes. I don't care if it happens through me, or through the family. But, if you try to interfere, I'll tell Lucianne that you deliberately kept Stevie from seeing her."

"And I'll tell her you're a fucking liar."

"Go ahead. Who do you think she'll believe?"

Gina's shoulders sagged. "You don't understand," she whined. "He was always the star, the genius. I could never compete. Even when he was crazy, she always paid more attention to him than to me."

I thought of Gina's life of wealth and privilege. She

could have had anything, done anything. "You're right. I don't understand."

She took my words the way she wanted, rather than the way they were meant, and with an arrogant tilt of her chin, said, "So, where are his papers?"

"You want all of his papers, or just the journal?"

"Might as well give them all to me."

"I'll think about it and let you know."

She made a movement toward me. I held out my arm like a crossing guard. "Stop right there. Don't make me hurt you. Go home."

She glared at me for a long few seconds, thinking it over, before she turned around and stomped off. As if on cue, the light over my back gate switched off. After the glare of the outdoor light, the darkness seemed total.

"Can I go home now?" Mitch asked from his perch on the front steps.

I turned and headed in the direction of his voice. "I'm sorry. I forgot you were there."

He sighed. "That's the life of a bodyguard. Hang around for hours, waiting for your chance to take a bullet for someone, and they forget you're there."

"I didn't mean for you to hear that. I was only trying to get information out of her."

"I know."

"I don't really think of you as a bodyguard, even if you did stare down Tony."

"I know."

"Okay. Just as long as you know." My eyes had adjusted to the dark, and I made my way past Mitch, up the stairs of my front porch. I felt in my pocket for the new key and fitted it into the lock. The key turned smoothly, the lock clicked open, and the door handle yielded to the pressure of my hand.

"By the way," he said from the bottom of the steps. "My middle name isn't Rottweiler. It's Stanton."

I turned around. "Yeah? Mine isn't Rottweiler, either. It's Pit Bull. Good night." I stepped inside without waiting for him to reply. I closed the door and turned the lock. It felt so good to be home safe in my own house. Which just goes to show you how wrong a person can be.

CHAPTER SIXTEEN

I'd forgotten to leave a light on. No matter, I could find my way around blindfolded. I crossed the living room to switch on the lamp and banged my shin on something hard. What the hell? I felt around in the dark. For some reason, the table that usually held the lamp lay on its side in the middle of the living room. I stumbled to the kitchen, flipped on the wall switch, and all became clear. Someone had broken in and trashed my house. The lamp I'd tried to find in the dark had been smashed against the fireplace.

I held still and listened. I was pretty sure that whoever it had been was gone now. No sound of movement or breathing. Even so, I moved cautiously into my bedroom, turned on the overhead and inspected the damage. The dresser drawers lay helter skelter on the floor, the contents dumped in a pile. The bedclothes were torn apart, and the mattress pulled half off the box springs.

The tiny second bedroom that I used as a study was in even worse shape. Every folder and sheet of paper from my metal file cabinet had been strewn across the floor, along with the contents of my desk drawers. Books had been swept off the shelves, and my computer monitor, screen fractured, rested on top of the books.

A cool breeze wafted across my face. I lifted my gaze to what was left of the study window. Shards of glass glinted from the windowsill and more on the floor. They'd come through one of the few windows with working sash cords that wasn't painted shut. But why? Not to steal, that was certain. The computer was just about the only possession of monetary value that I owned, so why wreck it? It was sickening to think that someone simply wanted to smash all my belongings. Literally sickening. My stomach gave a warning heave.

I moved quickly to the bathroom and leaned over the sink. The heaves stopped, thank God. I didn't want to add vomit to the mess I had to clean up. The medicine cabinet gaped open, empty. The contents lay in the sink. And something else, too--blood. Not a lot. Just about as much as someone would get from cutting her hand on a broken window. Gina had had a piece of terrycloth wrapped around her hand. I looked around. Naturally, no towels remained on the rack, so I sifted through the pile on the floor and found the other half of the hand towel she'd taken.

I'd been about to phone the police, but now I needed to think. I put everything back in the medicine cabinet. When I swung the cabinet door shut, I found a message lipsticked on the mirror--Fuck you. That had a familiar ring to it. Gina had wanted Stevie's papers back, and she hadn't planned on asking nicely, either. She hadn't planned on asking at all. And, when she hadn't found what she wanted, she trashed my house and lurked outside until I came home. Lucky for her I hadn't known about my vandalized house when I'd had her pinned down on the front lawn. I grabbed a handful of toilet paper and scrubbed the mirror until no trace remained. I'd do the same with the whole house. Eventually.

The clean mirror reflected my grubby and bruised face. A bleeding scrape on my chin had dirt embedded in it. I found a fresh washcloth from the pile on the floor and cleaned the abrasion with soap and water. Each dab of the washcloth set off waves of wincing pain, which was fine with me, because it helped clear my head.

I wouldn't report the break-in to the police. Not that I'd mind seeing Gina in jail, but I couldn't do it to Lucianne. I could find out what Gina was after, though. I stopped dabbing at the still oozing scrape on my chin and stared at my reflection. What if I found out that she'd killed her brother? Or had him killed? I gave my head a shake. I'd make myself crazy if I thought too much about those possibilities. I'd deal with it—once I knew what it was I had to deal with.

I took a quick and badly needed shower. My sore muscles would have liked a long soak, but if I gave in to that wish, I'd have fallen right to sleep. I needed to stay awake. The sooner I figured out what Gina was looking for, the better for me. I wasn't going to be blindsided again.

I dressed in clean jeans and a sweatshirt, closed the door to the study, ignored the living room, and did a minimal straightening of the bedroom and the kitchen. I brought in both boxes of Stevie's papers from the car and set up office on my kitchen table.

I made a pot of coffee and a sandwich and settled down to see if I could find what Gina had been looking for—if she'd told the truth about what she wanted, and that was a big "if." First I sifted through a large stack of manila folders, each one neatly labeled, containing notes, tests and papers from both undergraduate and graduate classes he'd taken at Berkeley.

Next came a smaller group of typewritten formal papers with his name and the date, but no course number. They had titles like, "Probability and Fractal Measures." There were comments written on them, but no grade. Paperclipped to each of these papers were pages of handwritten equations.

At a guess, I'd say these represented work he'd done on his own ideas. I'd never shied away from math classes, but these papers were way beyond my level of comprehension. I thumbed through the pages a second time and came across a note from Stevie to a Professor Lang, asking for an appointment. Lang had written in a time at the bottom and signed it "Hal." Maybe I should try to find this professor and see if he could tell me whether these papers were publishable or not.

Then I came to the computer printouts. These were even more impenetrable for me than Stevie's formal papers. I'd used the computer every day in my work at the Center, where we used specialized software programs like SPSS and SAS to test hypotheses about environmental influences on health. I could read those printouts the way other people read the newspaper, but not these. I didn't recognize the software program used, the procedures or the results. I'd need to get help with these, too. Stevie had made a big mistake leaving his papers to me. If I didn't get a lot of expert help, I'd never know what any of it meant.

I paged through the printouts, letting my eye drift across each page without much hope of understanding any of it on my own. At page six, I nearly jumped out of my chair. The letters RBPCE headed a column of numbers. The same letters from the hand-printed page Stans had found in the trunk of my car. I'd sat at this very table staring at those letters while Stans probed for answers I didn't have.

All along, I'd thought the paper had come from the Center's recycling. What had Stans said? Never assume. Okay, so now I wasn't assuming—I was simply completely confused. Why were the pages left with Stevie's body? Would anyone have even noticed them, if I hadn't used them to cover Stevie's face? Maybe no one was supposed to notice them.

The date on the top of the printout was in the same time frame as Stevie's last papers as a graduate student. So none of it was recent. I went through the entire printout again, to see if there was anything I might have missed. Finally, the print began to run together before my eyes. Time to stop.

I repacked the boxes and left them on the kitchen table. I kept out the computer printouts and the formal papers. These I put into two large manila envelopes, which I hid in the clothes dryer. As an afterthought, I stuffed the dryer full of dirty laundry, just in case anyone thought of looking in there. There was no reason to think that Gina had been searching for these particular papers, but I hid them anyway. Put it down to justifiable paranoia.

The broken window in my study presented the next barrier to peaceful sleep. It was just my rotten luck that Gina had picked a functioning window. Now that the glass was broken, the lock on it was useless. I secured it by hammering a nail at an angle through the sash into the frame. It didn't solve the problem of the broken pane of glass, but an intruder would have to break all the rest of the glass out of the sash before squeezing through the opening. As an added barrier, I closed the study door and jammed a chair under the doorknob.

I finally lay down fully clothed, not even bothering to take off my shoes, and pulled a blanket up to my chin. If I hadn't been so bone weary, I would have stayed up all night and dealt with the mess. As it was, I couldn't sleep. My body craved rest, but my mind wouldn't shut down. Never mind that I lectured myself over and over that Gina was long gone and wouldn't be back, I continued floating around in that weird space between sleep and wake for a long time, never falling off the edge into unconsciousness.

That was why I heard the turn of the key in the back door lock and the creak of the loose floorboard as someone stepped inside. It just went to show me how little I'd actually been expecting another break-in. I'd been playing around with little imagined terrors, like watching a movie about a maniac with a chain saw. If I'd really expected an intruder, I'd have prepared myself better. As it was, I froze in my bed and tried to turn my body into a giant ear so I could hear him coming.

I knew it had to be a man by the sound of his footsteps. Not Gina this time. Either a man, or a very large woman—the floorboards in the kitchen only creaked if a person weighed over two hundred pounds. But who, I couldn't imagine. Someone with a key. Frank? He could have kept a key after the divorce, the slime, but Frank never crept in anywhere. It was always the grand, look-at-me entrance for Frank.

Whoever it was, he kept still for a full minute before he moved toward my bedroom. Toward me. Too late it hit me that I should have taken that minute to get the hell out. I rolled off the mattress and tried to slide under the bed, just as I used to do when foster dad number three came home raging drunk looking to inflict pain on someone, preferably someone small and helpless. Only I wasn't small anymore, and the bed frame was too low for me to get under and hide.

That was where he found me two seconds later, one arm under the bed up to the shoulder, the rest of me exposed to the beam of his flashlight. His head was a black shape behind the dazzle of the light, but from his size alone, I could tell it wasn't Frank. I shifted my gaze away from the light and saw that he held some kind of long stick in his other hand.

"Huh?" he said, as if to himself. I didn't know if he was more surprised to see that I was on the floor or to see that I was awake. Surprised or not, he didn't hesitate to try to whack me on the head with the stick. The bedframe and the mattress blocked him from getting a direct shot, but even so the glancing blow that he managed to give me hurt and made little lights flash on and off behind my eyes.

I pressed my body harder into the narrow space between floor and bedframe, groping with my hand under the bed to get a purchase and pull myself further underneath. My hand found Tyler's squirt gun where I'd left it about a century ago. My brain had completely forgotten about it. In fact, I think the brain is a highly over-rated organ, because nothing I did after that arose from rational thought.

The man lifted the stick to give me another crack on the head, but I didn't give the bastard a second chance. What if I wasn't small enough to fit under the bed anymore? That meant I wasn't helpless, either, and no drunken son of a bitch was going to beat me up again. I clutched Tyler's squirt gun and rolled away from the bed and the man. I scrambled to my feet, and pointed the gun at him. It gave a reassuring gurgle as I lifted it.

"Back off or I'll shoot."

I know he saw the gun, because he dipped the flashlight toward it. Maybe he didn't believe I'd actually shoot, or else he knew a toy gun when he saw one. Whatever the case, before I could even blink, he swung at me, and I squeezed the trigger. His weapon connected at a point just below my right elbow. My arm went agonizingly paralytic, and the water pistol slipped from my fingers.

I backed against the wall, looking for a way to dodge the next blow, but instead of hitting me, he screamed and dropped both the stick and the flashlight. What was he yelling about? I was the one whose arm hurt like hell. I kicked the stick aside and dove for the light. I had to hold it in my left hand, because my right arm wouldn't obey instructions.

"My eyes, my eyes," the man howled. I tried to track him with the light as he staggered around the room, moaning, his hands cupped over his face.

"Oh God, my eyes. I can't see. Help. What is it? Acid?"

"Bleach, you stinking creep, and you're just lucky it wasn't a bullet." I finally managed to get him in the beam of the flashlight.

He jumped as if I'd touched him. "Get away from me." He headed in the direction of the bedroom doorway, but at the wrong angle and collided with the wall instead. He reached out with his hands to regain his balance.

I pointed the light at his face and just stared. I recognized him. I couldn't put a name to his face, but I'd seen him before. "I know you, don't I? What's your name? Why did you attack me?"

He turned away from me and groped towards the door.

"Stop," I said, to no visible effect. In fact, my words seemed to spur him on. He must have had vision in at least one eye, because he moved faster and with more certainty toward the kitchen. I followed him as far as the back steps. He hadn't bothered to close the door on his way in and now ran straight out, across the backyard and scrambled noisily over the fence, before I could think of any possible way of stopping him.

I remained rooted in the doorway for several long seconds while pain, terror, nausea and light-headedness held a tag-team wrestling match in my head. I stood, unable to move as long as none of the competing feelings looked like a decided winner. I was going to have to do something, but what?

"When in doubt, breathe." Good old words of advice from a mentor I'd had as a student nurse. I took a deep breath in and let it out slowly. That put nausea and light-headedness on the ropes, leaving pain and terror to duke it out. I figured that my arm might hurt less if I could support it somehow, rather than let it hang at my side. I put the flashlight down, and lifted my lower right arm, cradling it in my left hand. I felt rather than heard a grinding along the bone, and pain pinned terror to the mat.

Pain aids concentration in the most amazing way. The only problem for me was that I could focus only on one thing—how much my arm hurt. I leaned against the doorjamb and did the breathing thing again. A new focus came into my mind—get help. I moved backward one step and tried to fish my keys out of the fruit bowl on the kitchen counter. A tricky maneuver since I was still using my left arm to support my right. I solved that problem by pulling the bottom of my sweatshirt over my arm and tucking the hem into my jeans to make a sling of sorts. I grabbed my keys, pulled the back door shut behind me and headed towards help, which in my mind had a full beard and wore a baseball cap pulled down to his eyebrows.

Mitch took his time answering the front door. I stood in the glare of his porch sensor light and alternately pushed the doorbell and kicked the door. He pulled the door open and stood on the threshold, wearing jeans and nothing else. His hair, freed from ponytail and baseball cap, surrounded his face and fell to his shoulders like a frizzy blond aura.

"Alison? Something wrong?"

"You're not bald." The words just slipped out—inane and inappropriate.

He squinted at me and passed his hand over the top of his head, as if checking out if I was right. "You woke me up to tell me I still had hair?"

"No. I need help."

"What's the matter?" He stepped back and waved me

inside.

I crossed over the threshold into Mitch's front hall. "My arm's broken. I think. I'm pretty sure. Would you drive me to the emergency room? Please?" I added.

His gaze went straight to my arm, suspended in the sweatshirt sling. "Come in. I'll need a second to get dressed." He led me into his living room and switched on a floor lamp. "Sit down." He waited until I sat before he crossed quickly to his bedroom.

I smiled to myself. Good old Mitch. No wasted words. No fuss. Just the way I liked it. The pain in my arm went up a notch for some reason. I squeezed my eyes shut and breathed. As soon as my eyelids closed, a movie came on in my brain. A slo-mo replay of me pointing the gun at the man and shooting. I groaned.

"Hey," Mitch said softly.

I opened my eyes and found Mitch crouched in front of me, looking worried. "Maybe I should call an ambulance."

I shook my head. "I tried to kill someone tonight."

"That how you broke your arm?"

"He hit me with on the arm with a stick, and I pulled the trigger at the same time."

"Where were you?"

"In my bedroom."

"Was this someone you had over? Or… "

"He sort of broke in. He had a key, but where'd he get the key? That's what I don't get."

"Was it Frank, or that other guy, the one you insulted?"

"Not Tony, or Frank, either. I didn't know him, but I recognized his face. I just can't remember where I've seen him before."

"You're saying he broke in and attacked you?"

I nodded and closed my eyes. The slo-mo replay started up again. I forced my eyes open. "I can't believe I could have messed up that much."

"Don't beat yourself up about it. Anyone could have missed in those circumstances."

"That's what I'm talking about. I didn't miss."

"Where'd you hit him?"

"In the face."

"So he's at your place?"

"No, he ran away."

Mitch sat back on his heels. "Run that by me again. You shot someone in the face, and he could still run away?"

"It wasn't a gun with bullets. It was a water pistol I'd taken away from Tyler."

"A water pistol! Jesus, you had me going there. You said you tried to kill him."

"I did. I would have if it had been a real gun."

"But you didn't."

"You don't get it. I really hurt him. I'd added some bleach to the water. I hit him in the eyes with it and might have blinded him permanently."

Mitch raked his fingers through his hair as he took in this bit of information. "You didn't call the police?"

"No. They'll call the police at the hospital. If I call from here, it'll take me all night before I can get my arm set."

"Okay, I'm ready. Let's go."

"Wait. I'll never get past the front desk without my insurance card." I held out my keys to him. "My shoulder bag is locked in the trunk of my car."

He nodded, took the keys and headed out the door with a quick, "Be right back."

It was hard to concentrate on breathing and not gritting my teeth against the pain. I couldn't close my eyes without seeing myself shoot the man in the face. I didn't really remember him hitting me. I just remembered wanting to kill him, meaning to kill him.

Mitch came back with my bag. He held onto it and stood gazing at me for a moment. "Anything else you need before we go? Something to wear home?"

I blinked at him.

"Won't they cut off your sweatshirt?" he asked.

I blinked again. My mind seemed to be having a hard time taking things in. "You're right, and this is my favorite sweatshirt, too."

He nodded and crossed to his bedroom. He returned with a polar fleece jacket and a sweatshirt. "You look cold. Lean forward," he said and wrapped the jacket around me. He gently slipped my good arm into the sleeve and zipped me up.

"We'd better get going." He stepped back and let me get myself up from the chair.

I tried to move without grimacing, taking my time. Mitch didn't seem antsy when it took me several tries to get on my feet, and he didn't hover, thank God. We made it outside to his truck without me making a fool of myself, though by the time he'd buckled me in, I was at risk for TMJ syndrome from grinding my back teeth.

He must have started his truck when he went out to get my purse, because the motor was already running. Once he'd settled himself in the driver's seat, he fiddled with some buttons on the control panel, and a blast of warm air enveloped me. The warmth was balm. I hadn't realized how cold I was. I let my eyes drift shut, and the damn replay started up again. I willed my eyes open and stared through the windshield the rest of the way.

When we turned the corner on Webster, and Alta Bates Hospital rose up at the end of the block, I said to Mitch, "You can just pull up into that circular drive and let me off."

"Don't you think you can walk?"

"I can walk."

"Then I'll go into the parking lot across the street, because that driveway's an ambulance lane. They won't let me leave the truck there." He turned into the brightly illuminated patients' parking lot, nearly empty now in the dark hours before dawn.

"What I meant is that you don't have to come in with me."

He pulled into a parking space and turned off the engine. I fumbled left-handed with the unfamiliar seat belt release.

"Need help with that seat belt?" He reached over to press the button for me.

I batted his hand away. "I can do it," I snapped. I continued to struggle with it, unable to get the right degree of pressure with my left hand. I finally had to admit defeat. "Okay, you do it."

He pushed the release without comment.

"I could do it, but probably not before the sun came up. I meant it, though, about you not having to come in. I'll be fine. It'll be morning soon, and I'll be in there for hours."

"If you'd just wanted to be dropped off, you could've called a taxi. You asked me to take you to the hospital. I figure that means all the way inside. Now why won't you let me do it?"

"You're right. I'm not too rational right now. I'll be okay just as soon as I... as I... " I stopped. I'd never be okay, if I couldn't stop my mental movie. "I can't get over the fact that I did such an awful thing."

"You were defending yourself."

"I wanted to kill him."

"No one will blame you."

"I blame myself. I got him mixed up with foster dad number three. He used to come home late, drunk, and beat the shit out of us for no reason except that he liked to cause us pain. I'd hide under the bed where he couldn't get to me. And, it's the dumbest thing, but that's what I tried to do tonight. Only I couldn't fit, and he hit me on the head. I found the gun under the bed, and I think I went a little nuts."

Mitch cocked his head to one side. "You have a bump right there." He brushed a finger along my temple. "Does it hurt?"

My head hurt, but not as much as my arm, so I hadn't paid any attention to it. "I can't stop seeing myself shoot the guy in the face, knowing I was going to hurt him. It just wasn't me—but it was me, you know?"

"Yes, I know."

I believed him, though I couldn't have said why. I fumbled with the door handle.

"Wait a second." He reached across me to open the glove compartment. "I want to give you my cell phone number." He pulled out a stubby pencil and a small notepad.

"You have a cell phone?"

He patted a small leather case on his belt. "Right here."

"I thought that was some carpenter's thing, like a really big tape measure."

"It is a carpenter's thing." He jotted on the paper, tore off the sheet, and handed it to me. "Can you tuck that in your pocket? Have them call me when you're ready to go home. Okay?"

"Okay."

Mitch got out, came around and opened the door for me. I lowered myself out of the pickup, and we headed toward the brightly lit emergency room entry. A uniformed policeman stood just inside the glass doors. Mitch bent his head toward me. "When you talk to the police, just tell them what happened, not what you were thinking."

It was good advice, but as it turned out, I found it quite easy to keep my thoughts to myself. Alta Bates Hospital was just two blocks over the line into Berkeley. As soon as the Berkeley cops found out that the crime had taken place in Oakland, they stopped listening and put in a call to Oakland police headquarters. The Oakland uniformed cops didn't show up until I'd been examined and x-rayed. By that time, my arm hurt so much I could speak only through clenched teeth.

They took down my attacker's physical description, gave each other knowing glances when I told them that the attacker had entered by key, raised their eyebrows when I admitted I'd put bleach in the squirt gun, and nodded in agreement when I suggested alerting all the local emergency rooms. I also told them that they should contact Stans and Carney in homicide, because I was pretty sure that the attack was related to Stevie's death.

When they started asking for more details, I grimaced and pointed to my bruised and swollen arm. They backed off and let the transport orderly wheel me away to the casting room, where I waited in isolation until an anesthesiologist could be located. I'd mentioned that I was an RN in hopes that I'd get some preferential treatment. Pretty selfish of me, I supposed, and it didn't work anyway. At any rate, I had plenty of time to think about what had happened. And why. Finally, a nurse showed up and started an IV drip of saline and Demerol.

The anesthesiologist arrived, inserted a long needle into my armpit and injected anesthesia into the brachial plexus to deaden the nerves to my arm. With the stage set, the orthopedist breezed in. He whipped the x-rays onto the viewing screen and gave them a ten second inspection. "You have a clean break. A nice clean break," he pronounced, as if I'd made a special achievement. It didn't matter to me one way or another. Between the nerve block in my right arm and the IV dripping Demerol into my left, I literally and figuratively was feeling no pain, and I told him so when he tested the effectiveness of the nerve block by tapping along my lower arm.

"No pain? No pain at all? Good. Good." He had a tic of saying everything twice, which for some reason struck me as very funny.

"No pain. No pain," I said from somewhere inside my narcotic cloud and giggled.

He lifted his gaze and let it rest on my face, as if he'd just discovered that my arm was in fact connected to a person. "She has a lump on her right temple." He glanced up at the nurse. "What's the evaluation on that? What's her neuro status?"

The nurse stopped prepping the casting materials

and quickly shuffled through my chart. "She didn't report it," she said still scanning the chart.

"Run a neuro exam. Give me a preliminary neuro." He barked, "Now! Stat!" when the nurse didn't instantly respond. "And stop the Demerol drip. No Demerol."

"Oh hell, you're going to stop the Demerol? And I was just beginning to enjoy myself, enjoy myself." I giggled again.

The nurse checked my pupillary reactivity and my reflexes and asked me stupid questions to assess my neurological status. I'm pretty sure that I answered everything correctly, but I may have affected the assessment by having another fit of the giggles when I tried to describe how I came to get whacked on the head. In the end, the orthopedist proceeded with the closed reduction of the break in my radius.

I wasn't giggling by the time I was wheeled out of the emergency room with a small envelope containing a starter dose of Vicodan clutched in my good hand. The nurse had helped me into Mitch's sweatshirt, cutting a little way up the seam of the right sleeve to accommodate the width of the cast. The sling pulled uncomfortably at the back of my neck, and little twinges of pain bit through the fast-disappearing anesthesia of the nerve block in my arm.

A hospital volunteer had phoned Mitch for me. As she pushed me down the hallway in a wheelchair, she told me he would meet me outside in the patient pick-up zone. But when she wheeled me out, all I saw was a good-looking clean-cut blond guy, leaning against Mitch's truck with his hands in his pockets, like a model in a jeans ad. He noticed me, smiled and pushed away from the truck. "How's the arm?"

I lurched out of the wheel chair. "Mitch? Is that you?

What happened to your beard and your hair?"

"I decided it was time for a change." He opened the door of the pickup for me.

I stood rooted to the spot, staring at him. The volunteer said something I didn't catch, because I couldn't stop looking at Mitch. It was so weird. I'd tried to imagine what he'd look like without the beard and the baseball cap, but I hadn't come close.

"Need help getting in?"

"No." I climbed into the truck.

He closed the door, circled the truck and slid into the driver's seat. "What's that?" He pointed to the small envelope in my hand.

"Painkiller for when I get home." I shifted my hips and pushed the envelope into my jeans. "You decided, just like that, and went out and got it cut?"

"Decided last night. Went out this morning while I was waiting to hear back from you."

I couldn't stop staring at him.

"You don't like it?" He rubbed the back of his neck, where his ponytail used to be.

"You look pretty good," I said in deliberate understatement. "You just don't look like you."

"I'm not used to it yet myself." He reached behind the seat, pulled out his A's baseball cap, and jammed it onto his head. "That any better?" he asked.

"No, but I'm not a reliable judge. I'm still coming down from all the drugs they gave me."

"And that's on top of no sleep and no food, right?" He started the engine. "We'll take care of the food part right now."

I didn't argue with him. Too tired, too hungry, and too spaced out even to talk, I let my head rest against the seat and went along for the ride. Mitch stopped at the College Avenue Café and told me to wait, as if I could do anything else. He came out in a short minute, carrying a bag, which he put carefully on the seat between us. The bag filled the truck with good smells.

"Their special BLT, side of potato salad, some other extras." He nodded toward the bag. "That okay?"

"They had it ready for you?"

"I called ahead. Go ahead, dig in." He pulled out of

the parking space, headed up College, and hit the light at Claremont just before it turned yellow.

"Mitch?"

"Yeah?"

"What's going on?"

"What do you mean?"

"You're acting weird."

"If you don't like BLT's, just say so."

I let my head fall back against the headrest, too tired to pursue it. Mitch pulled the truck over to the curb. "Now what?"

"Cops." A black and white with its lights flashing, but no siren, streaked by. Mitch pulled out as soon as they passed. The police car turned at my street, which gave me a bad feeling. It must have hit Mitch the same way, because he pressed down on the accelerator. When we turned the corner, I could see the police car, lights still flashing, parked in front of my house. An unmarked car was already there. Two uniformed cops and my old friends Stans and Carney stood conferring on the front sidewalk.

Mitch pulled into his driveway. No sooner had he turned off the engine, than another police vehicle came into sight from the other direction. Mitch helped me with the seatbelt, and I opened the door, slid to the ground and hurried across the street. The cops had split up, the uniformed guys staying on the sidewalk, Carney going to the unmarked car, and Stans heading up my front walk. Why was my front door open? I sure as hell didn't leave it like that.

"Sorry ma'am, but you can't go past here," one of the uniforms said to me.

"Yes, I can. I live here." I walked past him. "Hey, Stans," I called out.

Stans turned around.

I walked up to him. "What's going on?"

"You had some trouble here last night, I hear."

"I told the cops at the hospital to let you know. Did

you find the guy?"

"We think so."

"Is he okay?"

He shook his head.

"Oh God," I groaned. The last wisps of mind-altering narcotic evaporated. Nothing remained to blunt reality. I'd blinded someone. How would I live with myself?

"Where is he?"

Stans jerked his head toward my house.

"He came back here? What an idiot. Did you call the paramedics? Get him to a hospital. Maybe they can still do something."

"It's way too late for that."

"What the hell are you talking about?" I tried to go past him, but he blocked my way. I feinted left, moved right, and jogged by him up the front steps.

"Ms. Weaver, don't go in there."

I didn't go into my house. Not because Stans had ordered me to stay out, but because of who I saw through the open doorway, sitting in the middle of my living room with a knife in his chest—Frank Avery, formerly my ex-husband, now my late ex-husband.

CHAPTER SEVENTEEN

I stood on the threshold, transfixed by Frank's blind, staring eyes and the horror of the knife in his chest. A dim buzzing started up in my ears. The porch vibrated with Stans' heavy tread as he approached. He came to a stop next to me. "Ms. Weaver?"

I shifted my gaze to his face. Any excuse to look away.

"Is this the man who attacked you?"

I shook my head.

Stans said something like "Are you all right?" but I couldn't be sure. The buzzing in my ears was too loud.

"I can't hear you," I said. Or, at least, I think that was what I said. Stans looked startled and stared at me, so possibly the words came out a little funny. I stared right back, stretching my eyes as wide open as possible, because the light had dimmed, and it was hard to see clearly. And then, for some reason, my legs decided to stop holding me up, and things got a little confused, with Stans gripping me by my upper arms, his voice urgent, someone else grabbing me under the armpits from behind.

The next thing I knew, they had me seated on my front step with my head between my knees. I tried to sit up and pushed against the hand on the back of my head. "Let me up. You're squishing my arm." The pressure released, and I straightened.

Mitch was crouched in front of me. "You okay?"

I gazed at him. It was weird. Without the hair and

the beard, he seemed like a different person, but when I just focused on his eyes, he was the same old Mitch.

"Alison, are you okay?" he asked again.

I nodded.

"Ms. Weaver?" Stans said.

I turned my head. Stans was down on one knee next to me. "What happened?" I asked him.

"You fainted," Stans said.

I knew I hadn't fainted. I'd never fainted in my life, but I didn't want to get into it with him. "I meant—what happened to Frank?"

"We were hoping that you could tell us."

I struggled to my feet, hauling my cast with the other arm, so it wouldn't throw me off balance. Stans got to his feet, while Mitch leaned in close to give me a hand. "You should keep your head down," he said softly but emphatically.

"I'm okay." I shook off his arm to prove it. I looked around. Carney had joined Stans on the porch along with three uniformed cops, and I was the center of their attention. "Who killed Frank?" I asked them.

"Frank who?" Carney asked.

"Frank Avery. My ex-husband. The guy inside."

"Recently divorced?" Carney probed.

"Couple of years ago."

"Not amicably, I take it?"

I didn't like his tone. "What's that supposed to mean?"

"Was it a friendly divorce, or were there bad feelings, arguments, fights?"

"I know what 'amicably' means. What are you implying? That I killed him?"

Carney exchanged a glance with Stans. What had Mitch said—that I should keep my head down? Too late I understood that he'd meant it figuratively. I faced both of them. "Well?"

"You reported an assault last night," Stans said. "Your house shows signs of a prolonged struggle. You have a broken arm, and your ex-husband is dead."

"Tsk, tsk, Detective. Remember what you told me? 'Never assume.' My house was broken into and trashed last evening while I was out, long before the arm-breaker arrived. The housebreaker also tried to mug me on my front lawn. The arm-breaker came later and stayed only long enough to crack my radius and get a blast of bleach in the face. Neither one was Frank. I have no idea what Frank was doing here."

I could have said more about the logical probability of a person with a broken arm effectively wielding a knife, but I was weary right down to the bone, including the broken bone in my arm. The twinges of pain under the cast had escalated to a steady ache. I needed pain medication and sleep. Most of all, I needed time in a quiet place to take in everything that had happened, but my home, my only refuge, was gone.

My neck ached from the weight of the sling holding my casted arm. I lifted the cast to relieve the pressure and rubbed the back of my neck with my good hand. Stans, Carney and the uniformed cops stood around, like tourists at the zoo. "What are you looking at? Don't you guys have work to do?"

Mitch cleared his throat. I glanced at him, and he gave me a small warning shake of his head.

Stans said, "We were just waiting to see if you were all right, because you fainted. But, if you're feeling okay now, we'd like you to answer some questions."

I rounded on him. "For your information, I didn't faint, but you don't really give a damn how I feel, do you? If it mattered at all, you'd never have paraded Frank's mutilated corpse in front of me with no warning, nothing. You could have stopped me going up to the house, if you'd wanted to. As far as I'm concerned, you can take your questions and shove them up… "

Mitch grabbed me by my good arm.

"... Up your official procedure. Look, I'm going to repeat this for the last time. I squirted bleach into my attacker's face. If you'd taken the time to check local emergency rooms, you'd have found him by now. Have the pathologist check Frank's eyes. No damage, no bleach, it wasn't Frank." I walked carefully down the front steps on shaking knees. Mitch held my arm until I reached the bottom.

Some neighbors stood in small groups across the street. At least I think they were neighbors. Only one of them was a familiar face, but they all seemed to know one another. Nothing like a murder in the neighborhood to build community feeling.

A taxi pulled up next door and Rose got out, hauling a plastic grocery bag with her. She turned and stared wide-eyed at the gathering of police cars, cops and neighbors. She spotted me and headed in my direction. A uniformed cop stopped her when she reached the edge of my property.

Mitch and I both moved forward to meet her. I tried to hurry and winced against the jostling I gave my arm.

"What happened?" Rose's face was creased with concern. "Are you two all right?" She looked from me to Mitch.

"We're fine. Frank's dead. Someone killed him in my house, while I was in the hospital having my arm set." I hoisted my casted arm to show her. "Mitch took me."

"You broke your arm?"

"It's a long story. I'm fine, now, really I am."

"I had no idea. I had an early doctor's appointment. Mitch, I didn't recognize you at first. You look very handsome. But Alison, my dear, you look done in."

"I'm just tired, that's all."

"She fainted," Mitch said.

I glared at him. "I did not faint."

"You poor thing. You'd better lie down," she told me. "Where will she go?" she asked Mitch.

"She's staying with me," Mitch said.

"No, I'm not."

Rose patted my shoulder. "That's the very best thing. Mitch will take good care of you. You go on now." She made little shooing gestures with her hand. "I'll come visit you later." She turned and bustled down the sidewalk to her house.

I gritted my teeth and faced Mitch. "I never said I was staying with you."

"Come on." He urged me to cross the street. "You don't want to stay out here."

I followed him across the street. "I need my bag," I said to his back.

"It's in my truck. Wait here. I'll get it." He veered off toward his truck, but before he could reach it, two groups of gawkers converged on him and started asking questions.

I would've moved closer to eavesdrop, but a passing car caught my eye. Not just any car—a silver Boxster. Maybe Frank's murder had already been on the news, and the lookie-loos were descending on the site. I'd bet that in the past two years Frank had met quite a few people rich enough to own cars like that.

The driver eased his car around the traffic jam in front of my house and pulled into the first available parking space. He got out and headed straight for me. Not a friend of Frank's after all. Not a friend of mine, either. Stevie Number's father, Jack Lind, in a suit, tie and shoes as classy as his car, walked up to me and asked, "How much do you want to make all of this go away?"

I stared at him. He seemed to be waiting for an answer, so I said, "What the hell are you talking about?"

"You heard me. Gina told me about last night."

"Let me get this straight. You're here on behalf of your adult daughter, the one who poses as a juvenile delinquent?"

"She's impulsive, doesn't think things through, that's all. No need to bring the police into it." He gestured at the gathering of cop cars in front of my house.

"You've done this before, right? Look, it's time to cut the cord. Your daughter has major psychological problems. You're only making things worse by covering up for her."

"I'm not interested in your two-bit psychoanalysis of my daughter."

"Okay, how about a hundred dollar psychoanalysis? I know big words, too, like 'narcissistic personality,' 'character disorder,' and, my favorite, 'sociopath.'"

He glared at me and said through clenched teeth, "I'm offering to let Stephen's will go through probate uncontested if you won't press charges."

"I don't get it. You're going to such lengths to protect your daughter, but you turned your back on your son."

"You know nothing about it. My son was past saving. Do you accept my offer or not?"

I nearly asked him if he really thought he could buy me off, but I glanced past his shoulder and saw Stans and Carney conferring with a third suit on the sidewalk across the street. Maybe I could play Jack Lind along until I could catch their attention. "I've never settled out of court, so to speak. How does it work? Do we shake hands on it, or what?" I asked. "Of course, I'll have to shake with my left hand. Do left hand shakes count?"

Jack Lind looked at my casted arm hanging in its sling as if he'd just noticed it. "I didn't know... " he spoke hesitatingly. "Gina didn't say anything about an injury. In fact, she said that you'd hurt her arms," he said without conviction.

"Mmm," I said non-committally. Interesting that he assumed it was Gina who'd broken my arm. Gina had probably lied about things like that before, or he would've protested more emphatically. I scanned the opposite side of the street for Stans and Carney. They were just turning away from the third man. "Oh look. The homicide detectives who're working on Stevie's case." I waved my good arm until I caught Carney's eye. He nudged Stans. They crossed the street together and planted themselves in front of us.

Stans glanced from me to Jack Lind and raised his

eyebrows. "What's going on here?"

"Jack... " I turned to Jack Lind. "You don't mind if I call you Jack, do you?" He gave me a steely look. "Jack has just convinced me that I should press charges against Gina for breaking into my house, trashing it, and then assaulting me in my front yard."

"Wait a minute," Jack said.

"I was concerned about the impact on her mother. She's been through so much already. But, you're right, Jack. Gina needs help, and she won't get it unless she's forced to face the consequences of her actions."

"You'll have to prove she did it," Jack said, his neck reddening as his blood pressure cranked up.

"No problem. I have a witness to the assault. He's right over there." I pointed out Mitch, still surrounded by curious neighbors. "And, I'm pretty sure she left her fingerprints all over my house. I just hope for your sake that they don't find them on the knife that killed my ex-husband."

"What are you talking about? Someone was killed?" Jack's red face suddenly drained of color.

"These are pretty serious allegations," Stans said to me.

"She did some serious damage to my property, which I guess you noticed. She was searching for Stevie's journal. When she didn't find it, she tried to beat me up. Do you suppose she hired the man who broke my arm, too?"

"You," Jack pointed a finger at me, "are going to regret this."

"Are you threatening me, Jack? In front of police officers?"

He glared at me. "You'll be hearing from my lawyer."

"I'm going to be busy. Have him contact my lawyer," I waited a beat for effect and added, "Andrew Duggan."

He clamped his jaw shut, spun around and strode off. Carney took off after Jack, stopping him before he could get into his car.

"You're in the middle of a very messy situation, Ms. Weaver," Stans said.

I narrowed my eyes at him. "I'm not talking to you."

"Okay, I can bring another officer over, if you'd like. We have a lot of questions, and you're it for answers as far as I can see. I think I should tell you up front, we might have to take you into protective custody."

"What are you talking about?"

"According to you, you've been attacked more than once. Your ex-husband was killed in your house. If you didn't do it, then we're thinking you might have been the real target. We're also thinking you could have crucial information about the murder of Stephen Lind that you haven't shared with us."

"I've told you everything I know."

"That's what you said before, then we find you at Florence Bing's place, only she's dead and we can't ask her anything. Then, you finally clue us in that you know where this GI Joe's been hiding out, but, guess what, he's moved without leaving a forwarding address."

"But now you have Joe, right? He's the one who knows about Stevie's murder."

Stans paused before replying, "The suspect is not yet in custody."

"Not yet? Didn't Frank tell you where he was?"

Stans remained silent.

"Omigod. Frank hid Joe, and now Frank's dead."

"We think you should come with us, for your own protection."

"Am I under arrest?"

Stans hesitated a fraction before answering, "No."

"Good. You want to question somebody? There's a little kid across the street with those rubber-neckers. His name is Tyler. Frank hired him to spy on me. He might know something. Go easy on him, though. He hero-worshipped Frank."

"Thanks for the information. We still need to sit down with you and go over all the details."

"Look at me. I've been avoiding mirrors like a vampire, because I know I look like holy hell. That's nothing compared to how I feel. I'm going to my neighbor's," I gestured with my thumb to Mitch's house. "If you want to protect me, let me take a nap. Then, you can ask me anything."

I turned and headed for Mitch's front door without waiting for Stans to reply. I had to concentrate to make the effort needed to lift my feet, because my shoes suddenly weighed about ten pounds apiece. I'd moved beyond tired into the realm of exhaustion.

Mitch caught up with me as I reached the front steps. "Here, let me get the door." He had my shoulder bag and the paper bag of food we'd stopped for earlier. "Don't look back," he said as he unlocked the door. "The TV news people just showed up."

I stepped inside as soon as he opened the door. Whatever I felt about being interviewed by the police counted triple for the news media. Mitch quickly followed me inside, shut and locked the door. He'd left the lights on inside when we'd left the night before. He circled the living room switching off lamps, but left the shades down. "Come in and sit down. Can I get you anything?"

I crossed the room and sat on the sofa next to an end table with a telephone on it, wincing as I settled against the cushions. "Just some water, please."

Mitch disappeared into his kitchen and reappeared carrying a glass of water. He held it while I dug the small envelope of Vicodin out of my jeans and shook out a pill. When I had the pill between my teeth, he handed me the glass.

"Will one be enough? You look pretty rough."

I swallowed the pill and finished off the remaining water. "I'll wait twenty minutes and take a second one if I need to. Thanks." I handed the glass back to him. "And, thanks, you know, for everything." The words were laughably inadequate, but I didn't know what else to say.

He shrugged. "You're welcome."

"I think I'd better call that lawyer you recommended. Ron somebody."

"Ron Kelso."

"Right. Could you give me his number again?"

"Sure." Mitch headed back to the kitchen.

I closed my eyes and rested my head against the back of the sofa while I waited.

When I opened my eyes, I had that weird disorientation that comes with falling asleep in an unfamiliar place. I turned my head and saw Mitch sitting in his easy chair, and it all came back to me.

"Hey," Mitch said. "You awake?"

"Have I been asleep long?"

"About four hours."

"Why didn't you wake me up?"

"I didn't tiptoe around. The phone's been ringing. I finally switched over to the machine a half an hour ago, because I got tired of answering it."

I tried to sit up. Somehow I'd ended up stretched full length on the sofa, covered with a blanket, a pillow under my head. I had to wrestle the blanket off with my functioning arm before I could get both feet on the floor and struggle to a sitting position. I rubbed my forehead with my fingers trying to clear the fog inside my brain. It didn't work. A four-hour nap wasn't nearly enough, but it would have to do. "Who called?"

"You name it. Cops. Reporters. Everybody on the street I've done work for."

"What did you tell the cops?"

He shrugged. "That you were asleep."

"Thanks."

"No problem. Can I get you something?"

"Is that coffee I smell? I could really use a jolt of caffeine right about now, if it's no bother."

He rose to his feet. "No bother at all. Want something to eat?"

"You still have that BLT with the side of potato salad?"

"I put it all in the refrigerator. It'll be soggy by now."

"Soggy's no deterrent to someone as hungry as I am."

He came back in an amazingly short time and placed a tray loaded with two sandwiches, a pint of potato salad, dill pickles, two chocolate chip cookies and a mug of coffee on the low table in front of me. I hardly noticed the sogginess and proved it by demolishing everything and getting refills on the coffee. Mitch kept me company while I ate and assured me that he'd fixed something for himself earlier and wouldn't even accept my offer of the second cookie.

When I'd downed the last of the coffee, I said, "I hope that my crashing on your couch didn't keep you from anything you had to do."

"It didn't," he said, without any of the give-away shifting around in his chair that said he wasn't telling the truth. In fact, Mitch had a capacity for being present, just totally there in the room that I'd seen only in really good nurses and a few chaplains.

"I'll be getting out of your way now.

"Stay as long as you like or need to." He gave me a level gaze.

"Don't worry. I'm not moving in on you," I said with a laugh.

"I'm telling you that you can. It's up to you."

Was I imagining it or were there layers of meaning in what Mitch was saying? I knew I didn't imagine the sudden feeling of warmth that unfolded in my middle regions that was more than the result of a full stomach. I gazed at the man who used to be the detested destroyer of my neighborhood. Somehow or other, he'd ended up being the one I'd turned to when I was in trouble. Had he meant "stay in his house" or "stay with him in his house?"

I rose to my feet. What did I care what he meant? I

didn't need any more complications in my life. Particularly the kind of complications I'd let myself in for if I started going goo-goo over Mitch. "Mind if I use your bathroom?"

"It's through the bedroom." He pointed to a doorway off the living room.

I followed his directions, checking out the refinished wood floors and freshly painted white walls along the way. He'd even fixed up the bathroom, using new fixtures that matched the house's original style. No question about it, Mitch had maintained the integrity of his home. Too bad I couldn't say the same about mine. It would take more than refinished floors and fresh paint to exorcise Frank's newly resident ghost.

I finger-combed my hair, which was the best I could do for it since I'd left my bag in the living room. After I used the toilet, I washed my face and hands. While I patted my face dry, I gazed in the mirror and did a quick inventory. One formerly black eye, now several shades of yellow and green, and the persistent question of why I hadn't told the cops about Joe's hideout sooner. One scraped chin thanks to Gina, and vengeful thoughts directed toward her on Stevie's behalf. One lump on my forehead from the mysterious intruder, and lingering regrets about squirting bleach in his eyes. All in all, a face well past benefiting from concealing make-up and a conscience that had taken all the scrutiny it could bear for the time being.

I left the bathroom and couldn't help pausing for a few nosy seconds to check out Mitch's bedroom. His bed was unmade, but everything else was very neat. Not the total order that ruled in his garage workshop, but still pretty tidy for a man. Or for a woman like me, for that matter. He'd even put the books on his bedside table in a neat stack.

The hardback on top lay title-side down. I stepped closer for a quick look, and damned if I didn't find myself gazing at a dust cover photo of Frank as the intense writer in a black turtleneck, looking a lot better than the last time I'd seen him. God, I remembered the day he sat for that picture. The poor photographer had sweated through three hours and five rolls of film for this one shot. I picked up the book and passed my hand over the image of his face. *Frank, you stupid idiot, why the hell did you have to go and get yourself killed?*

Something niggled in the back of my mind. I turned the book over, read the title, and it hit me. What was Mitch doing with a copy of All Through the Night? I gripped the book and strode into the living room. Thought he could soften me up with sandwiches, did he? Well, he had another think coming. I caught him in the middle of clearing up crumbs from the coffee table.

"You said you'd never heard of Frank Avery before, so how do you explain this?" I demanded, shoving the book in his face. "Bad short-term memory? Selective amnesia? Or could it be the Tony Dezzutti syndrome?"

Mitch took the book from me, opened it to the flyleaf, and held it up for me to see. "It's Mrs. Fiorelli's. She loaned it to me when I started working on your door. I just told her that I didn't know who he was."

I peered at the page. Rose had written her name at the top. She'd probably bought it when it first came out. Frank and I were still nominally married then. "Okay, so you didn't pay good money for it. But, why waste your time reading trash?"

"Mrs. Fiorelli said it was about your life."

"She's mistaken." I pointed to the book. "That is not about me. In fact, it's nothing more than a compendium of lies and distortions."

"What's not true?"

"For one thing, no nurse is planet Krypton's answer to Mother Theresa. You get tired and bitch and moan about your job like everyone else does. Every now and then, you might make a difference for a patient, and that keeps you going. Frank took the good ones and strung them all together. Then he sentimentalized everything so much it made me want to gag."

"So he exaggerated?"

"More like he fictionalized. Everything. He'd said he wanted to know the real me. I was flattered. It was so seductive to have this man's total attention. Not just any man, either. A writer. I fell for the mystique and just blabbed on and on. God, what an idiot I was. He took what he wanted and made up the rest."

"Like what?"

"Like, I didn't have to fight my way into college. I lucked out with Ruth, my fourth foster mom. She saw to it that I stayed out of trouble and in school. She paid for my SAT prep course herself. High enough scores will get you into college, plus money to pay for it."

"It must have helped that you were smart."

"Helped more that she believed in me and saw to it that I believed in myself, but that particular detail didn't fit Frank's story."

"Did he make up the part about your mom, too?"

"That was the worst lie of all. I didn't try to stop my mother from killing herself. I helped her. She wanted to die and chose me as her designated driver to the other plane. Frank thought it made a better story his way. So not only did he invade my privacy, parade my life in front of the world, he twisted it into a lie."

"You helped her?"

"She started off with pills and white wine, but figured she might need something stronger. So she had me bring in the vodka bottle for her. Then, when she threw up, she told me where to find some anti-emetic. She took more pills for insurance and went into a coma. She'd made me promise I'd stay with her, so I did. In the morning, I went to the neighbors and told them."

"But you were only six years old."

"True, and I'd like to think I didn't really understand what was happening, but usually I feel that I did. Anyway, I didn't even know Frank was writing about me until the book came out. He thought having a bestseller justified everything. I disagreed and filed for divorce. No problem for him, because he'd already social climbed his way into a rich woman's bed." I looked down at my toes. "I don't know why I dumped all of this on you."

"I'm glad you did."

"Glad? Why?"

"It means you trust me."

"I've made that mistake before."

"Not this time. Not with me."

I pressed my lips together to stop myself from contradicting him. I had to admit there was something there that made me feel I could confide in him. Maybe this time I could actually trust my instincts. "Thanks for every single thing you've done." We locked gazes.

"I have to tell you something," he said and stopped.

I waited. When he didn't say anything else, I asked. "What?"

He let out his breath as if he'd been holding it. "The police are waiting for you. Outside."

I gazed at Mitch for a beat. Why did I have the feeling that he'd intended to say something else?

CHAPTER EIGHTEEN

I crossed to the window and peeked out through the curtains. Stans and Carney stood on the sidewalk in front of Mitch's house. All the other cops had finished up and gone.

"They showed up while you were in the bathroom," Mitch said. "I didn't let them in, but they're not leaving until you talk to them."

I turned away from the window. "I haven't even called that lawyer, Kelso, yet."

"I called him while you were asleep. I told him what I know about it. He said he'd meet you when you have to talk to the cops. He's not in court today."

"I have a feeling they want to arrest me. Stans said something about protective custody, but that's just cop talk for jail, isn't it?"

"I'd trust Kelso and do whatever he says."

"That's easy for you to say. They don't have you fingered for the slammer, or whatever they call it these days." I looked around for my shoulder bag.

"What do you need?"

"My bag. If they arrest me, can I post bail with a credit card?"

Mitch found my shoulder bag behind the couch and held it out to me. "You're going to be all right. I won't let them put you in jail."

I took my bag and wedged it to my body with my cast

so I could root around in it with my left hand. "Look, I was in juvie for awhile. You know, juvenile detention. They told me juvie wasn't as bad as jail. That's when I knew I never wanted to go to jail." I kept trying without luck to find my hairbrush.

"Here, let me help," Mitch said and took the bag from me. "Don't say it. I know you can do it yourself, but right now you don't have the time. What do you need?"

"My hairbrush. Please," I added grudgingly.

"Don't fix up too much," Mitch said. "The worse you look, the harder it will be for them to justify questioning you for very long."

"Look, I'm not exactly vain, but there's no way I'm going to try to look worse than I already do. Even if it would make Stans and Carney go easy on me, which I seriously doubt."

"How do you ever find anything in here?" he said, holding the bag wide open and peering into the interior.

"Just dump everything out. It doesn't matter."

He tipped the contents of my bag out onto the sofa. My hair brush flew out in a rain of the assorted debris I'd gathered since the last time I'd cleaned out my bag—planner, addressbook, computer disks, several bunches of keys, lipstick, concealer, coins, a bottle of aspirin, a parking ticket, old toothpicks, business cards, many scraps of paper, and the picture of Stevie and Flo with their friends.

I picked up the picture. "I forgot I had this. Look." I held it up so Mitch could see. "That's Stevie, the guy who was killed, and that's Flo—his girlfriend before he had his schizophrenic break. She's dead, too. They say she committed suicide, but I found her body, and I can't see suicide. That's two dead, and Frank makes three. He was a real jerk, but he shouldn't have died like that." I sank down onto the sofa.

"You okay?"

"I'm okay, just so much pointless death is getting to me." I spread the picture out in my lap, and my gaze fell on one of the other figures in the photo, the only person not smiling, a man with a bulbous nose, overhanging brow ridges, and thick, fleshy lips. "That's the guy!" I jumped to my feet so fast that the picture fluttered to the floor.

Mitch bent over and retrieved it. "What guy?"

"The guy who broke my arm. I knew I recognized him from somewhere." I grabbed the picture from Mitch and headed for the front door. "I have to tell the cops about this."

"Wait. Call Kelso first. You shouldn't talk to the cops without a lawyer."

"I'll call him later, if I need to. Probably won't now. This definitely links the attack on me back to Stevie." I held the picture between my teeth and wrestled the door open with my left hand. Stans and Carney stood on the sidewalk and turned toward me as I emerged from Mitch's house.

"I know who attacked me." I waved the picture above my head like a banner. I hurried down the front steps and shoved the picture in Stans' face. "That's the guy. Second from the left. I knew I'd seen him before. That's what spooked him, I think. I said 'I know you, don't I?' and he took out of there like his hair was on fire."

"I thought it was dark. How could you see his face?" Stans asked.

"He dropped his flashlight when I sprayed him with the bleach. I picked it up."

"With a broken arm?" Carney asked.

"With my un-broken left arm."

"And you can ID someone you saw by flashlight from a photograph that's, what, five years old?" Carney asked.

I stared at them. "You don't believe me, do you?"

"We just want to get all the facts, that's all, before we decide who to believe and who not," Stans said.

"Here's a fact. The man in this picture, who by the way has a very distinctive face, attacked me and broke my arm," I said and rattled the page for emphasis.

Stans pulled the picture from my fingers. "This the same photo you gave us? The one you got from Mrs. Lind?"

"A copy of it, yes. Yours is probably sharper. Don't you see? This man is a link between Stevie and the attack on me. He might even be the killer. Stevie died from a blow to the head, right?"

"Could be a tie-in," Stans said. "Problem is right now we're trying to find out who killed your ex-husband. And he's not in this picture, is he?"

"So you're not even going to pursue it?"

"Sure, we'll follow up on it and on every single lead we get. We want to close that case. Our job right now, though, is to focus on the current case. The murder of Frank Avery. We thought you'd want to help us with that one, too. Am I right?"

"That's what I'm trying to do. Frank found out something about Stevie's murder. That's why he was killed."

"Maybe," Stans said.

"What do you mean maybe? And don't give me that line about not assuming anything. You know for a fact that Frank talked to GI Joe, and Joe very probably knows who killed Stevie, or at least why he was killed."

"Just because your ex-husband talked to Joe, doesn't mean Joe told him anything relevant to the murder. What I know as fact is that your ex was giving you grief. You threatened him with a restraining order within my hearing. I had the impression that he was stalking you, though you denied it."

"I still deny it. It wasn't me he was after, it was something to write about. That's why he tracked down Joe and hid him."

"Something to write about? What does that mean?" Carney asked.

"It means… " I began and stopped. "Look, ask his wife. Ask Tony. Neither of them likes me, and they adored Frank, so maybe you'll believe them. They'll tell you he was after his next book." I moved away from them. Enough was enough. If they didn't want to believe me, that was their problem. I needed at least ten more hours of sleep and would be happy to get some of it on Mitch's couch.

Stans caught me by the arm and stopped me. "Wait a minute. We're not done yet."

"You may not be, but I am." I pulled my arm free. "If you want to arrest me, go ahead, but I'm not putting up with any more of this bullshit. I give you a picture ID of the man who came into my house and attacked me, and you blow me off. I'd like that picture back, if you don't mind." I held out my hand. "You have the original already."

Stans gave me the picture. "Look, I know you're frustrated, but so are we. I promise you we'll follow up on the guy in the photo. It might be related to the Lind case. It might be related to Avery's murder. We don't know. In fact, we don't know squat, so help us out."

I rubbed my forehead. If they were at a loss and willing to admit it, I had no choice but to try to help, even though it grated. I glanced up and met Carney's gaze.

"We know it's hard to relive it, but we need to know what went on in your house before Avery was killed, and you're our only witness," Carney said.

"Okay, okay. Quit playing nice cop, nicer cop. Where should I start?"

"How about walking us through what happened last night," Stans said.

So I stood in my front yard and went over the past twenty-four hours for Stans and Carney, starting with the fact that I was home during the day, because I'd been as good as fired from my job. I told them about Tony's visit, and about eating dinner with Rose and Mitch next door, sitting in the backyard until dark. I described my encounter with Gina and recounted what she'd revealed to me. Carney wanted to know where Mitch was during this time, and I showed him, leaving out the by-play about being my bodyguard.

When I reached the point in my story of going into the house, I could think of about a million things I'd rather do than open the front door. Maybe Stans sensed my reluctance. "The coroner's people took the body away several hours ago," he said. He crossed to the door, opened it, and held the yellow plastic police tape apart for me to duck through.

"It's not locked?" I asked.

"Both doors were unlocked when we got here. We saw the body through the window, which gave us the right to enter your house, in case you're wondering. We'll have you lock it up before we leave, and we'll seal the doors."

I stepped inside, and he and Carney followed. I looked around the living room. I'd been wrong to worry about what I'd see. No bloodstains marred the easy chair Frank had occupied, though I probably wouldn't be using it again. My house was nothing more than a vandalized mess covered with a generous dusting of messy fingerprint powder.

"I know it's hard to tell, but is anything out of place or different from the way you left it last night?" Stans asked.

I looked around. The door to the study stood open. "That door was closed, and I'd jammed a chair under the door knob." I crossed and looked into the study. I pointed to the broken window. "That was how Gina got in. I nailed the sash shut afterwards."

I backed away from the study doorway and crossed to my bedroom, trailing Stans and Carney behind. I scanned the room. "The stick the guy hit me with is missing and so's the water pistol. No wonder you didn't believe me."

"They were here. They've been taken away as evidence," Carney said.

"What was it anyway? I call it a stick, but it might've been a metal bar. It was hard enough."

"It was a police nightstick, made of hardwood, just under two feet long," Carney said.

"Were his fingerprints on it?" I asked.

"A partial," Carney said. "The lab guys will see what they can do with it."

"He also put his hands on the wall and the door," I gestured to the places I meant. "He couldn't see and was trying to feel his way out."

"We'll bring the crime scene team back to see if they can pick anything up."

"I'm curious about the water gun with the bleach," Stans said. "Most folks would use pepper spray."

"Someone was outside my house the other night. I don't know if he was trying to get in or not, but it woke me up. I got out of bed and saw him leaving, crossing the front yard. It worried me. I'd confiscated the gun from Tyler, because even though it's plastic, it's black and looks like a real gun. Remember the kid in the school yard some years back?"

Stans gave me a grim look. A policeman had killed the boy, thinking he had a real gun. "They're illegal now."

"In this state. Tyler's dad brought it back from Hong Kong. So I filled it with water and bleach in case the guy came back."

"When was this?" Stans asked.

"The night before you came and towed my car off."

"You didn't call in and report it?" Carney asked.

"What was the point? I didn't see his face, and he hadn't actually entered my house. At the time, I wasn't sure he'd even tried to."

"You didn't mention it that morning," Stans said.

"It went completely out of my head. I was asleep when you came pounding on my door. In fact, I'd forgotten all about the water gun until I found it when I tried to hide under the bed."

"You what?" Carney asked.

"Let me show you," I said. I gave them an awkward demonstration of my face-off with the nightstick-wielding intruder, playing both parts. I showed them how I'd tried to squeeze under the bed, found the water gun, rolled away after he'd hit me on the head, and squirted him in the face at the same moment he hit me on the arm.

"I know I hit his eyes. He really yelled a lot and put his hands to his face, but I think he could see a little bit, because at first he kind of groped around, then he moved pretty fast. He ran out through the back door." I demonstrated by leading them to the kitchen. "I followed him as far as the door. He ran across the back yard and climbed over the fence. Maybe the neighbors over there heard something?"

Carney shook his head. "The house is up for sale. The owners already moved out."

My eye fell on the empty kitchen table. "Did you take Stevie's papers, too?"

"What papers?" Stans asked.

"There were two cardboard boxes of Stevie's papers that Lucianne Lind gave me. I had them in the trunk of my car. After Gina tore up the place, I thought I'd check them out. See if I could find what she wanted so desperately."

"Maybe you put them back in your car?" Carney suggested.

"No, I left them right there on the kitchen table. I was too tired to lug them outside again. Hang on a minute. Let me think." I closed my eyes and pictured in my mind retrieving the boxes, going through them, sorting the papers, and... I opened my eyes. "I forgot. I have them. Some of them. I hid them because—wait let me get them and show you." I crossed to the dryer, opened it and pulled the dirty laundry onto the floor. It was awkward with my left hand only. The papers slipped from my grip.

"Here, let me," Carney said. He brought the papers to the table.

I pulled the computer printouts from the stack. "Here," I said to Stans, "look at this." I flipped to page six and pointed to the top of the column.

"What am I supposed to see?"

"RBPCE," I read the letters that topped the column of numbers. "Don't you recognize it? From the page you found in the trunk of my car? It's the same. And that page was like the ones left with Stevie's body. I assumed the unshredded papers were from the Center. But they were Stevie's all along. I think that GI Joe left them with his body because they were important."

"What does RBPCE mean?" Carney asked.

"That's the problem. I don't know, but it's another link." I turned to Stans. "Isn't it?"

"Maybe. Right now I'm more interested in the fact that the rest of the papers were taken."

"Why'd you hide these?" Carney asked, gesturing to the pile on the table.

"The papers I left in the boxes were all notes and stuff from his classes. These were different. The computer printouts have to be connected to his murder somehow. The rest of it is part of my job as Stevie's beneficiary. They're his original work, and Lucianne Lind hopes I can get them published."

"You didn't answer my question. Why'd you hide them?"

"Gina trashed my house looking for some of Stevie's papers. She told me she wanted his journal, which may or may not have been a lie. I didn't find a journal, but I thought I'd better hide the important papers, just in case she came back."

Stans picked up the papers and tamped the ends on the table to make them neat.

"Wait a minute. You're not taking those papers, are you?"

"According to you, they have some bearing on the Lind case," Stans said.

"Just the computer printouts."

"Since the rest of Lind's papers were taken, it's likely they wanted these, too."

"Is this like my car? Evidence of a crime, so you can just make off with it?"

Stans hesitated. "Let's say it's a gray area. They look like evidence concerning the Lind case, but it's not clear what relation they have to Avery's murder. We're on the premises because of that crime. If you won't let us have them now, I'll have to get a court order."

"I don't mind sharing. I just want to keep control of the originals. What if I make copies and give them to you?"

"If they're evidence, we'll need originals," Stans argued.

"If you prove a link to the murder, you can have them."

Stans looked as if he'd like to argue the point, but his cell phone chirped and interrupted him. He pulled out the phone and snapped it open. "Stans here," he said and listened for a few moments. It must have been important, because he moved into the living room, tucked the phone against his shoulder, and pulled out his notebook.

I tried to eavesdrop on the conversation, but Carney started talking and drowned out Stans' voice. "Can you think of anyone other than Gina Lind or your ex-husband who might have had it in for you?"

"You don't listen, do you? Frank didn't want to hurt me. He wasn't stalking me. He wanted to use me to get information, that's all."

"You didn't answer the question."

"Ask a better one, and I will."

"Hey, partner," Stans said from the doorway.

Carney and I turned around, and Stans gestured to Carney to join him in the living room. They held a brief whispered conference, nodded to one another and moved back into the kitchen.

"Why don't we sit down?" Stans suggested, pulling out one of the chairs for me.

I sat and waited while Stans and Carney took seats on either side. Stans placed his notebook and pen on the table. "Let's see, we got to the point where your attacker ran out the back door, right? Then what happened?"

"When he was gone, I picked up my keys and left."

"Where'd you go?"

"Across the street to Mitch's house. I knew I had a broken bone in my arm. I couldn't drive, so I asked Mitch to take me to the ER."

"You didn't try to call the police? Or ask him to call the police?"

I cradled my casted arm in my lap gazed down at it. "No. He offered. I was in a lot of pain and wanted to get to the hospital as fast as possible."

"Is that the only reason you didn't call the police?" Stans asked.

I looked up and met Stans' gaze. Had he guessed that I'd been too terrified by ghosts from my past to stay in my house one more second? "I wanted immediate medical attention. If I waited for the police, I'd have been here for hours explaining what had happened."

"Okay, so you had your keys. Did you lock the door?" Stans asked.

"Yes… I think so." I tried to visualize what I'd done.

"With a broken arm?" Carney asked.

"I guess I didn't actually lock it. I just closed it behind me. All I could think about was getting medical attention."

"You went across the street. Then what?" Stans prompted.

"I woke up Mitch. He let me in. He got dressed and took me to the hospital."

"That's it?"

"He got my bag out of the trunk of my car. I'd locked it there the previous night like I always do when I work at the Mobile Clinic."

"Except for the night someone borrowed your car to move Lind's body."

I grimaced. Stans had a good memory. "Right, except for that night."

"Where were you when Kent was getting your purse?"

"Who's Kent?" I asked. "I told you—it was Mitch."

Stans flipped his notebook open. "That's his name," he said and read, "Mitchell Stanton Kent."

"I didn't know."

"You didn't know his last name?" Carney put in,

disbelief in every syllable.

"No. So what?"

"Just tell us where you were when he was getting your purse," Stans said.

"In his living room. Why? What difference does it make? My attacker had already run away."

"So you say," Stans said, sounding a little too much like Carney for my taste.

"Yes. So I say, because that's what happened. You don't believe me?"

"I think you're telling us most of the truth. I think you did recognize your attacker, and not from a five-year old photograph, but from life. He was your ex, who'd been giving you a bad time. Stalked you. Broke down your door. I think you told Kent that Avery attacked you, and he decided to deal with Avery himself."

"Mitch? You're kidding. Why would Mitch want to hurt Frank?"

"Why? The new boyfriend and the ex-husband. Couldn't be any love lost there."

"Don't be ridiculous. Mitch isn't my boyfriend. We hadn't even said two words to one another until I hired him to fix my door. I didn't even know his last name until just now, but I do know that Mitch is no killer."

"You're wrong there," Stans said and consulted his notebook again. "Mitchell Stanton Kent was tried, convicted and put in prison for murder."

CHAPTER NINETEEN

"You have some explaining to do, Mitchell Stanton Kent," I said the second he walked through the front door. I'd waited in his house two fingernail-biting hours after the cops had hauled him off for questioning, and I wanted some answers.

Once Stans and Carney found out that he'd served time for murder—a fact I still couldn't wrap my mind around—they were like dogs with a bone. Not an old dried out bone, either, but a big fresh one that still had bits of meat clinging to it. They wouldn't leave it alone, firing question after question at me, most of them repeats of what they'd already asked. I finally clamped my jaw shut, and they went for Mitch, hustling him into the back seat of their car, his face a blank mask.

He'd left his front door unlocked, so I waited inside. I tried to nap, but my eyes wouldn't stay shut. I found myself pacing the length and breadth of his house again and again. What if they arrested him? No matter what he'd done in the past, I knew Mitch hadn't killed Frank, the way I knew gravity held my feet to the earth, without thinking about it. Too bad Stans and Carney didn't have the benefit of my perspective.

I'd asked Mitch for help and had set him up for trouble. If only he'd told me he'd been in prison. I tripped on a throw rug on my millionth circle through the front hall to the kitchen. I kicked it out of my way. Damn it, why had I dragged him into this mess? And, why hadn't he told me?

He stood for a moment in the doorway. "You stayed." He closed the door and leaned against it, as if in relief.

"Where else would I go? My house is sealed. Besides, I want an explanation."

"I know. I should've told you." He crossed the living room and sank into a chair. Fatigue marked his face, but I wasn't going to let him off the hook, just because he was a little tired. I was tired, too, but I didn't sit down. I paced.

"So why didn't you tell me you'd been in prison?"

Mitch leaned forward and rested his forearms on his thighs. He didn't meet my gaze. "At first I thought you knew."

"How would I know? ESP?"

"Everyone on the block knows. I always tell people before I start a job for them. I thought you knew and that was why you never spoke to me."

The accusation stopped me in my tracks. "How could you think such a thing? You know I'm not that kind of person. I didn't talk to you because I hated the way you ruined my neighborhood. Prettied it up for a bunch of strangers."

"How was I supposed to know anything when you wouldn't talk to me? And, where'd you get the crazy idea I was ruining the neighborhood? I just do what I'm hired to do. Most people like to live in nice houses."

"I liked it the way it was, when everyone knew everyone else and helped out when someone needed it." I threw myself onto the sofa for emphasis, and because I was tired of pacing.

We sat, not looking at each other. After a while, Mitch said, "I finally figured out that you didn't know about me from the things you said. I knew I had to say something, but I was afraid."

I looked at him. "You don't strike me as the scaredy-cat type. What were you afraid of?"

Mitch lifted his gaze to meet mine. "That you wouldn't see me."

"How couldn't I see you? I see you every day."

"Come on, Alison, you know what I mean. I wanted to ask you out, spend time together, but I knew I'd have to tell you I was an ex-con first. I kept putting it off."

We sat in silence for several long moments. Of all the possible situations I could find myself in, Mitch wanting to date me was one I'd never have conjured up. Leaving his intentions aside, though, I owed it to him at least to hear him out. "How about telling me now?"

"I thought the cops filled you in."

"They said you'd been in prison for murder, that's all."

"I was convicted of manslaughter, not murder. I'm not making excuses, though. A man's dead because of me."

"What happened?"

"A bar fight. I was nineteen, being cool with a couple of low-lifes and a fake ID. I got drunk, and the next thing I knew I was in a fight with someone drunker than I was. I got him with a sucker punch and knocked him off his feet. He hit his head on a corner of the pool table on his way down. That was all it took. He never came to. Died two days later."

"That's a long way from being a cold-blooded killer," I said.

Mitch shrugged. "He's still dead. It's like you said last night. How you couldn't get over what you'd done. That's how I feel. Every day."

That was a lot of guilt for a man to carry around. I nearly reached out and patted him on the shoulder, but thought better of it and just asked, "What happens now? You're home, so the cops didn't arrest you."

"They wanted to, but they didn't have enough evidence. Ron thinks they're trying to put a case together against me."

"Ron?"

"Ron Kelso, my lawyer."

I snorted. "This the guy you were sending me to?

Some lawyer if he let a nineteen year old do hard time for a drunken brawl gone bad."

"He'd agree with you. He wasn't my lawyer at first. He's the one who got me a new trial. The problem right now is that I don't have an alibi for the time I took getting your bag out of your car or for an hour after I left the hospital. Ron says it'll probably depend on what the coroner decides about time of death."

"You mean they're putting all their energy into making a case against you? I can't believe the stupidity of it. I told them it's all related to Stevie's murder. If they solve that one, they'll solve them all."

"They don't see it that way."

"I guess it's up to me, then."

"To do what? You don't want to mess around with whoever this killer is. He's already made you a target. Maybe that knife was meant for you."

"I don't think so. And what makes you think the killer's a man? Gina Lind seems perfectly capable of murder to me."

"The girl you knocked down last night?"

"She's not a girl. She's in her twenties, and she knocked me down first."

"Still, it takes a lot of muscle to bury a knife in a man's chest."

I leaned my head back on the sofa cushions and gazed at the ceiling. "What do you suppose happened? Frank didn't look as if he'd struggled at all. You'd think he'd at least have tried to ward off the killer."

"I'm pretty sure he never saw it coming. The cops think the killer came up from behind."

I straightened and looked at him. "What do you mean?"

"Come over here. I'll be Frank, sitting in the chair. You go around behind the chair."

I did as he said. "Okay, now what?" I asked the top of Mitch's head.

"You pretend you're gripping a knife in both hands, raise it above your head and swing down in an arc toward my chest."

"All right, only you have to imagine both the knife and my right arm. This cast wasn't designed for crime re-enactments." I made a fist, lifted my arm and brought it down onto Mitch's chest with a gentle thump. Even one-armed and minus the knife, the action made it real. "Oh God," I breathed, unclenching my fist and flattening my palm against Mitch's chest. His heart beat reassuringly under my fingers.

He covered my hand with his. "You okay?"

I slid my hand out from under his and moved back to the couch. "I don't think I like re-enactments. I was right, though. A woman could have done it. You get a lot of force coming down that way. If I didn't have a broken arm, they'd have arrested me for sure. Open and shut for them. My house, my ex, and my knife. They asked me about that knife about fifty times before they gave up and decided to give you the third degree instead. I'm sorry I got you involved in this mess."

"Don't be sorry. I'm not."

I didn't have anything to say to that.

"Was the knife that killed Frank the same one I saw you with the day he kicked in your door?" Mitch asked.

"I guess so. I only had the one. That's the part that looks bad, isn't it? It seems like too much of a coincidence that Frank was stabbed with the same knife."

"Who else knew that you'd held him off with a knife that day? Besides me."

"Tony, of course, but he was a big fan of Frank's. And Rose, who's definitely not a suspect."

"Didn't you tell anyone? How about your friends?"

"I told Kenji. He's a friend of mine at work. My only friend there, actually, but he didn't even know Frank."

"You're sure about that?"

"Sure I'm sure, and Kenji's a good friend."

"Okay, if you say so. Can you think of anyone else? What about the friend who came by later? What's her name, Livvy?"

"Libby!" I sat up straight. "I forgot about Libby. I have to call her. She doesn't know how to reach me. She'll worry herself sick when she hears about Frank." I looked around for the phone.

"So she knew Frank? Did you tell her about the knife?"

"She knew about him. I don't know if they actually met. I didn't tell her about the knife, and it wouldn't matter if I had. Libby is goodness incarnate. You'll see what I mean, when you get to know her. Where's your phone? Wasn't it here by the couch?"

"I moved it when you were sleeping. Here, use my cell phone." He unsnapped the leather case on his belt and pulled out a small black plastic rectangle, which he flipped open and handed to me.

I reached to take the phone, but he held on to it.

"You said I'd get to know your friend Libby. Does that mean that you and me, we'll... ?"

I met his gaze. "That we'll see each other, date, whatever?"

He nodded and released his hold on the phone.

I leaned back and let my gaze slide away. "You'd do better to ask out someone who doesn't know so many recently murdered people."

"That's not what I want. Is it what you want?"

I still couldn't meet his gaze. How could I know what I wanted, really wanted, anymore? When it came to men, I'd have to plead impaired judgment. "Ask me after all this is over. Okay?"

"Okay." He stood up. "You go ahead and make that call. I'll get out some clean sheets and towels."

"What for?"

"Since you're staying here, I figured you'd like a shower, a bed, you know."

I narrowed my eyes at him. "Didn't we just have a conversation about not starting any kind of relationship right now?"

"I'm not planning on making any moves on you. I'm just being neighborly. Thought that was what you wanted—good neighbors."

I didn't have anything to say to that, and he left the room. I called Libby, who was just as upset as I'd expected. Not that Libby ever wasted time just being upset. I told her about having a broken arm and being temporarily locked out of my house, and before I knew it she showed up at Mitch's house with two complete changes of clothing and a half-gallon of ice cream.

"Hi, you must be Mitch. I'm Libby," she said when Mitch opened the door. She shoved the ice cream carton into his hands. "Here, you'll want to get that into your freezer pretty quick. It's starting to go soft."

Mitch disappeared into the kitchen, and Libby turned to embrace me. "I'm very sorry about Frank. Sorry about your arm, too. The whole situation is just terrible. I'm glad you have someone to help you. Isn't he the man who was working on your house the other day?" She lowered her voice to a whisper. "He's quite good looking."

"Don't start. Mitch is a friend."

Libby gave me a knowing smile, and I hurried on to ask, "What's in the bag?"

"Clothes. For you. I'm pretty sure these will fit all right. Tops and bottoms are pull-on so you don't have to fiddle with buttons and zippers. Why don't you take a shower and change?" She raised her voice. "Mitch? Can Alison use your shower? And, do you have some plastic, like a bag from the cleaners, we can wrap her cast in?"

And so, Libby organized my fractured life. I emerged an hour later with clean skin, hair and clothes. All I needed was a full belly to feel pretty good in spite of everything. Naturally, Libby was ready to provide that, too. "It's your favorite, rocky road," she said as she dumped three scoops into a bowl.

Mitch decided that ice cream wasn't a balanced enough diet and went after pizza. He ran into Rose on his way out the door. She'd come bearing a tray of antipasto and breadsticks. She found me at Mitch's kitchen table, spooning rocky road into my mouth.

"You're going to spoil your dinner," Rose said. She placed the tray in the center of the table.

"This is my dinner," I said. "And, this is, too. Thanks." I popped an olive into my mouth and followed it with a spoonful of ice cream. "You're staying for pizza, aren't you?"

Rose agreed to stay and sat at the table with us. Rose and Libby knew about each other, but hadn't ever met. They did the polite "heard so much about you" bit for awhile and then started singing Mitch's praises.

"Such a nice man. So concerned about you, Alison," Libby said.

"How would you know? You just met him."

"We had a good talk while you were in the shower. He filled me in on some things you'd omitted to tell me. I'm glad you had him to turn to last night."

"He's a wonderful carpenter," Rose put in. "Not one of those slap-dash types, either. A real old-time craftsman. Makes a very good living at it."

"Did you know he'd been in prison?" I asked Rose, while watching Libby out of the corner of my eye. Libby didn't bat an eyelash.

"Of course," Rose said. "He told me all about it. He doesn't make a secret of it." She turned to Libby. "He made a mistake and paid for it. He's a good man, nothing like the last one she hooked up with—may he rest in peace," she added, crossing herself.

"Mitch told me, too," Libby said. "He's worried that your staying with him might reflect badly on you as far as the police are concerned, but he thinks you need protection. I agreed with him."

I ate my ice cream and didn't comment.

Libby and Rose must have felt they'd made their

point, because they lapsed into silence. The doorbell broke through the quiet, and we all jumped.

"Maybe Mitch forgot his keys?" Rose asked.

I pushed away from the table and stood up. "Very unlikely. I'd better go see."

"Check through the window first," Rose said.

Libby stood up and followed me to the front door. I pulled aside the curtain over the small window across the top of the door. Detective Stans stood on the porch, finger poised to ring the bell again. I opened the door. "Now what?"

Stans' gaze slid from me to Libby, standing behind me in the hall, and back to me again. "Sorry to bother you, but I need your help."

"I'm not falling for that line again," I said.

"I wouldn't ask, but it's important. Please," he added.

Something in his somber expression alerted me.

"What?" I said and took a step back. "Someone's hurt? Worse than hurt?" I grabbed the doorjamb. "Not Mitch? He just went out for pizza," I added inanely, as if buying pizza conferred some sort of supernatural protection.

Stans shook his head. "No."

Libby put her arm around my shoulders. "It's not Joe, is it?"

"We haven't ID'd him yet. He doesn't match the description of GI Joe. We'd appreciate it if you could tell us if you've seen him before."

I let out a breath I'd been holding. "All right, I'll do it," I said.

"You're sure?" Libby murmured.

I nodded. "Save some pizza for me," I told her and followed Stans down the front steps.

"We have to go around the block. You okay for walking?" he asked as we headed for the corner.

"Yes, I had a shower and a bowl of rocky road ice cream. I feel like a new woman. That's a lie, but it's what

Mama Ruth, my last foster mom, used to say. 'Take a shower, eat something and you'll feel like a new woman.' Basically, I feel like an old woman who's clean and not hungry."

Stans didn't comment.

"Okay, I'm babbling. But I'm kind of on overwhelm right now. I'm assuming this is a homicide?"

Stans nodded.

"I usually try to limit my encounters with people who die violent deaths to one a day. What am I going to see when I get there?"

"Caucasian male, about six-two, hundred ninety pounds, brown hair, early to mid thirties, gunshot wound to the chest."

There was strange comfort in the de-personalized cop talk. Not an ex-husband, not a friend, just a Caucasian male. I could handle that. We walked around the block, and when we rounded the second corner, I could see where he was taking me. There was the now familiar traffic jam of cop cars, ambulance, news vans, and curiosity seekers in front of a house with a "for sale" sign on the front lawn--the supposedly empty house behind mine.

People turned to stare as we approached, but, at a gesture from Stans, parted to make way for us. Before we could reach the house, a cameraman hoisted his video equipment onto his shoulder and pointed it at us while a TV newswoman stuck a microphone in our faces and said, "What can you tell us at this time about the murder victims?"

Stans put one hand over the camera lens and another over the microphone. "For her own safety and for the security of our investigation, this witness's face can't be shown. Erase that tape, and I'll send out a senior detective to answer your questions on camera."

"Deal," the newswoman said.

Stans led me up the walk to the open front door. "Sorry about that."

"She said victims. Is there more than one?"

"No. She was just fishing for information, trying to get us to say something."

"How'd you find the body?"

"We didn't. The real estate agent did, when she brought some prospective buyers to see the house."

I followed Stans through the empty house to the kitchen toward the back. The sellers clearly hadn't used Mitch's services before putting it on the market. Ancient, stained wallpaper showed darker rectangles where pictures used to hang. The worn wood floors hadn't seen new wax in about a decade.

Idle police officers filled the kitchen, chatting among themselves. Carney wasn't among them, and the only one without a mustache was a woman. Everyone except Stans and me wore latex gloves. Stans shoved his hands in his pockets. "Don't touch anything," he warned. As if I would.

The body was already encased in a body bag, resting on a gurney. Nearby, a chalk outline and a pool of dry blood on the worn linoleum marked where he'd fallen. He must have been killed while standing at the sink. The sink, wall and floor in that area were spattered with brown-red blood.

A plainclothes cop approached us. "This the witness?" The cop asked Stans. Was I imagining things, or was there a tension between them?

"This is Alison Weaver," Stans said, but didn't tell me the cop's name. Instead, he turned to a police medic who stood at the head of the gurney. "Open it. Just the face."

The cop nodded and tugged at the zipper. The room fell silent around us as I gazed at the face, still recognizable even in death, of the man who'd broken my arm. I turned to Stans. "Guess you believe me now."

The other detective stepped forward. "Can you identify this man?"

"I don't know his name. He's the man who attacked me in my house last night. Today I recognized him from a group photograph I had of a friend who was murdered—Stephen Lind."

"Can you show me the photograph?" the detective

demanded more than asked.

"Detective Stans has it. I just have a copy."

The detective clenched his jaw and flashed an irritated look at Stans. What was his problem? I glanced at Stans, but his expression didn't give anything away. The medic started to zip up the body bag.

"Wait a minute before you do that, will you? I'd like to have a closer look. I won't touch him." I bent over the body and peered at the face. The eyes were almost completely closed. "Has the medical examiner looked at him already?"

The medic nodded.

"Did he look at his eyes?"

The medic nodded again. "Yeah, when the detective asked him to." He gestured toward Stans.

"And?" I prompted.

Stans said, "He could see damage to the left cornea, possibly some to the right. Couldn't say what from or how long ago it'd happened until he does the autopsy."

"Can I see the bullet wound?" I asked the medic.

The medic gave me a funny look, but Stans said "It's okay," and the medic unzipped the bag further. They must have opened his shirt to examine him and then folded it back over him without buttoning it. The front of the shirt was soaked in blood. I glanced up at the medic. "Mind opening his shirt?" He shrugged and pulled the flaps of material apart. I noted the gaping tear in the middle of his chest. "Exit wound, huh?" I asked the medic, more by way of conversation than needing confirmation, but the medic simply nodded and didn't add anything.

I gazed at the dead man's face. He'd injured me and might have intended worse than injury, though now I'd never know. But he'd also helped me exorcise some of my ghosts. Without meaning to, he'd done me a good turn. As I stood contemplating the ironies of my life, a uniformed cop came in and reported to the other detective.

"No one heard a gunshot. Several neighbors said a noisy motorcycle woke them up around 3 a.m. and then again about a half an hour later. The couple next door said that the second time, the motorcycle was parked with its engine running, but no one was around. They were about to call the cops to complain when someone got on it and drove off."

I turned around. "It was Frank's motorcycle. I'll bet you anything. He drove it here, and the murderer drove it away."

The detective folded his arms across his chest. "Who's Frank?" the detective asked.

"Frank Avery. The other homicide," Stans replied. "You done?" he asked me.

"Yes," I said, and Stans signaled the medic to close up the body bag. As soon as his face was covered again, the conversational noise in the kitchen upped a notch.

Carney came in through the back door, approached us and held up a bunch of keys. "It's a fit all right."

"What is?" I asked.

"This one," he said, separating out one key from the others and holding it up, "opens your back door. It's a master key. They all are. He could walk in almost any place he wanted that has a standard lock on the door."

"He—you mean that guy?" I gestured to the body bag.

Carney nodded. "I can hardly wait to ID his prints and pull his sheet."

The other detective moved in next to Carney, irritation sparking from him like static electricity. "Mind letting me in on what's going on?"

Stans remained impassive, but Carney replied without trying to hide his grin. "It's like I told you when I saw these. They're master keys. It's how he got into Ms. Weaver's house without breaking in. Ditto this house. It's a good bet that the guy who popped him also did Avery, which means you'll be working with us. Sorry," he said without sounding the least bit regretful.

The other detective jutted his jaw out and stepped close to Carney. "Fine, but this one's still my case."

"Sure, sure," Carney said, still grinning like a very irritating sibling, who knew just how to get under his brother's skin and intended to keep on doing it.

"Excuse me," the medic said. "Is it okay to remove the body now?"

"Yes," the detective said quickly and turned away from us. "I'll go out with you and talk to the media."

I waited until they'd left the room before I asked Stans and Carney, "What that was all about?"

Carney shrugged. "Politics. He's a glory hound, and we just happened to pull two high profile homicides in a row. Along comes this third one, which he doesn't want to see linked to ours because he thinks he'll have to share air time with us."

"So you don't yearn to see yourself on the news?" I asked.

"Better to keep a low profile, so you're not a target if there's backlash. There's no glory if you don't solve the case. I learned that from my partner here." He gave Stans a punch on the arm.

Stans winced and rubbed his arm. "You're in a good mood."

"Damn right I am. He's out the front door, and we're going out the back. Something I need Ms. Weaver to look at."

We followed Carney out the back door. He led us to the garbage cans, which were surrounded with trash. Not a very appealing view for prospective home buyers, but probably less of a put-off than finding a dead body while walking through with a realtor.

"Thought it wouldn't hurt to take a peek, and you'll never guess what." He pulled a latex glove out of his pocket and pulled it on his hand with a snap before lifting the lid of one of the cans. "Can you identify these?" he asked me.

I stepped forward and peered into the can. It was half filled with familiar manila folders, all neatly labeled. "Those are Stevie's, the ones left on my kitchen table."

"That's what I thought," Carney said.

"Only they were in cardboard boxes."

"Like these?" Carney asked, opening the second garbage can with a flourish. It held flattened cardboard boxes.

"I don't get it. It looks like the trash's been dumped out so the papers could be hidden. Why not just take them along?"

"Maybe he took the ones he wanted and threw away the rest, thinking we wouldn't find them and figure out that was what he was after," Carney said. He turned to Stans. "Guess we should have the crime scene boys do the backyard, right? Our man probably came over the fence. Brought the boxes with him."

"Why are you assuming it was a man? I told you that Gina Lind trashed my house looking for Stevie's papers. It's possible she came back and found them." I gestured to the trashcans.

"We haven't ruled out Gina Lind," Carney said. He didn't actually smile when he said it, but he looked very pleased with himself.

I'd never seen Carney so cheerful. It gave me the courage to ask, "What about Mitch? What about me, for that matter? Are we still suspects?"

Carney immediately sobered and exchanged a glance with Stans, and it was Stans who said, "We're looking at more than one homicide here, and until we figure out how or if they're connected, we're not ruling anyone out."

CHAPTER TWENTY

I walked into Mitch's house a while later. Libby, Mitch and Rose were seated cozily together on the couch. Rose's antipasto tray and three empty wineglasses stood on the coffee table in front of them. The three of them were smiling, as if they'd just been sharing some hilarious joke. "Too bad, you just missed it," Libby said.

"I missed it? You ate all the pizza? You couldn't save me even one slice?"

"We haven't eaten anything, yet. We were waiting for you. Now that you're back, we can eat." Libby heaved herself up from the couch.

Mitch stood up quickly. "You sit down, Libby. I'll get it."

"You're sure?"

"I'm sure. Who wants more wine?"

"Not for me," Libby said. She moved around the coffee table and settled herself into the easy chair.

"How about you, Rose?" Mitch asked.

I raised my eyebrows. So now they were on a first name basis, were they?

"Well, maybe just a half a glass," Rose said. "I don't want to get tipsy."

"Tipsy on half a glass? Come on, Rose."

Rose giggled and batted her eyelashes at him as she handed him her glass. Mitch took her glass and headed for the kitchen.

"Don't you want to know what you just missed?" Libby asked.

"Not particularly," I said, letting my grumpiness show.

"Come, sit over here," Rose said, patting the empty spot next to her on the couch.

I crossed the room and sat down stiffly "I'm the one who had to identify a body. Why don't you want to hear about that?"

"Because we already know it was the man who attacked you, but he didn't have any identification on him, so they don't know his name, yet." Libby said. "We saw it on the news." She gestured toward the small TV set in the bookcase on the other side of the room. It was on, with the volume turned all the way down.

"They showed them bringing out the body, but it was all covered up," Rose said. "Was it awful for you, dear?"

"Not too bad. I was mainly relieved to know that he won't be coming back to break my other arm. Guess how he got into my house? He had a set of master keys."

"We know," Rose and Libby said in chorus.

I threw up my hands. "Okay, fine, you know everything. You probably also know what they found in the trash."

Rose leaned toward me, her eyes wide. "They didn't mention the trash. What was it? The murder weapon? A body part?"

Mitch came into the room with the pizza and four plates. "What's this about body parts?"

"They found something in the trash," Libby said.

"It wasn't a body part, and I don't know where you get such gruesome ideas, Rose. It was Stevie's papers. Someone took them from my house last night."

"Oh," Rose said, clearly disappointed. They all paused for a beat.

"I'll get the wine," Mitch said, as if I hadn't made my

revelation. "You start with the pizza."

"Okay," Libby said, picking up a plate and pulling the pizza toward her. "Let me get you your slice, Alison, since you have only one working arm."

"Don't you get it?" I asked. "Who wanted Stevie's papers so much she was willing to break into my house to get them?" I took the plate Libby handed me. I rested the plate in my lap, picked up the pizza slice and took a big bite.

"Gina Lind," Mitch said as he came into the room. He handed a refilled wineglass to Rose and a tumbler filled with a soft drink to me.

"I don't rate wine?" I asked.

"Not while you're taking those pain pills," he said. "I had your prescription filled while I was out getting the pizza. The pharmacist said no alcohol." He sat on the couch next to me and accepted the plate of pizza Libby passed to him.

"You what? How'd you get my prescription?"

"It was in the pile of stuff we dumped out of your bag looking for your hairbrush."

"You couldn't ask first?"

He shrugged. "You'd have said no, then stayed up all night because your arm hurt." He tackled his own slice of pizza.

Libby laughed. "That's our Alison, all right. Now don't give me that look," she said to me. "Eat your pizza and let us tell you who we saw on the news. The police received an anonymous tip that Gina Lind was going to leave the country, and they took her into custody at the airport. They had a TV crew there and filmed the whole thing."

I stared at her. "They arrested Gina? I can't believe it. Those slippery cops told me they still hadn't ruled me out as a suspect."

Mitch shook his head. "I don't think they arrested her, just detained her. They said they wanted her for questioning."

"For which murder?"

"They said for an assault, and I guess that means her attack on you," Mitch replied. "But they sort of implied that it also had to do with her brother's death."

"And Gina was about to leave the country? That doesn't look too good for her, does it?"

"You should have heard the way she talked," Rose put in. "They had to beep over almost everything she said, but we could read her lips anyway, so I don't know why they bothered."

"How can they possibly consider you a suspect?" Libby demanded.

"They just told me they haven't ruled anyone out. I guess they'll say that until they actually arrest someone."

"I'm confused," Rose said. "Why would anyone kill the man who broke your arm? And, who killed Frank? And, why?"

"I'm with you, Rose," Libby said. "I've seen Gina in action. She definitely has a violent edge, but she doesn't seem big enough or strong enough to kill anyone." She turned to me. "Mitch said that you easily knocked her to the ground and held her down when she tried to attack you."

"Did Mitch also show you how the police think Frank was killed? Believe me, Gina could've done it. And she could've shot the man who attacked me, too. I saw the body. He was shot in the back. He never saw it coming."

"But why?" Rose asked.

I shrugged. "I'm not sure. Probably because he wasn't useful to her anymore, and she didn't want to leave anyone behind who could identify her."

"That makes sort of twisted sense," Libby said. "And, I guess poor Frank was just in the wrong place at the wrong time."

I shook my head. "I think he was lured to my house. He came on his motorcycle and met the killer at the house behind mine. I imagine they walked around the block to my house, let themselves in the back. Frank sat in the chair, all unsuspecting, when the killer came up behind him, and—whammo, a knife in the chest. The killer went back to the house behind mine, taking Stevie's papers along this time. And, get this, the killer's cold blooded enough to go through the papers before dumping them in the trash, along with the boxes they came in. Then, he—or very possibly she—takes off on Frank's motorcycle."

"I'm with Rose on this one," Mitch said. "You've described how, but we still don't know why."

"Frank was killed because he knew too much. I think GI Joe told him what he knew about Stevie's killer. It all goes back to Stevie. When I know why Stevie was killed, I'll know who."

"Where's Joe now? Do the police know?" Libby asked.

I shook my head. "They don't have a clue. Frank hid him some place. Didn't tell anyone, not even Tony, and he's the one who told Frank where Joe was hiding out."

We sat in silence, munching our pizza.

"Joe's the key," Libby announced suddenly.

"Yes," I agreed. "He knows something crucial, but no one knows where he is. He's not on the street, or we'd have heard about it by now."

"I'm willing to bet that one person knows where he is—his mother," Libby said.

"Barbara Reynolds—of course, she might know. She told me she'd hired a private detective to keep tabs on him, but I don't think she had him followed constantly. Just checked up on him. She can't have direct contact with him, though, or her ex-husband will file for custody of their other children."

"It's still worth a try," Libby said.

"Okay, let's go," I said, getting to my feet.

"Now?" Mitch asked.

"It's getting late," Rose said.

"They're right," Libby said. "It's too late to go ringing her doorbell. Let me go by myself in the morning. I think she'll talk to me." She stood up. "I should be getting along. I still have to find someone to take your place at the clinic."

Rose stood up and started picking up the dirty dishes.

"Leave those, Rose," Mitch said. "I play by your rules, and you wouldn't let me carry plates into your kitchen, remember?"

Rose reluctantly agreed to let Mitch do the cleaning up, gave me a hug, and set off for home. Libby followed her out the door, saying, "Wait up, Rose, show me which house is yours so I'll know which door to knock on when I come visiting." She turned and said over her shoulder, "I'll call you tomorrow, Alison, after I go see Barbara." She started down the steps, turned and added. "Mitch, thanks. For everything." Her words seemed weighted with significance.

"What was that all about?" I asked Mitch, when he'd closed and locked the door.

"You were right. I like Libby. She's great." He crossed to the coffee table, stacked up the dirty plates and carried them into the kitchen.

I picked up my empty glass and followed him. "You didn't answer my question."

He turned and took my glass from me and set it on the drainboard. "Tell you what. I'll answer your question, if you'll answer one of mine."

"Okay. What do you want to know?"

"What were you so mad about when you came in tonight?"

"I wasn't... " I stopped in mid-denial and let my gaze slide away from Mitch.

"Yes?" Mitch prompted.

"All right, I was a little mad, but I got over it right away."

Mitch just looked at me and didn't say anything.

His silence pressed in on me, until I was forced to say, "It's embarrassing to talk about. I feel stupid."

Mitch folded his arms and continued to gaze at me.

"Okay, okay, if you must know, when I came in, you were sitting on the couch with Rose and Libby. You were all laughing about something, and I felt left out. That's all. I told you it was stupid."

"Know what we were laughing about?"

I shook my head.

"You. Libby had just told us about the run-in you had with a pimp when you were handing out free condoms down on West MacArthur. So, I told them what you said to Tony, when he showed up and threatened you."

I winced. "I should never have left you alone together."

He turned to the sink, turned on the hot water and tipped some dishwashing liquid into the sink. "I like them both."

"Of course you do. There's Rose flirting with you, all girlish over a glass of wine, and Libby giving you the biggest slice of pizza. Don't think I didn't notice that. They clearly like you, so naturally you like them back."

Mitch deftly washed, rinsed and stacked dishes in the drainer for a few moments. "They like you better."

I let his comment pass. "Remember, you were going to tell me what Libby meant by what she said?"

He finished stacking the last dish, drained the soapy water from the sink and dried his hands on a dishtowel. "We're going to help clean up your house, when the police unseal it."

"Whose idea was that?"

"Libby's. She's worried about how you'll feel going back after Frank was killed there."

"That sounds like Libby, all right. Libby's children died in a house fire. She and her husband had to go through the ashes of the house to see if they could salvage any of their possessions. I think she still has nightmares about it."

"So she's married?"

I shook my head. "Widowed. Her husband committed suicide three months later. He left Libby broke and homeless. An old lady from her church took her in and saw her through the worst of it. When Libby asked the woman how she could repay her, the woman told her 'Pass it on.' So the next day she applied to college. Got a degree in social work and started the mobile clinic. But, what I don't get is, if it was Libby's idea to help clean up my house, why did she thank you?"

"Because I said I'd be the one to tell you."

"That's it? You say you'll tell me, and she gives you this intense 'thank you for everything?'"

"I also said I'd make sure you let us do it."

"And how are you going to do that?"

"Good question. Ask you nicely?"

"More likely, you'll just go ahead without telling me, like you did with my prescription."

"Speaking of which, you look like your arm's hurting." He moved directly toward me, and I sidestepped out of his way. "I was just getting your pills." He picked up a pill bottle from the counter and unscrewed the top. "Here you go." I stuck out my hand, and he tipped a pill onto my palm. He crossed to the sink, filled a glass with water and handed it to me. "I'm going to leave one pill out." He placed a tablet on the lid of the bottle, "so you can take it in the night if you need it. I have an idea that this child-proof cap will be hard for you to get off one-handed."

I downed the pill. "Thanks." I handed him the empty glass. "I appreciate your going to the trouble to fill the prescription. You were right. I wouldn't have let you do it, if you'd asked first. I don't mean to be difficult, you know. I just like my independence."

"It's a good quality to have. It's just that you sometimes take it to extremes."

"I can see that. I don't seem to know how to act any other way. Will you tell me something honestly?"

He nodded. "Sure, I'll try."

"Do you think that I might've prevented all this—my broken arm and Frank's murder—if I'd listened to you about locking my gate, or put better locks on my back door?"

"Aw, hell, Alison," Mitch said, with a gaze so soft I had to lower my eyes. "Don't go there. All those 'what ifs' will just wear down your soul." He stepped toward me, and this time I didn't move away. When he wrapped his arms around me, I let my head rest on his shoulder, pressing my forehead against the curve of his neck. I hadn't been held with such tenderness for a very long time. Maybe never, if I thought about it.

I could feel his carotid pulse against my forehead beating slow and steady and my own breathing slowed down to match his. We stayed like that for a long moment before I realized that his heartbeat had picked up speed and my own was playing copycat.

"Mitch?"

"Mmm?"

"You're not getting any ideas, are you?"

"Maybe." He caressed my back. "Are you?"

I was going to take the fifth on that one. "My idea is that I should get some sleep so I'll be ready to find answers tomorrow." I pulled away, and Mitch let his arms fall to his sides.

"Where are you going to look?" he asked.

"The University. That's where Stevie and Flo and the guy who broke my arm all knew each other well enough to pose for a group picture. I think I'll go see if I can find someone who knew them then."

"You're not going to the University tomorrow."

"Who's going to stop me?"

Mitch rubbed the back of his neck. "God and the state of California. Tomorrow's Sunday. No school."

"Oh," I said, turning away. "Fine. I'll think of something else, then."

"Alison?" Mitch said.

I looked at him over my shoulder.

"Why don't you back off for a little while? Let the cops figure it out."

I turned to face him. "You know what they're figuring? That you had means, motive and opportunity to kill Frank. They could easily arrest you just so they can look like they've solved his murder."

"They're not going to arrest me, and if they do, then they won't be able to make enough of a case to take to court. But I've got a feeling that you're not trying to protect me. You've just decided to go after this guy yourself, for your own personal reasons."

"So what if I have?"

"So you could be next on the hit list. You say Frank was killed because he knew something. The more you keep poking around, the likelier it is that you'll find out what that something was. Or maybe the killer won't wait until you find out. Have you thought of that?"

"That's a perfect example of why you and I shouldn't get involved. You'll think you can tell me what to do, and I'm not comfortable with that."

"Jesus H. Christ! What kind of twisted ideas do you have? Can't a man who cares about you even say 'Don't get killed'?"

I stared at him.

"Well?"

"Give me a minute. I'm thinking."

"Think all you want. I'm going to bed. I didn't get much sleep last night." He headed out the kitchen doorway.

"What about me?"

He turned around to face me.

"I mean, where do I sleep?"

He jerked his thumb over his shoulder. "Spare bedroom. Bed's made up. Turn off the lights when you're done."

"Okay," I said, but he'd already disappeared into the hallway. I heard the door to his bedroom click shut.

"And for your information, I don't have twisted ideas," I said out loud, but Mitch didn't reappear. I found the spare bedroom easily enough. It had a single bed in the corner and a large desk holding a computer, fax machine and a neat stack of books against one wall. The bathroom lay between Mitch's bedroom and the spare room. I could hear water running in the bathroom through the closed door. Stupid man. He didn't have any reason to be so huffy.

I collected my things from the living room, carried them into the bedroom, and dumped them in a heap on a chair. My pile of stuff stood in stark contrast to the orderliness of the rest of the room. A perfect image of how we would never get along. Neat Mitch and messy Alison. Couldn't he see that?

I made a last trip to turn off the kitchen and living room lights. This time, when I entered the spare bedroom, there were no sounds from the bathroom and the door stood open a crack. I guessed that was Mitch's code for "bathroom's all yours." That was like him, too. Thoughtful and, all right, caring. And, most of all, not like Frank in any way.

I straightened my shoulders, marched up to his bedroom door and knocked. "Mitch? Listen, will you?"

He pulled the door open. He was barefoot, but otherwise still dressed, thank God. "What?"

"By now you know that I don't often ask for help. But when I was standing at my back door with my arm broken and hurting so much I couldn't move, it didn't occur to me to call 911 or even Libby, and she's my best friend in the world. All I thought was... no it wasn't even a thought, it was a picture of you in my head, a picture of where I knew I'd be safe."

He shifted his feet and opened his mouth to speak. I held up a hand to stop him. "Wait, let me finish or I won't be able to say all of it. I'm not cut out for a relationship kind of thing, so don't take it personally, because, if I were any good at relationships, you'd be at the top of my list. But I don't want you to be wasting your time thinking that you and I could get together. I mean for a short thing, maybe, that would be cool, but probably not really, because it would be awkward afterwards, living across the street from each other. Unless I got it wrong, and that's what you want. Not the awkward part. The short thing part."

He peered at me. "You done?"

I nodded.

"Okay. Good night."

"Good night? That's it?"

"What did you want me to say?"

"I want you to acknowledge that I'm right."

"I can't do that."

"Why not?"

"Two reasons. One, because as crazy as it sounds, ever since you pointed a knife at me and told me to leave your door alone, I haven't been able to get you out of my head. And two, because you just told me that when you really needed someone, I was the one you turned to. Whether you want to admit it or not, something's already going on between us. So, you can either face up to it and come in here," he gestured toward the interior of his bedroom, "or you can let me get some sleep."

I took one step back.

He gave me a rueful smile. "That's what I thought. See you in the morning." He closed his bedroom door.

CHAPTER TWENTY-ONE

I retreated to the guestroom and sat on the edge of the bed. What had given me the idea we could talk about things in a rational way? I'd said the wrong things, and now Mitch thought we were leading up to something. A relationship with me was the very last thing he needed, couldn't he see that? My history alone should've been enough to send off danger signals. Maybe I ought to carry a written warning, like a pack of cigarettes.

I lay back on the bed, trying for a comfortable position for my arm. I had to find some way out of this situation. I didn't want to have to argue with Mitch every time I left the house. The fact was that if I'd at least talked to Frank, or returned his calls, I could've found out what he was up to. No matter what Mitch said, I carried some responsibility for Frank's death. If I didn't try to do what I could, who knew who else would die? Maybe Mitch thought I was in danger, but by my accounting, GI Joe was a more likely candidate.

I sat up. What was I doing lying here? I wasn't going to get any sleep. I rolled my head around to ease the tension in my neck. Even if my conscience didn't keep me awake with harangues, my arm would. The painkiller hadn't even blunted the edges of the pain in my arm, shoulder, neck and head. I returned to the darkened kitchen and turned on the light. Where had Mitch left those pills?

I found the bottle with the one pill resting on top. I swallowed the pill with some water right from the kitchen faucet. As I turned to leave the room, my eye fell on the telephone. Why hadn't I thought of it before? I didn't have to stay here. Libby could put me up until I could get back into my house.

I called Libby, speaking as quietly as I could. She wasn't as agreeable to having a houseguest as I'd expected. Something about needing to keep her spare room open for homeless emergencies, though why I didn't qualify, I couldn't quite figure out. She did agree to my going with her to see Barbara Reynolds, promising to pick me up right after church, and I had to be satisfied with that.

"Now get some sleep, you hear?"

"Sure thing," I lied and carefully replaced the receiver.

I switched off the light and returned to the spare room. I struggled out of my clothes, put on the sweatshirt Mitch had loaned me for the trip home from the hospital. It fell to mid-thigh and felt cozy. After wrestling out of my clothes and into the sweatshirt, my arm ached more than ever. I crawled into the narrow bed. *I'm not going to be able to sleep a wink* was the last thought that passed through my mind.

I woke up the next morning to the smell of brewing coffee. It pulled me out of bed as if I were in a weird sci-fi movie being mind-controlled by aliens. I staggered out of my room, eyes slitted open just enough to prevent collision with large objects.

"Hi," Mitch said.

"Mumph," I replied. Out of my peripheral vision, I could see him standing by the kitchen table, but my gaze was riveted on the coffee maker. I came to a halt in front of it and breathed in the steam. There was another thing I needed to do to be able actually to drink the coffee, but I couldn't quite remember what it was.

"Want some coffee?" Mitch rose from the table.

"Mmmm." An animal sound that came from somewhere in my throat.

He moved around the kitchen, opened and closed a

cupboard, while I continued to inhale deeply in front of the coffee maker. He poured the coffee into a cup and handed it to me.

I took a sip. Hot, but not mouth-burning hot. I took a gulp, and then another. I drained the cup and held it out for a refill.

"Whoa there, pilgrim. You want to take it easy with the hard stuff. It packs a wallop."

"Very funny." I nudged him in the chest with my empty cup. "More... please."

He took the cup from me and gave me a gentle push in the small of my back. "Sit down at the table. I'll bring it to you."

I moved to the table, lowered myself onto a chair, and rested my cast on the table. "It's that damned Vicodin. I feel like I've been in a coma for twenty years."

Mitch brought my coffee and a raisin Danish and placed them in front of me.

I stared at the Danish. "Where'd that come from?"

"The freezer," he said, lowering himself into the chair across from me.

"Know what's in my freezer? Ice cubes."

"Figures."

I sipped my coffee and chewed on a bite of Danish. "I don't usually eat breakfast."

"That figures, too."

"You know, we're nothing alike. And I'm not going to change."

He leaned back in his chair. "Are you trying to pick a fight, or is this just the way you are in the mornings?"

I rested my forehead in my hand. "Neither. I'm trying to finish last night's conversation." I lifted my head and gazed at him. "Can't we just be friends?"

Mitch leaned forward. "If you're breaking up with me, I want my sweatshirt back." He reached out and with his index finger, hooked my neckline and tugged.

"Hey!" I yelped and pulled the material away from him. "Watch it. I'm not wearing... " I stopped in the middle of my sentence.

"Nothing underneath, huh?" He lounged back in his chair. "Okay, you can keep it on. For now. It's more interesting when you make me use my imagination."

"I'm serious."

"Me too. A man talking about his fantasies is always serious."

I rolled my eyes. "Look, Mitch, I don't want bad feelings between us."

"Me neither."

"Good. That's good. Okay." I got to my feet. "I'm going to take a shower."

"What's your hurry?"

"I have some things to do, and, as I think I made clear last night, I don't want to have my comings and goings supervised—by anyone."

"Sure, whatever you say. I just thought you might want to tell Libby you're leaving without her, since she's been waiting for you for an hour."

"Libby's here? Where?"

"I'm in here," Libby called from the living room. "Reading about you in the Sunday papers."

And listening in on my conversation with Mitch, no doubt. I hurried into the living room. "I thought you said you were coming by after church."

She lowered the newspaper and peered at me. "I did. You were asleep, so Mitch very kindly gave me coffee and Danish and the paper to read while I waited for you. And, if you ask me, you look like you could use another twelve hours sack time." She gave me a knowing smile and looked meaningfully toward the kitchen.

I lifted a warning finger. "Don't start. I'll be ready in a few minutes."

I went to get ready and in a short time we were out the door and on our way across town to Piedmont. I brought the paper along with me and scanned it while Libby drove. Frank's murder had made the front page. A publicity shot of Frank was positioned next to a police arrest picture of my attacker. "His name was Ray Munsen," I said to Libby. "The guy who broke my arm."

"And he'd been arrested several times before, but apparently he always got off. He never went to prison."

The article was as close an approximation to the truth as could be expected. The description of the main facts of Frank's and Ray Munsen's murders was accurate, but when it came to speculations about what might link the men, the article veered into near fiction. Frank's widow made some nearly libelous remarks about my responsibility for the deaths. The article said I was a nurse and didn't mention graduate school or the Center. Daniel would be grateful for that.

I tossed the paper into the back seat with a grunt of disgust.

"It's better not to read news accounts about something that touches you so nearly," Libby said. I grunted again, and we rode in silence to Barbara house.

She answered the door, gazed at us with a frown and didn't invite us in. "What do you want?"

"We need to talk to you about Jason," Libby said.

Barbara shook her head and moved to close the door, but Libby, who could move fast for such a large woman, placed her arm and shoulder into the opening before Barbara could swing the door shut. "His life is in danger and so is Alison's. Please help us."

I'd never seen anyone say no to Libby. Apparently Barbara wasn't going to be the first. She released the door and stood back. We moved into the front hall before she could change her mind.

"I can't tell you anything." She folded her arms across her chest.

"Not even to save more lives?" I asked.

"Jason is safe," she said.

"But Frank wasn't and neither was I," I gestured with my cast.

Her brows drew together in a frown. "What?"

"Remember my ex? He visited you the day of Stevie's memorial service and offered to bring Jason to you. He was murdered."

She took a step back and stared at us. "Murdered?"

"Don't you read the papers?"

She shook her head. "I haven't had time. I've... " She broke off before finishing. "Please, just go. I'm sorry about Frank, but there's nothing I can do for you."

I dropped my gaze and stared at the floor. There had to be some way to persuade her to open up to us. "Where are your kids?" I asked, looking around the spacious front hall. When I'd visited before, the hall had housed a friendly jumble of kids' stuff. Today, the entire area was empty. Not a sneaker, sweatshirt, backpack, basketball or inline skate in sight.

She straightened. "What business is it of yours? Please just go. Now."

"It's Sunday. No school. I thought they might be at home."

"Well, they're not. They're... " She broke off, her lower lip trembling.

"Their dad took them, right? You said he had a court order."

Tears welled up in her eyes, and she seemed to fold in on herself. Libby put her arm around her. "There now. It's all right. We're here to help. Why don't we all sit down? How about the kitchen? I think I need some tea. How about you, Alison?"

We made our way to the kitchen and went through the soothing ritual of making and drinking a cup of tea. Barbara calmed down enough to talk, but stayed on the verge of tears. "Frank just showed up in the middle of the night." She glanced up at me. "Is he really dead? I can't seem to take it in." She took a sip of tea. "He brought Jason, but Jason was too ill even to get out of the car. I asked Frank why he hadn't simply taken him straight to the hospital, but never got an answer. Anyway, I rode in the car with them to the emergency room. It was very frightening. Jason was... was... " Her voice broke and she covered her face with her hands.

Libby patted her shoulder and we waited for her to recover and go on.

She took a deep breath and blew her nose. "He was raving and incoherent. He didn't recognize me. It turned out that he'd had a stroke. Apparently, it's one of the things that can happen with the drug abuse. Frank took off, just stranded me there in the emergency room. I remembered too late that you'd warned me about him. Anyway, the doctors weren't sure if Jason was going to make it. He was in very bad physical shape, dehydrated, malnourished. I guess you know."

I nodded.

"I couldn't leave him there. What if he died? But my other children were home alone. Ryan's fifteen and very responsible, but still I thought there should be an adult. So I called their father, thinking he'd want to help." She gave a bitter laugh. "Sure, he'd help. He took them and is suing for custody."

"But Jason made it?" Libby asked.

"Yes. They put him in ICU and he improved very quickly—physically. He has some paralysis on his left side, but they think with physical therapy he'll recover a lot of functioning. Mentally, it's another story. He's... " she paused and took a deep breath. "He's psychotic. It's from the drugs, too. They don't know if he'll ever be normal." She teared up again.

Libby did her shoulder-patting thing once more. I could've used some shoulder-patting myself. I'd been counting on getting information from Jason, but what would I learn from someone who didn't even recognize his own mother?

"Excuse me," Libby said to Barbara, "would you mind

if I used your phone?" She stood up. "I think I noticed one in the other room." There was a phone on the kitchen wall, but Libby apparently wanted privacy. She left the room to make her mysterious call, and Barbara turned her tear-stained face to me.

"I'm really sorry, Barbara," I said. "What hospital is Jason in? We'd like to visit him."

"He's not in the hospital now. They won't keep you unless you're really sick, you know. He's in a convalescent home in Walnut Creek—Sunnyside. Have you heard of it?"

"Would it be all right if we went to see him?"

"I suppose so. I could call and let them know, if you'd like."

"That would be great."

Libby returned to the kitchen, and Barbara left to make the call on our behalf.

"Will you take me to see Joe?" I still thought of him as GI Joe, even though I was learning to say Jason instead.

"Of course. We'll just have to wait a few minutes before we go."

"What's up?"

"I've been mending fences," she replied and wouldn't add more.

I didn't have to wait long to find out what she meant. A bare two minutes later, Barbara answered the front door and found a tearful Lucianne Lind on her doorstep. "I'm so sorry," she choked out. "I was wrong to blame you all this time. Please forgive me,"

Barbara gave her a stunned stare for a moment and stepped forward to embrace her. "Thank you, thank you."

The two women held one another and rocked from side to side in some ancient female ritual of exchanging comfort. I cocked an eyebrow at Libby. "Your phone call?"

She nodded and dabbed at her own tears. "They used to be best friends, and they need each other so much now, I had to try."

Barbara drew away from Lucianne and led her into

the house. “He took the kids. I don’t know what to do. I can’t afford a lawyer and Jason’s doctor bills.”

“We’ll get them back,” Lucianne said. She turned to Libby and embraced her. “Thank you.” She spotted me and released Libby. “I owe you an apology, too, for Gina. The police told me that she attacked you and vandalized your house. She’s been out of my control for a long time, but I believed Jack when he told me she was better.”

I shrugged. “Gina’s an adult now. It’s her responsibility, not yours. I saw on the news that they’d stopped her at the airport. I hope you don’t mind my asking—has she been arrested?”

She lowered her gaze. “She was charged with illegal entry, vandalism and aggravated assault. Her lawyer said he can get the charges dropped.” She lifted her gaze with a jerk. “I don’t know if I should tell you that, since you’re the, the… ”

“Complainant,” Libby filled in for her.

Lucianne shifted her gaze to Libby, looking relieved not to have to speak directly to me. “Yes. Her lawyer and Jack seem to think that they’re looking for a scapegoat for all the murders, but they don’t really have a case against her. I mean, no one could really imagine that Gina’s capable of murder, could they?”

Her question created one of those hugely uncomfortable black holes of conversational silence. Lucianne was probably the only one in the room who didn’t see—or didn’t want to see—that side of her daughter. I’d not only seen it, but felt it and had nothing to say. I left it to Barbara and Libby to murmur reassurances to her.

I made eye contact with Libby, who neatly shifted gears, thanked Barbara for her help, and got us out of there. Barbara had given me good directions and with Libby driving, we quite easily made the half-hour drive in twenty minutes.

“Do you think he’ll be able to tell us anything?” Libby asked, as she whipped into the parking lot.

“Sure. If he can talk, and if he recognizes us.”

As it turned out, he could talk—if you could call constant repetition of "name, rank, serial number" talking. They had him in four-point restraints, and he rhythmically jerked his left arm and leg against the padded leather cuffs with every monotonic repetition of his "rights." We couldn't get close enough to find out if he recognized us or not. The three Sunnyside employees who were gathered in his room turned on us as we came through the door and backed us into the hallway before we could approach the bed.

"I'm sorry, but Jason can't have visitors right now," said a tall African American woman dressed in a stylish pantsuit in shades of beige. The gold nametag on her lapel said "Shalawn Keasley, RN." The other two, a man and a woman, wore white pants and colorful shirts. I couldn't see their nametags from where I stood, but I guessed they were aides. I had the impression that the three had been arguing about something when we came into the room.

"I'm Alison Weaver. This is Libby Honeck. We're friends of Jason's and also of his mother, Barbara. Just so you know, I'm an RN, and Libby runs the Mobile Clinic in Berkeley. We want to know why he's in four-point restraints."

"His doctor ordered the use of physical restraints, because he didn't want to sedate him at this point."

"Why in the world not? Even with the padding, he's going to rub his wrists and ankles raw. Then you'll be dealing with potential infection."

"His mother insisted on no drugs, but I think the doctor will probably try anti-psychotics next week, because we're not happy keeping him in restraints."

"Yes," said Libby. "I can see that. It seems that all the other patients are dressed and out of their rooms."

"That's our normal protocol. I'm sorry you can't see Jason today. If you call ahead next time, we can tell you if he can have visitors."

"Why can't we see him now?" I asked.

Shalawn Keasley paused and pressed her lips together. I could tell that she didn't like having her authority challenged. Too bad. She'd have to get over it, because I had to try to find out what Jason knew about Stevie's murder.

Her hesitation gave the male aide a chance to speak his mind. "Because he's crazy, that's why. And he goes nuts every time someone walks into the room. Particularly me." He turned to Shalawn and the other aide. "So you have to assign someone else. Make Evelyn switch with me." He gestured toward the other aide.

Evelyn shook her head, "No way, Arthur. I don't take violent patients and you know it."

"We'll discuss this," Shalawn told them through clenched teeth, "after I finish talking with Jason's visitors." She turned to us with a good attempt at a smile. "Why don't you come to my office for a minute. I can answer any other questions you have and give you our phone number so you can call us first next time."

"No thanks. We want to see Jason today," I said.

"I've told you that's not possible," she replied, dropping the smile.

Libby edged forward. She didn't as much as glance at me, but we'd worked together long enough that I could read her body language—it was saying "shut up and let me handle this." Fine with me, as long as we talked to Jason. "I think we might be able to help. We've known Jason for the last couple of years. In fact, as long as we've known him, he's gone by his street name of GI Joe, because he's fascinated by anything that has to do with the military."

"Right," I said, not able to resist adding my two cents. "That's the reason he's chanting 'name, rank, serial number.' He thinks he's protected by the Geneva rules for prisoners of war from being held in four-point restraints."

"Is that why he calls me a gook every time he sees me?" Arthur asked. "I thought he was just a racist, and besides, I'm Filipino," he added, as if that clarified things.

"Your explanation of his behavior doesn't change the fact that it's psychotic behavior," Shalawn said.

"You're right, of course," Libby said. "But, what if we

simply acknowledge his reality? He might be more willing to respond to those around him."

Shalawn frowned. "It's not our policy to... "

Evelyn interrupted her. "Isn't that what we do with Mrs. Clark? If she thinks I'm her daughter when I'm feeding her, I go along with her, because that way she'll eat."

"We don't have to act out any crazy scenario," I said. "Just give him some indication in his own terms that he's safe."

"How do you propose we do that?" Shalawn asked.

"If he thinks he's a prisoner of war," Evelyn put in, when I didn't immediately respond. "Arthur could be from the Red Cross."

I nodded. "It's worth a try. And, do you have a VCR? Show him some war movies. I'll bet he'd at least hold still as long as they were on."

Shalawn agreed reluctantly to let us have a trial run. Libby left to get some war movies from a nearby video store. Evelyn made Arthur a Red Cross armband with some paper and a felt tip pen, while I crossed my fingers for luck and walked into Joe's room.

He'd stopped chanting and lay with his eyes closed, looking very frail and thin. I hardly recognized him. He'd always been so incredibly filthy before that his features had been blurred by the dirt. Now I could see a family resemblance to his mother.

"Hey, Joe," I said softly.

His eyes snapped open. He looked at me, then scanned the room. When his gaze returned to my face, I said, "It's Alison. Remember me? Stevie's friend?"

Recognition bloomed in his face. He took in the cast on my arm and bruises on my face. "You don't look so good. Guess, they got you, too, huh?" His speech was slightly slurred. Maybe that was from the stroke. His gaze shifted to someone behind me and he stiffened.

I turned. Arthur stood in the doorway. I gestured to

him to join me and he stepped forward. "This is Arthur. He's a nurse like me. He's going to take care of you, and he said I could help him today."

Joe narrowed his eyes at me. "This is a trick, huh? You're with them now."

I shook my head. "No trick. This is a Red Cross hospital, and they don't allow the enemy inside their perimeter. You're safe here."

Joe didn't relax his posture. His gaze darted between Arthur and me. For a moment, it looked like he was going to recede back into his rhythmic chanting, and I didn't know what to say to stop him.

Arthur took the initiative. "Hey, man," he said. "Look what I've got. Your dogtags." He held up the military ID by its chain. "They sent them over with your things from the hospital."

"Give 'em to me," Joe said, a desperate note in his voice.

"Sure, man. You can have them, no problem." Arthur approached the bed and lay the tags on Joe's chest. "What say we get you out of these?" he said, unfastening the restraint on Joe's wrist. "You want to get the other one?" he asked me.

I struggled with it left-handed, while Arthur moved to undo the restraints on his ankles. Joe waited patiently for me to release him. When his hands were free, he clutched the dogtags in his fist. His eyes filled with tears. He brushed them away with the back of his arm. "I needed these so bad," he gestured with his fist. "I had to give my name, rank and serial number, but I have trouble remembering, you know?"

I nodded. "I know. Your memory'll come back eventually." I hoped I was telling him the truth.

"Feel up to eating something?" Arthur asked. "You have to get some meat on your bones if you're going to get healthy, you know."

"Sure," Joe said. "You got any Jell-O?"

Arthur chuckled. "Oh yeah, we got Jell-O. Be right

back," he said and left.

"I have to ask you something," I said. "And I don't want to upset you, so let me check first. Is it all right to talk about Stevie and what happened to him?"

Joe dropped his gaze and said quietly. "I guess so."

"You remember what happened?"

He nodded. "They got him. I had to go out, and when I came back, they'd got him."

"You didn't see who did it?"

He shook his head. "Stevie knew them."

"How do you know that?"

"It's like they always say. He wouldn't open the door to anyone he didn't know."

"So you took him in the trunk of my car and left him where I work."

He began plucking at the bedclothes and wouldn't meet my gaze.

"It's okay. I know you took my car and the stuff in my trunk. You were scared and thought you had to hide. Jesus took care of you."

He looked at me in wonder. "How do you know that?"

"I figured it out."

"Stevie was right about you. You're real smart. Stevie was getting a job, and he said I had to clean up my act. So I borrowed your car and your stuff, so I could be on my own."

"You already knew I carried camping equipment and food in my trunk? Or did you just find it when you put Stevie's body in there."

"I'd seen it, because you'd put your bag in the trunk when you came to the clinic. And I was pissed off at him, you know? I was gonna borrow some money off one of you guys at the clinic, then Libby left your keys lying out. Seemed like it was meant to be. But, when I got back, they'd got Stevie, and I wished I hadn'a cussed him out before I left."

"Why did you take his body to the Center?"

"What Center?"

"Where I work."

"Couldn't take him to your house, could I? Someone would've seen me for sure."

"I mean, why did you want to bring the body so I'd see him?"

"Because of the papers. Stevie wanted you to see his papers." He tensed up and lifted his head from the pillow. "You got 'em didn't you? His papers?"

I nodded. "I got them."

He didn't seem reassured. He struggled to sit up. "I promised. You were his insurance. And I promised. But they got him. Goddam gooks. Goddam gooks." His eyes rolled back in his head, and his body jerked spasmodically, his arms banging against the bed rails.

"Arthur!" I yelled and tried to hold Joe's shoulders down with my good arm. Arthur came running into the room. "He's seizing," I said unnecessarily, since Arthur had already taken in the situation. He pulled the pillow from under Joe's head with one hand and reached for the tongue depressor taped to the wall behind the bed with the other. He wedged the depressor length-wise across Joe's mouth to keep him from biting his tongue, and then he placed a hand on his forehead and an arm across his chest. Arthur's grip was undoubtedly a lot more effective than my one-armed effort, but I couldn't make myself let go of Joe's shoulders.

It wasn't a long seizure as these things go, but it seemed to go on forever. Finally, Joe's convulsive movements stilled. Arthur and I slowly straightened and glanced at each other. "Has he had seizures before?" I asked.

"No, he hasn't," said Shalawn from the doorway. "And I'm going to have to ask you to leave. Now."

CHAPTER TWENTY-TWO

"Don't keep beating yourself up about it," Mitch said. He'd just seen Libby to the door. We'd had dinner together and hashed over the afternoon's debacle at Sunnyside nursing home. I sat slumped at Mitch's kitchen table, taking the last swig of my after dinner coffee. "From your description of the guy," Mitch went on, "it sounds like he could've had a seizure at any time."

"I know. I don't blame myself for that. At least, not too much. It's just that I really thought I was going to find out something about Stevie's murder. Instead, I'm back to where I started."

"Where's that?"

I looked up. "Huh?"

"Where did you start? Maybe if you go over it from the beginning you'll find out you know something you didn't know you knew, because you'll see it a different way. Like a jigsaw puzzle, you know? You're working on sky, so you only look for blue pieces. Only there's no more blue, and you think you're missing a piece. But then you start looking for pieces by shape instead of by color, and there it is. And it turns out it's green, because that part's a tree. You'd never have found it as long as you were looking for a blue piece."

"That's a great analogy."

"Think so?"

"I do. Except with this puzzle, I can't tell what's

shape and what's color. I don't even know which parts are pieces of this particular puzzle."

Mitch frowned.

"Here, I'll show you." I retrieved the group photo and Stevie's papers from my room, brought them into the kitchen and spread them out on the table. "There's Stephen Lind." I pointed to his face in the picture. "Mathematical genius, working on a graduate degree at age sixteen. Eight years later, he's schizophrenic, a Telegraph Avenue regular known as Stevie Number and is murdered by 'them,' according to Jason Reynolds, aka GI Joe."

I moved my finger to the person standing next to Stevie. "Here you have Florence Bing in happier times. She's Stevie's lover, and also a graduate student. Eight years later, never having completed her degree, she works as office manager at the Center for Biostatistical Studies. The day she learns that her former lover has been murdered, she goes home and kills herself. Only I still don't think it was suicide. In any case, the Oakland cops aren't interested, because it looked like suicide and it happened in Berkeley. Go figure."

"And the guy who attacked you?" Mitch asked.

"That would be this cutie." I tapped the photo above his face. "Ray Munsen, the papers said. He'd been arrested a few times, but no convictions. No clue what his connection to Stevie might have been, except that Stevie knew him well enough to have his picture taken with him."

"What about the other two guys in the picture?" Mitch asked, leaning over the table to peer at the photo.

"No idea. I don't know how Ray fits with Stevie and Flo, much less whether these guys are part of the puzzle, too. See what I mean?"

"And these?" Mitch tapped the stack of papers.

"There are four papers here that Stevie wrote before his schizophrenic break." I lifted the paperclipped pages from the stack. "I know that because they're dated and have his name on them. I think he wrote them on his own and not for a class. I went through two boxes of papers and notes from classes. These are different. No grade. No class number below the name and date. But someone read two of them." I leafed through one of the papers and held up a page with comments. "I thought I could try to track this guy down at the University. Maybe he can tell me something about what the papers mean. They're way beyond me."

"Do you think they might have something to do with why he was killed?"

"Who knows? I have a feeling that there are very few people who'd understand them in the first place, but maybe they hold some secret to the universe."

"You mean, like E=MC2?"

I rubbed my forehead. "I guess, although it sounds pretty farfetched. Stans and Carney would never buy it. I mean, who's our suspect then?"

"What about the rest of this?" Mitch picked up the last pages in the stack—the computer print-outs.

"These are even more confusing. This is the kind of thing I do in my work. Take this page, for example. It's an ANOVA—that's short for analysis of variance."

"Is there a way to say that in English?"

"Do you know what a correlation is?"

Mitch shook his head. "No, but that's okay. I think I'm out of my depth here."

"No, you're not. It's really not hard. People understood correlations before they knew how to compute them mathematically. Give me some paper and a pencil, and I'll show you."

Mitch handed me the pad and pencil he kept next to the kitchen phone.

"Okay, this'll be rough, because I'm not very good with my left hand, but imagine that this is a city map." I drew a wobbly oval on the page. I nearly blackened one area of the oval with little dots, then made a few random dots in other areas. "What if I told you that those dots represented an outbreak of cholera?"

"I'd want to know where that was, because I wouldn't

want to go there."

"Don't worry, you can't. This is London in the middle of the nineteenth century, and, in Soho," I tapped my diagram, "five hundred people died in two weeks. Most people thought cholera was spread through the air. But one man, Dr. John Snow, had a theory that it was spread through contaminated water. He went around the area and talked to people who'd lost family members and found out they all got their water from one source—the Broad Street pump. Guess what he did."

"You tell me."

"He took the handle off the pump. Actually, he didn't do it himself. He had to convince the local officials to do it. And, although they still didn't believe his theory about contaminated water, they were persuaded by the correlation—that's the relationship between the number of people who drank water from the pump and the number who died of cholera."

"Sounds like a pretty smart guy, this Dr. Snow."

"Yes. He's my role model. He didn't just study the problem. He went out and fixed it. Now, though, it's a lot harder. We're not tracking cholera, but birth defects and cancers and other diseases, and it can take years between the time of exposure and the appearance of the health problem."

"Like smoking and lung cancer?"

I nodded. "Right."

"So are these correlations?" He pointed to the computer printouts.

"No, but they're another way of figuring out a relationship. Correlations can be easy to see if you plot them out in a scatter diagram, which basically is what I did here." I pointed to my rough map. "Other relationships, especially if you have several groups, aren't so clear visually. So we do different statistical tests to see if there's a strong relationship, or if it's just something that could've happened by chance."

"So this page makes sense to you?"

"Yes and no. I recognize the statistical test. I can see that the results aren't significant."

"Significant?"

"That's jargon for saying that whatever relationship they were measuring here, it's very likely it happened by chance. See that letter p? It stands for the probability the relationship happened by chance. Any number over .05 wouldn't count."

"This one's .35. No good, huh?"

"No good at all. The problem for me, though, is that's all I know. This printout says 'page three of seven' at the top. I have three through seven, but where're the first two pages? The first page would at least spell out what this label stood for. See these labels at the top of the columns? That one—RBPCE—is a mystery. Not just because I don't know what it stands for, but because it also appeared on some papers that Joe left with Stevie's body." I sighed and pushed my chair away from the table.

"You still thinking about going up to the University tomorrow to ask questions?"

"Definitely. It seems pretty clear that I have to check around and see if anyone remembers Flo, Stevie or this Ray Munsen."

"That's what I thought. I have something for you to take with you, in case of trouble." He stood up and went into his bedroom.

"If it's a weapon or pepper spray, forget it," I called after him. "I can't manage anything tricky left-handed. I'm not even too good at things that aren't tricky."

Mitch returned to the kitchen and handed me a cell phone. "It's not exactly a weapon, but you can use it to call for help. I've programmed my cell phone number in already. You can speed dial like this." He demonstrated by pushing two buttons in sequence and the phone on his belt went beepbeep. "See? You do it." He stood over me while I pushed the buttons.

I held the phone up to my ear and said, grinning, "Hi Mitch. I'm in trouble. Could you call 911 for me?"

"You're not scared, are you?" he asked. It wasn't really a question.

I stopped grinning and turned off the phone. "It's a funny thing. I had this incredible realization when Ray Munsen was trying to crack my skull open. I was no longer that helpless little girl who had to hide from her drunken foster dad."

"No one would ever take you for a helpless little girl."

"I know, but that's all on the outside. On the inside I was always waiting for the punch or the kick, and maybe thought I deserved it because I'd watched my mother kill herself. I don't know. Anyway, I changed that night. I stood up to him—to Ray Munsen, but also to my ghosts, and it wasn't just a tough guy act I was putting on, either. The downside unfortunately was that I became a little homicidal. So now I've had to deal with that, but I just don't feel scared anymore. You think I should, though, don't you?"

"Seems only reasonable. Didn't Joe tell you that Stevie called you his insurance? What do you suppose he meant?"

"I think he thought that if anything happened to him, I'd take care of his papers. Get them published, maybe. That's what his mother expects, anyway. What do you think?"

"It seems pretty clear to me that there's something in here that someone wants, or else just doesn't want to get out. I don't know which, but they're willing to kill for it."

"So the sooner we find out which it is, the sooner we can stop them. Right?"

Mitch rubbed the back of his neck. "I should know better than to argue with you, but you'll take the phone?"

"Sure."

"Promise?"

"Okay, I promise. Look, I'll put it in my bag right now." I retrieved my bag from my room. "I even have a little pocket it'll fit right into. Of course, ever since you put everything back in here so nice and neat, I can't find a thing, but I'll certainly know where the phone is."

"And you should take a key to the house." He crossed to the corkboard above his phone, pulled a key from a hook and handed it to me.

"Thanks. I'll pay you for the phone. I should've thought of it myself. I can't even get into my house right now to see if anyone's left messages for me."

"No need to pay me."

"I want to."

"Let me do this one thing, okay?" he said with a kind of vehemence I hadn't heard from him before.

"What's the matter?"

He dropped his gaze to the papers on the table. "Nothing," he said, the way people do when they don't want to talk about what's bothering them. "Look, I'm going to turn in now. I have to leave pretty early for the job I'm working on. I'll try not to make too much noise. Night."

"Night," I called after him. He disappeared into his room and closed the door. I slouched down in the chair. What had gotten into him? Must have been something I said, but what? Maybe he'd just finally seen that I wouldn't be a very good bet as a girlfriend. I hadn't even asked him what he'd done during the day, I'd just obsessed about Joe, going over and over what had happened. That must have been it. He'd realized what he'd be getting into if he got involved with me.

I stood up, stowed Stevie's papers in my bag along with Mitch's house key, turned off the lights and felt my way in the dark to my room. It was a good thing that Mitch had finally caught on about me. He was a good man, and I'd hate to hurt him. Somehow, though, I really wasn't as glad about it as I should have been.

The next morning, Mitch was gone before I got up. I hadn't even heard him leave. I took the bus to the Berkeley campus. I missed having the use of a car, but given the impossible parking situation around campus, I knew I'd have a shorter distance to walk from the bus stop.

I started at the School of Public Health. I had the advantage there of knowing most of the administrative staff, so I knew who would be helpful. The only problem, of course, was that they also knew me. I could only hope they hadn't read the papers or watched the TV news or listened to the radio. I started with Gayle Walsh, long-time graduate student coordinator, who, I was pretty sure, had been around when Flo was a student. She was alone in her office when I stepped into the doorway.

She instantly quashed any hope I'd had of passing through simply as a student and not as someone involved in multiple murder investigations. "Good God. Alison Weaver." She pushed her glasses up on her nose to get a better look at me. "I've just been reading about you. You look like hell, my dear. Why don't you close the door, pull up a chair, and tell me what's going on."

Good old Gayle. Always got right to the point. I closed the door and sat. "The police won't let me talk about anything while they're investigating. All I can tell you is that the news accounts are pretty accurate."

"So it's true that you were once married to Frank Avery?" she asked, her eyebrows raised almost to her hairline.

I nodded.

"But you're not a suspect?"

"I have a pretty good alibi." I lifted my casted arm.

"I read about that, too. To be honest, it sounds like a very strange tale."

"Weird beyond description. Weirder yet to live through it, believe me. I'm here because I need your help." I pulled out the group picture and slid it across her desk. "Do you recognize anyone in that picture?"

She adjusted her glasses, peered at the picture and frowned. "Yes, the police asked me about them, too."

"Wait a minute. You've already talked to the police?"

"Yes, last week, only their picture had just the two of them, Florence and Stephen. I recognize him," she said pointing to one of the two unidentified people in the photo. "That's Dr. Aaronson. He did his graduate work in this department. He's at Brown now."

I stood up and leaned over Gayle's desk. "What about him?" I asked, placing a finger above Ray Munsen's head.

"Don't have a clue. Sorry. I wouldn't have remembered Florence if the police hadn't asked me to look up her records. I recognized Dr. Aaronson because he came here as a visiting professor a year ago. He's been very successful in his career. Florence dropped out of the doctoral program."

"How did you know Stevie, I mean, Stephen Lind? He was in the mathematics department."

"I didn't. The police told me who he was."

"Do you remember the police officer's name? Was it Carney or Stans?"

"I don't think so." She flipped through her Rolodex, pulled a business card free from a paperclip and handed it to me.

I glanced at the printed name. "Bakke? He's a new one to me... " My eyes took in the small print under the name. "Wait a minute, this guy's from the Berkeley police." I sank back into the chair and gazed at Gayle. "What did they tell you?"

Gayle fiddled with a paperclip. "I'm not sure whether I'm supposed to talk about it or not."

"Please, Gayle. Help me. I found Stevie's body in a dumpster behind the Center where I work. He'd had his head bashed in. I found Flo's body in her house. They said it was a suicide, but I told them they were wrong. Suicide didn't fit. Two nights ago, Ray Munsen," I pointed to Munsen's face in the photo, "attacked me and broke my arm. While I was having my arm set, someone stabbed my ex-husband to death in my house, and, then I'm pretty sure the same someone killed Munsen in an unoccupied house one street over from mine. There has to be a connection here, if I can only find it."

She dropped the paperclip and wrinkled her brow with concern. "All I know is that they're calling Florence Bing's death 'suspicious.' It might have been a suicide, but they weren't sure."

"That's progress, of sorts. Did they say why they needed to see her old records?"

"Yes, eventually. At first I was going to make them get a court order to see our files, but what if it wasn't suicide, and there's some madman out there putting cyanide in regular sleeping pills?"

"Cyanide! Holy shit!" I jumped to my feet and paced about Gayle's cramped office. I knocked against the chair I'd been sitting in, pushed it out of my way and kept on pacing. Why hadn't I thought of cyanide myself? It fit all the symptoms perfectly. I turned to Gayle. "May I use your phone? I'm pretty sure the Oakland police don't know anything about this."

"Of course." She pushed it across her desk.

I opened my bag to retrieve Stans' card. Mitch had put all my loose business cards and scraps of paper into one of the small interior pockets in my bag. I found the card right away. I also spotted the cell phone Mitch had made me take. "I forgot," I said, glancing up at Gayle. "I have a phone with me."

I punched in the number on Stans' business card. A man, not Stans, eventually answered the phone and told me Stans was off that day and would I like to speak with another officer? No, I didn't want to talk to anyone else. I'd have to go through endless rigmarole to make it clear why it was important. How about giving me Stans' home phone number? That wasn't possible. I finally settled for leaving Stans a long message, including my new cell phone number, which I made the message-taker read back to me to make sure he'd actually written it all down.

I put the phone back in my bag and reached across the desk for the picture.

"Wait a minute," Gayle said. "Why don't I send this to Dr. Aaronson and see what he remembers about the others in the picture?"

"Good idea. I have to hang on to this picture, but I'll make a copy for you."

"No need. I can scan it into my computer." She

swiveled around in her chair, slipped the picture onto a scanner on a table behind her desk and pushed a button. Imagine having her own scanner. I'd been under the restrictive influence of the Center's rules for so long, I'd forgotten that other people could have easy access to technology.

"What's your email address?" she asked as she handed the photo back to me. "I'll forward his answer to you."

I gazed at her for a long moment. I no longer had access to email through the Center. As for my home computer, even if I could get to it, I didn't know when I could have it repaired. "You'd better phone me, if you don't mind," I said. I pulled the cell phone out again and read the number off to her. It rang while I was holding it, and I nearly jumped out of my chair. I stared at the phone, and it rang again. I pushed the talk button. "Hello?"

"Detective Stans here. You had some information for me?"

"That was fast. They said it was your day off."

He paused. Was that a deep sigh I heard? "You made a strong impression on the officer who took your call. What do you have?"

"You should talk to the Berkeley cops about Florence Bing's death. It was cyanide poisoning. They're now calling it 'suspicious,' instead of definite suicide."

"Where'd you hear that?"

"From Gayle Walsh. She's the graduate student coordinator for the School of Public Health. Flo was in the doctoral program, so the Berkeley police were here asking about her. I'm in Gayle's office right now. She recognized someone else in the group picture."

"Maybe I'd better talk to her directly."

"Okay." I looked up at Gayle. "It's Detective Stans. He's with the Oakland police. He wants to talk to you." I handed her the phone and listened in to her side of the conversation. Unfortunately, she didn't tell him anything she hadn't already told me. She ended by promising to fax him copies of Flo's records and Dr. Aaronson's reply to her email.

She passed the phone back to me, saying, "He wants to talk to you again."

I took the phone. "I told you it wasn't suicide," I said to Stans.

"People have been known to kill themselves with cyanide."

"If she did it on purpose, why would she hide it in a Seconal capsule?"

This time I was sure I heard him sigh. "Look, I appreciate the information. I don't want to encourage you to keep going around asking questions, but if it occurs to you that you know something else that might help us, I'd like to give you another number to call. Got a pencil?"

"Just a sec." I grabbed a felt tip pen from Gayle's desk, tucked the phone between my ear and my shoulder and pushed up the sleeve covering my cast. "Okay." I scrawled the number he gave me onto the white plaster. "This your home number?" I asked.

"My cell phone."

"And the number you reached me on is my cell phone. Temporarily. Until I get back into my house. Any idea when that'll happen?"

"Today or tomorrow. I'll get back to you." He hung up without saying goodbye.

I ended the call and nearly turned the phone off, but Stans had given me an idea. I pressed the speed dial for Mitch's phone.

He answered on the first ring. "You okay?"

"I'm fine. How'd you know it was me?"

"Caller ID. What's up?"

"Okay if I have something faxed to your machine?"

"Sure." The well equipped carpenter. Mitch had more electronic equipment than I did. He gave me the number and I passed it on to Gayle, who wrote it down.

"Thanks. See you later."

He paused a moment, then said. "See you."

I turned to Gayle. "Will you fax me the same stuff you're faxing to Stans?"

"Well, I can send you Dr. Aaronson's reply, but I don't know about the records."

"It's okay. I'm helping the police. You heard me talking to the detective, right?"

"Yes, okay," she agreed.

I left her with a promise that I'd be back to fill her in on more details the following week. I slipped out of her office and hurried out of the building with my head down. Heaven help me if my graduate advisor spotted me. What could I tell him? He'd already given me two extensions on my dissertation. But he didn't see me and neither did anyone else who knew me.

I'd been very lucky with Gayle, but then I'd had an inside track, since I knew her. Finding Stevie's former professor, Harold Lang, was much more of a longshot, but it was one of those days when you think you should buy a lottery ticket, because the first person I asked not only told me Lang still worked there, but where I could find him.

He was seated on a bench in a grove of redwoods, just outside the mathematics department building, sharing his sandwich with a squirrel. At my approach, the squirrel whipped his wispy gray tail back and forth twice and took off up the nearest tree. He stopped about ten feet up and eyed me with unblinking black eyes. Dr. Lang swung his head around and gazed at me. He had a very round head, bald on the top and fringed from ear to ear around the back with dark brown hair. He was in late middle age and quite nattily dressed in a blue buttoned-down shirt and yellow tie.

"Professor Lang? Sorry to interrupt your lunch."

"I don't mind, though my lunch companion does." He gestured to the squirrel, which hadn't budged from the side of the tree. "Are you one of my students?" He squinted at me.

"No. I'm a friend, or I was a friend, of a former student of yours. Stephen Lind."

"Stephen, yes. What a tragic death. A terrible loss." He rubbed the smooth dome of his head and sighed heavily.

"You knew him well?"

He glanced up at me. "Better than anyone else here in the academic community. Why don't you join me?" He moved to make room for me on the bench. "I don't believe you mentioned your name."

I sat in the space he'd provided. "I'm Alison Weaver."

Lee straightened with a jerk and stared at me. "You're Alison? I'm so pleased to meet you at last. Stephen spoke of you often."

It was my turn to stare. I hadn't met Stevie until after his psychotic break, long after he'd left the University. "Are you telling me you talked to Stevie, I mean Stephen, recently?"

He nodded. "Yes, we had long discussions at least once a week for the last six months. Right here on this bench, as a matter of fact, because he was more comfortable outside. And you can call him Stevie. He told me that people knew him as Stevie Number. He liked the name."

"I had no idea. I'm so glad he had a friend who'd known him from before his illness."

"I'd always liked Stephen, but I have to admit to selfish motives. He helped me a great deal with some new work I've been doing on magic numbers."

"He helped me a few times with statistical theory. I'm glad he had enough lucid moments to maintain contact with you."

Lee tilted his head to one side and gazed at me with a half smile. "He said he wasn't sure if you knew or not."

"Knew what?"

"That he was in remission from his illness. He was no longer schizophrenic."

CHAPTER TWENTY-THREE

I stared at him. "What are you talking about? In remission from schizophrenia? Not possible. On meds regularly, maybe, but cured? It doesn't happen."

"I used to hold the same view, but I've since done some investigations into the mental health literature, and it's indeed possible. Not common, of course, but it has occurred in documented cases. He came to me just as you did, at lunchtime. He knew my preference for dining alfresco. He asked for my help. He told me that he believed he could conquer his madness if he could train his mind to stay away from insane thoughts."

"And you helped him steer clear of crazy thinking?"

"He said as much, though I confess I benefited as much or more than he from our discussions, which focused for the most part on areas of mathematical theory where our interests overlapped. He was immensely gifted."

"So he could have sane conversations with you. What about during the rest of the time?"

"It was quite difficult, but he found ways to manage—most of the time. I think he would have been wholly successful eventually."

I shook my head. I still couldn't quite take it in. "It's incredible. He never said anything to me about it. I just thought he was being more compliant with his meds. You said he talked to you about me?"

"He told me that you had initiated his self-therapy by

telling him that his genealogical pursuits were crazy, but that the probability model he'd developed was sane. I believe that he'd formed a strong attachment to you. He certainly respected you intellectually."

"He did?"

"He did, indeed. He told me he wished to wait until he'd secured employment before he 'came out as sane,' to quote his own phrase."

"So he really was looking for a job. His sister mentioned that, too, but she didn't take it seriously. Did he have any particular job in mind?"

"He purposely didn't tell me. He felt that there was some risk involved, but didn't elaborate."

"What do you mean—risk?"

"I don't know. That was the word he used. I assumed that he meant it was a risk for him to pursue employment because of his condition. Possibly too much pressure would be detrimental to his mental health. However, when I heard that he'd been killed… "

"You thought he might have meant something else."

Lang nodded in agreement.

I leaned toward him. "I think he did mean something else. He wrote a will the week before he died, naming me as his beneficiary. That's why I came to see you. I have his papers." I hauled my bag into my lap and struggled with my one good hand to open it and retrieve the papers.

"His papers?" Lang said, a tremor in his voice.

I glanced at him. "Yes. He wrote these before he became ill. You've seen two of them and wrote comments on them. That's how I knew to look for you. His mother wants me to get them published posthumously. I hoped you could tell me if it's possible." I held the papers out to him.

Lang stared at the papers without moving except for licking his lips. He turned his gaze away and folded his arms across his chest. "Yes, I remember. They were on the Rieman hypothesis."

"There's one on fractals and probability. It's all too

esoteric for me."

"They will certainly be published. You hold on to them. I'll ask two other reputable mathematicians to join me, and we'll look at them together, edit as necessary, and submit them."

I pulled my hand back and rested the papers on my lap. "I was really hoping that you'd look at them now."

He cocked his head to one side. "Did you have some particular reason?"

"Three other people have been killed besides Stevie. And some of his papers were taken from my house."

He gave me a startled look.

"Not these papers," I hurriedly reassured him. "They were just class notes, and they've been found. But I wonder if there's something in here, something important enough for someone to kill for."

Lang gave a shout of laughter. The squirrel, which hadn't abandoned his waiting position halfway up the tree, scrambled up the trunk and disappeared from sight. "That's an amusing thought." He laughed again and then rapidly sobered. "Amusing in a grim way, of course, considering the circumstances. I suppose some mathematicians might say they'd kill in order to do work as brilliant and original as Stephen's was, but I can't think of one who'd actually do it. And multiple murders are really out of the question. No, what you have to worry about among my colleagues is theft—intellectual theft, that is."

"Well, maybe that's it. Someone stole Stevie's ideas and published them as his own. If Stevie's original papers are published, the plagiarism will be discovered." As soon as the words were out of my mouth, I realized that I might be talking to the one person in a position to plagiarize Stevie's work.

Lang gave me an ironical smile. "I can see by your facial expression that it just occurred to you that I might be guilty of it myself. I hope you'll take my word that I'm not. For the most part, Stephen and I didn't pursue the same areas of mathematics. I'm primarily interested in functional analysis. Stephen's work was with number theory. However, our work overlapped in the area you're holding in your hand—the Rieman hypothesis."

"Okay, I'll take you at your word. You assemble your team, and I'll hand over the papers. Seems like it would be hard to pull a fast one that way."

"I think it's the ethical way to proceed. That way he will receive full credit and recognition for his work. Perhaps it will provide some small comfort to his family."

I stuck the papers back in my bag and pulled out the photograph. "Do you by any chance recognize anyone in this picture?"

Lang didn't even look at the photo. His gaze remained fastened on the edges of Stevie's papers sticking out of the top of my bag. "You have all of Stephen's papers?"

"Probably not. I have two boxes from his mother's house. His sister said he'd kept a journal, but it wasn't with the stuff his mother gave me. On the other hand, his sister could've been lying. She does that."

"He never mentioned keeping a journal to me, but that doesn't signify. You must make copies of everything and store the originals elsewhere. A safe deposit box, for example. It would be terrible if they were lost or stolen. They're invaluable."

"I'll take good care of them. I promise." That seemed to satisfy him, so I held out the photo again.

He took it and peered at it. "That's Stephen, of course. That's the woman he was involved with at that time. I saw them together quite a bit. I don't recognize anyone else. Should I?"

"No. It was a longshot. I still can't quite believe that he was coming out of his schizophrenia. It's wonderful, and yet, it's awful, too, that he was killed just at that point."

Professor Lang agreed with me, repeating "tragic" several times. We exchanged phone numbers, and I promised to call him the following week. I left him seated on his bench and hiked south across campus towards Bancroft Avenue.

The crush of bodies increased as everyone funneled from the open space of Sproul Plaza onto the narrow sidewalks of Telegraph Avenue. I usually strolled along the Avenue checking out the wares of the street merchants and talking to any Mobile Clinic clients I ran into. I ignored all of it that day, because images of Stevie kept strobing through my mind like a bad music video. I'd noticed that he'd stopped acting schizy, but I couldn't remember when I'd noticed it. At the time I'd attributed it to medication effects and figured his rational behavior would last until he decided to go off meds again. Stupid me. There should be a law against hindsight. The wisdom gained doesn't seem worth the pain of guilt and self-recrimination.

I might have gone along like this all the way to the bus stop if I hadn't seen a dog sniffing at something in the gutter. It took a second for it to hit me why I'd noticed the dog in the first place. It wasn't Dorris, Doris' beloved mutt, but close enough in its mongrel look to fire off a figurative lightbulb in my brain. Stevie had befriended both Doris and her dog. Joe had talked to Doris after dumping Stevie's body at the Center. And, Doris had known that Stevie was hiding out with Jesus. So why was I moping along, kicking myself for past mistakes when there was a source of information about Stevie I hadn't tapped yet?

It took me nearly an hour of repeatedly walking up and down the same four blocks of Telegraph Avenue, plus exploring the cross streets for several blocks in each direction before I tracked Doris down behind a church on Durant Avenue. I probably wouldn't have found her even then, if one of my street clients hadn't pointed me in the right direction. Marvilyn, who always wore a both a full beard and a full skirt in order to, in his words, proclaim to the universe his/her androgyny, told me that he/she'd seen Doris going through the dumpster behind St. Paul's a short while before.

I found the dumpster easily, but the only sign of Doris was Dorris worrying a paper bag and tearing at it with her teeth to get to the leftovers of someone's lunch. She cocked one eye at me, but didn't leave off in her quest to rip the bag apart. "Doris?" I called.

"Whadyawant?" she said.

I circled the dumpster and found her re-packing her cart. Blankets, clothing, papers, magazines, food containers and other assorted items were strewn on the ground nearby. "Hi Doris. Can we talk?"

She moved to block her possessions from my view. "Go away."

I took two steps back. "Is this better? Sorry, but I can't go all the way away."

She eyed me up and down. "You break your arm or someone do it for you?"

"It wasn't an accident. Worse than that, three more people were killed after Stevie. I need your help."

"I don't know nothing about it. Besides, I got work to do." She gestured to her half-loaded cart.

"Please, Doris. I need to know some things about Stevie. He was your friend, wasn't he?"

She shifted from foot to foot and turned her head twice to check on her possessions behind her. "Stevie was nice to us. He gave Dorris a big bag of food, and I... " She stopped in mid-sentence and her eyes darted in all directions.

She looked on the verge of bolting, but I was pretty sure she'd never leave her belongings behind. I took a chance that she might confide in me if I looked totally unthreatening. "Mind if I sit down?" I asked as if we were standing in her living room. I slowly lowered myself to the ground, groaning a little for effect. "I'm really tired and my arm's starting to hurt." I took a few seconds to settle myself comfortably on the pavement with my bag between my knees. "There, that's better. Now, you were saying that you did Stevie a favor, right?" It was just a wild guess on my part that was what she'd been about to say, but the way she stared at me told me I'd hit a bull's-eye. "Why don't you tell me about it?"

"It wasn't a big deal."

"Maybe not for you, but I'm sure it was important to Stevie. Maybe you were the only one he could ask."

"It was Joe who asked," she said.

"Yeah? Well, Joe was Stevie's best friend."

"I didn't know Stevie was dead. Joe said Stevie needed someone to protect his stuff for awhile. He said you were mad at him, so he couldn't ask you."

I let my gaze drop to the pavement. I'd had the right idea about Joe's intentions. If only we'd been able to make a connection before Tony Dezzutti and his garbage-collecting cronies had arrived on the scene. I lifted my gaze. "I need to see everything Joe left with you."

"See it? You can have what's left. I'm tired of lugging it around."

"What do you mean 'what's left?' Where's the rest of it?"

"Joe took it back. He and a friend of his."

I sat up straight. "What friend?" Except for Stevie, I didn't think Joe had any friends.

My sudden move startled Doris. She moved even further away from me, practically standing on top of her possessions. "I don't know. Some guy on a big Harley. I gotta go now. I have to pack up and go. Okay?"

"Did Stevie's friend have gray hair in a pony tail and a mustache?" I asked, although I knew the answer already.

"Yeah, that's the guy. You know him?"

I nodded.

"I think I'd like to get me one of them motorcycles," Doris said. "Only I don't know if Dorris would like it."

"What did Joe give you to keep for him?"

"Books and papers, that's all. Oh, and his gun."

"His gun!"

"Don't get your shorts in a knot. You already saw it. He told me."

"You're right. I did. I was just surprised that he gave it to you for safekeeping. That's a pretty big responsibility. I'd better take it and the other stuff, too." I tried to hit just the right casual note, but Doris was too canny for me.

"It was a lot of work, ya' know, hauling this stuff around. I think I deserve something for it."

"Okay, what kind of compensation are we talking about?"

"Let me think." She furrowed her brow. "I want an extra large pizza with everything on it—double cheese, too."

"Wait a minute—double cheese? You think I'm some kind of moneybags?"

"Yeah. And I want a small sausage pizza for Dorris. No cheese. Cheese gives her the runs."

"How about me? Do I get some?"

"Get your own. I'm not sharing."

I bent my head and looked like I was considering it. "Okay," I said, after a few moments. "It's a deal, but only if I can look at all of Stevie's stuff and Joe's gun while we're waiting for the pizza to be delivered."

"You gonna have it delivered? Here?" She clearly hadn't expected this turn of events. Maybe she thought she could take off while I was chasing down her pizza.

"Sure," I said and pulled out my cell phone. I was really going to have to remember to thank Mitch for getting me this phone. I pushed up my sleeve and punched in Stans' number. "Alison Weaver here," I said when he answered. "Got a pencil? This is very important." I spoke slowly and emphasized each word. "I need an extra large double cheese pizza loaded, and a small sausage no cheese pizza."

There was a very long pause before he said, "You okay?"

"Yeah. I need them delivered to St. Paul's church on Durant. Know where that is?"

"I can find it."

"Walk down the driveway into the parking lot around the back."

"Do I need backup for this?"

"No, just me and a friend going through a mutual friend's memorabilia. You know, that guy I knew who was killed? Stevie Number?"

"Sure you're okay?"

"I could use a pizza myself. I missed lunch."

"These aren't for you?"

"They're for my friends, Doris and Dorris. You'll see when you get here. And could you bring those bags with you? Like you used when you helped me clean out my car?"

"Okay, I get that you can't talk and that you want me to bring evidence bags. Convince me that you're okay, or I'm alerting the Berkeley PD to send its nearest cruiser straight there."

"I'm better than I've been since I first met you, except that I really need those pizzas ASAP, or I don't get the papers."

"I'm on my way," he said and hung up.

I turned to Doris. "Okay, the pizza's on its way. Where's the stuff?"

"In my cart," she said and added quickly, "I'll get it," when I made a move to get to my feet. She made two trips carrying books and papers in neat stacks, which she placed next to me. The second stack had Joe's gun on top.

I picked up the gun first. The barrel was solid. The trigger didn't move. "It's not real," I said.

"'Course it's not real. Who'd give a nutcase like Joe a real gun? It's just like the kind German soldiers used, though. Stevie bought it for him."

I turned to the books and papers next. The books were journals, every page covered with Stevie's close handwriting. I started by leafing through them, reading every fifth or sixth page. Gradually, I became absorbed in the unfolding story.

He'd documented his life, starting at a very young age. The earliest ones were in large printing, not cursive, and the spelling was often inventive. Gina's name appeared frequently. At first, he was pleased to have a baby sister, someone to play with and to teach. By the time she was three, though, she was only mentioned in relation to some injury or assault. First to him personally, and then as she grew older, to things he cared about—pets, science projects, a special present he'd made for his mother in art class. She always escaped punishment. She was adept at manipulating her parents—it wasn't her fault, or she didn't mean to do it, or she wasn't even there, and behind it all subtly laying the blame on Stevie for being the smart one, the special child.

"She was a real bitch, wasn't she?" Doris commented.

I looked up, startled. "You read these?"

"Sure. Didn't say I wasn't supposed to. It woulda made me crazy, too, living with someone like that. She always got away with it."

"I don't think she was the reason. They think that people like Stevie have some kind of predisposition, and when they get too stressed, they… " I hesitated trying to think of some layman's term that would convey my meaning.

"They crack up," Doris filled in.

"Exactly. And he wasn't living at home when he cracked up." I read some more, really unable to tear myself away, until Stans showed up, wearing a large, garish Hawaiian shirt and carrying a stack of pizza boxes.

"Here's your pizza, lady," he said, his eyes scanning the entire area. He froze when he saw the gun lying on the ground next to me.

"Don't worry," I said. "It's not real. This is Doris," I said, pointing to Doris who'd backed up all the way to her cart, when Stans had appeared. "She gets the extra large. That's Dorris," I pointed to the dog, who needed only one whiff of the pizza smell to know she liked Stans. "She spells her name with two R's. She gets the small sausage, no cheese."

Stans approached Doris, but seemed to sense that he couldn't get too near. "Ma'am," he said, and held out the pizza box at full arm's length. Doris snatched it and moved to the other side of her cart. He flipped open the small box and placed it on the ground. Dorris was on it before it touched the pavement. He turned to me and handed me the third box.

I took it and peeked inside. "Mmmm, pepperoni. Good choice," I said. "What do I owe you?"

"An explanation."

"How about a motive for murder?" I held up one of Stevie's journals.

Stans reached out to take it from me and his Hawaiian shirt rode up on his hip, revealing his holstered service revolver.

"You're not a pizza deliveryman," Doris shouted. She glared at me. "You called the cops." She abandoned her orderly packing, dumped her remaining belongings into her cart, plopped the pizza carton on top and got out of there as fast as the bent wheels on her rusty grocery cart would go. Dorris hung around long enough to see if I'd share some of my pepperoni pizza with her. When I made it clear I wouldn't, she took off after Doris.

Stans hunkered down next to me, while I did show and tell with my loot. "Joe's gun." I passed it to him. "A gift from Stevie, according to Doris." I placed my hand on the stack of journals I'd read. "All these bound books are Stevie's journals. They're what Gina broke into my house for, and, from what I've read, I can see why. She hated Stevie and did what she could to make his life miserable. You'll have to read them yourself to see what I mean."

"Okay," he said, without enthusiasm. "What about the rest of it?"

I leafed through the small stack of lined notepaper. "These are just like the papers that Joe left with Stevie's body. Different data, but same handwriting. I think it's Stevie's writing, judging from those journals."

"And you still don't have any idea what those numbers mean?" Stans asked. "You're not holding out on me?"

I shook my head no. "Doris said that Frank brought Joe to collect some of the papers from her. This is just what's left," I said, then I remembered that I hadn't told him about Joe yet. I bit my lip. "Oops, I forgot."

Stans sighed. "Okay, out with it."

"I talked to Joe yesterday. He had a stroke, and his mom put him in a convalescent home in Walnut Creek. He's not real coherent."

Stans puffed out his cheeks and blew out some air. "That's what I could say about this whole case—not real coherent. You couldn't have called me yesterday to tell me you'd found him?"

I dropped my gaze. "Sorry. His mom's been sort of hiding him. Not a bad idea really, since Stevie's killer might try to get to him."

Stans shook his head. "Not now, he won't. The killer's dead."

CHAPTER TWENTY-FOUR

"What are you talking about?" I demanded.

"We got the pathologist's report. Munsen's nightstick matches the dent in the victim's head. They found some tissue embedded in the wood and are checking to see if it's a match."

I lifted my hand and fingered the sore spot on my temple. "You're saying Munsen killed Stevie?"

"Looks like. He might not have meant to kill him. Two of his arrests were for assault. He'd used the nightstick both times in drug deals gone bad. Everyone we've talked to who'd admit knowing him has mentioned the nightstick. Sort of his signature. He liked to hurt people."

"But, what about Flo? Did you talk to the Berkeley police?"

Stans nodded. "Sure, right after you called the first time. Turns out they had an eyewitness. One of the neighbors saw a guy coming down the path from Ms. Bing's place about the right time. Her description of him sounds like Munsen. They're taking photos over to her. I'm betting she'll pick him out. Like you said, he has a pretty distinctive face. We searched his place, but we'll go back and look for cyanide, now we know what to look for."

"But why would he kill them?"

Stans shrugged. "Haven't figured that out yet, but one possible motive is money. Turns out your friend Florence was loaded."

"What? That's not possible. I don't know what she was paid, but it wasn't enough to get rich on. And, you saw where she lived."

Stans nodded. "She owned the house, rented it out and lived in the cottage in back. In fact, she owned several properties. Also had a couple mil stashed in an offshore account."

"It doesn't make any sense."

"It will—eventually, when we get all the facts. Maybe some of the papers you've turned up will explain it. You've caused me some headaches, but you've helped, too." He stood up. "Come on. I'll give you a ride home."

He picked up the stack of journals and papers with Joe's gun on top and headed down the driveway. I scrambled to my feet and followed him. He stowed everything in the trunk of his car and let me into the front passenger seat.

"So Munsen was a drug dealer?" I asked, when Stans was settled into the driver's seat.

"Not a street dealer. More like a drug entrepreneur."

"What about Stevie's journals?"

"What about them?"

"They're a motive for Gina to kill Stevie. Maybe she knew Munsen and hired him."

"Maybe." He made it sound like a very distant probability.

"You're not going to follow up on it, are you?"

"We're going to pursue our investigation anywhere it leads. We still have Munsen's murder and your ex-husband's as unsolved homicides. Lind's sister might have a motive and might've known Munsen. Hey, we might find out that you knew Munsen. Or maybe your boyfriend did."

"He's not my boyfriend," I said automatically, "and he didn't know Munsen. He was just trying to help me, or he wouldn't be involved in any of this."

"Yeah, yeah. I know. We checked. Between the two of you, you've got more character witnesses than the Pope."

When we reached Mitch's house, I said, "Thanks for the ride," and opened the door. "By the way," I added as a parting shot, "you're really something in that Hawaiian shirt. Is that your undercover outfit?"

Stans gazed down at the expanse of floral fabric spread over his belly as if he'd just then noticed what he was wearing. "My wife bought it for me. We were going to a luau." He checked his watch. "With any luck, I might still make it, after I log in this evidence."

"Sorry to ruin your day off," I said and meant it.

"I couldn't have played pizza delivery boy if it wasn't my day off. You should take a day off yourself. Better yet, give me a break and take a week off."

I slid out of the car and said, "Aloha," before closing the door. Stans made a face and drove off.

I climbed the steps to Mitch's house. His truck wasn't in the driveway, so he was probably still out working. I hoped he wasn't just avoiding me, now that he'd figured out he didn't want me as his girlfriend after all. I'd opened my bag to search for Mitch's house key, when I heard someone calling my name. I turned to look.

Kenji's car was stopped in the middle of the street. He leaned his head out of the driver's side window. "Hey, Alison. Wait up. I have to talk to you."

I waved to him. "Come on in."

He parked his car, bounded up the steps and grabbed me in a bear hug. As fate would have it, Mitch pulled into the driveway at just that moment. I caught a glimpse of his face when he first saw us. He didn't look happy.

I struggled to free myself. "Whoa, Kenji. Fragile goods here. Handle with care."

He released me but kept hold of my shoulders. "Sorry, babe. I've been so worried about you. I've been phoning, but you haven't answered any of my messages. Then, when I drove by and saw the crime scene tape, I thought the worst."

"I can't get inside to check my messages yet, because Frank was killed there. You heard about that?"

He nodded. "And some other guy, too, right? And you don't look so good yourself, babe."

Mitch came up the stairs. I glanced at him over Kenji's shoulder. "This is Kenji."

Kenji dropped his hands from my shoulders, and turned to shake hands with Mitch.

"Kenji, Mitch" I said, completing the introductions. "Kenji works at the Center."

Mitch nodded to Kenji, unsmiling. "Lose your key?" he asked me.

"No, it's right here. Somewhere." I looked into my bag.

"Excuse me." He shouldered past Kenji to get to the front door. He pulled his keys out of his pocket, found the right one with no effort and opened the door.

While Mitch was busy with the front door, Kenji shifted his gaze back and forth between Mitch and me, his eyebrows raised. Kenji was out on a fact-finding expedition, no doubt. He might've wanted to make sure I was all right, but he was going to take back some tidbits about the murders and my social life, too, while he was at it.

We followed Mitch into the house. "Would you like something to drink?" I asked Kenji. "Coffee? Tea? I need a glass of water myself. I just had a pepperoni pizza and I'm dying of thirst." I led the way to the kitchen. Mitch came too, still unsmiling and with hints of the bad-ass look about his eyes. Maybe he thought that Kenji was going to be another Tony.

"Nothing for me, thanks," Kenji said.

I opened a cupboard, looking for a glass, and found breakfast cereal and crackers. Mitch produced a glass from another cupboard, filled it at the sink and handed it to me.

"Thanks." I smiled right into his eyes as I took the glass. His tough guy expression softened into a weary sadness, but hardened again when Kenji spoke.

"I really need to talk to you, Alison. I have some news, and… " he hesitated, eyed Mitch and nervously licked his lips, "... and I owe you an apology."

I pulled out a chair at the kitchen table. "Why don't we sit down. You too, Mitch," I said, when he made no move to join us.

"You sure?" he asked me, ignoring Kenji.

I nodded, and he pulled out a chair and sat down.

Kenji lowered himself slowly into a chair across from us. "I'm leaving the Center. I've accepted a position at the CDC," he said.

"That's great. Is it a big step up?"

"Bigger than I'd expected."

"You deserve it. Your work is first rate, and you've published in all the right journals."

"True, and I can represent whichever minority they need a token for, if tokenism ever comes back into fashion," he said with a touch of his old humor.

"A man of many talents," I said, raising my glass in a salute. "I had no idea you were even looking for another position."

"It was time to move on. The Center is just a way station. You know that. You either move on or move up, but you don't stay. Daniel likes to keep bringing in fresh talent, so to speak. He's spread a wide net of influence in the field by seeing that so many of us get the right support for our work and then find positions of power."

"I guess so. I hadn't thought of it that way. It certainly can't hurt to have friends at the CDC."

"Daniel already does," Kenji said. "That was why I didn't stick up for you. I'd already interviewed with their hiring team. They were in town early for the PHS meetings. Remember that sick day I took? The interviews went very well, but they wanted to talk to Daniel. He has a lot of influence. I'm a little junior for the job I'd applied for. If Daniel had said I wasn't up to it, they wouldn't have offered it to me."

"So you didn't cross him when he said I had to go," I said.

"It was a lousy thing to do, and I apologize. I'm not sure I could've made any difference. When Daniel gets his mind set against you, that's pretty much it. But, you really have the potential to be a brilliant researcher. You did the work of three field workers on the refinery study, and Carolyn said that Daniel's having her follow your data analysis proposal without revisions."

"Speaking of Carolyn, how is she?" I asked, glad to change the subject. I was squirming a little under all the praise.

Kenji smiled broadly. "She's fine, just fine. I think I've met my match. No, I lie. She's more than a match for me. Actually, she wants to apologize to you, too. She didn't understand your situation. Daniel didn't really give her the full picture, when he hired her."

I shrugged. "That's okay."

"So now you have your new job?" Mitch spoke for the first time.

Kenji nodded. "I'm just finishing up a couple of loose ends at the Center this week, and I'm out of there."

"So maybe you could hire Alison?"

Kenji glanced nervously at him. "Well, not hire her myself. She has to finish her dissertation before she can go on the open job market. But," he said, turning to me, "you know I'll give you a glowing recommendation when you're ready to job hunt."

Mitch snorted and resumed his bad-ass expression.

Kenji avoided looking at him. "I think I'll be on my way." He got to his feet, and his eye fell on the papers on the table. I'd left Stevie's computer printouts there the night before. "What's this? Are you working on something?"

"No, those are part of the mystery of Stevie's murder. He was mainly a theoretical mathematician, but he apparently was also interested in applied statistics. Papers of his with these variable names keep showing up all over the place." I pointed to the letters I couldn't decipher. "Do you have any idea what that might mean?"

Kenji's eyebrows went up. "No idea at all. Sorry." He

checked his watch. "I didn't realize it was so late. I'm supposed to pick up Carolyn. Nice meeting you, Mitch. And, Alison, stay in touch. Okay?"

"Sure."

I followed him down the hall and watched him walk out the front door. He didn't look back. I closed the door and turned around. Mitch stood at the other end of the hall, watching me.

"What?" I asked.

"You tell me. Old boyfriend?"

"Not an old boyfriend." I brushed past him on my way back to the kitchen.

"He called you 'babe.'"

"That's just his way. He likes to tweak the establishment's nose by being a little outrageous, but you'd never know it from his research or his published papers. I appreciated his style, and we became buddies." I finished drinking my water and got some more.

"Some buddy. Couldn't even stand up for you, when it mattered."

"He apologized."

"Right, so now he can live with himself. Noticed he didn't offer you a job, though."

"I can't apply for that kind of job until I finish my dissertation. Besides, I wouldn't want to move to Atlanta anyway."

"Is that where he's going?"

I nodded. "The CDC—Centers for Disease Control—is in Atlanta."

"And you don't want to move, even for a job like his?"

I shook my head.

"Good. Not that it's my business. I really get it now. How smart you are and everything. You were trying to tell me that, and I just didn't hear it. But I'm glad you're not going to be moving away just the same."

"What are you talking about?"

"I'm talking about me falling for someone who's way out of my league."

"Me? Out of your league? Are you kidding?"

"I wish I was."

"But you've completely misunderstood me. Do you think I admire someone like Kenji more than you?"

"Hey, I said I get it. You don't have to let me down gently or anything,"

"What matters to me is being a good person, like you are. You found a way to fix Rose's screen door without her thinking she was accepting charity. That's being smart with your heart. Sometimes I think that all I know about my heart is that it has four chambers and pumps blood."

"It's okay, Alison. Don't worry about it. You don't have to try to make me feel good. That guy, Kenji? He just glanced at that piece of paper and knew what it was. You deserve to find someone like that. Only try to find someone who doesn't lie."

"What do you mean?"

"He was lying. Couldn't you tell? He recognized those letters."

I stared at Mitch. He was absolutely right. Kenji had been lying. I saw it, but just didn't want to believe it, so I ignored my gut instinct. I lowered my gaze to the printout and saw what Kenji had seen. "You're right. He lied. You were right last night, too. I was looking for sky when I should have been looking for tetrachlorethylene."

"What's that?"

I pointed to the variable name. "PCE. That's the abbreviation for tetrachlorethylene."

Mitch leaned over the table and looked at the letters. "What about the RB part? It says RBPCE. Is that another chemical?"

"I'm pretty sure not." I picked up the page. My hand was shaking and made the paper rattle as I lifted it.

"What is it then?"

"I have to think about it. I'm just going to lie down for

awhile and think." I headed for my room.

"How about some dinner?"

"No, thanks. That pepperoni pizza pretty much took care of my eating needs—for several days." I went into my room and closed the door. I crossed to the bed and sat down. I was a liar myself, and a coward. I didn't want to think. I wanted not to think. Make my mind a blank. I breathed in and out slowly and tried to push thoughts out of my mind, but they pushed and shoved and elbowed their way back in again, like shoppers at a department store the day after Christmas.

It took awhile, but I finally achieved some order in my brain. I forced each thought to march in separately. I examined it, questioned it, and compared it to previous thoughts.

Mitch took a shower. I heard the water running in the bathroom. After awhile he fixed himself something to eat. The cooking smells held no appeal. I might never be hungry again and not just because of the pizza. Betrayal can be a real appetite depressant.

I realized that the sun had gone down and night fully established in the time I'd spent sitting and thinking. I stood up and flipped on the light switch by the door. In the sudden illumination, I noticed papers in the tray of Mitch's fax machine. I picked them up. Gayle had kept her word and faxed me Flo's records and Dr. Aaronson's reply to her inquiry. Would Stans see these tonight, or was he off eating roast pig and doing the hula?

I took the faxed pages back to the bed and read them. I didn't reach any different conclusion than the one I'd finally settled for, sitting in the dark and marching my thoughts up and down like trained soldiers. It all went back to the Center, but there was one piece of evidence missing. I suppose I could call Stans and tell him, but what if I was wrong? Unthinkable to make such an accusation. I had to know the truth for myself, first. And to do that, I needed help.

I opened the bedroom door and crossed to the living room. Mitch sat in his chair, reading a book. He looked up when I came into the room.

"Get your thinking done?"

I nodded. "I need your help. Will you drive me to the Center?"

"Isn't it kind of late? I was just about to turn in."

"Now's the best time for what I have to do."

"Is it something dangerous?"

"No danger at all," I said, which was true if I didn't count the danger to my ideals.

"How about illegal? You're not proposing a little breaking and entering, are you?"

I hesitated. "That's sort of a gray area. Literally speaking, no breaking. I have a key and an entry code, but we might need a flashlight."

Mitch drove me to the Center and held the flashlight while I unlocked the outer door with the extra set of keys that had resided, forgotten, in my bag. I punched in Kenji's doorcode—the number palindrome I'd noted for no particular reason except that numbers had a way of sticking in my memory.

"You don't have to come in with me, if you don't want to," I said.

"I'm coming in." He followed me through the door and it swung shut behind us.

"Look, I don't want you involved if the police show up."

"I thought you said this wasn't illegal."

"I said it was a gray area." I led Mitch by flashlight to the data room. "This room's called the fishbowl, because of that big window. They keep all the really good equipment in here, and Daniel limits access. No one could sneak in here and use the scanner or the color copier without Flo seeing. Her cubicle's right outside the door."

I punched in Kenji's code and entered the room. "I think it's okay to turn the lights on in here. There aren't any windows to the outside." I turned the lights on and crossed to the bookshelf. "These are copies of all the dissertations of people who've worked here. I used to look at this shelf and imagine the day I'd add mine to the lineup."

"Are you going to tell me what this is about?"

"I'm pretty sure Stevie was killed because he found out about faked data. Remember when we were talking about statistics and measuring whether an association could've happened by chance?"

"You're talking about tetrachlorethylene?"

I nodded. "You're a fast learner." I lifted Daniel's dissertation from the shelf and carried it to the table in the middle of the room, pulled the printouts from my pocket and sat down.

I'd read this dissertation three or four times. It was my model for the work I'd hoped to do someday. Kenji must have studied it harder than I had, though, because he recognized the variable label when he saw it, and then lied to me about it.

I flipped to the appendices and found the one with all the data tables. The one I needed was Table III. It was titled "Levels of Tetrachlorethylene (PCE) in Wells at Rio Blanco." The first column of figures was headed with the variable label RBPCE. The numbers in the columns were different from the ones on Stevie's printout. Just as I'd known they would be. In Daniel's version, all the associations between PCE levels and subsequent birth defects and childhood cancers were significant.

Someone in the main room outside the fishbowl sniffed loudly. The sound raised the hairs on the back of my neck. I jerked my head up and stared at Mitch. He frowned and opened his mouth to speak. I quickly put a finger to my lips and strained to listen.

Suddenly, light flooded the main office, illuminating all the empty cubicles. "Come on out, Alison," Daniel called to me. "I know you're in there."

I motioned to Mitch to get under the table and hide. He shook his head. I stood up and backed toward the door. I mimed a phone with my hand and mouthed the words "nine-one-one" and again gestured for him to stay in the fishbowl.

"Ah, there you are," Daniel said behind me.

I spun around.

He stood just outside the door of the fishbowl, a crowbar in one hand and a gun in the other. "And not alone, I see. That's a complication, but not an insurmountable one. Come out of there, both of you." He backed away and gestured with the gun for us to follow.

I moved slowly through the doorway into the aisle outside. "How did you know I was here?"

Daniel backed away from us, keeping his distance. "I have an alarm on my computer at home that sounds when anyone opens the door after hours. Every doorcode and the time it's used are recorded. And, it so happens I'd just spoken to Kenji by phone at his home. When his code showed up on my computer, I guessed that you'd tricked him into giving you his code."

"No. I simply noticed it once and the number stuck in my head."

"And the keys?"

"I had an extra set I forgot about until recently."

"Who are you?" Daniel addressed himself to Mitch for the first time.

"He's just a neighbor," I said quickly before Mitch could answer. I stepped in front of Mitch. Why had I let him come in with me? Now I'd put his life in danger. "He gave me a ride, that's all."

Mitch stepped forward, elbowing me aside. "Name's Rottweiler," he said and gave me a sidelong glance, as if checking to see if I remembered when I'd given him that name.

I gritted my teeth. All I needed was Mitch going all testosterone on me. If I'd thought rushing Daniel and overpowering him was a possibility, I'd have tried that by now. But he was too far away from us, and he held two weapons in terrifyingly steady hands.

"All right," Daniel said. "Why don't you be a good

doggie, Mr. Rottweiler, and sit down on the floor. That's it. Right where you are. Sit. And keep your hands above your head, if you don't mind, or I shall shoot your girlfriend."

Mitch slowly complied, and Daniel smiled in satisfaction. "Just a neighbor indeed, Alison. You know what an irrepressible gossip our Kenji is. He described the man you're living with perfectly."

"What's with the crowbar?" I said to divert his attention from Mitch. "Going to try to bash my head in like your friend, Ray Munsen, did to Stevie?"

"This?" He brandished the iron bar. "Not at all. I'll tell the police that this is how you broke into the Center. Just so they'll know what a desperate and irrational woman you were. I've already jammed the front door open for realism's sake, so I don't need it any longer." He tossed it aside and it hit the linoleum with a clang. "Ray was fond of his nightstick. He was a bit of a sadist, actually. That quality had its uses, but I've found that there's nothing like a knife and a gun for really getting the job done." He waved the gun at us to emphasize his point.

"You killed Frank," I said. It seemed like a good idea to keep him talking, though I didn't exactly like the topic of conversation. I tried to check out Mitch in my peripheral vision, because I didn't want to look directly at him. He sat like stone, but his hands seemed a little lower than before.

"I thought you'd puzzled out what happened to Avery."

"What I figured out is that your entire career is based on a lie. You submitted fraudulent data about the PCE levels in the wells at Rio Blanco. There wasn't a significant association between the PCE levels and either birth defects or childhood cancers."

"Fraudulent, you say? Do you know what's fraudulent? Letting women bear deformed babies, allowing children to be exposed to carcinogens simply because they're poor. I know that the PCE was responsible for those children's suffering, and you know it too." He spoke more emphatically with each sentence.

"You have to prove it," I said, to goad him on. He might get so involved in the argument, I could distract him. "Those are the rules, Daniel. We're ethically bound to adhere to the rules of what counts as proof."

"You want to preach ethics to me? I'll tell you where our society is, ethically-speaking, now. Drug companies had stopped producing eflornithine, the only cure for sleeping sickness, because they couldn't make a big enough profit from the poor Africans who're afflicted with it. A stupid name for the disease, by the way, since it drives people horribly mad before it sends them into a terminal coma. Then the drug companies discover that eflornithine eliminates facial hair in women. Suddenly, it's profitable for them to produce it, because vain, stupid, American women have nothing better to do with their lives than obsess about the hair on their upper lips. Drug companies now have a bonanza, and maybe, just maybe, they'll produce some extra eflornithine for the poor afflicted Africans."

"Forget what the drug companies do, Daniel. It was wrong to fake your data. Killing Stevie, Flo, Frank and Ray Munsen was wrong, too."

"By what measure? Stephen Lind was an arrogant little boy. He didn't care about my work, about alleviating human suffering. He cared about winning. He thought he had a new approach, a new method. He wanted to name it after himself—the Lind probability estimate."

"What about Flo? She worked for you for years. You knew her even before. I saw her school records. You taught at Berkeley, and she took your seminars."

"Flo betrayed me. She went into my personal computer and gave Stephen access to my original data, so he could demonstrate the value of his statistical approach. However, it was a simple matter to see that the numbers I'd reported were different from those in the computer. It didn't take a mathematical genius to grasp that."

"Lucky for you that Stevie had a schizophrenic break."

He sniffed. "Luck had very little to do with it. Ray provided me with a strong hallucinogen."

"Oh yes, your sidekick, Ray Munsen. I heard from David Aaronson today. Another one of your former students. He told me all about Ray, that he was already involved in dealing illegal drugs when he was in graduate school. He said that you took that group picture."

"Yes, Aaronson's one of my early products. Very successful. We're in touch."

I shook my head. Daniel wasn't in touch with anything, especially reality. I had to think of something soon. "So you gave Stevie a hallucinogen?"

"A very large dose, in fact, and told him that Flo wanted nothing more to do with him. I'd hoped for suicide, though I never did understand what he saw in her. However, the resulting schizophrenia was more gratifying to me."

"Then he went into remission."

"Unfortunately, yes. He might never have bothered with me at all, but he heard about me and the Center from you, and it gave him ideas."

"He asked you for a job."

"Yes, he actually thought I would employ him. He was perhaps not so fully in remission as he thought." Daniel allowed himself a small chuckle at his own joke. "He was trying out a mild blackmail on me. Of course, he didn't know that I'd spent the past eight years being blackmailed by an expert."

"Who?"

"Flo, of course. She bled me and the Center. I wouldn't have been able to run my studies if I hadn't had Ray's business to rely on. I laundered the money from his drug operations while Flo squeezed every cent she could from me."

"Why? She lived a very Spartan lifestyle."

"For the sake of her beloved Stephen. She was going to spirit him off to some secluded isle and care for him, broken mind and all. The way she went on about it was sickening."

"She thought he was in Conway House, right? She had no idea he was living nearby, did she?"

Daniel gave another of his chuckles. I wasn't used to hearing him laugh, and in the context, it was a scary sound. "Ironic, isn't it? The day you told her Stephen had been killed, I had to move fast."

"You poisoned her."

"Not I. I was lunching with Brian Perry from the NIPH, remember? But my friend Ray kept special potions for emergencies. She was going to tell all. Ray offered to help expose me. For a fee. She gave him the incriminating evidence. He mixed a drink for her, and that was that."

"I found her."

"I know, but what's another dead body to a hospice nurse? Certainly, you've seen worse. Of course, I could've wished for a little more lag time. I'd planned on cleaning up loose ends before the police started making inquiries. You made that difficult. You've made a number of things difficult for me. Your stupid husband being a prime example."

"Ex-husband."

"He managed to procure some very incriminating papers from a crazy bag lady, not that he understood what the papers really were. He kept hoping you'd explain. Fortunately, he asked me to help him make contact with you, and I obliged. You were supposed to be arrested for killing him. Kenji spread it all over the office that you'd threatened him with a butcher knife."

"But Ray had to go and break my arm."

"You were simply supposed to be knocked unconscious. It would have looked like a marital spat then. Open and shut. What did you use on Ray? Mace?"

"Bleach."

"He was quite hopeless after that. Hysterical, in fact."

"So you shot him."

"I had to think on my feet."

Thinking on my feet was what I had to do, too, but

the gun that Daniel kept pointed at my mid-section kept interfering with my thought process.

"Hey, man," Mitch whined. "My arms have gone to sleep." He lowered his arms and held them out, palms up, as if they were completely useless.

"Hands up," Daniel ordered.

Mitch raised his hands marginally. "I'm telling you, they've gone to sleep. My legs are all pins and needles, and my back is killing me. I've got a bad back. I can't take sitting like this." He rocked forward and back, as if to ease an ache.

"Very well," Daniel said. "Lie down. Face down. That way it will make things easier for all of us." He smiled as if he'd said something funny.

When Mitch hesitated, Daniel gestured with the gun. "Face down on the ground. Now."

"Okay, okay." Mitch looked scared. Definitely very un-Mitch like. What was he up to? He moved in little increments, wincing with each shift. Still keeping his hands at about shoulder height, he managed to get on one knee, but lost his balance, and one shoulder tipped against the wall. He put out a hand and caught himself with a grunt.

Daniel took a step backward and straightened the arm holding the gun. "On your belly, doggie," He ordered. "Now."

"Don't shoot," Mitch pleaded. "I'm moving as fast as I can. It's my back." He put one hand at the small of his back, as if to brace it so he could move.

And he did move, but so fast I could hardly take it in. His hand whipped forward, sending something hurtling toward Daniel. At almost the same instant, he sprang sideways, slamming into me, knocking both of us through the doorway of the fishbowl, and Daniel fired his gun.

I put my hands out instinctively to break my fall. My broken arm screamed in protest when I hit the floor. Mitch landed on top of me, rolled off and kicked the door shut.

"Get the lights," he said, "And help me with this table."

I scrambled over to the wall and flipped the switch. Light still filtered into the room through the window, but at least we'd be harder to spot. Mitch shoved the conference room table to block the door. I hurried to help him. "This table's way too light," I grunted, as I jammed it against the door. "It wouldn't keep a toddler out, much less a maniac with a gun. Speaking of maniacs. Where is he?"

"Maybe I knocked him out," Mitch said. He was on the floor next to one of the computers.

"What did you throw at him?"

"My flashlight and I could use it right about now," he mumbled, and then more urgently, "Alison, get down!"

Daniel loomed up on the other side of the window, blood dripping down one side of his face. I dove under the table just as he fired into the window. The bullet punched a hole through the acrylic pane with a deafening crash.

"Damn," I said, peeking out from under the table. "I thought that stuff was supposed to be bulletproof.

"Acrylic, huh?" Mitch said. "Good thing it isn't glass."

"Supposed to be burglar-proof." Suddenly it hit me that there'd never been a burglary. Daniel had just sold everything off, filed for the insurance, and replaced everything with old used equipment.

"Come out, you two," Daniel screamed. I'm not going to let you or anyone else destroy my life's work." He fired another eardrum shattering shot. A second hole appeared in the acrylic, but the pane, as a whole, still held.

"Mitch, how about calling 911 now, on your handy cell phone? You did bring your cell phone, didn't you?"

"In a second. I'm busy right now."

"With what?"

"Booby trap," he whispered and crawled toward me, keeping below the window. "Talk to him. Distract him for a second." He levered himself silently onto the table.

"Daniel," I called through the door. "Wait a minute. Let's talk about this. Maybe we can work something out."

"It's too late for talking, Alison. You're a threat to my

work. You want to undo all the good I've achieved. I can't allow that to happen." I heard the little click-click sound of the electronic lock release. "He's going to try to come in," I whispered to Mitch.

"Good," he said, and slid from the table to the floor. "I hope this reaches. Tell me exactly when he has his hand on the door handle and don't touch anything," he warned.

I scooted from the shelter of the table and looked at the door. In the light coming through the bullet-riddled window, I saw the door handle turn. "Now!"

Sparks flew. Daniel screamed, and the lights went out.

"What happened?" I asked.

"I wired the door handle and it gave him an electric shock when I plugged it in. It's only 110 volts, but it'll give him something to think about," Mitch said, his voice coming out of the blackness on the other side of the room. "We can only do it once, because it tripped the circuit breakers. I'm calling 911, and then we'll barricade the door some more." I could hear his phone beep as he punched in the number.

"I think the lights are still on in the other part of the office." I could see dim glow coming through the window.

"Must be on another circuit."

I held still and listened for Daniel. Not a sound. I crawled over to the window and lifted my head enough to peek out.

"Stay away from the window. He still has a gun."

Daniel lay sprawled on the floor of the cubicle opposite. He didn't move. I couldn't see the gun. I couldn't see him breathe, either, but the light was dim.

"No, he looks knocked out. I don't think he's breathing." I stood up and pushed the table out of the way.

"Alison, wait for the cops."

I opened the door and peeked out. The light was dim, but enough to see. Daniel still didn't move. Behind me I heard Mitch talking to the 911 operator. I knelt beside Daniel's inert form, felt for a pulse. Nothing.

He lay with his arms outflung. Just the same pose I'd found Stevie in. He'd had Stevie killed. And Flo. He'd stabbed Frank with my kitchen knife and shot Ray Munsen in the back. I stared at the face of the man who'd been my hero. "Dying's too good for you, you son of a bitch," I told him and started CPR.

The compressions were difficult because I'd really done a number on my broken arm and could only press with my left hand. But I could do the breathing okay and quickly got into the four-count compression rhythm.

"Alison?" Mitch called from the fishbowl.

"I'm... out... here... four," I said, punctuating every compression, then I did the two breaths. "Come... and... see... four," I said and did two more breaths.

"I don't think I can. Is he alive?"

I heard the tenuous note in his voice and remembered that he lived every day with the memory of having killed a man. Not surprising that he didn't want to witness another death.

"He's... not... dead... four." I did two breaths and checked for pulse and breathing. Nothing. "Son... of... a... bitch," I swore to my CPR rhythm. I heard sirens, in the distance, but quickly drawing near. I felt the first thready pulse when the cops entered the building. "Here. I'm over here," I yelled. Daniel took a solo breath.

The paramedics came on the heels of the two cops. "Where's the light switch?" one of them asked, while the other bent over Daniel's body.

"Check the circuit breaker," I said, and one of the cops took off. I straightened and backed out of the cubicle, which was going to be too small for all of us.

"What happened here?" a paramedic asked.

"Electric shock. Pulse and breathing just re-started. Pulse thready. Breathing shallow and irregular," I said in verbal shorthand, which the paramedics took in while they moved smoothly through their own assessment of Daniel's condition.

The cop must've found the circuit box, because all the

lights suddenly came on. A third paramedics hurried up. "Where's the gunshot vic?" he asked the cop.

"It's not a gunshot wound." I gestured to the paramedics around Daniel. "It was electric shock, but he's breathing on his own now."

"The 911 caller said there was one heart attack and one gunshot. Both males."

"He had a gun, but... " I stopped in mid-sentence as what the paramedic said sank in. I turned and ran into the fishbowl.

Mitch lay with his back propped against the wall, his legs stretched out in front of him. One blue leg. One red leg. And blood everywhere. On the rug next to his pocketknife and the bits of plastic he'd stripped from the wires. In streaks marking the path he'd made crawling across the room. On the table where he'd perched to wrap the exposed wires around the door handle.

"Hey," Mitch said. "How's the crazy guy?"

"Oh God," I breathed. "Oh shit. He shot you. Why didn't you tell me?" I threw myself onto my knees, my gaze riveted to the red pool of blood that had spread out beneath him.

Bullet wounds. I had to think about bullet wounds. What do you do? I had to fix this. Okay, now I remembered. Assess. That's first. I had to check the site. I reached for Mitch's belt and tried to unfasten the buckle. Stupid arm. It wouldn't work. Even my fingers were all goofy. Useless. And my eyes wouldn't focus. Why was it so hard to see? I couldn't help him, unless I could see the wound. My eyes were about as useless as my arm. But I could see the blood. So much blood. Too much. I had to help. I had to see the wound.

The paramedic knelt down across from me and snapped open his kit. "Hey, buddy," he said to Mitch. "How's it going?"

"Been better," Mitch said.

I kept struggling with the belt buckle. I almost had it, then it slipped.

"Ma'am?" the paramedic said. "I need you to stand back now so I can see what's going on with your friend."

"Don't touch him," I snarled not leaving off my battle with the buckle. "I'm a nurse. I'll take care of him."

"If you're a nurse, ma'am," the medic said, "then you know it's time for you to move aside and let me do my job."

I wouldn't answer him, wouldn't even look at him. I couldn't stop. What if Mitch died?

Mitch covered my hands with his. "Alison, look at me."

I lifted my gaze to meet his. "Don't die. Please don't die," I choked out.

"Okay, you win. I won't die, but you have to stop crying."

"Cry? Me? I never cry."

He lifted one hand to stroke the tears on my cheek. "If you're not crying, then somebody better fix that leak in the roof, because I'm getting all wet."

"He's going to be okay," the paramedic said. "Didn't hit the artery. Lucky."

I looked down at Mitch's leg. The paramedic had moved swiftly and cut Mitch's pant leg open from the bottom while Mitch had me distracted.

"That's right," I said, blinking. "That's how you do it. Cut off the clothes. Why couldn't I remember that? All I could think of was that I had to get his belt unfastened."

"I don't know about you," Mitch said to the paramedic, "but today's women are too much for me. She hasn't even kissed me yet, and all she can think about is getting my pants off."

"That's cold, man," the paramedic said with a grin, not pausing in his efficient movements. He pulled out a thick pressure dressing and began to strap it on. "I think the least you could do is give the man a kiss," he said to me.

Mitch looked at me. Such a look. Hope, tenderness, desire. "You cried over me," he said. "I have witnesses. You're mine now. Sorry, but there's no backing out."

So I kissed him. What else could I do? Besides, backing out was the last thing I wanted. He returned kiss for kiss and didn't do too badly either, for a man with a bullet in his leg.

Of course, he did a much better job later, when he got out of the hospital.

To my Readers

If you have any thoughts, comments or questions about *Odds of Dying*, I'd love to hear from you. You can contact me at judith@judithjaneway.com. For information about events and upcoming books or to sign up for my newsletter, please visit http://www.judithjaneway.com/.

About the Author

Judith Janeway believes that she was born with a Ticonderoga no. 2 pencil in one hand and a canary yellow lined pad in the other, because she can't remember a time when she wasn't writing stories.

She attended the University of California, Berkeley, the University of Bordeaux, France, and San Francisco State University and emerged with a Master's degree in Comparative Literature. She took up teaching at a men's college, which wasn't as much fun as it sounds. After seven years it finally occurred to her that having a passion for literature didn't correlate with having a passion for *teaching* literature.

She left teaching in favor of the study of Health Psychology and the Philosophy of Science. She received a PhD from the University of California, San Francisco, and has pursued a career in social science research, studying people coping with serious/terminal illnesses and their caregivers. Just to be clear, she is a research psychologist, not a clinical psychologist. She has she never been reimbursed for handing out advice to people foolish enough to tell her their problems.

During this time of teaching, not teaching, pursuing an advanced degree, conducting research, and publishing scholarly articles, she married, divorced and acquired a number of children—not necessarily in that order. And, of course, she wrote fiction.

She wrote in the library when she should have been studying for comprehensive exams. She wrote in hotel lobbies while attending professional meetings. She wrote while waiting for children at swimming, piano, violin, and guitar lessons, or at soccer, baseball, and basketball practice. She wrote while on the commuter bus to and from work. She wrote while family members waited impatiently for food to be put on the table.

She entered a romance novel in a contest and won

first prize—an opportunity to show her manuscript to an editor. The editor bought the book and a second one. Since then, Judith has turned her writing focus to mystery/suspense, which has always been her favorite genre. *Odds of Dying* is the first of the Alison Weaver mysteries. *The Magician's Daughter,* which will be published February 2015 by Poisoned Pen Press, is the first in a series of *Valentine Hill Mysteries*.

Currently, she lives in the San Francisco Bay Area and continues to write in the interstices of a life that encompasses work, travel, fun with family and friends, and far too much Sudoku.

20115246R00194

Made in the USA
San Bernardino, CA
27 March 2015